# RAVEN
## EVELYN ROGERS

**ZEBRA BOOKS**
**KENSINGTON PUBLISHING CORP.**

ZEBRA BOOKS are published by

Kensington Publishing Corp.
850 Third Avenue
New York, NY 10022

First Printing: February, 1995

Printed in the United States of America

*To my brother Jim Graves
and sister Loretta White
with love and thanks.
I couldn't get by
without your support.*

# *One*

Raven leapt from the bed screaming.

In the dark, invisible hands groped at her gown, hands that threatened hurt, hands that signified death. Heart pounding, her belly hot and tight, she fought a second scream. She must escape . . . she must . . .

Suddenly she jerked awake and the scream settled into a sigh. Swaying, she saw reality in the surrounding shadows. Dreams assaulted her, nothing more, dreams and the breeze from the open window of her safe, familiar room.

She pressed a hand to her heart. How foolish to feel so terrified, yet the danger had seemed so real. Eyes closed, she remembered the image of clouds slashed with red shifting to embrace her naked flesh, stroking, inflaming. Nothing as distinct as a Yankee uniform or a soldier lunging out of the mist.

But he was there, waiting to strike. A small cry escaped her lips. Night thoughts, she realized with a shudder. After two years, the night thoughts had returned.

Shame washed over her. The year was 1876, not 1863, and she a twenty-seven-year-old spinster, not a child. In an alley behind her home, the soldier had robbed her of innocence; but that had been a lifetime ago. Why did she dream of him now?

And why, oh why, did she feel this curious tightening in her stomach and a heat that pumped through her veins?

"Raven," Angel called through the bedroom door, "are you all right?"

Her sister's voice startled her. Slipping back into bed, she huddled beneath the covers and fought her fright and shame.

"Raven," Angel called again.

Cursing her frailty, she took a steadying breath. She was not given to cowardice, nor to fear. Above all, she never begged solace from anyone, not even her beloved family. Her confidences were her own.

But she needed her dear sister's presence now. With Angel nearby, instead of thinking, she could slip into her habit of pretense.

"Come in," she called out.

Angel stepped through the door and moonlight flooded the room, falling on her long, golden hair, turning her gown ghost-white as she eased toward the bed. Despite her thundering heart, Raven smiled. Angel was so good, so sweet, so precious that her presence lightened the dark.

With a sigh born of relief, Raven settled beneath the covers to let her sister's goodness drive away the dream. At twenty, Angel was the youngest of the Chadwick daughters—fair where Raven was dark; small and softly rounded where Raven was slender and tall; soft-spoken where Raven was blunt. Shy, she seldom saw ugliness in the world. Raven saw it everywhere.

"You cried out," said Angel.

"Just a bad dream." Raven pushed a tangle of ebony locks from her face and propped her pillow against the iron headboard. She patted the bed where Angel could sit. "It must have been the pork at supper."

"It seemed all right to me," Angel said, worry in her eyes.

"I probably overate."

"You never do that. Papa says you're as thin as Paddy's post." A frown wrinkled Angel's brow. "He's right, you know."

How dear she was, thought Raven with a rush of love, as gentle and caring at twenty as she had been at two.

She was, however, no more respectable among Savannah's gentry than her more outspoken siblings, daughters of an Irish-born Savannah shopkeeper and his genteel English wife. The Chadwick girls, everyone said, did not know their place.

Which was to stay away from the bachelor sons of the old-money elite. It wasn't the fault of the Chadwicks that their nabob sons patronized the store. Before Flame Chadwick's marriage, they'd swarmed around her like moths. Now it was the baby sister's turn, though she gave them no more than her smile.

It was enough, thought Raven, to draw the men for miles.

"You look hot," said Angel. She laid a palm to Raven's cheek. "No fever."

"I told you it was just a dream."

"You always make light of your troubles."

"I don't have troubles. I'm the tough one, remember? Strong, dependable, loyal." She grinned. "Like the family dog."

"Who reads Shakespeare better than any actress in the world and who sings sweeter than any bird. You should have stayed in Charleston last summer with that repertory troupe."

Raven shrugged. "It didn't work out."

"Why? You never said."

*Because the director decided to rape me.*

Raven shuddered at the memory. He had lurched at her from the shadows of the deserted stage. For just a moment she had returned to childhood, to the tender age of fourteen. Unlike that earlier time, nothing bad had happened; but she had been terrified and she had run.

Her journey to Charleston was the first and only occasion she had tried to become an actress. Despite her ambitions, she figured it was also her last. She had a small inheritance to make her fancies come true, but she didn't have the nerve. She was safe in Savannah. Here she would remain.

"Maybe I'll try some other place," she said, knowing she wouldn't. "After Papa and Mama get back from their trip."

"Papa's like a child, so proud of his anniversary gift. Just think. Thirty years together, and they act like lovers. Just last week I caught them—"

Angel broke off, blushing. "Never mind. They were in the back of the store and didn't know anyone was about."

She fell silent, her pale brow furrowed.

"What's bothering you?" asked Raven.

Angel attempted a smile. "You read me the way you do your plays. It's probably nothing. Mama seems awfully quiet lately. I asked her today if something was wrong. She said no."

Raven had noticed the same change, but she saw no purpose in contributing to Angel's worry. "Believe what Mama says. Like you, she couldn't lie to save her life. She probably misses her grandson in Texas. He must seem a million miles away."

Angel circled a finger on the bedcover, then looked at her sister with serious, thoughtful eyes. Here, thought Raven, comes the real reason for the midnight visit.

"Or maybe she's worried about returning to England after thirty years. Imagine Mama being thrown out of anywhere. What foolishness that was. And all because she fell in love with Papa. How could she not?"

"He was poor Irish. To the Pickerings, he carried the plague."

Angel settled more comfortably on the bed. "We don't know much about Mama's family, do we? It never bothered me before, but now, with her going back . . ." Her voice trailed off as she stared into the moonlight. "I'm sure everything will be wonderful when she returns."

But the most optimistic of the Chadwicks sounded unsure.

"Of course it will," said Raven, unused to her role as cheer-bringer.

"So why didn't her cousin answer the letter she wrote?"

*Because,* Raven might have answered, *Elizabeth Pickering Bannerman, wife of the eleventh Earl of Stafford and Mama's favorite kin, thought herself too important to acknowledge the wife of a lowly tradesman.*

"The letter could have gotten lost at sea," she said,

hedging. "And what if they're snubbing us? Papa said that if he and Mama weren't welcomed, they would see the sights of London, like any other American tourists, and sail back home."

Angel looked unconvinced, and Raven took her hand. "As far as I'm concerned, Chadwicks need only each other. Who cares what anyone thinks?" A sudden melancholy settled on her. "I suppose you'll fall in love one day and let some rascal carry you off."

"Not me," said Angel. "He'll have to be as honorable and brave and good as Saint Patrick to tempt me from home."

"You'll be a spinster like me if you wait for an earthly saint."

It was a familiar argument between them. Angel stifled a yawn.

"Go back to bed," said Raven. "I promised Mama I'd finish my gowns tomorrow, and I'll need you to work in the store for me in the afternoon."

"Of course." Angel smiled. "You're so beautiful, Raven. All dark and mysterious, and you have the most wonderful black eyes. You may have chosen the plainest styles from the Butterick catalog, but you also picked out the most brilliant colors of cloth in the store. You're going to look superb. Forget about me. A handsome man is going to come along, look at you, and—"

"Out!" commanded Raven.

Angel scrambled for the door, then paused. "One of these days—" she began.

"Out, out, damned child," said Raven, affecting her Lady Macbeth voice and making as if to rise from the bed. "No matter how handsome he is, if he does more than look, I'll punch him in the nose."

Alone, she wondered just how far she would go to defend herself, now that she was full grown.

An uneasiness settled around her heart. Another attack was not impossible, especially if she ventured again from home. Men didn't look at her in admiration and gentle longing the way they looked at her sister. They looked at the would-be actress with lust, taking her ambitions, her black hair and eyes, her disreputably tawny skin as signs of a lascivious woman. They were wrong.

Ever since the assault in the alley, she had found comfort in reading, in pretense. She had decided long ago on the single life; she couldn't imagine anything—or anyone—changing her mind.

In her gentle way, Mama occasionally let her know she shouldn't be afraid to feel, especially when it came to loving a man. It was easy for Mama to talk. She had Papa. And she didn't know about the soldier.

Only Papa knew, and he didn't talk about it. For Raven, the memories were so ravaging, she banned them from her mind. Except when the night thoughts came, a rare occurrence. Why had they returned tonight? They seemed an omen, a warning that something bad awaited.

But nothing could harm her, not while she stayed in her beloved, protective home, dreaming about playing famous roles on equally famous stages, in her maturity continuing the pretend games of her youth. Mama was right. There was much she was afraid to feel.

\* \* \*

The day dawned unseasonably warm for November. With a steady stream of customers patronizing Chadwick Dry Goods and Clothing, Raven worked all morning behind the counter.

After the two o'clock meal, with the other Chadwicks at the nearby store, she settled in the parlor to finish hemming the gowns begun weeks ago. Mounds of red and green and lavender silk surrounded her. Unable to find her mother's sewing box in its usual place by the rocker, she went in search of thread.

She found it by the hearth in her parents' bedroom. She also found a letter tucked beneath a skein of yarn.

She studied the English stamp and the childish scrawl on the envelope: *Anne Pickering Chadwick, Savannah, Georgia, U.S.A.*

Despite the warmth of the day, a chill swept through her—and a return of the dread she had experienced during the night. The letter shook in her hand. Mama's letter hidden in Mama's room, discovered by accident. More than anyone else in the family, Raven understood the importance of privacy. Conscience told her to put the letter back unread.

But it came from England and it was postmarked with last September's date. The least secretive of the Chadwicks, Mama had been hiding it two months.

Glancing through the open window at the unseasonably clement afternoon, she thought about Mama working close by, about her strong yet gentle ways, about her recent retreat into herself.

Cousin Elizabeth . . . Countess of Stafford . . . had once been like the sister Mama never had. With both parents dead, she had begun to reminisce about her, going as far as to write after the long separation.

And now there was this letter Mama hid.

Could it be from the countess? If so, why keep it a secret? Unless it contained bad news. Mama never lied. Deep worries might drive her to do so now. Whether she asked or not, she needed help, the kind only Chadwicks could give. Above all else, Raven was a Chadwick. Reasoning thus, she opened the envelope before conscience could make her return it to the yarn.

Engraved at the top of the single page were the words STAFFORD HOUSE, 22 BOLTON ROW, LONDON. Just as she'd thought, here was the reply to Mama's letter to London, the answer she had said never arrived. Its message was simple, without signature, written in a hand similar to the scrawl on the envelope.

*Do not write again or make further contact, else you will die.*

Ignoring the glances of passersby, Raven held her cloak tight and strode through the tree-lined park near her home.

*You will die.*

With each step, the words drummed in her head. She'd opened the letter a scant hour ago; the message refused to leave her mind.

Mama's life had been threatened, and by someone too cowardly to sign his name. Dear Mama, keeping such a terrible thing to herself. Sharing her mother's pain, Raven guessed at the cause for secrecy. Mama didn't want Papa to worry or to cancel the journey he had been planning for so long.

The returning dream really had been an omen, a warning that bad times lay ahead. So what was she to do? Leave the matter alone? Pretend to ignorance? Impossible. Mama needed help.

"I'll go to the store and ask her about this," she whispered to herself.

But Mama would be crushed at the betrayal of her privacy.

"I'll talk to Papa."

Worse. To reveal Mama's secrets without permission would be equally wrong.

The dilemma weighed heavily in her heart. She couldn't return to ignorance any more than she could regain her innocence. One question kept pounding in her head—what was she to do?

"I'll just sail right over there and tell those uppity snobs that anyone who hurts Mama will have to answer to me."

A small voice mocked her; she wouldn't be much of a threat. Besides, she couldn't go to London. She wouldn't even travel to Charleston again.

No, London was definitely impossible. No matter that it was the city of Shakespeare, home of Drury Lane, the Lyceum, places she had read about for years. She had planned a safe life here in Savannah, and it was here she must remain.

"Miss Chadwick, what a pleasant surprise."

Startled, she looked up to see her path blocked by the short, squat figure of Harold Gash, Savannah's most prominent banker, and by the ivory-handled cane he tapped at his side. His complexion was pocked and his pale eyes narrowly set; but in his top hat and double-breasted frock overcoat with its velvet lapels, he looked every inch the prestigious citizen.

"Mr. Gash," she said with a nod, prepared to pass him by.

"How fortuitous that we should meet," he said, continuing to stand in her way. A gloved hand brushed at his neatly trimmed moustache and whiskers. "You have been on my mind, young lady. We have matters to discuss."

His words were issued innocently enough, but experience made Raven eye him carefully. Nothing in his small smile suggested a leer, yet his presence caused her uneasiness.

"Later, perhaps," she said.

"I am a busy man, Miss Chadwick. Surely you can spare a few moments of your time." He glanced toward the bank, which faced upon the park. "I think of your inheritance, small though it may be, which you have intrusted to my establishment."

"Is something wrong?" she asked, alarmed.

"Of that, you must be the judge."

Raven's heart sank. Of course something was wrong. At the moment she could think of nothing that was right.

A sense of doom sat heavily on her shoulders as she accompanied Gash to the bank. The building was empty of workers. "They're on holiday," Gash explained as he led her to a large room at the rear. When he closed the door behind her and turned the key, she whirled to face him, the alarm she should have been feeling gripping her heart.

"Mr. Gash—" she began, stopped by his leering smile.

Slowly he unbuttoned his coat. "Forgive the locked door, but we must avoid awkward intrusions."

He tossed coat and hat aside, along with the cane. Raven glanced at the door; the key was gone. "I would like to leave now. Whatever we have to discuss can wait."

"Please sit down," he said, gesturing toward an over-stuffed sofa against the side wall.

Raven took in the room at a glance. One window, draperies closed, dark walls and leather furniture, a wide desk, shelves of papers and books—everything neat and businesslike . . . except for the banker's smile.

And the watchful glint in his close-set eyes.

Raven held her ground. "You mentioned my inheritance."

Gash chuckled. "It's quite safe. Fortuitous investments could increase its value, however." He stared at her mouth, then looked down at her cloak. She held it close.

"You're an actress, Raven, a woman of the world. Surely you don't mind if I call you Raven, do you?" He advanced. "Let me help with your wrap."

"I prefer to keep it on."

"For the while. Your father is quite fortunate to have such lovely women underneath his roof."

Raven thought of Mrs. Gash, a woman of formidable stance and bombastic nature. She was also one of the biggest snobs in town. Never had she set foot in the Chadwick store, leaving that chore to her servants.

The look in her husband's eye gave evidence he wasn't quite as aloof.

He left her for a moment to pour a glass of whiskey. "Might I serve you?" he asked.

She shook her head. "I want to leave."

"Not just yet." He swallowed the liquor and set the glass aside. "Enough. Too much would blunt the pleasure of the day."

Raven fought a rising panic. "Please, Mr. Gash, unlock the door."

"Not just yet," he repeated. "Did you know, my dear, your father requires loans from time to time? He pays them off, of course, but one day I might have to turn him down."

Raven knew a threat when she heard one. "If you touch me, I'll—" Her voice broke. She didn't know what she would do.

"You are truly lovely, my dear." He drew close. They were of the same height, but he outweighed her by fifty pounds. She would be no match in a fight.

"And experienced, I'm sure," he continued. "Don't play the virgin, Raven. Any woman who leaves home to go upon the stage is hardly pure. Especially one who ventures into a deserted office with a man." He touched her cheek. "You have the look of a wanton. You make my blood boil."

She jerked away, rubbing her skin. The terror of the night returned, except that the banker was not a dream. "I'll scream," she said.

"In pleasure, I hope. Besides, no one will hear you. These walls are thick, and we're quite alone."

He removed his suitcoat and began to unbutton his vest. His neck lay in reddish folds above his stiff high collar, and he licked his lips with a small, pink tongue.

Raven shuddered.

"Your cloak," he said, no longer gentle. "Take it off."

"If you rape me, I'll tell the world."

"Rape? How blunt-spoken you are, my dear. Who would believe you? I'll claim you asked special favors for your father in exchange for favors of your own. Everyone knows there's nothing too base for the Irish."

She could feel his hot breath on her. He smelled of beef and garlic and a cloying cologne reminiscent of rotted roses.

She closed her eyes. *Not again,* a voice within her cried. Sex for her was linked with violence, and with death. Dark, red-streaked mists swirled behind her lids. She parted her lips, but a jangling bell stilled her scream.

"Goddamn," the banker muttered. Again the bell jangled. "Stay here," he ordered, moustache quivering from his anger. "I'll be right back."

Alone in the locked room, she flew to the window and parted the draperies. Despite her frantic efforts, the bolt at the sill refused to budge. She used the banker's cane to break the glass and gingerly climbed through the jagged opening, emerging in the deserted alley behind the bank. Without a backward glance, she hurried to the brighter light of the nearby street.

All was quiet at home. In the parlor, surrounded by the brightly colored mounds of unfinished gowns, she gave way to her tears. The dream . . . the letter . . . the bank . . . all formed a crushing chain. The dream would return. She knew it in her heart.

And so would Harold Gash, with his implied threats of financial harm to Papa if she did not submit to his wishes. Never, she told herself. At best, the situation was awkward; at worst, disaster for Papa lay ahead.

And all because of her . . . if she stayed. She wanted

to live in Savannah forever, but forever was proving a
very brief time.

*You will die.* For just a moment, she wished that she
could.

But that was the coward's way. When her tears dried,
she saw what she must do. Impossible as it had seemed
during the night, she must say goodbye to her beloved
home.

In London, Gash could not reach her. And she could
prepare the way for Mama, whose anniversary journey
was only months away. The difficulty lay in convincing
her parents she truly wished to leave.

She was an actress, wasn't she? It was time she put
her acting skills to work.

# *Two*

Theaters brought out the lecher in Marcus Bannerman.

Even in a deserted wing of the Lyceum, on a cold, damp January morning with the scent of past performances in the air, he felt a familiar tightening in his loins.

Past associations, past pursuits. He remembered them far too well, as he had known he would. For close to a year he had avoided the London theater district as purposefully as he once had sought it out. If it weren't for Amy, he wouldn't be here today.

"Be on your guard, Marcus."

He cocked an eyebrow at the dark-suited man beside him.

Simon Normandy, the Lyceum's masterful stage manager, returned a rueful smile. "One of your former . . . er, companions lurks backstage."

"Female?"

"Most definitely," the manager replied with a wave of his hand. "No telling where she'll appear."

Though Normandy was four inches shorter than Marcus's six feet, his arms were long and his gesture dramatically wide, taking in the full sweep of the stage wing. He bore strong features, a mop of curly brown hair, and eyes that glinted with both intelligence and humor. He had been Marcus's friend for years and though changing circumstances had separated them, he remained a sympathetic acquaintance.

"You're a legend around here, you know," Normandy added.

Marcus laughed in protest.

"I speak no more than the truth," said Normandy. "I recall the night after a performance of *Henry VIII,* you demonstrated to the players how a rakish king should be played. Very instructive you were, too, striding about the stage and into the darkened theater, quoting God knows what. I think you made up most of the dialogue. You had the women tearing off their clothes."

"Under the influence of brandy," Marcus explained with a rueful grin. "All of us."

"Don't underestimate your appeal, my friend. You've a presence about you that no woman can resist. I'm a contented husband and father, but you were an inspiration to watch."

The man exaggerated. . . . Yet those were the days of indulgence Marcus could not regret, the days before his uncle died and passed on a legacy of responsibilities and debts. Good days indeed, and one of his former paramours lurked nearby.

Nostalgia washed over him, diluting his lust. Sadly, *all* his paramours could be described as former. For a man who lived in a household of women, celibacy was an ironic state of affairs.

He needed a wife, and soon—not a lusty one, unfortunately, but a rich woman willing to wed an impoverished peer. The candidates on his list seemed to prefer respectability over passion, in themselves and their mate. Actresses—the ones of his acquaintance—need not apply.

Slapping his top hat against the folds of his cloak, he tried to decide who might be prowling off the wings.

"Althea Innocent," he said and gave thought to the inaccuracy of the buxom redhead's name. Althea had knowing hands that could put a sailor to blush.

"Right-o," said Normandy.

He stepped past Marcus to turn up a gas jet on the wall beside them, casting a pale light on scattered boxes and trunks, the high scaffolding, the fall of a dozen ropes, and, in the far corner, an open door leading to the back-stage cubicles.

"She's in the sewing room with one of the seam-stresses. The play opened last night. She wants more décolletage."

"Being upstaged, is she?"

Normandy shuddered. "Dreadfully, and by the French maid who has not a word of dialogue. She's not taking it well at all."

Marcus understood the shudder. Althea was a beautiful, passionate star of the London stage. She reveled in her conquests, but at age thirty-five—the same as Marcus—she felt the passing of years, a sense that translated itself into temper. He recalled with clarity her response to the news their six-months' relationship was at an end.

*May your entrails rot within your ugly flesh and destroy the appendage that gives you pride.*

There was nothing equivocal about Althea. The words, flung at him almost a year ago, still rang in his ears.

He'd been ambivalent about severing their ties. Althea enjoyed a romp in bed as much as he, but she also expected expensive gifts, baubles Marcus could no longer provide. Respectability had become his goal. He had been forced to reform.

But damnation, life had lost its zest. He would far prefer a woman's bare breasts against his chest than the hair shirt of duty.

He shook off the thought as fruitless. Too many people depended upon his strength and judgment and, most demanding of all, upon his good name. Like Althea, self-indulgence must remain in his past.

"Retreat would seem advisable," he said.

Normandy nodded.

A rustle of taffeta broke the stillness of the stage wing, drowning out the hiss of the gaslight.

"Trapped," said Marcus as the actress burst through the door.

"The alterations *will* be finished by four this afternoon." Althea Innocent tossed the high-pitched command over her shoulder. "It's out on the streets for you if they are not."

With the threat hanging in the air, her green cat's eyes swept the stage wing and settled on the two men. Even in the dim light Marcus could make out the carefully applied paint that altered the coarseness of her features. Her gown, green to match her eyes, was low-cut, tight-waisted, and full-skirted, and her fiery hair fashioned in a mass of curls beneath a feathered hat, giving height to her short, ripe curves.

"Cussie!" she said as she swished toward them.

Marcus grimaced.

"Cussie?" questioned Normandy under his breath.

"I fear so," said Marcus, his eyes pinned to the approaching actress. He concentrated on the expanse of flesh visible above her neckline. Her ample white breasts jiggled as she walked. He gazed at them in fond remembrance.

She halted in front of him, green taffeta brushing against his black cloak. Her full lips twisted into a smirk, and a self-satisfied glint lit her eyes. "I knew you would return."

Marcus shifted slightly, and from the corner of his eye, he caught a shadowy figure moving in front of the stage curtain to his right. For a moment his attention was diverted. A woman, he thought. Another paramour? Was he being out-flanked?

He pushed the newcomer's presence from his mind. "You're looking well," he said with a short bow.

Althea pouted. "Come now, my pet. You can do better than that. *Well* could describe one of those horses you race."

*Used to race,* Marcus thought with a sigh as he remembered another lost pleasure.

"I can add nothing to what your mirror has already told you," he said.

"Really, Marcus, you should have been a diplomat. I look an absolute fright." She fingered a curl against her cheek. "Curse this damp weather. I can't do a thing with my hair."

She glanced at Normandy. "Simon, darling, do be a precious bunny and hop back to that impudent sewing girl. I asked the simplest of tasks. She acts as though I demanded a new wardrobe. I wouldn't do such a thing ten hours away from curtain."

Marcus recalled she had done exactly that the previous

year; but if he had learned anything in his association with women, it was the wisdom of silence.

The stage manager shrugged at Marcus, as if to say *Sorry, old boy, but you're on your own.*

Marcus patted an inside vest pocket. "Thanks for finding my sister's bracelet. She was certain she'd lost it here earlier in the week."

"It was nothing, m'lord," said Normandy, a formality in his voice now that they were no longer alone. "I believe the clasp is broken."

"I'll see to its repair." Marcus knew how much the piece of jewelry meant to his only sibling. Not that she would be grateful he had located it. Gratitude had not passed between them the past five years.

With a nod to Althea, Normandy hurried across the stage wing and disappeared through the door.

The actress placed a hand on Marcus's arm. "I simply had to get Simon away." She moistened her lower lip. "We have so much to talk about in private."

"Althea, I came by here to collect my sister's bracelet. Our meeting was purely by chance."

"Fate, I'd call it. Surely my Cussie remembers the nights we spent together. And the days, too. How like a lion you were, with your magnificent golden hair, and oh, the things you demanded of your little lioness! You really were a naughty boy to upset me so, although I knew you would return." A calculating glint lit her eyes. "What took you so long?"

Marcus removed her hand from his sleeve, an action that took more force than he had expected. "You are a beautiful woman, Althea, and you deserve someone far more worthy than I."

"Nonsense. Last winter I was the envy of all London—"

She paused, as though she had revealed more than she intended. "Of course, I have been besieged by suitors, but none"—she ran her fingers across his chest—"with your particular charms." Her gaze dropped to below his waist. "They don't even come close."

Again he shifted her hand to her side. Escaping Althea was very much like trying to get rid of flypaper. She kept sticking to whatever she touched.

"Then you must, by all means, continue your search."

Althea's answering shriek bounced against the walls. Marcus flinched. She paced before him, her gown rustling like leaves, her feather bouncing in rhythm with her steps.

"No man insults me in such a way twice. You tell me to look elsewhere. I say you are a cad, a lying, slithering snake, a worm, a jackal who preys on the defenseless—"

She paused for breath, and Marcus wondered if she shouldn't explain the analogies. Cad, snake, and worm he would accept, but jackal was going a bit far.

"This time," she said, her voice thickened to a stentorian tone, "it is I who will leave. Do not attempt to approach me again, for it will do you little good."

In haughty grandeur she stepped past him, headed toward the stairs that led from the stage into the darkened auditorium. She'd always been keen on grand exits, Marcus recalled, grateful his entrails and manly appendage had not been condemned.

The woman he had spied a moment ago remained standing in silence by the curtain. She stepped out of the shadows into the edges of gaslight, a tall and somber figure, her tightly pinned-back hair as black as her bonnet and cloak.

Pausing beside her, Althea glanced over her shoulder. "How fortuitous, Your Lordship. Already a replacement." Then it was back to the newcomer, and a quick, thorough perusal. "What a drab thing you are. Good bones, I grant you, but men prefer ripe flesh. I give you a month."

With a swirl of her skirts, she hurried down the steps and swept up a fur-lined mantle from a front-row chair. The rustle of taffeta slowly faded as she disappeared up the center aisle.

In the ensuing silence, Marcus looked at the woman and shrugged. "Please accept my apologies for Miss Innocent's outburst. She's been under a great deal of stress lately."

"I'm sure that she has. She makes no secret as to its cause."

An American, thought Marcus, and one with an unusually throaty voice. He stepped forward to study her more closely. Drab? Not in the least. Eyes as black as her hair, tawny skin, high cheekbones, a strong, purposeful set to her mouth, all in all a regal bearing, and one he found not only attractive but compelling as well. For the life of him, he could not look away.

Old habits rose within him. He gave her a provocative grin. "She also said we wouldn't last a month. Althea has greatly undervalued your charms, Miss—"

The woman's eyes widened in alarm, as though he'd threatened her. Had he known her sometime in his wastrel past? Had he offended her in some way that startled her months later? He wasn't given to offending women, but in his former life he had been foxed often enough to dally with the female populace of Kensington without an inkling of remembrance.

He must have been unconscious to forget this one.

Thick lashes lowered over finely formed cheeks. When she looked at him again, the alarm was gone, replaced by the light of aggravation. Too, the woman had a defiant tilt to her chin.

"Introductions are not necessary," she said. "I may share Miss Innocent's profession in the theater, but I'm not in contention to be a lioness."

An actress, he thought. A year ago he would have pursued her until she became his . . . for a while at least. Knowledgeable about the latest fashions, he looked over her plain bonnet and cloak. Apparently not very successful at her chosen career. Stage-struck, though. Burning with ambition. Except to be—

What had she said? A lioness. Marcus had to think a moment.

"Ah, yes, one of Althea's menagerie comparisons." He glanced at the woman's white knuckles clutching her cloak. As though he would tear it open and have his way with her.

"You're perfectly safe," he said with an edge of irritation. "I've had to give up ravishing actresses, especially on these wooden floors. Too rough on the knees."

The chin went up a fraction. "If you think I'm afraid, you flatter yourself," she said with more defiance than conviction.

Normally an even-tempered man, Marcus found himself growing angry. First Althea with her histrionics, and now this American acting as though he were a sex-crazed fiend. All he'd come in for was a lost bracelet and a brief visit with an old friend . . . a *male* friend, that is.

Despite his monkish existence, a streak of devilment survived in his soul. He stepped close, until he could smell the clean scent of soap on her skin and see the spark of a matching anger deep in her remarkable black eyes.

"If not a lioness, then what role would suit you?" He stroked her cheek. She flinched but held her ground. "A purring kitten?" he said softly, letting his breath warm her cheek. "One with claws, to draw blood across a man's back when you lie beneath him."

"Oh!" She slapped his hand away. "I've got claws, all right. I've also got sense enough to know when I'm being baited. If you hurry outside, I'm sure you can catch up with Miss Innocent. Or some love-starved ninny who would appreciate your approach. I have all the men I can manage just now."

She allowed her gaze to travel the length of him. "Another would be superfluous."

She stepped back to allow him to pass, and Marcus shook his head, disgusted with them both. Settling his hat low on his forehead, he stared at her for a moment, but anything he thought to say would only make him out a bigger fool.

A pox on all women, he thought as he bowed his goodbye. Taking the stage stairs two at a time and making his way up the center aisle, he marveled at how much he really had changed in the past year.


Raven stared at the flowing cloak disappearing into the darkness of the theater, listened to the fading footsteps, the creaking of a door as it opened and closed. She hugged herself and, for the thousandth time since her ship had docked at Portsmouth a week ago, questioned why she had ever left home.

*Mama.* The answer always came swift and strong. Mama, and the realization that her safe life in Savannah was done.

All right, she conceded, she had justification for being here, but whatever had made her react just now in such a ridiculous way? She'd been rude and then provocative, as though a dozen lovers waited to crawl into her bed. Raven the Wanton was a role she was poorly equipped to play.

She blamed the man who had provoked her, a smoother, more menacing version of Harold Gash. He had started off politely enough, giving her a smile that must have melted many a female heart. Tall, wide-shouldered, with a self-confident bearing, he had a raw-boned, almost boyish look about him, even down to a thin vertical scar in the cleft of his chin.

Boyish, that is, except for incredible blue eyes, insolent, daring, all-seeing. He wasn't an actor, of that she was certain, but he had an actor's eyes, reflecting whatever he chose.

And he had chosen to mock her. She should never have let him see that she was shaken. Just why he had that effect she wasn't sure, but the instant he had stepped close she hadn't been her usual in-control self.

London, that was the problem. As naive as Angel, she had pictured a larger version of Savannah. She couldn't have been more wrong. The city was dirty, crowded, noisy, its constant fog a bilious shade of yellow. The

stench was proving the worst—the sour smell of sewage
in the gutters, of unwashed bodies, and of burning coal
from a million fires. What she wouldn't give for a breath
of clean Georgia air! And a comforting Chadwick smile.

Instead, she was getting leers from total strangers, far
more obvious advances than any she had encountered
back home. This latest boor—this Cussie—wasn't the
first to cast a lascivious eye her way. But he was the
most unsettling.

The actress had called him Your Lordship. Had she
been speaking sarcastically? Or was he really possessed
of a title, like Cousin Elizabeth's Earl of Stafford? Lacking a description from Mama, she had pictured the earl
as pale and thin-faced and slightly balding, his countenance carved with the evidence of dissolute living . . .
or else he was tight-lipped, judgmental, austere.

Either type would be typical of such a lofty personage.
She blamed it on in-breeding. Like the world's lesser animals, the upper classes on both sides of the Atlantic
mated with their own kind.

Certainly no aristocrat was ever tall and ruggedly
handsome, graceful yet athletic in his movements, a
shock of wheat-colored hair falling carelessly across a
high forehead.

And an all-too-friendly smile gracing both his lips and
eyes. No one like him had ever walked into Chadwick
Dry Goods and Clothing, that was for sure. Harold Gash
hardly seemed a member of the same sex.

Something trembled inside Raven, something almost
like the night thoughts, but that couldn't be. That particular terror did not attack during the day. The possibility
that it might now do so was enough to paralyze her heart,

and she thrust the trembles aside. She was neither fourteen nor innocent, and she hadn't come all the way from Savannah to fall victim to her past.

Suitable employment, that was the first order of business, more from a practical standpoint than order of importance. She had told her parents that when her inheritance money ran out, she would return home. A job would extend her stay.

She would find that job, and then it was on to the letter that burned in her pocket. The letter Mama didn't know she had.

Without revealing what she knew, she had tried to confront her parents with arguments against their planned journey. "Old hurts might be stirred," she had said.

"We're mature enough and strong enough to take their slights, lass," Papa had countered.

Slights? *You will die* hardly fit into that category.

One evening shortly before leaving, she'd watched from the bedroom door while her mother threw an empty envelope into the fire, thinking she was destroying the letter itself. Raven had kept her silence, wondering if she were worsening her original betrayal of confidence. She knew only that since Mama planned to ignore the warning, she had to investigate it herself. And so, almost grateful to Harold Gash for forcing her into action, she had declared she was sailing months before them.

"You've given me the courage to seek out what I want. I'll be performing at the Lyceum by the time you get there."

They had been dubious, Mama most of all, but she had assured them she wouldn't visit Cousin Elizabeth or her titled husband or any other Pickering. She would concentrate on her career.

They were lies piled on top of lies. She would find employment if she could, and then it was straight to Bolton Row.

*You will die.* She had to remind herself of the letter night and day. Mama would eventually find out the full extent of her duplicity. Papa, too. She prayed they would understand.

Raven turned toward the sound of footsteps offstage. Simon Normandy, she hoped. She had been given his name at the box office outside. Assistant to the famous Lyceum director Henry Irving, he could help her if anyone could.

She smoothed her hair, straightened her bonnet, and wearing a false smile of confidence, she strode toward the golden glow of gaslight beckoning from the stage wing.

# *Three*

A week later Raven stood before Stafford House, a pale stone edifice in Mayfair's Bolton Row. *I won't visit Cousin Elizabeth.* The lie rang in her ears, but not so loudly she considered leaving.

A very fashionable address, she thought, quite different from her boardinghouse in Soho and definitely suitable for the Earl of Stafford and his countess. Mama had visited here as a child. What awaited her when she returned?

Wrought-iron rails protected the stoop, and Doric pillars flanked the carved door, from the center of which snarled a brass lion's-head knocker. It was no more a welcome sign than the gray mist that swirled about her, chilling her blood and bones.

If only Mama had corresponded with her beloved cousin. She had heard from her only once, in a letter reporting her father's death. At least that had been the one letter anyone knew about. Maybe the Countess of Stafford had penned *You will die.*

Raven pulled her wool cloak close and brushed an errant curl from her face, attempting without success to anchor it back into the twist of hair beneath her bonnet. Her heart pounded with unaccustomed heaviness. Only the letter in her purse kept her from bolting after the hansom cab from which she'd just alighted.

Papa planned to walk right up to Stafford House and ask for Lady Stafford. *Big as you please,* he had said. Raven could do no less. The clip-clop of horses' hooves and the creak of leather and springs echoed in the dense afternoon air as she stepped within the shelter of the portico. Lifting the lion's snout, she let it fall with a bang.

Who awaited her inside? What kind of greeting could she expect? She feared it would be no more friendly than the reception she'd gotten from Simon Normandy and a host of similar managers at the legitimate theaters of London.

She had failed in her attempts to find employment. Irrationally, she blamed the arrogant aristocrat she knew only as Marcus. Unless she counted Cussie, a name that suited him better. He had unsettled her beyond all reason, and she'd made a bad impression on Normandy, setting the pattern for the week.

All that must change.

In her heart she knew the fault lay with herself. She had allowed Cussie to rattle her. Thank goodness she would never see him again.

A minute crept by, and she was about to reach once again for the snout when the door opened with an ominous creak.

A gray-haired man in the formal black worsted suit and stiff white shirt of a butler greeted her with a questioning glance. Thick gray eyebrows swept back in wings above a pair of searching brown eyes, and his lined face reminded Raven of Savannah's most austere and dignified banker.

"Lady Stafford, please," said Raven.

The butler's winged brows raised. "Lady Stafford?"

"Right," said Raven, wondering what she was doing wrong. "Is she at home?"

A gust of wind caught her from behind and the fullness of her cloak snapped through the open door where she had not yet been given admittance.

The butler stepped aside and gestured for her to enter, then closed the door against the cold. He glanced at her gloved hands, but she had no calling card to present.

"Tell her Raven Chadwick, Anne Pickering's daughter, is here."

He hesitated a moment, then his lips twitched, almost into a smile, and his eyes warmed. "Miss Anne?"

Raven felt a surge of hope. "You knew her?"

"I've been with the family since I was a boy. Oh, my."

Raven wanted to ask him a hundred questions about the girl her mother had been, but he gestured for her to wait and hurried across the entryway and up the stairs.

She took in the high carved ceiling, the crystal chandelier, the winding staircase, the gaslights hissing from brackets on the dark-paneled walls. A lone, straight-legged table rested beneath one of the gas sconces; in the center was a single silver salver for the cards of visitors more prepared than she.

All was elegant, but more simple than she had expected from her reading. Where were the dark ancestral portraits, the suits of armor, the massive pieces of furniture she associated with Victorian decor? And where was the hint of evil she feared lurked under this fashionable roof?

Moisture condensed on the folds of her cloak and

dripped onto the marble floor. She stirred nervously. What was taking so long? In Georgia she had thought about her approach, about how she would stride into 22 Bolton Row and demand to know who wanted to harm her mother. In England she wasn't as sure of herself. A softer, ingratiating approach might work better. Besides, at the moment she could be soft far more easily than she could be demanding.

The butler returned to take her cloak and guide her upstairs to the drawing room. She smoothed the skirt of her emerald-green day dress. The style was modest—square neck, natural waist, without a touch of lace or trim on the long sleeves, and only a narrow ruffle at the hem of the straight skirt and short train—but it compensated for its plainness in the color.

Angel had been right in her assessment of the cloth she'd selected. Its brilliance, the result of the new chemical dyes, looked superb. It must have been her sense of the dramatic that had made her choose it. She certainly didn't care to draw attention to herself.

Stepping inside the drawing room, she was again struck by the simplicity of the furnishings . . . few antimacassars on the sofa and chairs, less fringe and clutter than the sitting room of her boardinghouse, no crystal drops on the light fixtures. A small, rectangular piano in the far corner and a delicately patterned pastel Chinese rug, its colors matched in a porcelain vase on the mantel, gave the room both warmth and grace.

"Miss Raven Chadwick," the butler said, then withdrew, closing the door behind him.

Raven stared in dismay at the young woman sitting with book in hand before the fire. Slight of build, with

fair hair outlining a delicately formed face, her complexion pale and pink tinged, her eyes wide and blue, she
reminded Raven of an English rose.

For a moment Raven thought she looked vaguely familiar, but a closer look convinced her she was wrong.

"You're not Lady Stafford," she said, then felt foolish.

"For which I am grateful," the young woman said.
"Lady Stafford died eight years ago."

No wonder Mama hadn't heard from the woman. "I'm
sorry," she said and meant it. "Elizabeth Pickering was
my mother's cousin and her dearest friend. I had been
so sure of meeting her at last."

The young woman looked at her with curiosity. "Lady
Stafford was my aunt by marriage. Her husband, the late
earl, and my father were brothers." Her brow creased.
"The name is Chadwick? It's unfamiliar to me."

"The earl is dead, too?" asked Raven, her heart heavier
than ever. "My grandmother died before Mama left England, and Cousin Elizabeth wrote about my grandfather's death. But we'd thought that others remained who
would remember her."

The young woman stood, tall and straight, and Raven
assessed her more closely. Her gown was fawn cashmere
with a fringed yoke of sage and a matching knife-pleated
underskirt. Her golden hair, parted in the middle, swept
back into a cascade of curls falling from the crown of
her head to the nape of her neck. She couldn't be much
above twenty, certainly not yet twenty-five, but for all
her delicacy there was a tightness around her mouth and
a hardness in her eyes that spoke of an unhappy life.

Or perhaps Raven was reading too much into her countenance and her rigid stance. She had the habit of assessing people as though they were part of a play.

The young woman's eyes suddenly widened. "Chadwick. Of course. How foolish of me. Frederick said something about your mother, but I barely listened. You're the daughter of the disgraced woman, aren't you? The one who ran off to America with that terrible Irishman."

The unexpected criticism stung. Raven could not let it pass. "I'm sorry if that's all you heard. Papa is the most wonderful man in the world."

To her surprise, the young woman smiled. "You're absolutely right," she said, not in the least embarrassed. "I of all people ought to know not to listen to gossip. I'm Amy Bannerman, sister to the present earl. Your mother left long before I was born."

Raven looked at her in surprise. "Lady Amy?" she said.

"Not quite. My father was the late earl's younger brother. He died ages ago, out of a title, out of the money. I'm a simple *miss*." She reached for the bell cord close to her chair. "Please sit and I'll ring for tea."

Apparently Miss Bannerman was quick to change moods, Raven decided, and she had an honesty about her that was disarming. Momentarily at ease, she drew her first deep breath since she'd lifted the lion's-head knocker. She had barely settled herself onto the sofa when the door opened to admit a short, plump, gray-haired woman in beribboned black bombazine, her wide, gray eyes resting in a round and wrinkled face, a kindly smile gracing her lips.

"Frederick said Annie's girl was here. Is it true?" She

caught sight of Raven. "Goodness," she said, pressing fat fingers against her cheek, "the coloring is wrong, Annie was so fair, but the features . . . oh yes, the features are just as I remember them."

"Aunt Cordelia, this is Raven Chadwick," Amy said. "Miss Chadwick, this is my late mother's sister, Miss Cordelia Halstead."

"Raven," said Cordelia. "A perfect name."

"Papa chose it as soon as he saw my dark hair."

"Oh, yes, your Papa." She came around the sofa and beamed down at Raven. "He was quite naughty, you know, in taking away our Annie. Not that we were related by blood. It must be so confusing to you. I can hardly keep it straight myself."

As the woman spoke, Raven caught a strong whiff of gin and noticed the heightened streak of color in her cheeks. Given her condition, it was surprising Cordelia could keep anything straight. But there was something gentle about her, something warm and friendly that made Raven forget the gin.

Again the door opened and closed. This time the woman who entered was tall and thin to the point of emaciation, her black silk dress as plain as Raven's. Dark hair, streaked with gray, was pulled back from her face and twisted into a tight bun at her nape. Her mouth was pinched, her pale eyes sharp as they cut across the room.

"Aunt Irene," said Amy, "I suppose Frederick has told you, too, about our visitor."

Irene, thought Raven in relief. At last here was someone her mother had mentioned. Cousin Irene Pickering, spinster sister to Elizabeth. Mama hadn't remembered her fondly. Unwilling to give a reason, she'd said only that Irene preferred keeping to herself.

She rose to face her mother's cousin and, by extension, hers as well, wondering if she might be greeted by a smile, a hug, even a peck on the cheek. As far as she knew, Irene and her brother Ralph Pickering—if he still lived—were the last of her mother's blood kin.

Irene Pickering made no move to come deeper into the room. "You look like your father," she said.

"Oh, no, Irene," said Cordelia in immediate protest. "She's got Annie's nose and chin and she holds herself just the same way, proud and sure of herself."

"Bah!" said Irene. "Your memory's pickled. Black Irish, that's what she is. What brings you here, girl? Come from the colonies, I take it."

Angry words sprang to Raven's lips, but she swallowed them with a smile. "The English theater beckoned. Ever since I was a young girl, I've longed to go on the stage."

"The stage?" the three listeners said at once.

"The stage," said Raven.

"Oh, dear," Cordelia said with a soft hiccough.

"How unfortunate," Irene said through pursed lips.

It was left to Amy to throw back her head and laugh. "How wonderful! My brother will be furious."

Irene shot the young woman a withering glance, then turned her attention once again to Raven. "Why on earth would you choose to be a public woman?"

"A public woman? That sounds like a—"

"No need to be vulgar, Miss Chadwick," Irene said. "Such women are all on the same level."

"Have you actually performed?" said Amy. "In America, I mean. Oh, this is too marvelous for words."

Raven felt like a ball tossed back and forth, from the critical Irene to the overly delighted Amy. She wasn't sure who was the worse.

"I've performed little outside the parlor of my home."

The arrival of tea interrupted further comment. It wasn't until they were settled down, Amy and Raven in the chairs before the fire and the two older women on the sofa, all balancing cups and saucers and plates of bread and butter, that the issue was raised again.

"An actress," said Amy with a satisfied glint in her eye. "How marvelous! And how brave of you to begin your career in London."

"Humph," Irene said. "Foolishness, I'd call it. If not worse."

Cordelia sipped at the tea and pulled a face.

"Do you have plans for tomorrow evening?" asked Amy.

"None," Raven said.

"Most of London is still in the country, but I'm having a small gathering for dinner. There will be dancing afterwards. Do say you can come."

Raven suspected Miss Bannerman of multiple reasons behind the invitation and not all of them owed to hospitality. Still, she had multiple reasons for accepting.

The rest of her visit was spent in a discussion of her family and the kind of life they led in Savannah. She didn't think it overly dishonest to stress the importance of Chadwick Dry Goods and Clothing to the local economy, skipping over the gentry's superior attitude toward a middle-class shopkeeper and his family who lived in a frame house behind the store.

If Mama and Papa did make it over here, she wanted them viewed in the best possible light.

With such an attentive audience, she quickly described her two sisters—redheaded Flame, now living in Texas, and the sweet, fair-haired Angel, barely twenty, who remained at home—making no attempt to hide the love she felt for them both.

The aunts seemed most interested when she described how Papa had named each of his daughters for the color of her hair.

"How sweet," Cordelia said.

"How strange," said Irene.

Lost in thought, Amy did not speak.

When Raven tried to put forth questions of her own, she met with evasions. Even when she raised the possibility of a summertime visit by her parents, she elicited no more than polite responses, certainly nothing that indicated a possible source of Mama's letter.

Her detecting skills, she decided a half hour later as she walked through the quickening mist toward Piccadilly and a hoped-for hansom cab, definitely needed work.


Having little idea the manner of dress required for the evening, Raven chose a silk crimson gown. Only a flounced overskirt and lace-trimmed off-the-shoulder neckline kept it from being as unadorned as the emerald-green. She would have preferred a cloak grander than the black limousine, but it was serviceable enough, the only truly important consideration.

For jewelry Raven wore a pair of her mother's teardrop

pearl earrings, forced upon her at the last minute of packing by an insistent Anne. Long white gloves came to the edge of the rounded short sleeves, and she had exchanged her sturdy boots for black-satin evening slippers.

She arrived at Stafford House later than she'd planned; but on a clear, brisk Saturday night, with most of London gadding about the town, summoning a hansom cab had proven difficult. Miss Bannerman had said most of London remained in the country. She must have meant the fashionable set. On this one evening Raven had passed more people than she would have seen in a month in Savannah.

A footman greeted her at the door. Tall and sharp-featured, with eyes reminiscent of a hawk's, he gave Raven a personal survey as he took her cloak. Word of her would-be occupation must have spread among the servants. Obviously, a public woman deserved whatever looks she received.

Raven swallowed her natural reticence to meet strangers and shifted into a queenly stance. She hadn't much of a bosom, but she possessed height and a long slender neck to give her distinction. Too, she was confident of the coiffure over which she had labored, an upsweep of fragile curls that tumbled to her bare shoulders and soft tendrils that outlined her face.

She had considered enhancing her complexion with the lightest touch of paint, but cosmetics were worn only by women of lowest morality, according to the landlady at her boardinghouse. She relied on the natural blush of anticipation to lighten her tawny skin.

Whatever was working, the footman seemed impressed. With full respect he directed her toward the butler, who in turn guided her once again to the drawing room. The furniture had been pushed aside to accommodate the crowd, and in the alteration the room had lost its warmth.

"Frederick," she said as she looked over the expanse of jewels and medals glittering in the gaslight, "we must talk sometime about Mama."

"Whenever you wish, miss," he said with deference, but there was a decidedly pleased glint in his eye.

"Miss Raven Chadwick," he announced from the door.

Several heads turned. Gradually the laughter and talk ceased. Raven stood somewhat awkwardly for a moment, then forced a satin slipper forward, and another, searching all the while for a familiar and mercifully friendly face. She spied no one but fashionably dressed strangers.

If only she had gotten out socially more often, she might have known how to conduct herself, but she was such a private person that she rarely spoke to anyone outside the store. Savannah people thought she was haughty. Little did they know.

Haughty more aptly described the crowd she now faced. This was for Mama, she told herself. She could not turn and run.

The air in the room was close. Perspiration pooled between her breasts, and a line of moisture beaded on her upper lip.

"Miss Chadwick," a female voice trilled. The crowd parted as Amy Bannerman hurried toward the door, her ruffled and flounced cornflower faille gown rustling as she moved. Her thick-lashed blue eyes sparkled as she took Raven's hand.

"Come, there's someone I want you to meet. You're my surprise of the evening. I can hardly wait to see his reaction."

A brittle edge to her voice made Raven want to tug free and dash for safety, but the crowd closed behind her, cutting off retreat. They headed for an open window at the far end of the parlor. The other guests stepped aside, and Raven had the feeling she was being led to the scaffold and a waiting hangman.

When she saw the man directly ahead, she realized she wasn't far wrong. He spoke with another gentleman, his head thrown back in laughter. When he caught sight of the approaching women, the laughter died.

He was taller than Raven remembered him, blonder, more angular, and overall more like the lion he had been called. His eyes—actor's eyes, she'd thought them, capable of dissembling—were an icy blue as he studied her.

She was struck anew by the handsome picture he presented with his rugged features and the small scar at his chin. All in all, he looked uncompromisingly seductive, even to her. A rush of night air wafted through the open window. Raven shivered, but not from the cold. It was the old darkness stirring within her. She used all her self-possession and acting skills to return his steady gaze.

"Marcus," said Amy, "this is Raven Chadwick. Anne Pickering's daughter. You were only a boy when she ran away to America, but surely you've heard the family talk."

In none-too-friendly fashion, she turned to Raven. "Miss Chadwick, this is my brother Marcus Bannerman, since last year declared the twelfth Earl of Stafford and master of all he surveys. You must tell him of your ambitions in London. He'll be fascinated to hear."

# Four

Marcus stared into a pair of remarkable and all-too-familiar ink-black eyes.

Impossible, he told himself, yet the woman standing before him truly was the brazen actress from the Lyceum. He had thought of her more than once during the past week. What in bloody hell was she doing here?

Amy, he thought. This was one of her little games.

"Miss Chadwick," he said, outwardly calm. The name puzzled him. Had he heard it before? Something had been said about family, but knowing his sister's approach to conversation, he had paid it little mind.

"Lord Stafford," the actress returned, her voice level and controlled as she raised her eyes to his. Was that a glint of panic he saw in those black depths? Was she not as composed as she appeared? She was up to something, of that he was sure.

A hush settled over the room, as if everyone awaited a scene. Which they probably did, courtesy of their hostess. Amy had probably hinted there would be a special entertainment tonight. This was low, he thought, even for her, since the guests included several prospective brides and a few fathers as well. He'd be damned if he would react in any way that played into her hand.

"Isn't it wonderful Miss Chadwick has returned?" said Amy with more brightness and volume than Marcus thought necessary. "You remember, brother dear, the family scandal back in the forties."

"No, I do not."

"And I thought you were up on everything. Anne Pickering, Aunt Elizabeth's cousin, ran off with the Irishman—"

She broke off as she met Miss Chadwick's eye. Around them whisperings spread like leaves in a breeze.

Marcus gave grudging approval to the actress for cutting off his sister's less-than-kind ramblings, something he could seldom accomplish. Amy smiled at him, all innocence, but he didn't trust her. Somehow she had laid a trap to embarrass him, using a beautiful actress as bait, and she stood by quietly, waiting for the moment he would explode.

He wanted nothing more than to disappoint her. His explosions, should there be any, would come when he got Miss Chadwick alone.

"I would be most interested in hearing your story," he said. "But there's no need to bore our guests."

"They wouldn't be bored," said Amy. "Besides, you can't go off alone with her. Propriety demands a chaperon."

"Thank you for reminding me. I'll summon the aunts."

With a quick nod to the man beside him, he took Miss Chadwick by the elbow and guided her toward the door. He felt a tug on his hand, but he held firm, sensing through the thickness of her glove the softness and warmth of her arm.

Without a word, he took her downstairs to the library,

past a bemused butler and footman. He glanced at his prisoner. She wanted to cry out for help—the urge was there in her eyes—but she settled for an accusatory glance.

She walked ahead of him into the dimly lit room. A single gas jet burned, and the fire in the grate was low, casting grotesque shadows across the bookshelves that lined the walls. He watched her study the worn volumes, the heavily upholstered leather furniture, the wide oak desk that occupied much of the room. In her scarlet gown, with her fine features proudly set and her hair as intricately arranged as the pattern in the wine-colored rug, she looked very feminine and very out of place.

Her dark gaze shifted to him. "This is a man's sanctuary."

"Yes, it is."

"Then why did you bring me here?" she asked with what looked like worry in her eyes.

She was good at her craft, he thought, but not totally convincing. Perhaps rather than worried, she was disappointed she didn't play her role before a larger audience.

"I brought you here to have my way with you. Unlike the Lyceum stage, the rug is thick enough to protect my knees."

Her gasp sounded genuine enough. "Do not mock me," she said, twisting her hands at her waist. "You promised to summon the aunts."

"I lied," Marcus said, smiling. "I trust you don't mind."

She dropped her trembling hands to her sides. A nice

touch, he thought. So too was the tilt of her chin, as though she were summoning courage to confront him.

"Are you trying to charm me, Your Lordship? Do the hearts of English women melt beneath your gaze? Do they beg to run their fingers through your golden hair? I'll bet they don't notice your smile doesn't make it to your eyes."

She goaded him without mercy. Marcus rose to the challenge.

"It can, Miss Chadwick. Just tell me you've changed your mind about being a lioness."

There was no mistaking her indignation. "You really do take that lion comment seriously, don't you? As I recall, Miss Innocent also called you a worm and a snake and a jackal."

"You have a remarkable memory."

"I'm an actress, remember?"

"How could I forget?" He stepped close. "Where are all your lovers tonight?" He rested his hands lightly on her shoulders, to let her sense the heat but not the weight. "Perhaps you decided one more would not be superfluous?"

Something close to panic fluttered in her eyes. "Have you noticed we respond to one another in questions?" she asked.

He bent his head close and tightened his hold on her shoulders. Satin skin warmed beneath his fingers. His thumb sought the pulse point at her throat. His loins tightened at the pounding of her heart.

"Then it's time we came up with some answers," he said, a sudden hunger eating at him. He'd like to give

her what she wanted, all right, here on the carpet, and
now before he remembered his resolve.

Her lips parted, and he watched a play of emotions in
the depths of her ebony eyes. Surprise, curiosity, perhaps
a hunger comparable to his—in kind if not in intensity.

He also saw fear. Cursing, he released her as though
she were a firebrand.

"You're safe enough," he said. "I prefer willing part-
ners."

"Which hardly describes me."

"Stop the lying, Miss Chadwick. Or whoever you are.
You weren't all that disinterested." His gaze turned icy.
"Amy's outdone herself this time. How much is she paying you to participate in this charade? And how in hell
did you two meet? That had to be your doing."

"Paying me?" she asked. "I had no idea you would
be here."

"You do righteous indignation very well, but you really
ought to speak louder. With a little more volume, we can
entertain everyone at Amy's gathering. That is what you
two planned, is it not?"

"You are insane." She tried to step past him, but he
gripped her shoulders and held her in place. Damnation,
he couldn't keep his hands off her.

"I don't know what the trouble is between you and
your sister," she said, "but I seem to be caught in the
cross fire. I repeat, I did not know you would be here
tonight. If you will release me long enough to summon
your aunts, they can describe my first visit. You may not
want them here, but I do."

For the first time he felt a flicker of doubt. "Tempting,
but they've retired to their separate pursuits."

Studying the face lifted to him, he saw outrage in the set of her mouth and the fire in her eyes. Could this display of emotion be genuine? Perhaps his presence had truly been a surprise. A gentleman would give her the benefit of the doubt, and he was supposed to be a gentleman. Reluctantly he released her. She stepped away.

"You've accused me of lying, Your Lordship. What in the world do you think I'm lying about? That my name is Raven Chadwick? That I'm Anne Pickering's daughter? Why should I claim such an identity if it weren't true?"

He settled back on the arm of a chair and crossed his extended legs at the ankles.

"Prove it," he said.

"What?"

"Prove you're who you claim."

She glanced at her hands, clutched at her waist, and he could have sworn she muttered the beginnings of Portia's "mercy" speech.

Her thick lashes lifted.

"You'll have to accept my identity, Lord Stafford, because I say so."

"Ha!" he barked in a most unearl-like way. "You sound like my father whenever I questioned his word."

His gaze traveled over her features, the slope of her bare shoulders, reddened where his hands had pressed. He concentrated on the rise of her breasts above her fire-red gown. "You don't look like him, however, for which you can be grateful. He was short and fat."

"If you're trying to compliment me, don't bother. I'm not interested in pretty words."

"If I were trying to compliment you, Miss Chadwick, I could conjure up images that would whirl your lovely head."

"Please, Your Lordship, spare me from a sampling." She looked at him a moment, then sighed. "Oh, very well. If I must, I must."

She gave him a wide berth as she moved closer to the dying fire. In profile, with the soft glow of firelight detailing her features, she was maddeningly lovely. As she surely must have known.

"Your father married money," she said. "Mama didn't remember much about your parents except that they had a young son. I suppose that was you."

He kept his surprise to himself.

"I called here yesterday, believing that your uncle, the late earl, still lived. I hoped to meet his wife. Cousin Elizabeth had been my mother's dearest friend. Instead I met her sister, Irene Pickering. It seemed curious to me that Miss Bannerman introduced her as her aunt when she is not blood kin."

"Aunt Irene is a legacy that came with the title. She has long made her home at Stafford House."

"Is her brother Ralph alive? If so, they must be the only living relatives Mama has in England."

"Ralph Pickering lives at his club not far from Bolton Row."

"At least there are two relatives for Mama to see," she said, so low he barely caught her words. "Elizabeth wrote of the death of my grandfather, I think it was in 1863. The war was still going on then and we didn't get the letter for a long while. It broke my mother's heart that they hadn't made peace. My grandmother died years before Mama met Papa. You couldn't have known her. Mama said she was lovely—"

"Enough," said Marcus, raising his hands in surrender. "I concede you're who you claim to be."

He was graced with the actress's smile. She really ought to smile more often, he thought.

"You've come to England to meet the family," he said.

"That's right."

"And to find employment on the stage."

"You make my quest sound unworthy."

"It will be judged so, which is why Amy asked you here. Embarrassing her lordly brother has become her favorite game." The look on her face stopped him for a moment. "I had assumed you were part of her little scheme, but you seem wounded. Could I have been wrong again?"

"I don't know what you are. From what I saw at the Lyceum, I didn't think you always found actresses unworthy."

"Ah, you're remembering Miss Innocent. You're thinking what a hypocrite I am. And you're right. Hypocrisy is a basic tenet upon which English society is based."

"Cousin Irene said I would be a public woman. It's a sentiment you seem to share."

"Aunt Irene does not travel much about town, but she reads a great deal. She knows the prevailing attitudes."

"Which include the fact that it's all right to sit in awe of an actress, to applaud her talents and allow her to stir an audience to tears. It's even all right for a man such as yourself to share her bed. What is not all right is to allow her in the front door of your home."

"Congratulations, Miss Chadwick. You have picked up

on the fine points of Victorian morals. Except that words such as bed are rarely spoken in mixed company. You must admit, we're about as mixed as company can get."

"For which I am grateful."

His gaze traveled lazily across her figure. The inconstant light from both lamp and hearth cast interesting highlights on the rise and fall of her red silk gown. "I share the sentiment."

"Must you turn everything into a sexual taunt?"

"Tsk, tsk. Another blunder. Bed and sex in the same conversation? You'll never meet with success in the parlors of London."

He stood and closed the distance between them. "But in more private quarters—"

"You're testing me, aren't you? Using innuendo when outright accusations fail to elicit the response you're after."

"And that is what?"

"That for some reason you have not yet specified I wished to embarrass you tonight. That your sister made the suggestion and I leapt upon it as the low-class American I am. Miss Innocent was right. You are not a very nice man. Please move, Your Lordship. I wish to leave."

God, she was magnificent. She fired his blood.

"No," he said.

She shoved him, a very un-English act. When he did not move, she shoved again.

"Would you care to arm-wrestle, Miss Chadwick? You might meet with greater success."

She held herself very still. "What am I doing?" she whispered, staring at her hands as though they had acted on their own. She looked up at him with an anguish that seemed straight from her heart. "I've never behaved this way."

Marcus felt a twinge of uneasiness, but it did not linger. He knew well the deviousness of human nature. Miss Chadwick claimed she had traveled across an ocean to meet a family that had tossed her mother onto the street. He would accept that story when Queen Victoria opened a brothel in the Windsor Castle keep.

"Indulge me, please, Miss Chadwick. I have a few questions."

She nodded, her anguish softened to a lost look in her eyes.

"How long have you been in England?"

"Almost two weeks."

"And you are only now seeking out your long-lost family?"

"I wanted to settle in before I called."

"Ah, I see. Settle in."

"I couldn't show up at your door with luggage in hand. You would have thought I wanted a place to stay."

"And where have you . . . ah, settled in?"

"Soho. I know it's part slum, but I've found a perfectly respectable boardinghouse that I can afford."

"And have you found a position in a nearby theater? I understand they offer performances that are quite unique."

He tried to picture Miss Chadwick in one of the orgiastic displays that took place in that vice-ridden quarter of the city. Even in his most debauched moments, he'd never been tempted to attend a performance. For him, sex was not a spectator sport.

If Raven Chadwick were on the stage, however—

"As of yet," she said, "I have not been employed."

"Simon turned you down, did he?"

"He suggested a theater requiring little experience."

"A music hall, I'll be bound. Don't try to deny it. The indignation is there in your eyes."

"Lord Stafford, I have memorized most of Shakespeare's plays and many of his sonnets. All I want is a chance to demonstrate what I can do."

"It is entirely possible your accent is a handicap. Taking on a Shakespearean role is a lofty goal."

"Lofty but not respectable."

"It's another example of our hypocrisy. But we speak of you, not my country's shortcomings. Do you mind if we review what you have told me? I'm having difficulty assimilating it all. Without a chaperon or companion, you sailed from the colonies, arriving here several weeks ago."

"Two."

"Alone, you rent quarters in Soho, seek employment in the theater district, and after meeting with failure, find your way to Mayfair and your mother's estranged family."

"You make it sound as though I expected your help."

"You most certainly expected something. Not, I think, meeting with someone who had already observed your comportment." He took a step forward, and then another, not stopping until her back was to the wall beside the hearth, her chin tilted against his assault. "Under the circumstances, Miss Chadwick, you should have expected being tossed out on your ear."

A momentary panic in her eyes sharpened to anger. "I'm beginning to wish I had been."

"What a nice tremor you put to your voice. Admit you came here after weeks of frustration, hoping to foster a connection that might aid your ambitions. Even an American must realize that having the support of the peerage would be advantageous."

"Oh," she cried, then slapped him. He grabbed her by the shoulders and shook her. A curl fell loose across her cheek, giving her a wanton look. Her lips were full and red and parted. Desire knifed through him.

"Damnation, you make it difficult to be a gentleman."

"In your case, it must be impossible."

"Always a retort—"

He knew of one way to silence her. He kissed her. She stiffened, twisted, then seemed to melt into his arms. A year's worth of suppressed hungers destroyed Marcus's control. He'd meant only to end their argument, but she provoked him beyond endurance. His tongue sought hers and tasted honeyed sweetness. To hell with respectability, he thought savagely. The soft, warm woman in his arms obliterated common sense.

His hands sought her back, the curve of her waist, the flare of her hips. His palms cupped her buttocks, pulling her against his loins as his tongue ravaged her mouth. She was incredibly yielding.

And then she became a wildcat, slapping and clawing, writhing to escape. From aggressor, he shifted to defender, grabbing for her wrists, protecting his face from her feral nails and his body from her relentless knee.

At last he was able to back away. They stood facing one another, drawing ragged breaths.

"Don't you ever touch me again," she said.

He stroked a line of blood on his cheek. "What made you decide you didn't like it?"

A look of such dark terror flashed in her eyes that Marcus was momentarily stunned.

"I have no use for men." Trembling fingers smoothed her dress and tugged the neckline higher on her shoulders. "You took me by surprise, but it will not happen again."

Marcus stared at her long and hard. She had certainly been willing, at least for a moment. He credited her with retrieving a sense of propriety first.

A poor sort of respectable earl he was turning out to be.

"Accept my apology, Miss Chadwick."

"I wish you sounded more sincere."

"I do the best I can. Perhaps if I were a more skillful lover, you would not have taken offense."

"Again you mock me." She looked at him with tears in her eyes. "I—"

She broke off, as though what she wanted to say was too painful to put into words. She could not have chosen a more effective way to make him feel like dirt.

She circled around him and stepped toward the door. He touched her arm. She jerked away.

"I said do not touch me."

"I meant only to warn you that your hair needs tending. I will get your wrap and see that a carriage is summoned to take you back to Soho."

She cast a sideways glance at him. "Get me out of Mayfair, is that the plan? I assure you, it is my most urgent wish. But I must warn you that I will visit with my mother's cousins whenever I am able. Do you have a regular kind of job that takes you away from the house during the day? I would dislike inconveniencing you again with my presence."

"A job? What a curious idea." Marcus almost smiled. "I'm a peer of the realm. I have this ancestral house and a host of relatives to support, as well as an estate in Sussex. It's supposed to be enough."

"You English honor the idle rich, don't you, and scorn those who must work for a living."

Marcus could have told her he was neither idle nor rich, but he doubted she would listen.

"I wish you well in your search for employment," he said. "You should take Simon's advice and try the music halls. They truly are less demanding in their requirements." His eyes raked her for what he supposed was one last time, and he admitted to a moment of regret. "You are a beautiful woman, Miss Chadwick. I would be most surprised if you do not meet with success."

Lord Stafford left the room before Raven could respond. In the silence of his departure, the enormity of her weaknesses overcame her. She was such a reserved creature, quiet, withdrawn, outspoken with only her family. Around Marcus Bannerman, a stranger, she turned into a witch, a wanton, behaving in ways that brought her the deepest shame.

He frightened her because he turned her into a woman she did not know, a brazen shrew who needed only his touch to feel a heat in her blood she had never imagined, not even in her dreams. The touch of his lips still lingered on hers, the moist warmth, the delicate sensation that had the power of a thunderbolt. For a moment she had been powerless to struggle.

And then the terror had returned. She should have run for the front door when she had the chance, but she had reminded herself of Mama. *You will die.* Its message was all-important. She had much to learn about the Bannermans before Mama returned to these shores and into the arms of danger.

Not, however, by submitting to the earl's all-too-obvious charms.

What was he doing here anyway, she asked herself with little consideration for reason. She would never forget the shock of seeing him standing by the window, so tall and proud, the handsomest man in the room—and head of the household she must invade. No wonder Amy Bannerman had seemed familiar to her when first they met. She looked just like her brother.

Raven cringed to think of all she and the earl had said to one another at the Lyceum. But she'd had no idea—

She sighed. Of all the bad luck in the world, hers must be the worst.

As the butler Frederick escorted her to the front stoop, she did not catch sight of the earl, nor did she meet with any other residents of Bolton Row. Climbing into the cab summoned by the footman, she glanced at the carved front door of Stafford House. An outside light fell on the lion's-head knocker.

The snarling lion. The moment she had first spied it, she should have known the kind of animal lurking within.

With a sigh she admitted the truth. Bad luck wasn't

her problem. She herself was to blame. She had gone to Stafford House with the highest of intentions, but she had ended up making a mess of everything.

nothing would stand in their way. Together they would find the book. And when she had the diary in her hands . . . but everything in time, she reminded herself.

# Five

Marcus summoned Amy to the library shortly after noon the next day. As usual she kept him waiting. Listening to the storm outside his window, he had awhile to think, to study the bills and reports on his desk, to consider last night. Raven Chadwick, more than anything or anyone, refused to leave his mind.

He had spent a restless night going over all that had passed between them, regretting he had ever met her, wishing he knew her in ways that would pleasure them both.

Life certainly took unexpected turns. This time last year, with several lovelies vying for his attention, he had had nothing more weighty to consider than the best race in which to enter his stallion Lightning. Then he had come into his title, and Lightning had been sold.

The death of his cousin Arthur, the late earl's only child, had made the succession possible. His uncle had been young enough to sire other heirs. With that thought in mind, he had remarried after the first Lady Stafford's death.

He had died in bed in the arms of his young bride, who promptly took another husband and sailed for Australia, leaving a mound of debts in her wake. Marcus had come into possession of those debts, a once-great fortune dwindled from poor investments, the London town house, a bankrupt farm, a family to support.

Amy and Cordelia had always been there, of course, since his own parents had died; but they had lived a simple country existence on the Bannerman land that had been his father's legacy as second son. Marcus's gaming provided them a few luxuries. Now he had Irene and Ralph and a host of servants, long-time family retainers, the farm tenants. . . . The list of salaries went on, extending across the channel to France.

Amy had taken to spending enormous sums, claiming she did so only to further their reputation as leaders in society, leaving him to pay the bills. He ought to deny her; but whenever he tried, the image of a small house in Paris changed his mind.

Responsibility. A hair shirt. He'd love to pluck it off.

Yet, in another way, he found it a curious comfort and a welcome challenge. It wasn't anything he had admitted to anyone. He had barely admitted it to himself. Marcus the family man? Former friends would laugh.

His own and Amy's had never been a loving home, their parents wrapped in their own concerns. Since his adolescent years, his father had encouraged his wild ways.

"I never had much freedom," John Bannerman had said in his sole fatherly talk. "Remember, I was forced to marry young. Sow those wild oats, boy, while you can."

Raven Chadwick had said his father had married money. And so he had, to Gwenda Halstead, Cordelia's older sister. With the Bannerman and Halstead wealth depleted, it fell upon Marcus to follow his father's example. He had never planned to marry for love—except for his affection for Amy, love was a foreign emotion to him—but the woman who received his mother's locket should share his passions, all of them. Like the land in Sussex.

It was unfortunate none of the candidate brides showed the least interest in the country life since his time for wife shopping was close to an end.

Amy's arrival brought an end to his reflections. He watched her cross the room. Dressed in a simple blue gown, her hair free-flowing, she was a lovely young woman. Without artifice, she looked no older than eighteen.

He saw a little of himself in her height and in her face—the Bannerman bone structure, the Bannerman mouth—except that on her it all looked far more dainty, more precious. Something caught within him, something at once sharp and soft.

If only he could turn back the clock five years . . .

But he couldn't. And he wouldn't do things differently.

Everything in his life seemed fated, both the good and the bad, and most certainly it was out of his control.

He glanced at the rain pounding against the window at his back, condensation on the beveled panes obscuring the view of dead leaves in the garden. Despite the fire in the grate and the thickness of his morning coat, he felt a sudden chill.

Amy halted in front of his desk and eyed him boldly, as she always did, a familiar stubborn challenge hardening her delicate countenance. Then came puzzlement and, at last, a small smile.

"Brother dear, what is that mark on your cheek? Could it be a scratch? Let me guess. You've brought a kitten into Stafford House as a surprise."

"I'm not the one who brought in the surprise. Sit down. We have matters to discuss."

"I'm sure we do. Is that why you didn't return to the party last night? Because that ferocious actress attacked and you couldn't staunch the blood?"

The truth of the observation did little to remove its sting. He gestured toward a chair. "Sit down. Please."

"Avoiding the issue, are you? Secrecy will do little good. I'll find out what happened. And while the 'please' is almost charming and must have fluttered the hearts of a dozen women this week alone, I'd rather stand. Surely this won't take long. I was just beginning the invitations for a ball."

"Another one?"

"Last night was a small gathering, with only a pianist to provide music. This one will be done right, with an orchestra and a late supper, and . . . oh, you know, everything that's in fashion. The list of guests already contains two hundred names, and I'm not yet done."

Marcus riffled the bills before him. "And how do you propose to pay for it?"

"The way I always do. I'll send the creditors to my brother, who in his wisdom takes care of all problems. No matter how big or how small."

Marcus refused to be goaded into old arguments. Tossing his pen aside, he leaned back in his chair.

"And what was that problem you presented me last night?"

Amy's eyes widened. "A problem? You can't mean the charming Miss Chadwick. You've become so zealous about familial ties that I felt certain you would be ecstatic to meet her."

"We're alone, Amy. Out with the truth. You thought I would be furious."

"Which was it, fury or ecstasy? You left the room so fast, dragging the poor woman after you, I was unable to tell. Gossip leaned first toward fury; but when neither of you returned, ecstasy seemed favored."

"I sent word she had taken ill and I was called to business."

"Do you think anyone believed your excuses? You haven't yet lived down your reputation, Marcus, although the world knows you're trying to be a good boy."

She studied his scarred cheek. "At least you claim you are. If only you hadn't been bad for so long."

Sometimes Marcus wondered if his only sibling and primary responsibility didn't need a good spanking; other times, he was certain of it. He knew, too, that once he lifted a hand against her, the rift between them would be permanent. Foolish though the idea was, he kept hoping they would make their peace.

"You have an uncanny way of turning the conversation to your own ends, Amy, but this time I want the truth. What was Raven Chadwick doing here?"

"Bah. You want a confession. It's not at all the same thing. Miss Chadwick came here to announce she was visiting from America. She said her mother was a cousin and close friend to Aunt Elizabeth; and since you always seemed so fond of the countess, I thought you would want to meet her."

"You thought I would welcome her, ask about her presence here, and learn, with your carefully gathered assembly as witness, that she was an actress. The men who haven't dallied with such romantic creatures harbor fantasies about them, and the women are convinced they're all immoral. It would have led to a very interesting scene."

Amy sighed. "Yes, it would. And you forced her from the room before she could say a word. That wasn't in the least bit fair."

Marcus snapped his fingers. "I understand these latest invitations now. After last night's disappointment, you want a second chance for a scene."

Amy paced in front of his desk. "Really, Marcus, you make me sound calculating. In truth, I found Miss Chadwick a rather pleasant person. It doesn't bother me in the least that she wants to go on the stage. But you know what a flighty child I am."

"Don't provoke me any further than you have already done, little sister. What you did not know was that Miss Chadwick and I had already met."

Amy came to a halt and stared at him. "Already met?"

"When I stopped by the theater for your bracelet, she was there seeking employment. I took her for nothing more than an ambitious American. To her, I might have been the Prince of Wales. Or, I suppose, the Prince of Darkness. We did not introduce ourselves, nor did we become friends."

"Neither at the theater nor here last night." She broke

into a smile. "I knew you were angry when you saw her. I couldn't understand it. Now I do."

"If my anger pleases you, Amy, am I to be grateful?"

Her smile died. "I'm glad to get any kind of emotional reaction from you."

Brother and sister stared at one another for a moment, then Amy looked away. Marcus cursed silently. What in the devil was wrong that he couldn't talk to the person who meant the most to him in all the world? They couldn't converse five minutes without being at each other's throats.

"Amy—"

A clap of thunder stopped him. With the windowpanes rattling in their frames, the door opened to admit Irene.

"I thought I'd find you two together. Talking about Miss Chadwick, I should imagine."

She brushed an invisible hair from her face. As always, she was dressed in black, her gown straight and plain, accenting her tall, skeletal build and the hard lines in her face. Irene had a dry look about her, as if her body had been robbed of fluids. She'd never had a suitor that anyone could recall; ever since moving into Stafford House twenty years before, when the eleventh earl was in residence, she had satisfied herself with books.

Marcus had no complaints, even though she was related only to the former earl's deceased first wife.

"We were indeed discussing our American cousin," he said. "Or yours, to be more accurate."

"She's a stranger to me," Aunt Irene said with a sniff. "An upstart who doesn't know her place."

"And where might that be?" asked Amy.

Aunt Irene studied the shelves of books lining the library walls. At last her gaze fell to the window behind Marcus. "She belongs with her mother and that insufferable man she married. There's no place for her here."

"Aunt Irene," said Amy, "she just arrived. Can't we give her a chance?"

"Humph. Don't see why we should."

"I found her rather nice."

Everyone turned to the latest speaker, who had slipped unnoticed into the library and was standing just inside the door.

"Aunt Cordelia," said Amy, "come in and cast your ballot. Do we buy Miss Chadwick a ticket on the next clipper to America? If not, we could take her to our collective bosoms, as no doubt my brother has already tried. Or do we try sending her to the Tower? Which shall it be?"

"You're enjoying this, aren't you?" said Marcus.

"At least she has introduced a new topic of conversation. One does grow weary of hearing how much we should all economize and how you're going to take care of us if we'll only cooperate and place our lives into your hands."

He couldn't dispute a thing she said. God, what a straight stick he had become. He who had once bet his bank account on the turn of a card. No one appreciated— or hated—the irony more.

Again the library door opened.

"Mr. Ralph Pickering, m'lord," the butler Frederick announced.

Marcus felt a moment's relief. Here at last was a man to take his side . . . if he only knew what in hell it was. How did he feel about Miss Chadwick? At times last night he had tried to take her to his bosom, as Amy had said, and at others to send her to the devil, failing dismally at both extremes.

Today, assailed by memories of her eyes and her scent and of how she had tasted, he wasn't sure about anything concerning her. Except that she probably had legs in proportion to her long and slender arms. It was a trait he admired.

He knew one thing. This celibacy must come to an end.

Ralph strode into the room, went immediately to the sofa where Aunt Cordelia was seated, and took her hand.

"Cordelia, you're looking charming as ever."

Cordelia blushed . . . or perhaps it was just the gin that stained her cheeks. Marcus was never sure. To him his aunt looked the way she always did, round and kind with friendly gray eyes and gray hair that was never quite in place and a face that was quick to wrinkle into a smile.

Ralph turned to his sister, who stood behind him. "Irene, you appear in excellent health."

"As do you," she said.

Ralph did look fit. No taller than Irene, he sported neatly trimmed Dundreary whiskers and thick brows pewter in color like the rest of his hair. He always managed to dress in a dapper manner, despite the fact he was as much without funds as everyone else. This morning he sported a forest green single-breasted morning coat over a canary waistcoat, brown trousers tight to the knee, then flaring over patent-leather boots.

At sixty, he was two years older than his sister and the same age as Aunt Cordelia. Like the women, he had never wed, but there had been rumors in his youth of a great, tragic love.

He greeted Amy as cordially as he had Cordelia, then shifted his attention to Marcus. "It lacks only the boys here to make this a true gathering of the clan."

"That it does," said Marcus, thinking "the boys" aptly described his two rapscallion distant cousins, although one was just under thirty and the other just over. Each had inherited a baronetcy without benefit of money to go with the titles.

The passing on of such financial legacies was, Marcus had long ago decided, a family trait.

"I heard there was a bit of a dust-up here last night," Ralph said. "Something about a long-lost relative showing up at the door begging alms. The story's all over the club."

"I knew it," snapped Irene as she sat beside Cordelia. "That woman will bring us little good."

Amy started to reply, then caught herself when Marcus's eyes met hers. Strolling to the shelves at the side of the room, she removed a book at random and carelessly turned the pages.

"Was anything mentioned about her profession?" asked Marcus.

"Not that I heard," said Ralph. "She remains something of a mystery woman."

"Not for long. She plans to go on the stage."

Ralph whistled in surprise.

"What do you plan to do about her?" asked Irene.

"Yes, Marcus," said Amy. "Do tell us your plans."

"I don't know that there's anything for me to do. I can hardly lock her away somewhere."

Deep pain flashed across Amy's face. "Why not Paris? I understand it's good for such things."

"That's enough, Amy," said Marcus. The air crackled between them for a long moment. Ralph broke the silence.

"Unless Chadwick earned a fortune in the colonies, and anything's possible in that savage land, the girl can't have an endless supply of funds. There's the inheritance, of course—"

One of the aunts inhaled sharply; Marcus wasn't sure which one.

"What inheritance?" he asked.

"It went to Anne's girls, as I recall," said Ralph. "A year or two ago. Two, that's it. It was before you became the twelfth earl. No reason for you to know about it. Had nothing to do with the Bannermans. Pickering business all the way. There was some sort of jewelry supposed to be involved, set aside some time ago by Anne's father, but it was never found."

Marcus looked at his sister. "Did Miss Chadwick mention this inheritance? Or anything about the financial status of her father?"

"Really, Marcus, I hardly audited her accounts. She said her father owned a store of some kind. Chadwick Clothing, something like that."

"A tradesman," Irene said, "that's what he turned into. I wasn't in the least surprised."

Marcus kept his opinion to himself. Irene, dependent upon the charity of her late sister's in-laws, was a genuine snob.

"The store sounded profitable enough," Amy said. "Miss Chadwick was more expansive about her wonderful family, so loving and supportive. You should have been present to hear."

Marcus ignored the pointed tone of her voice. Miss Chadwick might have described with great conviction a loving home that did not exist. She was, after all, an actress.

He drummed his fingers on the desk. An inheritance had very likely funded Raven Chadwick's journey to America. A small sum, Ralph said, but perhaps it was enough to fuel the fires of avarice. And ambition. Human weaknesses, both.

As was lust. He had seen signs of it smoldering in her eyes. And he had tasted it on her lips.

She was a captivating woman, tremulous and exciting at the same time. It mattered not that the shyness might well be feigned. He would like to have her alone in this room right now for further investigation. This time he would watch out for her claws.

He lost himself to musing, then realized that Amy had proposed tea in the drawing room and the others were preparing to leave with her.

"I'll beg off, if you don't mind," he said, waving vaguely at his cluttered desk.

One by one, they filed out, an ofttimes fractious group that needed him more than they would admit. He would like to bring them to a level of tolerant harmony, if not outright affection, but it seemed a goal forever out of his reach.

He turned his chair to stare out the opaque window. The rain continued, although the fury of the storm had abated.

So, too, had his confusion over Raven Chadwick. The

one thing he understood was actresses. And she was an actress. Ergo, he understood her. She was, simply put, an opportunist.

So was he. That was why he had asked Amy to invite his prospective brides last night, wealthy women with an eye on becoming his countess. All respectable, and with fathers who demanded he be the same. And so he lived an austere existence.

Or he tried to. In this very room he had come close to failure, and all because of a black-eyed actress who had strayed into his life. A greedy, ambitious schemer. The more he thought about her, the more he knew he was right. Oh, she looked innocent enough, but he remembered her sauciness at the Lyceum. Ignorant of his identity, she had shown her true self. All the tremors and the worries and the panic she had demonstrated here were nothing more than enhancements to the picture she wanted to present, of a poor lost soul who needed help.

Last night she had admitted to seeking out the Bannermans only after failing to find employment. She had vowed to return to Stafford House as often as she wished. Trading on the family name, looking for more funds which might be shoveled her way. There could be no other reasons, since she had hardly been greeted with open affection and she'd made an issue of the idle rich.

He saw too easily how her presence could shatter the fragile Stafford calm. He would take great pleasure in proving her innocence false . . . and all in the name of family honor.

Marcus leaned back in his chair and smiled, for the

first time in a while facing a task he could welcome. Oh, yes, he would do whatever necessary to send her scurrying across the Atlantic.

Even if he had to get beneath her skirts.

"He thinks I'm a greedy, scheming witch!"

Raven jostled her cup of tea, spilling the liquid onto her lap.

"Let me get 'at, Miss," said her landlady, Mrs. Goodbody, who sat in the chair beside her.

The two were gathered in the boardinghouse parlor, taking a light repast to ward off the chill of the storm.

"Please don't bother," said Raven. "I've got a napkin. It's just that he makes me so angry, I forget myself."

"Gor," Mrs. Goodbody said, "yer in a terrible state. Don't let the nobs get ye down. Mr. Goodbody, may he rest in peace, allus said they's good 'uns and bad 'uns in all walks o' life."

"And so there are."

Raven smiled at the woman, a middle-aged matron who had taken a frightened foreigner into her establishment and, for a modest sum, offered sympathy as well as a roof and two hot meals a day. With the weather so bad, Raven had been unable to pursue her search for employment; with the disastrous meeting at Stafford House only the night before, her heart still stung over how badly everything had gone.

More and more, she was making a mess of everything.

When Mrs. Goodbody had invited her into the parlor for a "cuppa" as she called it and a womanly chat, she had almost broken down in tears.

"I normally don't let go like this," she said with an apologetic smile. "My sisters say I can keep a secret better than a statue of Robert E. Lee. For some reason, I haven't been myself since I arrived here."

"London's a right enuf fright fer most o' us. Tea and talk, they's been the savin' o' many a woman."

Raven drank the last cold drops in her cup, barely tasting the bitterness. "He suggested I try working in a music hall."

"There's plenty 'as done just 'at, an' lived t' tell the tale."

"Do I sound snobbish to you? It's just that I've always wanted to pursue something more serious."

" 'Tis true ain't nothin' much serious goin' on at the 'alls. But they gives people a laugh. These days they's plenty 'at needs t' fergit their troubles."

A bell tinkled in the hallway.

Mrs. Goodbody stood and smoothed her skirt. "That'll be somebody askin' fer the room what opened up. Take yer time wi' the tea. I may be awhile."

Alone, Raven stared into the dregs in her cup. An image formed in the leaves. Mocking eyes, grinning lips, a lock of hair across a wide forehead.

She blinked, and the image went away. She must be losing her mind. Or edging close to hysteria, which would be further from her true self than she could allow herself to go.

She thought about the cast of characters abiding at Stafford House. Marcus, Amy, Cordelia—all related by blood—and the outsider Irene, the unpleasant sister to

Mama's favorite cousin. Irene's brother Ralph she had yet to meet.

One of them had written the letter to Mama or, if not, it was someone with access to the stationery of Stafford House. She suspected all of them and none of them. The few times she had mentioned Mama, they had seemed politely interested. Only the butler showed signs of real affection for Miss Anne. The more she thought about the situation, the more she got confused.

And she had a new worry—the way the earl would treat Mama and Papa when they came for their visit next summer. It was possible he might be cavalier, suspicious, even insultingly curious about their private concerns, the way he was with her.

Or at least he would try. In self defense, she had scratched his face; there was little predicting what her quick-tempered father would do if Marcus Bannerman treated his beloved Annie with less than courtesy.

Raven cringed to think she had behaved on a level with the earl. She knew better. When Miss Lillian's Academy for Young Ladies decided Chadwicks weren't good enough for its hallowed halls, Mama had taken over her social training. Dear, genteel Mama who for once in her life had become a harsh taskmaster.

Mama, who had been threatened simply because she wrote home. Had the earl sent the warning letter? He seemed cruel enough, although she was inclined to believe he would have signed his name. Still, she didn't know him very well.

No more than she knew his unhappy sister Amy or

his unusual aunts. And there were others she had not met. Any of them could be the author. She had to find out.

Resolution lightened her spirits. She moved to the window and stared out at the rain. In the condensation on the glass she drew a circle, gave it shaggy hair, button eyes, and fangs hanging on either side of a small chin scar. For good measure, she added a pair of horns.

"You think you've driven me off, Marcus Bannerman, but you'll find that Chadwicks are a tough breed. I'll take whatever work I can find and I'll return to Stafford House as often as I must."

Should their paths cross, she wouldn't let him goad or tempt her into conduct she knew in her heart was not for her. She would ingratiate herself to the family, let them see the good qualities of the Chadwicks, all the while she listened and observed. Somehow she would learn the truth behind the words *You will die.*

She felt a surge of elation and a newfound sense of purpose. The Earl of Stafford had taken her by surprise with his kiss, but now she was forewarned. The man was a devil and a rake. He had intimidated her, as had the size of London and the closed society that was the theater world.

No more.

"You're like the conquering Yankees who came down to Savannah after the war. They were in charge, and there wasn't much the Rebs could do about it."

She smeared his image until it was little more than wet ripples on the glass.

"There's a war between us, too, Your Arrogant Lordship. Only this time a softspoken, mannerly Southern woman shall win."

# Six

Even in the wings, the music hall smelled of fish and smoke. Raven swallowed her queasiness; at the same time she rearranged the black feathers covering her bosom.

"Ticklish bastards, ain't they?"

Her eyes darted to the woman who'd suddenly popped up beside her. "I'm sorry—" she began.

"All them li'l edges. Like wearin' a bed o' ants." She smoothed the skirt of her purple dress over her rounded hips. "Gi' me somethin' ordinary so's I c'n prance about wif'out scratchin' meself raw."

Despite her anxiety, Raven had to smile. Only in the wings of Camden Cockloft, she thought, would a low-cut, calf-length gown of sequined satin be considered ordinary.

She studied her own costume. Black feathers tenuously attached to a lining of black satin covered far too little of her bosom, and there weren't enough feathers in the skirt to make a pigeon's wing. Flesh-colored tights covered much of her skin, but from the audience she would appear practically naked.

Legs and arms and breasts, that's what she was, with plumage in between. Too, there was the absurd headpiece that sat atop her wildly curled hair—a twist of wire over which gold taffeta had been stretched to resemble a beak.

By comparison the purple did, indeed, seem ordinary.

Sensible Raven felt as far from sensible as she could get.

"You're one of the dancers, aren't you?" she asked the woman beside her.

The woman nodded, her painted face breaking into a grin. With brown hair and eyes, even features and yellowed teeth, she looked no older than Raven's twenty-seven years, but there was a hardness about her that said she'd traveled far more miles.

"They said you wuz a lady from the States."

"Raven, the American Songbird. That's what it reads on the poster out front. Is my nationality good or bad?"

The dancer waved toward the dozen off-stage workers and performers bustling around the wing.

"All's welcome at the Cockloft. Just wonderin' why ye ain't at the London Pavilion. Newest an' fanciest 'all in town. Seems more t' yer style."

"They wouldn't hire me. Camden Cockloft did."

"Yer an 'onest one. There's some 'at'll swear they wouldn't work nowhere else, but in truf, 'at's why we're all 'ere."

A roar from the audience temporarily stopped her. "Ye won't find a better crowd t' watch yer, neither. Even the swells comes in. Not on a reg'lar basis, o' course, but it ain't un'eard of. 'As a good time, too."

Raven's heart sank. Swells . . . gentry . . . members of the peerage. Earls.

No, she told herself. The arrogant man who had advised her so sneeringly to seek the music halls for employment would never lower himself to visit one. Of that, she could be sure.

"Ah choo!"

"Bless yer."

Raven stifled a second sneeze.

" 'Ere now, yer wearin' it wrong," said the dancer. "Can't get too close t' the nose." Her experienced hands adjusted the plumage a couple of inches lower across Raven's chest, until two mounds of tawny flesh spilled over the black quills.

" 'At's better," she said, patting Raven's shoulder. The stage manager, a potbellied, baldheaded man in shirtsleeves, edged up behind her.

"Ouch!" the dancer yelled.

"Quiet," he hissed. "They'll be hearing you out front."

"Keep yer 'ands t' yerself, or they'll be 'earin' a lot more."

He winked at Raven. "Have t' give 'em a little pinch now and again, else they forget their place."

Raven watched him sidle off. "There's a manager in Charleston much like him."

"They's everywhere." The dancer excused herself with a parting word of advice. "Yer'll be the 'it o' the show. Just remember not t' scratch."

Alone, Raven listened to another roar from the crowd.

"Higher, higher," came the shouts to the background of rhythmic applause.

Raven edged to the side of the stage and peered around the corner, past the footlights and the pit orchestra, to the shadowed hall. A thousand people sat around the tables, their eyes directed to the trapeze suspended over the tables and to the scantily clad young woman swinging by her heels from the bar.

"Higher," came the cry.

With a tightening of pelvic and thigh muscles, the performer swooped over the crowd and arched toward the chandeliers. Down and up, down and up, her head coming dangerously close to the beer bottles on the tables, she roused an appreciative cheer.

Raven's breath caught at her daring.

" 'Ere's a pair o' legs 'll squeeze a man fer all 'e's worth," a gravelly voice shouted out over the tumult.

"In yer case," a woman yelled back, " 'at'll be a ha'penny."

A roar of laughter shook the walls of the big old building. Raven eased back into the protection of the wing, as much a stranger to this city as she had ever been. Despite the dozen people close by and the thousand more only a few yards away, she felt alone.

A sensation little short of terror took hold of her heart. This was the assembly she was supposed to entertain with a song. Genteelly presented, she'd been told at the lone rehearsal only three hours before. She hadn't seen the costume yet. She hadn't heard the crowd. Her heart sank to her toes. She had truly mired herself in a muddy mess this time.

She absolutely refused to consider what Mama and Papa would think of their prudent eldest daughter. Nor how the earl would look at her and say, "You're just what I thought you were."

A drum roll and a clash of cymbals marked the conclusion of the aerial act. The performer dashed past her, face beaded in sweat, her costume damp against her muscular form.

The stage manager patted her ruffled rear.

" 'At's a good way t' lose a 'and," she snarled, keeping to her pace.

"Get t' your place, blackbird," the showman barked. It took Raven a few seconds to realize he referred to her.

She forced her feet to move. Taking her position center stage behind the closed curtain, she told herself this was what she had always wanted, this losing herself in another character, this sharing of emotions behind the armor of pretense.

The difficulty lay in pretending to be a bird.

Or maybe not. Maybe all she really wanted to do was work in Papa's store, then later, in the Chadwick parlor, entertain the few people in the world who loved her, avoiding even the nearby park. She was a private person. Not a public woman at all. It was, she knew, a poor time to consider a change in careers.

Eyes closed, she remembered her true purpose in leaving home. Mama's image gave her resolve. If only she could remember the lyrics of her song.

Oh, yes, the trapeze. Tonight's presentation centered on a circus theme. Nervous, she barely heard the master of ceremonies introduce her. Something about an American cousin . . . could he have mentioned an earl?

The curtain parted, robbing her of time to think, and the footlights robbed her of vision. The orchestra struck the first notes of her song as she stared into the smoky dark. Except for the music, all was quiet.

The orchestra stopped, a baton tapped against a stand,

and the first notes sounded again, reminding Raven she was supposed to sing. A few catcalls came from the void.

Blowing a runaway feather from the vicinity of her mouth, she began the first verse.

"Louder," someone shouted, and others joined in.

Her sweaty palms gripped a handful of plumes. As she neared the chorus, she imagined herself back in Savannah singing only to the Chadwick clan. The image gave her courage and her soprano rang out loud and clear.

*He flies through the air with the greatest of ease . . .*

A lovely tune, if not exactly Verdi. Additional lights illuminated the trapeze. She watched as a dark-suited man climbed onto a table beneath the bar, grabbed hold, and hefted himself to a standing position above the crowd.

*That daring young man on the flying trapeze . . .*

Raven kept on singing as a wave of laughter and applause rose in the hall.

*His movements are graceful, the girls he doth please . . .*

The trapeze began to sway, gained momentum, and within a few measures had surpassed the previous performer's heights.

*And my love he has purloined away.*

As the orchestra took over, she stared up at the aerialist. Unlike his scantily clad predecessor, he was fully clothed in formal wear, from top hat to black-patent boots. He waved and winked at the women in the audience, then with a mocking glance in her direction, gave a swipe of his hand, as though he would banish her from sight.

There was no doubt he represented the twelfth Earl of Stafford, especially since he wore a large number 12 on his back. He lacked the earl's broad shoulders and elegant bearing, but he compensated with the correct degree of arrogance. The audience loved it.

For the second chorus, Raven was supposed to go down on her knees. She was too stunned to move. Did all of London know about her quarrel with the earl? How could they? Why would they care?

She scratched at a feather; two dropped from their appointed positions, and then the whole of her top gave way, littering the stage with tufts, exposing the portion of her breasts not already on view.

"The bird's moltin'," someone yelled out, and a hundred more cried out encouragement.

Covering herself with her arms, she turned to flee, slipped on a plume, and stumbled to her knees. The headpiece shifted to cover her eyes. Thumbing the beak into place, she spied a table directly in line with her vision. Two men stared back. One she did not recognize, the other she knew all too well.

Studying the scene upon the stage with a mixture of anger and satisfaction was Marcus Bannerman.


"You have a visitor, m'lord," Frederick said from the library door of Stafford House the morning after the music hall debacle.

Marcus looked up from his desk. "Who is it?"

The butler hesitated a moment. "Miss Chadwick."

Marcus leaned back in his chair. Only a twitch of his

lips revealed his surprise. "Wait five minutes, then show her in."

"Give her credit, Marcus. She's got mettle."

Marcus glanced at the man standing by the fire across the room. Daniel Lindsay had been a family friend for years, but he'd spent the last five of them making a fortune in India. He'd returned only this week, leaner and harder and seemingly older than his thirty years.

Seeing Daniel again was like revisiting his youth. He had wanted company on his excursion last night, and Daniel had consented to accompany him.

"You think she shows mettle?" he said. "Audacity is closer to it. That's what she showed on the stage." He pictured her stumbling to her knees a few feet in front of him. He pictured her breasts, dark-tipped and tempting. He'd felt a sharp erotic jolt, then fury because he wasn't the only one watching.

"She didn't fall on purpose, Marcus. Didn't you see the look on her face when she realized who the trapeze artist was supposed to represent?"

"You keep forgetting she's an actress."

"Which seems to explain everything to you."

Marcus tapped the papers in front of him. "I told you I wanted to prove her an opportunist and a schemer. I had no idea she would do my work for me in such a public way."

"Perhaps the damage to your new reputation isn't serious."

"We'll see."

Daniel grinned, and for a moment he was the boy who used to follow Marcus around the Sussex countryside.

"What I'll remember most from all this is the look on

your face when her costume slipped. And then the look on hers when she saw you. I'll bet she's here to offer apologies and ask how she can make amends. I've yet to meet a female who would deny you anything."

"It's possible you're about to meet one now."

The library door opened to reveal the object of their discussion, wearing black bonnet and cloak, looking much as she had the morning they'd first met.

"Trying to make yourself drab, Miss Chadwick?" Marcus asked. "It seems rather too little and far too late."

She paused in the doorway, then walked the width of the room, holding her response until she reached his desk. This afternoon she was everything that was respectable, but Marcus knew too well how quickly her respectability could change.

"You are a most unusual woman, Miss Chadwick. Your feathers do not ruffle easily."

Her lips tightened. "I deserve your jibes, Lord Stafford. I ask only that you let me say my piece and then I'll leave."

"It may take awhile. There are so many facets to the notorious Raven, the American songbird, that I have yet to explore."

"Lord Stafford—"

"Call me Marcus, and I will call you Raven. I feel I know you so well."

Daniel cleared his throat. "Marcus has forgotten his manners, Miss Chadwick." Abandoning the fireplace, he strode to her side. "I'm Daniel Lindsay, a long-lost friend recently returned to England."

Raven offered her hand, then gasped. "Oh, you were there with him."

"What a charming blush," Daniel said, bringing her gloved hand to his lips.

"Don't you have business elsewhere?" asked Marcus, a shade of irritation in his eyes. "Maybe Amy is in the drawing room. You haven't seen her in years. You'll find her changed."

Daniel's countenance hardened for an instant, then returned to amiability. "So are we all," he said. "Tempting though the suggestion may be, I'd best get back to my search for a residence. If I don't see your sister, please give her my regards and say I'll call upon her soon."

With a nod to Raven, he was gone and her eyes shifted slowly to the earl.

"Daniel is right," he said. "That is a most charming blush. I noticed it last night."

She held her silence.

"Forgive my ungentlemanly behavior. I should, of course, forget the unfortunate incident at Camden Cock-loft." He patted the paper on his desk. "But I've been reminded of it all day. And we both know I'm not really a gentleman, don't we?"

She continued to stand in silence, but he noticed a definite twitch to her right eye and a tightening of her lips.

Getting a reaction out of her was a challenge he could not resist.

"Allow me to compliment you, Raven. Your legs are all that I imagined them to be, and you have extraordinarily fine breasts."

She closed her eyes, but not before he got a glimpse

of rage, so hot he wondered whether she might come over the desk at him. Good, he thought. He would wrestle a round or two.

"Still no comment?" he asked.

He could see her stiffen beneath the cloak. Despite himself, he admired the regal bearing that must have been close to impossible for her to assume under the circumstances. But she was, he reminded himself, an actress.

Her lashes lifted; the anger was gone. "Please, Lord Stafford, this bickering is getting us nowhere."

"And where, little songbird, did you want to go?"

She cleared her throat. "I've come to apologize for last night."

In one sentence she had managed to make him feel like a cad. He glanced at the papers on his desk to remind himself he was in the right.

One of the papers, a small playbill that had been distributed throughout the theater district, played up last night's appearance by the Earl of Stafford's American cousin. The author erred in the relationship, but he got the performance right.

*See the beautiful songbird in her feathered finery.*

*Hear her plaintive cries for love.*

*Behold the scorn of the earl as he soars above the crowd.*

The upper left corner was decorated with a remarkable likeness of Marcus, pistol in hand. To the right, directly in line with his aim, was a bird twittering on the bar of a trapeze.

The second paper, featuring the same artwork, was one of the penny scandal sheets which appeared on the streets hours following a sordid or lurid or violent occurrence, particularly if the gentry or, better yet, a member of the peerage was involved.

Falling well within the requirements were the incidents at Camden Cockloft, particularly the singer's unorthodox exit in front of one particularly exalted member of the audience.

He held the playbill aloft. "Do you apologize for this?" He held up the newspaper. "Or this?"

"Mrs. Goodbody showed me those this morning. As humiliating as they are they help explain what happened last night."

"Mrs. Goodbody?"

"My landlady."

"Ah, yes, in Soho. These must have littered the streets. They certainly made their way to Mayfair and Kensington, and I would think most of London. Mine were delivered anonymously, the playbill yesterday, the scandal sheet in this morning's mail."

"So you saw the playbill earlier in the day. That's why you were at the performance."

Raven loosened the clasp of her cloak, easing it away from her throat. Marcus thought of what lay beneath her garments and felt a momentary desire, partial as he was to dark-tipped breasts.

"By all means, Raven, make yourself at home. Take off whatever you wish."

Her hands fisted at her sides. "As a boy did you tie cans to the tails of dogs and toss kittens into moving streams?"

"When things are slow around here, I'm wont to do it still."

She backed away from him and, to his surprise, sat in a facing chair. "I'm sorry, Your Lordship. I did not mean to lose my temper. What happened last night was inexcusable. But I did not know about the playbill. And I did not tell anyone about our relationship, except for Mrs. Goodbody, but I revealed only that you thought ill of me. She swears she passed nothing on."

"And Mrs. Goodbody wouldn't lie."

She gripped the arms of the chair. "The manager at the music hall learned of our difficulties and used that information for publicity, although why anyone would care is beyond me. They used me, too, requiring that I wear that absurd costume. When I agreed, I hadn't yet seen it; and then it was too late. One night, I told myself, to prove I could sing. Then I would ask for something more modest."

"And have they agreed?"

"I gave them no choice. I quit. Believe it or not, the man was actually quite nice about the whole thing. He gave me something you need to see." She pulled an envelope from her pocket and placed it on his desk, then settled back into her chair.

*Camden Cockloft* was written in a childish hand across the face of the envelope, which bore a London postmark and the date two days past. There was no return address.

Inside was a brief description of Raven and of her visit to Amy's party, exaggerating the number of people who had witnessed their meeting in the drawing room, making it sound as though half of London had been there.

The writer had also gotten their confrontation wrong:

*She begged him to give her money, tearing off her clothes and promising all sorts of things. The Earl said he was too good for the likes of her and threw her into the street.*

## Seven

Raven held her breath as she watched Marcus read the letter, as tense over his reaction as she was over the man himself.

She looked at the strong, blunt hands holding the slip of paper; and she looked, too, at the gray frock coat and jacquard waistcoat, the stiff white collar with its perfectly arranged tie, the muscular neck, the strong, scarred jaw and prominent cheekbones, the not-quite-so-perfectly arranged hair, and lastly the piercing blue eyes of the man who was distorting everything she had believed about herself.

He defeated her at every turn, making her feel beholden to him, making her feel ashamed. *No, Raven,* her voice of conscience said, *he just sits back and watches you defeat yourself.*

The letter, she told herself. Concentrate on the letter.

His tight expression indicated he was surprised by its existence, and more, by its contents. She wasn't much of a detective, but she didn't think he had ever seen it before.

Since the scrawl was the same on this letter and her mother's, it meant he hadn't written either one.

A wave of relief swept over her. She had been afraid

he was the guilty party. The feeling was not just for him. She didn't want *anyone* to be guilty. She wished the whole problem would go away," including the disaster at Camden Cockloft. Whatever the emotions were that had brought her to Stafford House this morning, shame was uppermost.

She had yet to consider fully the effect all this would have on her parents. Her disgrace was still too raw.

Marcus looked at her over the letter. "This does put another light on your performance."

Was that supposed to be another of His Lordship's sarcastic comments? He had thrown so many at her, she wasn't sure. Today she had no complaints. They were all deserved.

"What do you make of it?" she asked.

"Your visits here had already started rumors. Apparently someone with knowledge of this household took it upon himself to embellish the facts, someone who understood that Camden Cockloft would seize a bit of scandal to draw in the crowds. Someone who would take great pleasure in seeing one or the both of us embarrassed."

Raven shook her head in disbelief. "That doesn't make sense to me."

"London is a big city, but in some ways it's like a small town. Gossip is a favorite pastime, including the ruining of reputations. Have you made any enemies since you arrived?"

"Just—" She stopped herself.

"Just me, is that what you were going to say?"

She looked down at her hands, then forced her eyes

to his. "Are you my enemy? You would know it better than I."

He flicked at the letter. "If I were, I'd show it in more effective ways than this."

Raven thought about the Cockloft's raucous crowd, the applause, the smoke, the smells, the laughter. Mostly she thought about the wild cheering at her exposed flesh and about one man staring at her out of the dark, his silent fury screaming louder than all the rest.

"It's effective enough," she said with a shudder. "I want to crawl in a hole somewhere and not come out."

"We've all felt that way at times."

He sounded compassionate and bitter, too, as if he understood from personal experience the hard time she was having. Though they came from different worlds, she felt a precious moment of shared sympathy, and she allowed herself a small laugh.

"It's impossible for you to believe, Lord Stafford, but I'm really quite withdrawn when I'm back home."

As soon as the words were out, she sensed a change in the air.

"Withdrawn?" He looked at her in surprise, and suddenly she felt more ill at ease than at any moment since her arrival.

"I lead a very orderly and quiet life," she said, pulling her cloak tight, as though she could hide herself from the cynical light in his eye, wishing she had kept her personal revelations to herself. Shared sympathy, she realized, had quickly returned to scorn.

"You're right. It is hard to believe. You had me almost supportive of your cause, then you say withdrawn. I think of feathers and other more pleasurable images. They stayed with me much of the night."

Raven's heart pounded. She couldn't breathe. How dare he say such things, and yet he remembered nothing he had not seen.

*Mama says I'm afraid to feel.*

What would Mama say if she knew the emotions raging through her dispassionate daughter? Humiliation, guilt, remorse, and not only because she had represented the family so badly. She kept ruining herself in Marcus Bannerman's eyes. She didn't want to, not because of Mama but because. . . . She didn't know why.

The realization had come without warning when she had first seen him sitting behind his desk, mocking censure etched onto his face. The hurt of that moment returned a hundredfold. It seemed impossible that only a few days ago she had decided to ingratiate herself with the residents of Stafford House and show them the stuff Chadwicks were made of. She had shown them, all right, in ways she could never have imagined.

What had happened to her confidence? It lay in a fall of feathers on a music hall stage.

What to do now? She hadn't the vaguest idea.

"I never know what is going on in that lovely head of yours," he said, standing and walking around the desk. Raven edged back in the chair. "You are a surprising woman, or could it be that enterprising is more the word?"

Her heart caught in her throat. "What do you mean?"

"Is everything you do calculated or as innocent as you sometimes appear? Don't look so startled. I'm sure the letter is authentic. I refer to your humiliation, your apology, your worry over my reputation."

He forced her clutched hands apart and lifted her to her feet as though she weighed no more than mist. Deft movements shifted the cloak from her shoulders and onto the chair seat; strong hands rested on the shoulders of her lavender gown, and a pair of determined lips parted and eased toward hers.

The scent of earthy sandalwood wafted over her. It was a pity, she thought in a moment of lucidity, that Marcus smelled as good as he looked.

"You're a dilemma." His hands circled her waist. "Another music hall might invite a disaster similar to the Cockloft, and the legitimate theater has rejected you. So here you are."

Fury rescued her from humiliation. "I was trying to be nice."

"Give it up, Songbird. It isn't in character. You need work, don't you? And a roof over your head. Perhaps Stafford House. That's why you've come." His hands eased onto the flare of her hips. "I, too, have needs. Perhaps an arrangement can be made."

"You can't mean—"

"Oh, but I do. Reciprocity, it's called. You cooperate with me, and I'll cooperate with you."

She tried to summon the indignation she'd felt in a Savannah banker's office, but the earl was no Harold Gash.

"No," she managed. To her own ears, the protest was weak.

"Lavender becomes you," he said. "Everything does." His lips touched hers. Sparks crackled between them.

Here I go again, she thought.

He delivered the second kiss with greater authority. She held her stiffness for as long as possible—a moment no more extended than an intake of breath, a stifled cry, a softening of her resolve.

Her hands clutched the sleeves of his coat as she leaned into his strength. The kiss deepened. What a curious feeling it was to have a man's tongue touching hers, she thought, and she touched him right back. He pulled her tight against him. The room whirled until she knew nothing but his surrounding arms, broad chest, warm breath against her cheek.

And the taste of him as he tasted her.

A heat exploded within her, taking a shape all its own, its assault as sudden as it was intense. Desire became an entity separate and distinct, with claws that tore at her control. *Marcus* echoed in her mind until it was the one word she perceived.

A stranger to herself, she wanted to tear aside his clothes until she could touch his naked skin, stroke the ripples of muscle, explore the ways his body differed from hers. Her heart pounded in her ears with such driving power she could not hear the small inner voice that told her this was wrong . . . not until Marcus broke the kiss and leaned his forehead to hers while his ragged breath gradually slowed.

"I would have taken you here on the desk," he whispered. "What kind of power do you have over me, witch? I meant only to tease."

Heat became shame that tasted bitter on her tongue.

She edged away until they no longer touched. "You blame me for this? Never have I allowed a man so much as an intimate word. Not until I met you." She made no attempt to keep the anguish from her voice, the distress from her eyes. "Look at me. I'm a woman I do not know."

Hugging her waist, she turned her back to him and walked to the fire where Daniel Lindsay had stood when first she had entered. If only he had never gone. Flames licked upward, their light reflected in the folds of her moiré gown. The glowing coals that edged the grate seemed no hotter than the passions Marcus had aroused. It seemed there was no end to her shame.

She faced him. Across the room, she sensed his power over her. Oh, how she wished she could read the thoughts behind his stare.

"How we feel, or do not feel, about one another is not the issue between us," he said. "The well-being of this family is. It's my charge. And right now I'm doing a damned poor job."

He reached for her cloak. "The trouble is I can't keep my hands off you. And it's too easy to prove you're not the respectable woman you claim. Something isn't right. I will help you, of course, in your predicament. Please forget my suggestion. I spoke unwisely."

The library door opened and Amy strode into the room. "What suggestion?" she asked, then spied Raven by the fire. "Oh, Miss Chadwick, I didn't know you were here.

"I was just leaving."

A mischievous gleam lit Amy's blue eyes. "You can't. I want to hear all about last night."

"Amy—" Marcus began.

"Don't looked shocked, brother dear. Surely the subject has already come up this afternoon." Then back to Raven. "I'll bet the suggestion concerned Camden Cockloft. What a wonderful name for a music hall. Is it really like an attic, all low beams and cobwebs and scurrying mice?"

"I appreciate your attempts to make light of this," Raven said. "I am here to apologize for the embarrassment I caused."

"The gossips must be having a great time of it today."

Raven shrank from her words, wishing she could crawl under the rug.

Amy shifted to Marcus. "We've got to help her. She wouldn't have been on that stage if we had been more generous when she came to call."

Marcus leaned against the desk. "It's a rare thing to see you interested in someone else, Amy. Why do I feel uneasy?"

"Perhaps it is your conscience pricking at you. I doubt you've offered support."

"As in other things, little sister, you're wrong."

Both fell silent. The hostility Raven saw between them continued to baffle her. She loved her sisters enough to lay down her life to protect them. The Bannermans had difficulty remaining in the same room.

"How would you like to move in here?"

Raven stared openmouthed at Amy. "I beg your pardon?"

"Move in here. We've plenty of room."

"I can't."

"Of course you can." Amy crossed the room to take her hand. "We'll let the world know we're not ashamed of what happened. We'll spread word we're standing by our unfortunate guest who was taken advantage of by wicked Londoners."

Raven could not look at Marcus. "That's kind of you, but—"

"Not at all. We'll also be showing what generous souls we are, sure enough of our good character to ignore the talk."

Raven ought to refuse, but the temptation was too great. To clear her reputation and remove the shame that would fall to her parents when they arrived, she would do almost anything. Even reside under the same roof as the man who was proving to be her downfall.

The library door opened. "Mr. Lindsay," said Frederick.

Amy's grip threatened to break Raven's fingers.

"Marcus," said Daniel, striding in on the butler's heels. "I was still in the neighborhood and thought to ask you about tomorrow night."

He glanced at Raven, then saw Amy. "Oh, Miss Bannerman. I didn't know you were here."

Amy faced him with a smile. "Since when am I Miss Bannerman? Amy, please. It's what you used to call me when I was a child."

She swept to his side and planted a kiss on his cheek. "How wonderful to see you again. Have you met Miss Chadwick?"

Raven held her breath.

"We were introduced when she first arrived today. Miss Chadwick, a pleasure to see you again."

Thank goodness, thought Raven with a sigh, no one was mentioning last night. Daniel Lindsay really was a pleasant man, tall and even featured, leaner than Marcus but still broad-shouldered and somehow more manageable. She was learning that manageability was a much desired trait in a man.

Amy clapped her hands. "I've a splendid idea, Daniel. After Raven moves in here, you can come to call. It would be a great help. You two can show particular attention to one another at next week's ball, and then there will be no more rumors about Raven being interested in the earl. And vice versa, of course."

"If that's what you wish," said Daniel.

"Definitely," Amy said. "Come for dinner tonight and we'll start the campaign."

Daniel nodded solemnly to Raven. "I would consider it an honor if Miss Chadwick would allow me to call. Fair warning, though. I'm lately come from India, where I've worked mostly with men. Investments, shipping, that sort of thing. You might find my social skills a bit unpolished."

Raven almost laughed out loud. "Mr. Lindsay, I could say the same about myself."

"Then it's settled," Marcus said. "We'll have the aunts informed and prepare a room for our visitor from abroad. Let no one say that a Bannerman failed to do all he could to make a guest feel at home."

Amy paced the length of her bedroom, impatient for the afternoon to end. She'd already arranged for the preparation of a spare bedroom, a footman had taken Raven to collect her belongings, and Daniel was continuing his search for a town house. Marcus was "testing the gossipy waters" as he put it, meaning he was roaming the casinos for a game of cards.

He could put on all the fancy, reformed airs he wanted to; she knew he still gambled. No doubt to finance her forays into the social world. Such endeavors bothered her not a whit.

Whatever worries he harbored or difficulties he faced, he deserved them every one.

She stopped herself, for the moment admitting the truth. How fine it would be, just once in awhile, to have his love and respect. He would laugh if he knew she felt this way, laugh and tell her to accept the way things were.

Her gaze fell on the easel stand by her bed and on the blank canvas beckoning from across the room. The night table held the lacquered box containing her watercolors and brushes. Painting passed the time. She loved it, too, but it took a steady hand and clear eye, two things she did not possess today.

She sat in front of the mirror just as her maid entered. "Oh, Nancy, whatever shall I do with my hair?" She pulled the yellow curls this way and that, combed them high on her head, let them tumble to her shoulders. "Nothing looks good."

*Daniel looks good.*

The thought came from nowhere.

*He's lost weight in the past five years, but then so have I.*

"Miss Amy," said Nancy, standing behind her, "you can wear your hair any which way you please. I allus say so."

Amy smiled at Nancy's image in the mirror. A flighty young girl of eighteen, she provided service for the women of the household. Eighteen. Only slightly older than she had been when Daniel sailed for India. At twenty-three, she couldn't recall ever having been so young.

"The gown for the ball arrived while you and His Lordship were in the library. I was helping Cook, but I hurried on up 'cause I thought you might want to try it on."

Weariness settled on Amy's shoulders. "Not today, Nancy. In the morning. See to Aunt Cordelia or Aunt Irene."

"I already seen to 'em. Don't take much caring, those two. They'd rather not have me hanging about."

"Then run along to Cook. With guests for dinner, she'll appreciate the help."

Alone, Amy threw down the comb and settled herself in the window seat overlooking Bolton Row. It was an address far more fashionable than the Sussex farm where she had been reared, but after a year of residence she still couldn't call it home.

Not like the farm, isolated from traffic and visitors but never lonely, never dull. Right up until their death, her parents had been concerned primarily with each other, but she had found ways to occupy her time. In honesty she admitted that what attention they spared was offered to her and not to Marcus.

Their neglect had not weakened him in any way. Or brought doubt to his heart he could ever be wrong. Five years ago he had made decisions that changed her life. He made them still.

She sighed. As fashionable as Stafford House was, she could never be happy here. Despite the parties, the theaters, the social scene, each day seemed worse than the day before.

Today had been the worst of all.

What a Godsend Raven Chadwick was proving to be. For several reasons, few of which had been discussed.

"Miss Chadwick," she said to her reflection in the leaded pane, "be warned. You may think you're walking on carpet when you tread these floors, but it's Bannerman quicksand that'll trap you if you don't take care."

Cordelia Halstead rummaged in the nightstand by her bed. Her hand settled on a small, leather-bound flask, and a smile settled on her face.

"I thought you were hiding in there," she said as she poured the clear contents into the Minton teacup that was placed each day on the table. When she was alone, Cordelia always talked to her gin. It made the hours seem less lonely.

Gathering her shawl about her, she settled into the rocker by the grate and watched the low flames fighting among themselves.

"I wish I had a penny for every hour I've spent this way," she said. "A penny's all I'd need. Marcus cares for me so."

She had lived with one Bannerman or another most of her life, ever since her sister Gwenda had married John Archibald Bannerman and settled on his Sussex farm. Humble Hall, the place was called, named for someone generations past. It had been grand enough, but not as grand as the neighboring property of his brother the earl.

Younger son of the tenth earl, John had never worked hard on his land. The estate had dwindled, but it had sustained them.

When Marcus had come along, Gwenda had shown little interest in parenthood, and her husband far less. Marcus had been a lonely boy, then a wild one, always getting into scrapes. Fighting, swearing, and later gambling and wenching, although Cordelia, the spinster aunt, wasn't supposed to know about such things.

"But I had to know everything," she said to the dwindling drops of gin. "It was how I got by."

She had never cared much for her brother-in-law, nor, truth to tell, her sister Gwenda, but she had owed them allegiance and gratitude. Marcus received her love. She'd seen that he was properly clothed and fed and tutored, though he ran off several instructors in the process.

Amy had been different. A fair-haired beauty, cared for by both parents as much as they could harbor such affection, she had been born when Marcus was twelve. A spoiled child, she had wanted her way since she first opened those blue Bannerman eyes.

"She needed me as much as her brother, but she's never owned up to it. Needs me still, more than ever. Poor child. My heart breaks for the two of 'em."

She thought about the newest resident under the Stafford House roof. Anne's daughter. She remembered Anne Pickering fondly, although they hadn't been close. When Anne's tyrannical father had allowed her to visit Sussex, she had stayed with her cousin Elizabeth on the adjoining estate.

How much, Cordelia wondered, did Raven Chadwick

take after the woman who had defied a domineering father for the man she loved?

"There's potential there for trouble. The American has her own reason for being here. Something she's not yet revealed. Can't fool Cordelia."

With the warmth of the liquor stealing through her, she loosened her shawl, edged back from the fire, and slowly began to rock. Two thoughts occurred before she dropped off to sleep.

Miss Raven Chadwick had best watch her step around Amy and Marcus Bannerman. They were Cordelia's charges and she would protect them in any way that she could.

Second, she must ask her special, secret friend to replenish her cache of gin.

Irene Pickering gripped the post of her tester bed and cursed the day Raven Chadwick ever stepped foot in Stafford House. Cousin Anne should have kept her an ocean away.

Not that it was up to her to complain. Aunt Irene—a name she secretly hated—was a guest here as much as the prima donna would be. Except that she had been a guest most of her life.

The Pickerings had been a noble family, if not possessed of great wealth, and Irene appreciated fine things. She could have married well, but the dowry money had gone to her older sister Elizabeth when she had had a chance to become a countess. Like a charity case, the earl had taken her in, kept her under his roof even after

Elizabeth died, but the new wife hadn't liked her. He'd been about to ask her to leave when he died.

A fortuitous death. Marcus was a kinder earl, but stubborn. Hard to manipulate. Too much of an eye for the young women. He would pay her little mind if she advised him to keep Miss Chadwick away.

Men could be such fools.

She felt a headache coming on. Only one way to cure it, the way she always did.

Kneeling on the rug, she tugged a locked leather chest from beneath her bed and pulled out the key she wore suspended around her neck. The lid lifted easily and she stared at her treasures. A faded fan, a diary, a small wooden box that she stroked lovingly, reassured by its presence.

And, of course, the books. She thumbed through them, selected one that was a particular favorite, and returned both chest and key to their respective hiding places.

Locking the door, she sat in the straight-backed chair by the fire, pulled up the small footstool to support her kid leather boots, and opened the worn pages. They fell as if by will to a particularly entertaining passage.

Everyone thought she was such a dull creature, given to reading geographies and remembrances and, when she felt particularly daring, one of the gentle romances that were both scandalous and all the rage.

What hypocrites the citizens of Queen Victoria's times could be. There was scandal to be had in books, all right. One simply had to know where to find it.

Irene knew very well.

She had chosen a remembrance, but not one to be found in any lending library. She moistened her lips. Already her heart was pounding. She could recite the words by heart, but she preferred to see them on the printed page.

*I stripped off my coat, made it into a bundle, and placed it for her head. "There—there," I said and pulled her down. She made no resistance. I saw white thighs and belly, black hair . . .*

# Eight

"You've been here only a week and that's the second letter you've received from home." Amy toyed with her plate of eggs and toast as she glanced in open curiosity at the envelope beside Raven's plate. "Why were they sent to Soho?"

She and Raven were alone in the morning room, lingering over a late breakfast. After being in the young woman's company for days, Raven was no longer surprised at her bluntness.

"Because that's the address I sent as soon as I arrived."

"Surely you didn't plan to remain there."

"Oh, but I did." Raven had certainly never planned to reside at 22 Bolton Row, even on a temporary basis. The Chadwicks believed she hadn't even called. Yesterday she had written that one of the Bannermans met her at a concert and invited her to stay. It was close enough to the truth to satisfy her uncritical conscience, especially when they would learn everything soon enough.

"This one's from Angel," said Raven.

She smiled as she thought of her fair-haired youngest

sister, the gentle one everybody loved. Her letter had been waiting for her on the breakfast table. She had scanned it quickly, planning to read it several times when she was alone.

Amy's expectant air prodded her to continue. "She writes that Mama and Papa are well. The store is busy, and they've hired three Irishmen Flame met in Texas."

"And the other letter?"

"From Mama, saying much the same thing. Not a great deal happens in Savannah—"

She glanced out the window. "I miss them."

The words fell short of the hollow sensation that beset her whenever she considered what she had left behind. Especially when, on this gray and misty afternoon following Amy's ball, she had nothing to anticipate.

Not even a verbal sparring with Marcus. In her first week at Stafford House, their paths had seldom crossed. Last night he had been polite, even charming when they danced their one quadrille. With two hundred pairs of eyes watching and every ear in their vicinity alert, they contented themselves with talk of the weather and the parks of London that he recommended she visit, enriching the descriptions with tales of duels and robberies in the city's less civilized days.

He was, as she should have known, a graceful dancer and a skilled raconteur. If his hand—surprisingly callused for a gentleman—seemed roughly arousing and altogether too warm whenever he touched her, she gave no indication. Nor did he exhibit any special interest in her.

"I thought everything went well last night, didn't

you?" said Amy. "It was just as I expected. You were a curiosity at first, but you conducted yourself splendidly. You certainly scotched the talk."

"It was a role, Amy. I'm an actress, remember?"

"You're also an American, for which allowances had to be made. That dreadful scandal sheet has already been forgotten."

She pierced an egg with her fork, freeing the golden yolk. "Daniel was properly attentive and should be calling on you today. You do like him, don't you? Not the most accomplished dancer in the city, but a pleasant-enough sort."

The words carried a sharp edge, as if she dared Raven to contradict her. Raven was convinced Amy and Daniel had once shared more than just a casual friendship, but she was equally convinced neither would appreciate her speculations.

For all her brusqueness, Amy looked fragile and lovely in the fawn cashmere gown she'd worn the day Raven first called, her golden hair brushed into a simple fall of curls at the back of her head; but there were added shadows under her eyes and lines around her tightened mouth.

Raven sipped her tea. "I agree the evening went well, although I'm not certain what you wanted or expected."

"I wanted—"

Amy fell silent, joining Raven in studying the misty day. She rubbed her arms as if to warm herself. "Never mind what I wanted. I'm pleased with what I got." She thrust her food away. "You've never married, have you?

You're what, twenty-seven? I suppose you've given up hope."

Raven started at the insensitivity of the comment. Even for Amy, it was rude. What would she do if Raven told her that she hadn't given up hope? A woman couldn't give up something she never had.

But she wasn't about to reveal to any Bannerman anything private and personal. She had tried once with Marcus; he hadn't believed a word she'd said.

"Sometimes I think you want to be friends, Amy, and other times that you want only to intimidate me. Why?"

Amy looked past her, as if she could find a response hanging in the air. After a moment, she shrugged. "Because it's what is expected of me."

"And what is expected of me?"

"None of us really knows. That's why I ask questions."

The girl's hands brushed at imaginary crumbs on the linen cloth. She was jittery this morning, instead of triumphant as Raven had anticipated. And vulnerable, despite her bluntness. She was, in truth, like no one Raven had ever met.

"I'm a private person, Amy. I'm not used to revealing things about myself. I'll tell you this much. I never held girlish dreams of a man to love and children to cherish. I have my family. They are all I want."

"I, too, have no wish to marry."

"Have you informed your suitors? There were a dozen men hovering near you all evening."

"If that is how they choose to waste their time, it's

hardly my fault. I shall be content with Marcus and the aunts. We each have our special interests, of course. I paint; Cordelia drinks, and Irene reads. That's probably what they're doing now, if they're awake, Cordelia talking to her gin in a teacup and Irene pouring over one of those dreadful geographies she loves. Marcus's chore is to manage us all. That's varied enough for any household, don't you believe?"

To Raven's astonishment, Amy's eyes filled with tears. "He's gone to Paris, did you know? He took the boat train early this morning."

"I didn't know."

Amy wiped her damp lashes. "What a silly goose I am. Upset because I'm confined to London. I should be used to it by now. Business takes him there every few months. He's usually gone a couple of weeks."

Her distress made no sense. Why weep for Marcus when the two of them seldom spoke?

And why the news of his absence should depress *her,* Raven had no idea. She poured another cup of tea, stirring in a lump of sugar.

"He's looking for a wife," said Amy. "I don't mean in Paris, although if he found someone suitable over there I doubt he would hesitate to import her."

Raven added two more lumps.

"I didn't know you liked sweetened tea," said Amy.

"Oh," said Raven, realizing what she had done. "I seem to need the energy all of a sudden. It was a late night." For good measure, she added another lump, then forced herself to sip the syrup.

"He's after a rich bride," said Amy. "He doesn't talk

about it, but since he inherited the title, he's had his eye on several prospects."

Quite unbidden came an image of Marcus staring at her as she sprawled in disgrace on the Cockloft stage. Even now, more than a week later, she burned with shame.

"These prospects are very respectable, I'm sure," she said.

"I don't expect that's one of his criteria. But the women with money usually are quite beyond reproach. Marcus's title is tempting, but he's got a terrible reputation to live down. Gambling, drinking. He had a stable of horses he raced himself; but when the earl died, he sold them all. Women were the worst. He must have bedded every actress in town under the age of fifty."

Raven wasn't hearing anything she hadn't already known or suspected, so why was she suddenly chilled? Like Amy, she rubbed at her arms.

"Why tell me all this? It isn't my business."

"You said that sometimes I seemed to want you for a friend. I do. It gets lonely around here. You've had your sisters and your parents. I've had—" She stopped, and for the second time her eyes filled with tears. "I've had Marcus."

Raven wanted to take her hand, to give her the comfort she desperately needed; but before she could do so, the footman entered with the silver salver. "Another letter has arrived."

Sharp-featured and watchful, more than ever he reminded Raven of a hawk.

"Thank you, Hammond," said Amy, the tears gone

as quickly as they had appeared. "It's probably for Miss Chadwick."

"Beg your pardon, miss. The envelope is addressed to you."

She blanched. Raven was certain of it, even though Amy didn't once look at the salver. Pushing from the table, Amy stood. "We'll be having callers in a couple of hours. I need to select a gown."

Hammond extended the tray. Amy thrust the letter in a pocket without giving it a glance. The footman stepped aside as she walked from the room. His narrow eyes sought Raven, and she could have sworn his lips twitched into a smile as he turned to leave. His thick lips, she noticed for the first time, out of proportion to the rest of his face. Lips that could be described as sensual. A shiver ran down her spine.

In the solitude of her room, she pondered the sense of doom that had settled over her. It wasn't any one thing—Amy's loneliness, the servant's impudence, her own frustration because she hadn't done anything about her investigation. It certainly couldn't be blamed on the absence of the earl. Or his search for a wealthy wife.

And not even on Mama's letter, at least not entirely.

"I don't have enough to do," she told herself. "I'm used to working, and all I've done during my week here is arrange sprigs of holly for Amy's ball."

The argument sounded solid. She had read too many plays; too easily she let her imagination roam. Yet she could not erase from her heart the knowledge that something in this fashionable house was terribly wrong.

\* \* \*

The afternoon went as Amy had predicted, with several gentlemen and a few ladies dropping by, in Raven's opinion more to get another look at the scandalous American songbird than to foster friendship.

Daniel Lindsay stayed the longest, not leaving until he extracted Raven's consent to ride in his carriage through the park the next day, weather permitting. Raven suggested Amy join them, but she retorted she had better things to do. If Lindsay took offense, he didn't show it, but he did excuse himself soon afterwards.

Over the next few days she managed to get samplings of the women's handwriting; none matched Mama's letter, but the fact didn't exonerate them completely since the childish scrawl could have been faked.

She learned nothing more about Marcus. After that one burst of revelations in the morning room, Amy changed the subject when his name arose. Frustrated, Raven tried to throw herself into the excursions Amy arranged to the city's seemingly endless museums, galleries, cathedrals. She took special delight in bribing a guard to let them onto the grounds of the Tower of London.

"I want you to see the ravens," Amy explained. "Legend has it they've been here since the Tower was first built. If they leave, it's believed both the Tower and the kingdom will fall."

Raven tried to be enthusiastic, but she found it difficult, even when Amy pressed upon her a long black feather that had been lying in the grass. She kept the gift, but to her the birds were just scavengers. Since she was doing nothing to earn her bed and board, she decided her name was particularly apt.

When she wasn't touring the city or worrying about Mama or castigating herself about her sloth, she thought about the earl, about his prospective brides, about his eyes as he had looked at her on the stage. She thought, too, of his holding her during their dance. It all jumbled together in her mind until she thought she would go mad.

Worst were the dark hours of solitude when she tossed in her bed. The night thoughts hadn't returned since the early days when Marcus had dared to take her in his arms . . . had dared to kiss her. Still, there were long stretches of time when sleep wouldn't come.

With the days moving inexorably toward the time he would return, she found herself returning again and again to the library, where she felt his presence most. Flame would have said she was sucking on a sore tooth; she would have been right.

On an afternoon in late February, six weeks after her ship had landed in Portsmouth, she sat behind his library desk and relived the scenes that had taken place here between them, all of them, from the arguments to the kisses. With Amy calling on a friend, the two aunts pursuing their separate hobbies in their rooms, and the servants inventorying the linens and wine cellar, she knew she would not be disturbed.

In the silence, broken only by the hiss of gaslight and the snap of the fire, she touched her lips and thought about touching his. Longings stirred within her. She couldn't deny them; she wouldn't try.

He fascinated, aroused, disturbed, yet how little she knew him. Sitting here taking in the lingering scent of him, feeling the warmth of the leather chair as he had done a thousand times, she wanted to know more. The desk was clear of papers. As if moving of its own volition, her hand tried the center drawer. Locked. That ought to be the end of that.

But what if back in Savannah she had returned her mother's letter without reading it? Sometimes principles had to be compromised. What if there were information inside the drawer that would reveal who had written *You will die?* What if she found out it had all been a hoax and everything was wonderful?

What shameful rationalizing, she told herself, as she pulled a pin from her hair and went to work on the lock.


"The painting is definitely missing, Ralph. Frederick wrote as soon as he noticed it was no longer in the library. Much as I hated to do so, I ended my visit immediately."

Marcus paused on the walkway a half-block from Stafford House. He had sent his luggage on ahead from Victoria Station, but sought out Ralph in his Piccadilly club to see if he had any ideas about the theft. Rather than taking a cab, the two elected to walk the mile to Bolton Row.

"A small Landseer of a collie bitch and her pups,"

he said. "Quite charming and too valuable to lose. Since he's become the Queen's favorite, his works are bringing high prices."

"Landseer's dead, too," said Ralph. "That raises the value even more. I suppose the servants have all been queried."

"Frederick assured me that's the first thing he did."

"Has anything like this happened before?"

Marcus shook his head. "Not that there's much to steal. A few porcelains and another painting or two that have been in the family for years." Helpless rage overcame him. "Damn it, I'm supposed to guard the Stafford heritage, poor though it may be, not let it walk out the door."

A carriage rumbled by, its wheels clattering on the cobblestone street.

"You've visited Stafford House during my absence. How goes it?"

Ralph cleared his throat.

"That bad?" Marcus asked.

"The house is still standing, as you can observe. I can't get a word out of Cordelia, and Irene stays in her room. Amy's the one. Sometimes she's as gracious as anyone could want, and other times she's prickly as a hedgehog. I came across her in Green Park the other day—taking a stroll, she said. Who should come along but Daniel Lindsay? Since they seemed to want a private chat, I excused myself; but when I glanced back, they were having a jolly good row. Quiet kind, but I know your sister's moods. Lindsay's face turned as red as a cherry tart."

"She has a way of raising a man's ire. Don't give any thought to it. They never got along. We all grew up together, Daniel tagging after me and Amy resenting the both of us."

Remembering, Marcus grinned. "I was a hellion in those days, and proud of it. I hated like the devil anyone imitating my youthful swagger." The grin faded. "I'd be damned glad if anyone listened to me now."

"The lot of 'em don't act much like a family," Ralph said. "They never have, I suppose, but it seems worse since Anne's girl arrived."

He scratched his whiskers. "I say, Marcus, you don't suppose she filched the Landseer. I wouldn't have thought Anne would raise a child to steal, but you never know. American, half-Irish, she could be capable of anything. As she's already proven with that music hall disaster. You're a fortunate man to have gotten out of that unscathed."

The idea of Raven as a thief depressed Marcus more than he would have thought. "Women are hard to figure."

"Don't say that, m'boy. You're the expert. If you don't know 'em, what's an old bachelor like me going to do?"

"Enjoy what they offer and doubt what they say."

Ralph's pewter brows lifted. "Cynical advice."

"But not faulty." An image of black eyes and black hair flashed across his mind. "Consider Raven Chadwick. You've already mentioned her as our thief. Do you really believe she would have called if I'd been a struggling shopkeeper in Soho?"

"You're a struggling earl."

"The title, Uncle Ralph, is worth more than the man. I've no delusions about that."

"Best stay away from her," said Ralph. "She's trouble. I can tell it. Duty calls you, lad. You've said so yourself. A man's only got so much vigor; that's what my father always claimed. He swore semen was worth forty ounces of blood. Spend it too often, and you might as well open your veins."

Marcus had never considered a lack of vigor his problem, especially where Raven was concerned. Curse his black heart, his blood raced to think of her waiting behind the Stafford House door.

Poor Ralph was only spouting popular beliefs. Duty and Abstinence went together, both capitalized as was their due. And Continence as well. A man couldn't even think about sex, much less do anything about it, else he risked permanent fatigue.

To an unwilling celibate about to face a black-eyed beauty with breasts shaped to fill his hands, it was a concept hard to accept.

They reached the front walk of Stafford House.

"Come in for a brandy?"

"Thanks, but no. I'll stroll for a bit. Give Amy and the others my love. If you can gather them together."

Marcus let himself in the front door. All was quiet. He thought about the Landseer and its accustomed place on a library shelf. He'd like to see for himself the spot where it had been.

Tossing cloak and hat onto the stairway, he walked across the marble floor and eased the library door open.

Raven sat behind his desk, her tongue caught between her teeth as she worked at the top drawer. An unexpected disappointment struck him, and then anger. Arms crossed, he leaned against the frame and waited for her to see him.

Thick lashes were lowered over tawny cheeks, blocking a view of her eyes. Her hair, normally tightly bound, was pinned loosely to the top of her head, wisps edging her face. Her sea-green gown lacked adornment. He liked it better than the fancy Parisian styles.

It was better to wear for breaking the lock on his desk.

He ought to . . .

Several options came to mind. He liked the idea that while none came under the heading of Abstinence, adherence to Duty would be meticulously fulfilled.

"You're scratching the wood," he said.

Her gaze flew to him. She didn't move. He crossed the room and tossed a key onto the desk. "Here, use this." Still, she did not move.

Hands splayed on either side of the key, he leaned forward until he could see the flecks of fear in her eyes.

"Do you mind telling me what you're doing?"

She cleared her throat. "I'm—"

"Looking for something else to steal? There's nothing in there besides stationery and a few bills. Some personal correspondence, nothing of much interest."

She sat back, her eyes wide. "I'm not stealing."

"Righteous indignation becomes you. But then, so do feathers. You really are a remarkable woman."

"Lord Stafford—"

Marcus snapped his fingers. "I have it. There's also the flyer and scandal sheet proclaiming the brief but noteworthy career of Raven the American Songbird. Perhaps you wanted to mail them home so that your beloved family could keep up with your progress."

Loosening the top buttons of his shirt, he removed his cravat and came around the desk. She stood and stepped away. He grabbed her hand and, before she could fend him off, bound her wrists with the strip of white silk.

"You are my prisoner, Raven Chadwick."

She twisted her arms. "This is ridiculous. Let me go."

"I can't. I've just made a citizen's arrest. Besides, you might overpower me."

She closed her eyes. "Please let me go and I'll try to explain."

"Not yet." He eased her back in the chair and placed his hands on the armrests. "Don't fight me, Songbird, or I'll have to bind your legs, too. Shame to tie them together when they're so much more useful apart."

Her fists jerked upward and caught him on the chin. He bit his lip and tasted blood.

"Damn!"

She looked as surprised as he was at her successful strike. Marcus abandoned his taunts. He had her right where he wanted her. A trapped quarry, whether she realized it or not.

"The painting, Raven. What did you do with the painting? Sell it to a fence you met in Soho?"

The surprise gave way to confusion. "I don't know what you're talking about."

If she was acting, she was good. He told her as much.

"I'm not acting and I'm not lying. I don't know anything about a painting. I assume one has been stolen."

"Frederick wrote me in Paris. That's why I've returned. Unexpectedly, it would seem."

She had the grace to blush.

"I admit to breaking into your desk. Or trying to. The drawer has a strong lock."

"Nothing but the best for the peerage."

"You're a strange man, Marcus Bannerman. Sometimes I think you poke fun at yourself."

"It saves others the trouble. Now quit changing the subject. The painting. The desk." He rubbed his swollen lip. "The truth, willingly given, or I will do things to your body to force you to speak."

"You wouldn't. That would be—" She broke off, and he saw genuine alarm in her eyes. She looked away. "I can't breathe."

He studied the rise and fall of her breast. "You make a good show of it."

Her gaze flew back to him. "Don't you ever think of anything but bodies?"

*Not lately.*

"The painting."

"I am not a thief."

He picked the bent hairpin off the floor. "This says otherwise."

She slumped in the chair, all signs of fight in her gone. "Please let me go and I'll tell you the truth." She sighed, without spirit. "Don't worry. I'll not overpower you."

Her concession robbed the scene of its already dwindling pleasure. He loosened the tie, then gave her room to stand. As though catapulted, she escaped to the far side of the desk, but she made no move for the door. Instead, she walked to the hearth to stare into a mound of smoldering coals.

She looked at him, dark eyes wide and wounded, and Marcus's breath caught. She could overpower him, all right, but not with fists or claws. One glance left him ready to take her on the library floor. And the desk and the sofa and against the wall if they tired of horizontal positions.

He had to remind himself of the business at hand. Abstinence. Continence. Hellish requirements, both.

"The truth, Songbird. Why are you here?"

# *Nine*

*I want to know who threatened to kill my mother.*

Raven couldn't bring herself to tell Marcus the truth. He was so quick to misjudge her, he might think she had made the whole thing up. If she showed him the letter, he might accuse her of writing it herself, and the second letter to the Cockloft as well.

The more she thought about it, the more she was certain that was exactly what he would believe. Mama had tossed the envelope into the fire, leaving her unable to prove the threat had been received in Savannah. As to the music hall, the scandal over her performance had passed, and she lived free in more luxury than she had ever known.

He would have her bound again in a second, and this time he might do some of those things he had threatened. She got tight inside thinking of what the things might be.

"I'm waiting," he said. He might as well have added *while you make up your lies.*

She couldn't tell him everything, but everything she said could be the truth.

"There are secrets in this house I wanted to uncover."

A pair of cold blue eyes seemed to look right through her to the waves of heat rising from the hearth.

"Inadequate, Songbird. Try a different tune."

How sure of himself he appeared, standing behind his desk, tall and strong and handsomely tailored in his gray frock coat with its velvet lapels, every inch of him an aristocrat—except for the shock of hair on his forehead and the open throat of his shirt where his cravat had been.

And here she was, cowering by the fire in her homemade dress, a small-town woman not only crude but criminal.

Pride came to her rescue.

"How can I say anything else? I don't know what the secrets are."

He took a step toward her. "And if you did . . . assuming there were any to find . . . what would you do? Threaten to tell all to the scandal sheets if I didn't offer recompense?"

"That's a terrible thing to say."

Another step. "It's a terrible thing to contemplate."

"And it's wrong, wrong, wrong." She twisted her hands in anguish. Why did everything concerning Marcus Bannerman turn to disaster?

"I'm not a villainess. Just a plain and simple woman from a small town far away."

"You're neither plain nor simple, and you know it."

Raven ignored him. She had begun, and it was too late to stop. "All of you lead such separate lives. Why?

Why does Aunt Cordelia drink and Irene keep to her room? And why does Amy dislike you so?"

The pain in his eyes took her by surprise. As much as he was hurting her, she had had no idea she could hurt him in return.

"Amy is my concern. You are an intruder here."

For some reason, these last words hurt most of all. "I'm sorry. She asked me to stay, and that's the only reason I'm here. I'll leave immediately."

By now he was halfway across the room. "Don't be a fool."

"You accused me of stealing. Why not toss me out on the street?"

"Because we've unfinished business between us."

Her heart pounded. "What do you mean?"

"Amy, for one thing. I understand she's been agitated more than usual lately. You wouldn't know anything about that, would you?"

"You really do care about her. I knew you had to. Why don't you show her?"

"As you pointed out, there are secrets in this house you do not understand. And quit changing the subject back to me."

He was close enough to her now for the candor to show in his eyes. And hidden worries that seemed incomprehensibly deep. Money would be one of them, of course. Amy had been clear about that. But something worse . . . far worse . . . had hold of his heart. All of the sharp-edged emotions that tore at her softened. Infinity separated them, yet she wanted to touch him in reassurance that all would be well. She who doubted much in her own life would turn out right. Best keep her condolences to herself.

"It's Paris, isn't it?" she said with sudden insight. "Something about Paris. Amy cried when she told me that's where you'd gone."

A shuttered look darkened his eyes. "A coincidence. She grows emotional at times."

"She's rarely emotional, not below the surface where emotions count. That is what has worried me about her. She's brittle. And things that are brittle tend to break."

"Ah, all is clear. You broke into my desk to learn about the Bannerman siblings."

"I wanted to know more about you." Surely he could sense the truth in what she said.

"I fascinate you, do I?" The self-mockery was back in his voice.

*More than you know.*

"You're a hard man."

"I tend to be that way around you."

He stood a whisper away. She caught the scent of sandalwood, of soot from the train, of the outdoors, of Marcus himself.

"Is there no gentleness in your soul?" she asked.

"None. I do not possess a soul."

He took her in his embrace; she could not pull away, even had she tried.

She looked at his lips, still slightly swollen where she'd struck him, and his strong, scarred chin. Another woman's mark? Perhaps. She could not look into his eyes.

"It always ends like this between us," she said.

His lips twitched into a partial smile. "It's the only way I can stop your accusations."

At last her eyes met his. "And what about the things you say to me? You think I want them to continue?"

"I don't know what you want." He slanted his lips across hers. "This?" Again, more firmly. "Or this?"

He tightened his embrace. "Or maybe this."

He kissed her fully, his tongue against her lips, her teeth, her tongue. Warm anticipation tingled through her . . . nothing else, no conscience, no dark images, no anger. Just a strangely contented feeling that this was right and what she wanted more than anything else in the world.

She leaned into his strength. He growled; she sighed, their lips and tongues together. With the room whirling and her body heating, Raven knew not what to do except hold onto him and take each moment as it came.

His hands were on her back, her waist, her hips. His mouth eased from hers, and he kissed her eyes, her cheeks, the sensitive skin behind her ear. Still, she clung to him, her breath ragged, her body alive as it had never been before. Every part of her yearned for pleasures she had never tasted.

Determined hands adjusted her body until she was pressed against him, her hips against his, something hard and insistent against the juncture of her thighs. A warning . . . a promise . . . a sampling of what he offered her. He was a man who wanted her, a man ready, here and now, to accept her wanting him.

A feeling like hot, wet velvet captured the intimate parts of her. Her breasts tingled, their tips tight. Darkness swirled around her. This was part of the dream, she thought, the part that awakened her to a pounding heart and a belly tight with desire. Marcus was the cloud surrounding her, pulling her into his own person, his own demands.

With the dream always came a sense of death. Even now, when she shared his heat, his hunger. She was not so far under his spell that the night thoughts failed to penetrate. Fear conquered passion, and the tremblings of shared longings turned to the tremblings of panic.

She stiffened in his arms. He held her tight, but his hands ceased their exploration. She listened to the slowing of his breath.

"I can't keep my hands off you."

He spoke as if his were the only will that mattered. She felt inexplicably hurt, and a coldness settled over her heart where only a moment ago heat had dwelled.

"You've said that before. I'm not your victim," she said to the collar of his shirt. "Anymore than you are mine."

His hands dropped to his sides and he stepped away. "Meaning what?"

"Meaning that I don't purposefully entice you. And you haven't forced me into anything."

"I haven't had to."

The truth of his words stung. She looked away. "We're two adults who must avoid temptation. That's all."

"I tempt you? An admission at last."

"Oh, Marcus," she said, not trying to hide the anguish in her heart, "you knew you tempted me the first time we met. Believe what you will, but no one else has ever aroused such a feeling."

"I'm flattered."

"No, you're not. My reactions are what you expect. The first time I saw you, I knew you were a man women wanted. Althea Innocent indicated that clearly enough." She walked around him and began to make her way to the door, but she couldn't leave without one last declaration.

"Let me relieve you of one worry . . . or at least one accusation. I have no plans to seduce and then trap you into another scandal. I plan to give myself to no man."

She saw the idea was not foreign to him. A fist clutched at her heart.

"Amy says you're searching for a wife. I won't get in your way." A sense of futility settled heavily on her shoulders and she laughed softly, her derision self-directed. "As if I could. My moving in here was a mistake. I know it now. As soon as possible, I'll make arrangements to return home."

"Too late."

"What do you mean?"

He closed the distance between them. "I said we have unfinished business. You wanted employment on the legitimate stage. Before I left, I made arrangements for just that with Simon Normandy. You didn't ask for my help. That's why you got it."

Raven's brain seemed filled with cobwebs. She hardly understood what he said. "I have a role in a play?"

"That's right."

Inconceivable. "And you arranged it?"

"Yes."

Unbelievable. "Th-thank you," she stammered, still trying to assimilate what he'd said.

"Don't thank me too much. It's a very small part requiring a very large costume. In fact, you don't speak a line. But it will call for a great deal of acting ability." He brushed a lock of hair from her cheek. "The Lyceum plans to present a new play based on the story of Héloise and Abélard. You play the part of a nun."

Over the next few weeks, rehearsal kept Raven busy and away from Marcus. Rarely was he home for dinner, and she assumed he was out courting a prospective bride. Restless energy took hold of her. She yearned for pages of dialogue, grand gestures, even a mad scene to absorb the energy. Instead, she walked about the stage, hands folded, eyes lowered, feigning piety while Althea Innocent extolled the lines of the medieval abbess Héloise.

It was a role for which Miss Innocent was infinitely miscast. Raven kept the opinion to herself, even at breakfast on opening day.

As usual, she and Amy ate in the morning room alone.

"Are you nervous?" Amy asked as soon as they settled down to a cup of tea and toast.

"Not in the least," Raven lied.

Amy reached for the butter. "This is the story of two lovers who've been separated, right?"

A question casually asked, yet Raven saw a tension behind the young woman's bright eyes.

"Right," she said, with equal nonchalance. "They fall in love; but since he is a canon, the birth of their son and subsequent marriage are kept secret. To protect his career, she retires to a convent."

"Oh," said Amy. "How sad. And how stupid."

"Perhaps. It's the way it really happened, you know. The playwright had to make up very little of the story. Héloise's letters to Abélard are quite beautiful."

Except when Miss Innocent was overdramatizing them.

"What happens to the unhappy couple?"

"Believing she's been betrayed, her uncle breaks into Abélard's quarters and mutilates him."

"This grows more interesting. How?"

Raven tried to think of a delicate way to express it. "By reducing his manhood."

Amy's eyes widened. "You mean—"

"I do."

"Like a gelding."

"Closer to a eunuch," said Raven, then impishly added, "It takes a rather sharp knife."

The two women stared at one another.

"It sounds terribly painful," said Amy.

"I'm certain that it is."

Amy grinned first, then Raven. Both broke into a fit of giggles. Raven couldn't believe she was acting this way; she hadn't giggled in years.

"He becomes a monk and she takes the veil," she said when the laughter had faded. "It happened about seven hundred years ago. They've been entombed together in Paris ever since."

Amy snorted. "Reunited in death. Rather late."

"I suppose you could look at it that way."

Amy spooned marmalade over her buttered toast, then set her plate aside. "We'll be there this evening. Marcus has arranged a box."

"How kind. It's not a very good play, I'm afraid. You'll be bored."

"Not in the least. The aunts are coming, along with Uncle Ralph. And Daniel Lindsay. Oh, and I'll be accompanied by a gentleman you met at the ball."

"Which one?"

"What difference does it make? Someone entertaining, you can be sure."

"And your brother?" She asked the question casually, as though she little cared where he would be.

"One of the candidate brides, I believe, will join us."

She should have expected nothing else. So why the heaviness around her heart?

She looked at the toast, the butter, the marmalade, and felt a definite queasiness in the pit of her stomach. The play, she thought. Opening night had her unnerved.

Excusing herself, she went to her room, where she spent the day writing letters, reading Shakespeare, pacing, arranging her hair as if anyone would see it beneath her wimple, and imagining a pair of blue eyes following her about the stage while a woman in fancy finery rested a hand upon his arm.

Two hours before curtain time, the footman drove her to the Lyceum in the earl's carriage, complete with crest upon the door. A few eyes raised as she stepped to the ground, but she was too busy avoiding the helping hand Hammond offered to take much notice.

In the wing, she passed Althea Innocent arguing over a stage direction with the manager Simon Normandy.

"Miss Chadwick, good evening," Normandy said, separating himself from the vocal actress.

Althea's green and watchful eyes settled on Raven. "I know you from somewhere, don't I?"

Raven pulled her cloak close. "I'm in the opening scene of Act Two."

Althea waved an impatient hand. "Before. I keep thinking we've met before."

*You warned that Marcus would grow weary of me within a month.*

Raven turned. "I must get in costume."

"Marcus Bannerman!" On Althea's lips, the name rang out like thunder. "That day he came to see me here, to beg I take him back. You're the drab little thing who wanted to replace me."

Raven caught Normandy's eye. The stage manager shrugged.

"No one could take your place," she said, calling on all the skills of diplomacy Mama had taught. "I didn't even try."

With a nod to Normandy, Raven hurried away from the wing as quickly as her feet would carry her. Marcus's presence in her life followed wherever she went.

That was the reason she couldn't get him out of her mind.

The evening did not go well. She missed her cue to enter from stage left, although no one but the other performers could know she arrived late. Panic chilled her heart as she trod the familiar and oft-rehearsed steps in the background of the action.

Her fifteen minutes on the stage lasted an eternity, yet ended in an instant, and she found herself backstage waiting for the close of the second act, barely remembering her first appearance on the legitimate stage.

At last the curtain descended and the house lights went up for the final intermission. Using a spyglass borrowed from one of the stagehands, she peeked through an opening in the curtain. She picked out Marcus's box right away.

It was filled as Amy had predicted, the aunts in black to one side, behind them Uncle Ralph with the prominent Dundreary whiskers, then Daniel Lindsay, Amy and her companion. Most noticeable of all was Marcus, splendid as ever in evening attire, and beside him, a slender woman in white, her pale shoulders bare, a white feather waving from out of a mass of brown curls.

A prospective countess? She looked the part. And her hand rested upon Marcus's arm.

Raven backed away and hurried to change into her street clothes, seeing little need to wait around for the final curtain. The return trip to Bolton Row was in a hansom cab far less grand than the Stafford carriage, but it got her to her destination just as quickly.

Hammond let her in. She didn't bother to notice if he leered at her, instead rushing up the stairs to the safety of her room. Shedding garments and hairpins to left and right, she changed into her nightgown and jumped beneath the covers of her bed.

Her night of triumph, she thought as she stared at the canopy overhead. If Mama and Papa and her sisters had been there, perhaps she would feel more exultant. Her pragmatic self said no. She had a less than minor role in a poor play, and she hadn't made it to the stage on time.

Tomorrow she would do better. And with a different audience, perhaps enjoy the evening more.

Sleepless hours later she heard footsteps in the hall and doors that opened and closed. The Bannerman party had returned.

A knock at her door brought her upright. Amy, perhaps, come to talk over the evening . . . or perhaps to tease. With Amy, one could never be sure.

Easing into her slippers, she tiptoed across the room. "Who is it?" she asked through the crack in the doorframe.

Marcus's deep voice caressed her. "It's your proud sponsor. I had hoped to offer a congratulatory drink."

"I'm already in bed."

"A tempting picture. You've learned to throw your voice across the room."

She pressed her fingers to the cold, hard wood as if she might touch his words and the lips that said them. Realizing what she was doing, she jerked her hand away.

"Congratulate me tomorrow, Marcus."

A pause. "You stole the show."

"Don't be absurd."

"You were certainly the most pious person on stage."

"I kept my clothes on, you mean."

He laughed. And then another pause. "I've never had an actress under my roof before."

Raven's blood ran cold. "Meaning you've never had one so convenient?"

This time the pause was longer. "Congratulations. That's all. And lock your door. I may lose all control during the night."

She listened as his footsteps receded. What had that been all about? Was he once again mocking himself or was he mocking her? He sounded a trifle tipsy, but Marcus seldom drank. Perhaps he'd been toasting his newly acquired betrothed.

With sleep impossible, she paced the floor beside her bed. She had read every book in her room at least a dozen times. Too bad she'd never taken up needlework, else with the energy stored inside her she could knit an afghan before dawn.

Maybe Irene would lend her one of her geographies. At two in the morning, geography sounded unappealing. The volumes in Marcus's library called to her. Pulling on a wrapper, she peered into the hallway. All was quiet.

Slowly she walked the long route to the head of the stairs. She had never been about the house at night, never known there were shadows flickering in every nook.

She took the first step, then hesitated. Someone was behind her.

"Who's there?" she called out in a stage whisper.

Only the creaks of night answered.

"Must be my imagination," she said to herself. "Too much excitement"—although in truth she had found the whole evening sadly flat.

A shadow, a footstep, then from her darkest nightmare an indistinguishable mass flew at her. It was no cloud that struck her, but a solid force. She flailed for balance, then with a cry of panic plunged into the darkness down the stairs.

# Ten

A cry of distress stirred Marcus from his decanter of brandy.

"Raven," he thought, recognizing the voice right away. A chill pierced his alcohol fog. In an instant he was out of the fireside chair and through his bedroom door.

He found her lying against the banister halfway down the stairs, legs twisted beneath her, her nightgown a pool of white against the dark spray of her unbound hair.

He cried out her name, then more softly, "Raven," as he knelt beside her. So still, he thought, when she did not move. His trembling hands touched her. She felt warm and small and vulnerable.

What was she doing here? She was supposed to be safely barricaded in her bed. And why didn't she open her eyes and order him away?

Disbelief gave way to horror and then icy fear. He felt for a pulse at her throat. Faint but steady.

"Thank God," he whispered as he brushed the hair from her face. Cursing the liquor he'd been consuming all evening, he felt for broken bones. She moaned when he touched a swollen ankle.

A feeling of overpowering protectiveness took hold of him. Whatever had happened, she needed him. He must see that she was all right. Heart pounding, he lifted her in his arms. Light as a feather, he thought as he stood, a poor joke he might have made in their times of sparring.

If only she would snap something at him now.

She stirred, then settled quietly against him, cheek against his shirt. Dependent, helpless. His throat tightened. In the dim glow of a lone gaslight on the stairway wall, she looked pale . . . deathly so.

Except for the line of blood on her chin. She must have cut herself in the fall.

He met Amy in the dark at the top of the stairs.

"I thought I heard—" With a small cry, she broke off.

"She's hurt," he said. "Get a doctor."

"But what—"

"Now!"

She nodded and hurried past him. He carried Raven to his room. Easing the wrapper from her limp body, he laid her on the bed just as her eyes fluttered open.

"Oh," she said, staring up at him. "What happened?"

He pulled the covers to her shoulders, then with the tail of his shirt dabbed at the blood on her chin.

"You fell."

She closed her eyes for a minute. When she opened them again; she seemed to shrink back into the mattress.

"I can't remember—"

She tried to rise, then fell back with a moan. "My head—"

"Don't talk. The doctor's on the way."

She stared up at him in silence, her eyes as black as the night that pressed against the house. She seemed to be asking something, but she did not put the question into words. At last her lashes lowered over colorless cheeks and her breathing steadied as if she were asleep. But Marcus saw the twitches of her mouth and the whiteness of her knuckles as she clutched at the covers.

She was frightened. Or in pain. He didn't know which was worse.

Amy burst into the room.

"Hammond is going for the doctor. What happened? What was she—"

Spying Raven lying quiet and still, she ceased her questions. Marcus took her aside to tell what he knew, then explained again to the aunts, who came in separately.

"Wait in the hall," he ordered, then pulled the chair beside the bed to await the doctor, his hand at her wrist to touch the beat of her heart.

He waited with the others in the hallway during the examination.

"She's got a nasty bump on her head and a small cut on her chin," the doctor reported a quarter hour later. "Her ankle's badly sprained, I'd say. It doesn't appear to be broken. To be safe, she shouldn't try to walk for a couple of weeks."

"Have you told her all this?"

The doctor grinned. "Oh, yes. She had a few things to say about my instructions."

He adjusted his glasses on the bridge of his nose. "She seemed most concerned about getting back into her own room."

"I wondered about that myself," said Amy.

Marcus declined to comment, except to echo the doctor's prescription. "Two weeks of bed rest, you say."

"Once the head pains go away, she can sit up. She can move about in a carriage, if she gets restless. But nothing more."

"Oh, dear," said Cordelia. "Poor thing."

"Fimble-famble," said Irene. "She shouldn't have been wandering around in the dark."

"The hallway was unlit," said Marcus, "but not the stairs. And that is where she fell."

"Tripped over her own feet, like as not," Irene said.

"She never seemed particularly clumsy to me."

"Humph! What are you saying? She was pushed?"

"Oh, dear," said Cordelia.

"Not in the least," said Marcus. "Maybe she suffered a dizzy spell."

"Possibly," said Irene. "Women in a certain condition do, so I'm told."

"Aunt Irene!" Amy said.

"Don't sound so shocked. She's an actress. She could have had a dalliance after rehearsal one night." Irene looked at the doctor. "What's your professional opinion? Any chance she's increasing?"

The doctor stiffened. "My examination was not designed to answer such a question, Miss Pickering. In a fall such as she suffered, any pregnancy would most likely have been terminated. There was certainly no indication of such." He looked at Marcus. "Would Your Lordship like me to return to the sickroom?"

"No," Marcus snapped. "We are concerned with Miss Chadwick's head and ankle. Nothing in between." He glared at the assembly. "Nothing of this conversation is to be repeated. I will not have it."

Even Amy nodded agreement.

"The important thing is Raven's hurt," she said. "And needs rest. She can scarcely return to her play."

"Oh, dear," said Cordelia. "I hadn't considered that. She did such a fine job."

"From what I could see, little was required," said Irene. "Even I could have played the nun."

Amy's eyes widened. "Or I. Of course. That's what I'll do. Until she's up and about again."

"No, Amy, you will not." Marcus stared at his sister. How stubborn she looked with determination firing her eyes, and how fragile. No more able to care for herself than when she'd turned eighteen.

Some decisions must be left to him. This was one of them.

"Marcus—" she began.

"No. Now everyone get to bed. We've had a long day and it's almost dawn. I'll see the doctor out and leave orders with Frederick for the morning."

"Where will you sleep?" asked Amy, all the belligerence back in her voice. "You could hardly bother Raven tonight."

"Rest assured I will take care of our guest."

He looked past them all to the closed door of his room and thought of the woman lying in his bed. The protective feeling stirred within him as strong as ever. Over the past weeks he had thought several times of assaulting her himself—in several ways. Exploiting the family name, assaulting his desk, perhaps filching the painting—all had been cause for censure and for punishment.

Now that she was hurt, he wanted nothing more than to know she was safe.

\* \* \*

The red-streaked mist surrounded Raven as thickly as it had ever done. Her leaden body refused to stir, despite the terror gripping her soul. This time the mist took human shape. A face, obscure but for the leering mouth, came close, teeth bared. She saw the tattered blue uniform of the Yankee soldier, saw the thin, twisted lips ease apart.

*You will die.*

She tried to cover her ears against the condemnation, but her arms refused to move.

*You will die.*

The words came at Raven in waves, along with the throbbing head pain that threatened to split her skull.

*You will die.*

The thin edge of reason cut into her terror. These were not the words of the soldier . . . not his first and, God help them both, not his last. They had been penned to her mother, she thought as she drifted closer into unwilling consciousness. Her precious mother who would be under this same roof in only a few months.

With the memory of the fall returning in all its horror, she knew the words were also directed to her.

In the dark that preceded dawn, with the Bannerman clan behind the nearby doors, she had been shoved down the stairs. Before this moment, she had never considered herself in danger—except from her own weakness for a man. One man, whose aura permeated everything around her.

She felt his presence. Anvils rested on her eyes, yet she forced them open. He sat beside the hearth, no more than a dozen feet away. She saw him in profile, the strong, straight nose and angular jaw, the lock of flaxen hair across his forehead, his eyes directed toward the bright fire.

His fire, his room, his bed. Each particular set off an alarm in her already overwrought mind.

He shifted his gaze to hers. Steady, worried, questioning. She felt his heat more than the warmth from the fire.

*Did you push me?*

The question came without warning. She looked away into the shadows apart from the firelight. "Is it still night?" she asked.

"Afternoon."

"How long have I been asleep?"

"Twelve hours."

"Impossible." She tried to sit up, then fell back, the throbbing behind her eyes unendurable.

"Don't rush your recovery."

She waited until the waves of pain receded. "Would you mind opening the draperies?"

She watched him stand, watched his long legs take the length of the room in a half-dozen strides. He was dressed in tailored trousers and shirtsleeves, his collar open at the throat. Bristles darkened his lean cheeks and hid the scar on his chin. She'd never seen him unshaven. Despite the fear, the pain, the exhaustion, something stirred inside her.

*Did you push me?*

The question would not go away.

The draperies opened onto dim daylight, but still the winter rays hurt her eyes. She must have grimaced because he darkened the windows again, then returned to stand beside her bed.

"You're supposed to take a teaspoon of medicine," he said, gesturing to a small vial on the bedside table.

"It's not opium, is it?"

"An anodyne of quinine, I believe. It's either this or a cup of tea."

"I'll take the tea."

Ringing for a servant, Marcus eased Raven to a sitting position. Under his gentle hands, she was able to shift without terminal pain. Could these be the hands that had shoved her? It seemed impossible, and yet so did all the other possibilities.

After the tea had been served and drunk, he pulled his chair beside the bed.

"What happened?" he asked.

Raven ran a forefinger around the patterns on the coverlet and considered her response. With the terror easing from both her mind and heart, an icy, hollow feeling took their place. She was afraid, and she was alone.

"I don't remember."

Marcus leaned back, his long legs stretched in front of him, his eyes watchful.

"I doubt you've forgotten everything. Why did you leave your room?"

"I wanted something to read."

"Ah, you were off to the library."

A frown in his direction cost her a throb or two. "Without a hairpin. I was after a book. I must have tripped. The next thing I knew I was in your bed and some strange man was poking at me."

"Would you have felt better if I had been the man?"

"Marcus—"

"Just testing if you're really getting better. Glad to see that you are."

"Thank you, Doctor," she said, thinking that if a pounding heart and a rush of blood to her cheeks indicated good health, she was indeed getting better.

"I examined the carpet at the top of the stairs," he said. "No bumps, no tears, nothing to trip over."

"Probably my own feet were the culprits."

Like the time on the music hall stage, she almost added, but this was not the time to be glib . . . and the conditions were not the same at all.

"You fell at an angle. Good thing. The banister stopped you from going all the way down."

She shuddered. "I don't want to talk about it anymore. It's bad enough being confined—" She stopped herself. "What am I doing in your room instead of mine?"

"It was closer. Besides, I granted myself permission to rest in your bed. Too good an opportunity to pass up." He leaned forward in the chair. "Got damned little rest, though. I could smell you in the sheets."

Raven's gaze darted to his face, to the parted mouth, the lean, shadowed cheeks, the eyes lit with blue fire.

She looked away. What a ninny she had become. Even suspecting him of attempted murder, she yearned to stroke his skin. Irritation, directed at them both, gave her strength to put aside her fear.

He shifted to sit on the bed. He touched her face. She started.

"What are you afraid of, Songbird?"

"You startled me, that's all."

"Are you sure you don't remember more about the fall?"

She couldn't look at him. "I'm sure."

His thumb stroked her chin. "I'm afraid you'll have a scar like mine. No doubt it will look better on you."

"Yours isn't so bad," she said without thinking.

"Is that a blush on your cheek? You really are getting better."

He stood. "It's time you rested. I've sent word to Simon Normandy that you're out as his nun."

In vain Raven tried to summon regret. "It wasn't much of a role anyway."

"A practical woman."

"I used to be," she said in a whisper.

"Good," he said as though he hadn't heard. "Then you'll agree with my plans. I spent a great deal of time thinking yesterday and last night. Drinking, too."

"I decided you were celebrating your betrothal."

"To the woman at the theater?" Marcus grimaced. "I didn't ask her. She had the right pedigree, but unfortunately she didn't understand the references to Abélard's emasculation. She kept thinking the play was a comedy. She laughed at inopportune times."

Guiltily, Raven remembered how she and Amy had giggled when the details of the monk's amputation had been discussed.

"That's an unusual test for a bride," she said.

"But an effective one. The decision didn't help my finances, however. Somewhere between the rebuff at your door and your cry, I decided to abandon the paperwork that's kept me in town. From correspondence received yesterday, I learned that the Stafford country estate and farmlands in Sussex are deteriorating to an incredible degree. I need to oversee them personally."

"You're leaving London," said Raven, wishing the information filled her with relief.

"I'm not the only one. Amy has agreed, far more readily than I would have expected, as have the aunts. Frederick, Hammond, even the upstairs maid will be joining us."

Raven glanced up at him with all the nonchalance her acting skills could summon. "I wish you success and a pleasant journey."

"Oh, we're not leaving until you can travel. Don't look surprised, Songbird. On the stairs in the wee hours of the morning, I vowed to watch over you. And that means taking you to Sussex with us. Whether you believe it or not, a Bannerman does not go back on his word."

He left before she could respond. In her confused state, she was grateful. He suspected her fall had not been the accident she claimed. Did he know for sure? Had his hands really been the ones that came out of the dark?

Despite all her self-directed warnings, she couldn't believe it of him. Not in her heart. Not that she felt he truly cared for her well being; but if he ever chose to end her life, she believed he would attack face on.

The realization brought both comfort and pain. It was the pain that lingered as she drifted into the balm of sleep.


Irene took it upon herself to summon the servants before dinner and tell them of the plans. Most had heard rumors, but she wanted to see the look on one face in particular when she announced who would be included in the party.

Before retiring, she stopped by the drawing room to turn the Chinese vase toward the wall. An hour later, dressed in a frilly gown and wrapper, her long, gray-streaked hair brushed until it crackled with electricity, she responded to a soft knock at her door.

She opened it quickly to admit her visitor.

"I see you got the signal. I thought you might want a reading lesson tonight."

Without waiting for an answer, she went to the bed, pulled out the chest, and selected the printed matter to be studied, taking a moment to touch the small wooden box she kept hidden away.

"Put it back. I've got a new one for you."

She smiled up at her pupil. Roger Hammond smiled back.

"You're a devil," she said, her body tightening as she stared into the all-seeing eyes of the footman.

"It's called *The Lustful Turk*. In the bed with you, like a good girl, and I'll do the reading."

Meekly, Irene did as she was told, slipping off her wrapper and pulling the covers to her throat.

"Naughty girl, teasing old Roger like that. Down with the covers, down with the gown."

He reached out to tweak a nipple. She drew back before he could touch her.

"Must I tell you every time?" he asked.

Oh, yes, he must. And he knew it.

Her breasts were small and sagged only a little, but he claimed he liked them that way. To look at, of course.

She never let him lay his hands on her, but she could see he wanted to.

He sat on the bedside and opened the book. Heat was already building between her legs.

" 'I quickly felt his finger again,' " he began to read. Irene settled back to be entertained.

# *Eleven*

On the train ride out of London, Raven couldn't stop studying hands.

Amy's, slender with pale, smooth skin stretched tight over tapered fingers, nails rounded and buffed to a shine;

Aunt Cordelia's, blunt, brown-spotted, the nails chewed to the quick;

Aunt Irene's, thin and wrinkled and pointed like talons.

Raven shuddered at the comparison.

She had to picture Marcus's, since he had traveled to Sussex two days earlier with the domestic staff. Strong, broad hands that had helped to lift her when, at her insistence, she had moved from his bed to her own. He had carried her himself, which was not what she'd had in mind. With equal sureness he'd brought her to the drawing room in the afternoons, then back again to her room.

Strong, *warm* hands, at once hard and gentle, handled her with ease. She could feel them against her body now.

Whose hands had shoved her down the stairs? Ten days had passed since the almost tragedy and she was no closer to the answer than she had ever been.

With Amy beside her in the first-class compartment, the aunts facing them on the upholstered seat, she looked out the window into the cold morning of early March, watching the city's yellow fog give way to soot from the London, Brighton and South Coast Railway's laboring engine. The heaviness in her heart remained.

"We don't have to go all the way to Brighton," Amy had explained when they discussed the details of the journey. "There's a station a few miles from Ditchling, the village nearest the estate. Only a thousand souls in the whole area, not counting the witches and their ghost hounds."

"Witches?" Raven had asked from the chaise longue where the Bannermans, brother and sister for once in agreement, insisted she rest. The chair had been brought to the drawing room from Aunt Cordelia's room. Nothing Raven could say convinced anyone to take it back.

"Witches," Amy repeated. "Lots of stories abound concerning them. The natives will tell you. They do it well."

Raven promptly pictured the three witches of Macbeth in the midst of thunder and lightning and harsh, craggy land, standing in the shadows of wind-tossed trees, stirring a boiling cauldron, and chanting dire predictions. Instead, after the four women had changed from the railroad car to the Stafford carriage, she saw rolling meadows marked with patches of green winter grass and brown bunches of hay, grazing sheep, a cloud-studded winter-blue sky.

It was a pastoral scene to calm her bruised soul. Not at all like the lush vegetation of her Georgia home, it was, nevertheless, country and she loved it. If she leaned slightly out the window—and ignored both the dust from the road and Irene's censorial glance—she could catch a whiff of the sea, which lay only a few miles to the south.

Just the way she could smell the sea from the docks along the Savannah River. Papa said it was brine caught in the sails and planks of the ships, but she knew better. Tears burned at the back of her eyes. She longed for home.

Perhaps if Marcus had met them at the station, she would have had his blunt words and tyrannical manner to distract her. But he'd sent Hammond in his stead. The hawk-eyed footman was a poor substitute, she thought, then chastised herself for missing the earl. The countryside really had her confused.

"It's beautiful, isn't it?" Amy said, a smile of pleasure softening her face. "The South Downs lack the drama of the northern landscapes, but there's a gentle sweep to the land that surpasses even the Weald. One can look at a forest only so long. Here, the world seems on view."

Sitting beside Raven in the crowded, rocking conveyance, her eyes directed to the passing countryside, the young woman looked younger than she had in London. Happier, too.

Across from them, Aunt Cordelia nodded in agreement, and even Irene appeared complacent for a change.

Raven did not respond. Since the fall, she had slipped into her old ways. Withdrawn, quiet, observing, speaking rarely unless spoken to. Mostly asking herself questions . . . and studying hands.

As the days passed, the fall had become harder to remember, the details blurred. Perhaps she really had tripped, as she'd insisted to Marcus. Perhaps she was the one at fault.

But no. It was the easy solution. Nothing had proven easy for Raven in a long, long while . . . except staying home and working in the store and performing before a nighttime fire for a loving audience who thought her the best actress and singer in the world.

If not for Papa's plans and Mama's safety—and an embarrassing episode in the bank—she would be there yet.

How sad it was that nothing stayed the same. One sister wed, the other sure to follow the same path.

If only they could all be children again, in those innocent days before the war brought the Yankee soldiers to Georgia, before the Chadwick girls knew they weren't considered equal to the gentry, before the men started noticing them, before the night thoughts came.

A return to last summer would suffice. Last summer Mama's letter hadn't arrived and Raven hadn't journeyed abroad or met the earl.

The thought startled her. Encountering Marcus Bannerman was no more important than her experiences in the theater, no more dramatic, no closer to her heart. Why should he keep intruding into her mind?

She was grateful he hadn't tried to kiss her again or make forward suggestions concerning her availability. It was as though her injuries had made her too vulnerable. Now that she was healthy again, would he renew the heated advances? The thought brought a tightening of her belly and a quickening of her breath. He frightened her, not as a possible assailant but as a man.

When the carriage veered from the main road onto a narrow, winding lane, Raven caught her first glimpse of Beacon Hall.

Named for the nearby high point of ground known as Ditchling Beacon, it sat on a small crest, thick evergreen shrubs protecting its base. Red brick partially covered in ivy, the hall's four floors rose out of the landscape like a crimson ship adrift on a sea of green. A dozen chimneys rose higher still, half of them emitting a stream of smoke into the crisp, clear air. The white-framed windows were dark, sullen eyes, unwelcoming and cold.

As they rocked their way closer to the front steps, she looked for the master of the house. Only one man awaited, the butler Frederick. When the carriage came to a dusty, creaking halt, he hastened down the steps and opened the door. With his assistance, the aunts exited, and he offered his arm to help Raven to the ground.

"I'm fine, thank you," she said, stepping onto the gravel drive and putting her full weight onto the damaged ankle to prove her claim. Other than an occasional weakness if she stepped wrong, she was healed.

Except for the memories and the questions and the night thoughts. These she kept to herself.

Her gaze swept over the front facade. "It looks newer than I imagined," she said to Amy, who had alighted to stand beside her.

"The land's been in the family for two hundred years, but the original house burned when the seventh earl got a bit tiddly and built a bonfire in the great hall. There were enough wooden support beams to satisfy even his pyromania."

"Was anyone killed?"

"Miraculously, no. He died two weeks later when he fell into an abandoned well. God will protect the feeble-minded only so long."

Amy turned to supervise the distribution of the luggage, piled precariously atop the carriage. Raven gave a moment's thought to what it must be like to know such details of one's ancestry. It was understandable that Mama never cared to discuss the family that had rejected her. Papa was a different situation.

"We're in the New World, lass, and have left all else behind," he had said in response to her few inquiries; and in Georgia, she'd been content.

But she was in England now, where the past seemed as important as the present. Perhaps Irene knew something of the Chadwick clan as well as the Pickerings. Perhaps she could be persuaded to talk.

She glanced at the woman, who was hovering over her box of precious books, demanding that Hammond carry it immediately to her room. If Raven ever caught the woman in a solicitous mood, she would ask.

It was, she knew, a very large *if*.

They were halfway up the stairs when a deep, rolling bark came from the side of the house. All eyes shifted toward the sound.

"Albert," muttered Frederick. "What's gotten into the beast?"

Beast indeed, thought Raven, who estimated the bark to be an octave below the lowest note in her range.

Looking more like a pony than a dog, Albert rounded the corner and lumbered toward them along the graveled drive. A bloodhound, Raven noted, with ears flopping on a head as large as her valise.

"Albert," Frederick commanded, "halt!"

The beast kept on running in a straight line for the newcomers, bounded up the steps, and halted before a wide-eyed Aunt Cordelia. Rearing onto his hind legs, he planted a forepaw on each of her shoulders and lapped her cheeks.

Raven rushed to brace her against a fall, while Frederick grabbed the dog's collar and Aunt Cordelia squealed her distress. Hammond remained stationary beside Aunt Irene, guarding the box of books balanced on his shoulder. Amy assisted Raven, who was certain she saw a glint of laughter in the young woman's eyes.

With the bloodhound dragged to a safe distance away from the house, Amy asked, "Are you all right?"

Cordelia straightened her bonnet. "Oh, my, I do believe I should like to wash my face."

"You must have encouraged the dog in some way," said Irene.

"Aunt Irene," said Amy in protest, brushing the dusty pawprints from Cordelia's black cloak.

"I speak what everyone else is thinking."

Raven glanced at Albert. He sat in the pathway firmly in Frederick's grasp, his giant tongue lolling sideways over a row of blunt molars, his large brown eyes pinned on Aunt Cordelia. His head came to the butler's waist, and he seemed to have enough loose skin about his ears and neck to cover a pack of dogs.

Cordelia did not return his gaze.

"Albert's a gift from Squire Clifton," Frederick explained. "We've not yet learned the dog's peculiarities."

"Then perhaps we ought to return him," said Amy with a sharpness she did not try to hide.

"His Lordship's taken with the beast, Miss Amy," said Frederick.

"He would be," said Amy, shrugging as though she'd lost all interest in the subject.

"Hammond, tie the dog behind the house," said Frederick. With a show of reluctance, the footman set down the box to comply, and the women entered Beacon Hall, all but Irene, who said she needed to retrieve something. They left her hovering over her books.

As Raven stepped into the great room immediately inside the front door, she caught a musty scent that two days of airing had not removed. Closed doors appeared at intervals along the paneled walls on either side of the broad sweep of marble; and at the back of the room, a winding staircase led to the upper floors. Overhead hung one of the largest chandeliers she had ever seen, its crystal drops shining, two hundred candles waiting to be lit.

"The hall's been closed up since Uncle Philip remarried and took his young bride to London," said Amy. "She didn't care for country life."

"But you do," said Raven.

The two women looked at one another for a moment. Amy was the first to look away.

"I used to," she said, then strode toward the maid Nancy standing at the base of the stairs.

A door to the right opened, and a flush-faced matron in a pale cotton gown and apron hurried to greet the newcomers.

With a curtsy, she brushed a strand of graying hair beneath her cap. "Sorry t' have missed your arrival, Miss Bannerman," she said to Raven. "Trying to break in the new cook is a chore, t' be sure."

Behind them, Frederick cleared his throat. "This is Miss Bannerman," he said, indicating Amy.

The woman's face flushed a brighter red as Frederick introduced her. "Mrs. Reardon is our housekeeper. Another contribution of Squire Clifton." His tone put the woman on a level with the dog.

"The squire has been busy the past two days, has he not?" said Amy.

"He and Miss Clifton have been present at Beacon Hall each day."

"The daughter's still unwed, is she?"

Frederick sniffed in reply.

"And is the cook his suggestion also?"

"His Lordship, I believe, has employed one of the farmer's wives."

"And difficult she is, too," broke in Mrs. Reardon.

"That will be all," Frederick said, sending the woman scurrying back through the door from whence she had come.

Raven didn't blame her for running. If the butler had spoken to her in such a manner, she would be dashing up the stairs, weak ankle and all.

The four women started toward the stairs, where Nancy awaited them.

The maid curtsied, hands crushing the corners of her white apron. "The rooms is ready. All on the second floor. There's water for them that wants to take a bath."

Irene's nose wrinkled. *"Those,"* she muttered, then shrugged. "Oh, what's the use?"

Raven stared up the stairs, which seemed to wind into the heavens. If she stood at the top of them, would she think they led down into hell?

She shivered. Thinking about the fall did little good, except to remind her she must be cautious and watchful.

"How many bedrooms does this house have?" she asked.

"Seventeen," said Amy. "Not counting the servants' quarters, of course. Rather small for an earldom, but we shall make do."

Raven thought of the four small rooms that seemed so comfortable in Savannah. "I imagine we can."

Upstairs, she found her room larger than the one she had occupied at Stafford House, the bed canopied, the wardrobe grander, and instead of one window, there were two, between them a small rocking chair and footstool. There was also a second room for bathing, with a hip bath half full of lavender-scented water.

As much as she wished to wash the grime from her body, she gave first attention to the windows. They opened onto the back of the house, onto a series of fenced pens beside a stable and then a stretch of rolling hills that ended in a copse of English oak.

Marcus was not to be seen.

She opened the sash to the winter sun. Warm enough, she decided, to allow a walk without her heavy cloak, her first outdoor venture since the—

She stopped herself. Since the accident, she finished. If she thought of it like that, she might handle the memory better.

Shaking out a green-wool gown, she hurriedly bathed and dressed, brushed her hair loose, and in a moment of recklessness decided to leave it unbound. She saw not another soul as she hurried down the stairs and out the front door. At the base of the stairs she took a deep breath

of the fresh country air. How wonderful it was to be
outside alone. She didn't care where Marcus had hidden
himself, didn't wonder why he hadn't bothered to meet
them, felt certain that whatever he was up to was no
concern of hers.

Her feet took her around the house in the direction of
the stable. He couldn't possibly be there, not the noble
earl, unless he were saddling a magnificent stallion for
a gallop across the meadows. Perhaps that was where he
was now, gamboling without a care or visiting the helpful
squire.

Not to mention the squire's unwed daughter, whose
existence seemed to have irritated Amy.

Not Raven. Wherever Marcus was, she thought it no
concern of hers.

She wouldn't mind a gambol herself. Papa had made
sure that his girls took riding lessons. From him they
had inherited a love for a fast ride.

Not today, of course. And with Mama's lessons of
courtesy as her guide, she'd have to wait until the offer
of a horse was made. Still, she might find out what animals were available.

At the open stable door, she knew that Marcus was
inside. She couldn't see him and she couldn't hear him,
but she knew without understanding how or why.

A lantern hung from a post at the back of the stable;
otherwise, all was dark. In the stalls to her right she could
barely make out the two bays that had been hitched to
the carriage; to the left two other horses nickered softly
as she passed. Hugging herself against the indoor chill,
she walked toward the light.

A baritone voice startled her. She had never heard the

earl sing, but it was most definitely his voice. And crooning a lullaby, too! She couldn't have been more surprised if he had swung from the rafters naked.

The words of the song were difficult to determine . . . something about apples and cradles and rosy-cheeked babes. It was the tone that mattered. Gentle, deep, steady. Warmth curled within her, and she slowed her step, lest he hear her and fall silent.

She found him in a small pen at the rear of the stable, beneath the lantern, his back to the rough plank wall. Light flickered over his lean, bristled face, highlighting the strong cheekbones and prominent chin. Coatless, shirt opened at the throat and sleeves rolled halfway to his elbows, his wheat hair uncombed, he sat on a small stool feeding a bottle of milk to a small black lamb.

He looked boyish, the way he had that first day she'd met him on a theater stage. He looked masculine, too, as masculine as any man she'd ever seen. Her breath caught. She wanted nothing more than to stand there forever watching the scene.

As if she had called to him, he raised his eyes to hers. Neither spoke for a moment. Raven feared he could hear the pounding of her heart.

"We've arrived," she managed at last. Foolishly. But she could only speak of the obvious. The sensations coursing through her were too private—and too unsettling—to put into words.

"Yes," he said. He laughed softly. "You caught me playing shepherd."

"You do it very well."

An invisible force pulled her to his side. She knelt

beside the stool and watched the lamb suckle at the bottle.

"Sophie's an orphan," he said.

"Sophie?"

He shrugged. "I had a nanny once by that name," he said. "Lasted six months in my father's employ."

"Why such a short while?"

"By Bannerman standards, she was remarkably long-lived. I went through nannies rather quickly, I'm afraid."

"Hard on women, were you?"

"Not all of them."

Again their eyes met. Flustered, Raven forced her attention to the lamb. "She's done."

With a pop Marcus forced the nipple from the animal's mouth. Sophie responded with an angry squeal.

He set the lamb on her feet. She rocked unsteadily, then with a bleat tottered to a bank of straw in the corner, curled into a fuzzy ball within its depths, and promptly went to sleep. All in the space of a minute. Raven sighed in envy at such innocence.

She felt Marcus watching her. Slowly she lifted her lashes. In the lamplight the blue of his eyes had darkened to deep cerulean. In their depths she saw no hint of mockery or teasing. She saw only heat, so penetrating she had to look away.

How foolish it was to remain kneeling beside him, to see from the corner of her eye the golden hairs at his throat, the span of white linen across his broad chest, the stretch of his trousers against his abdomen and thighs. If she touched him, she knew his body would be as hard as the ground on which she knelt.

She started to rise. One hand on her arm, gently put, held her in place.

He touched her unbound hair. "Soft as the lamb, Songbird. You ought to wear it like this more often."

She stared at his throat. Two days in the country and already his skin looked tanner than she remembered, his neck strong and corded as though he had been working hard.

"It's an unseemly style for the city," she said. "The country air made me feel reckless."

"I share the feeling."

He stroked her chin. "The cut has healed. I see no sign of a scar."

"How did you get yours?"

He grinned. Her heart took a small leap.

"I wish I could say it was in noble battle. Actually, it happened in a rambunctious fencing lesson with Daniel."

"I had imagined an angry husband attacked when he came home unexpectedly."

"If I said such a thing was impossible, you'd think only that I had a better sense of survival than to get trapped and a more precise reckoning of time."

Always self-mocking, she thought. And tempting beyond the limits of her self-imposed restraint.

Her gaze lifted to his lips. Tempting. His head bent to hers. She closed her eyes as he drew nearer, her hands resting upon his thighs. They were, as she'd known, hard as the ground.

She heard his sharp intake of breath. Her heart pounded in her ears as his thumbs played with the high collar of her dress.

She had barely felt the beginning of his whisper-soft

kiss when a loud commotion came from the yard outside the stable. She jerked away at the sound of shouts and a barking bloodhound.

"Aunt Cordelia," she whispered.

"Damn," Marcus said.

She stumbled to her feet. With Marcus close behind, she hurried the length of the stable and burst into the dying light of day.

Amy hurried past toward a small outbuilding beyond the stable. She followed a grizzled, barrel-chested man who in turn chased after the bloodhound Albert.

Albert came to a halt at the door of the shed and set up a howl to waken a sleeping lamb.

With Raven and Marcus falling in behind her, Amy shoved past the stranger and ordered the dog to desist.

Albert turned mournful eyes to her and, incredibly, fell silent. Crouching by the closed door, he stared at the handle, as though he would take it between his formidable teeth and enter the shed.

"What the bloody hell is going on?" asked Marcus.

Amy glanced sideways at her brother. "The mutt's got Aunt Cordelia trapped inside."

"Whatever for? I can't imagine her teasing the brute."

"Not purposefully. She and I were conducting an experiment to see why the dog attacked her as soon as she got here. The experiment was a success."

"Not to Cordelia," said Marcus. "We have to let her out. The potting shed is filled with a fertilizer that is most unpleasant even in the open air."

"Only after Albert is securely leashed," said Amy. "After all, she's still carrying the flask."

She reached down to stroke the folds of skin between

the bloodhound's ears. "I'm sure the squire has given you a fine hunting dog, brother dear, but he has one fault. A decided appetite for gin."

# Twelve

Raven had no idea how close she had come to a thorough lovemaking on the stable floor. Marcus decided to tell her, the next time they were alone.

Hours after their encounter, sequestered in the Beacon Hall library, he could still picture her kneeling beside him, a cloud of black hair framing her lovely face, her tawny skin as smooth as satin in the lamplight. Those magnificent eyes had glinted with pleasure at the lamb, and then she had turned them on him.

Portraits of her should grace the finest halls.

Better yet, that hair ought to be splayed against a bed of straw, face lifted to him, eyes smoldering with passions he had aroused. Marcus got hard just thinking of what he would do . . . should have done . . . almost did.

He shook his head in disgust at the abrupt ending of their kiss before he'd barely gotten a taste of her. The object of his desire—the only woman he had really wanted since she first walked out of the Lyceum's shadows—had been saved by a gin-loving dog.

Marcus stopped himself. Was *saved* what she would have called it or was *interrupted* closer to the truth? He still wasn't sure.

No matter how he phrased it, Albert and his pursuit

of Aunt Cordelia had altered the natural sequence of events. It was a plot right out of a music hall farce.

Always something intruded upon them. Marcus wasn't in the habit of being frustrated with such regularity. Nor was he given to losing his temper and self-control, yet around her he didn't know himself. Raven Chadwick. Songbird. He *never* bestowed women with pet names.

At first he'd meant it as a taunt, remindful of her brief career as a singer, but its use had taken on another nuance. *Affection,* he would have called it, except that he was not an affectionate man. Women called him lusty, yes, but none had ever accused him of being loving. Or seemed to wish that he were, their interest inclined more to his generosity.

At the moment the object of his lust was asleep in a room two floors over his head. Amy and the aunts were likewise at rest. Their first evening in the country had been quiet; they had retired early, leaving Marcus to his thoughts. And to his worries, which went beyond the visitor from abroad.

He stared at the papers on his desk and thought of the myriad worries they represented. Times were bad all over England, but nowhere worse than here in the south. Imports of grain and beef from the United States, unbothered by the bloody rains, were driving down the price of British products. Everything from cheese to whole carcasses could be shipped in the new cold-storage rooms.

Corned beef in tins, an abomination in Marcus's opinion, also hurt the market, a market Sussex needed to survive.

A sense of *déjà vu* swept over him. He had sat like this by the hour at Stafford House, poring over bills and reports. His predecessor had been an unwise business-man, having sunk most of the family fortune in Lanca-shire cotton mills during the Yanks' War Between the States. Blockades had kept the necessary cotton bales in the southern ports, and the mills had failed.

The first Lady Stafford had been a careful manager, but the second had increased the estate's debts to a dis-graceful degree. The late Lord Stafford must have felt he was buying the heir she was supposed to give him. He had spent his money in vain.

Damned if Marcus didn't wish she had given birth to triplets. Let one of the infants take on the headaches of being earl.

Gradually he was bringing the accounts to a healthy level—if he could overcome his sister's fondness for spending money as fast as he made it. He could deny her little, and she knew it—except the one thing she wanted most. She asked the impossible. And so she lived an indulgent life.

He had hoped that Daniel Lindsay's return from India would remind her of the happy days she'd known in Sus-sex, but the two had renewed the animosity that had ex-isted between them when they were children. If anything, she spent more money now than ever.

Sometimes Marcus resorted to a game of cards and a cautious bet or two to pay for her extravagances, but that was in the city where he felt more sure of himself. The country estate was another matter. Here, there was work to be done. Hard, physical work—and changes to be made.

The door to the library opened to admit Frederick. "Mr. Seed, Your Lordship."

Marcus nodded, then sat back to watch the entrance of the land agent for Beacon Hall. Ten thousand acres, all under his control. For the while.

Graham Seed entered, hat in hand, a short, gaunt man in his early forties with thinning brown hair and narrow brown eyes and a scaly red skin that gave him the look of an insect. Most curious was the complete absence of eyebrows. He minced forward, shoulders rounded beneath the coat of his ill-fitting suit, as though he would pay full deference to his exalted employer. Marcus was not impressed.

"Mr. Seed," he said, "take a chair."

Seed rotated a bowler hat between his fingers. "If it's all the same, Your Lordship, I'd just as soon stand."

"Oh, but it isn't. We might be here awhile."

Seed blinked twice, then lowered his slight frame into one of the high-backed chairs facing the desk, the hat in his lap.

Marcus looked at the stacks of invoices and receipts spread before him, then settled a cool gaze on the agent.

"These records go back several years, before my uncle hired you, yet there are few dated within the past twelve months."

Seed cleared his throat. "I'm a man o' the country, Your Lordship. I keep some accounts in me head."

"An acceptable practice, if you work for yourself."

Seed stiffened. "The late earl never had no complaints."

"And neither should I, is that it?"

"Beggin' your pardon, Your Lordship, but you ain't a farmer." He raised his hands in apology. "No fault in that. There's need for all kinds."

"Perhaps not all," said Marcus. "But do go on."

Seed shifted about in the chair. "Maybe Lord Stafford should tell me what concerns him in partic'lar."

"With relish, Mr. Seed. I took a ride around the estate yesterday and this morning. The tenants live in hovels unsuitable for pigs."

Seed shrugged. "Some folks can't take care o' themselves, that's fer sure. They've got good land to till—"

"Very little of which has been touched," said Marcus with open irritation. "Spring planting, it would seem, will be late this year."

"It's been dreadful rainy, as Your Lordship knows. Turned good Sussex land into a bog."

"In the low areas, I'm certain you are right. But the Stafford land is blessed with much high ground that drains well."

Seed's eyes widened, as if he were surprised his employer knew so much about the landscape. Marcus was certain he would have raised his brows, too, if he'd possessed any to raise.

The land agent should have known better than to assume Marcus's ignorance. He had grown to manhood on the neighboring estate, his father's land, which he had long ago inherited and shamefully neglected during his carousing days. Squire Clifton leased it now, adding its acreage to his already formidable holdings. It was a letter from the squire that had alarmed him about the condition of Stafford lands.

"What about the fertilizer I authorized you to purchase?" Marcus asked. "There's no record of it anywhere that I can find."

"I can get you the paperwork right handily. Distributed

to the tenants, just as you wrote. Can't say what they done with it."

"And the new steam-plow? Have they sold it as well?"

"They'd sell their children for a price. They're a stupid lot, if'n you don't mind my saying so. Hardly seemed to know what it was for. I'd gamble me commission they've sold it for a pint or two of ale in the Ditchling pub. Unlikely they'll admit it, but I'll do me best to learn the truth o' the matter, that you can be assured."

"These tenants are very convenient, aren't they?"

"Beggin' Your Lordship's pardon?"

"If the fields aren't tilled or properly treated, we've only to cast blame upon the poor souls whose existence is dependent upon good crops."

"Birds what'll foul their own nests, that's what they are," Seed said with a sniff, giving little evidence he had caught Marcus's sarcasm.

"I hired the wife of one this morning to serve as cook."

"In Beacon Hall?"

"Yes. Why does that surprise you?"

"They're an untrustworthy lot. Best be careful, Your Lordship. She'll be spittin' in the stew if she ain't watched."

"You know whom I've hired?"

"The name don't matter. They're all of a kind."

Argument against the agent's prejudice was both foolish and futile, and Marcus shifted to a new topic.

"This afternoon I found a young lamb wandering in the field behind the stable. An orphan not weaned from the teat, so weak she could barely walk. Have we stock enough to waste such a creature?"

"A gang o' farmers' boys is supposed t' take the herd to the fields for grazing of a morning and bring 'em home at night."

"The greenest grass would have done this foundling little good. She wanted milk."

"There's bound t' be loss on a place the size of Your Lordship's estate. And we've a fair share of orphan sheep since the winter births."

"Little consolation that sentiment is to the lamb."

"Your Lordship's got a city heart. In the country we expect loss. Still, I'll speak to Quirke."

"Ah, yes, Arthur Quirke." Marcus pictured the bailiff, a brutish young man in his late twenties. He'd been present at the rescue of Aunt Cordelia. He'd wanted to beat the dog.

"What," asked Marcus, "will you ask him to do?"

"Punish the boys what let that lamb escape."

"With a stick, no doubt."

"Quirke has his ways."

"I'm certain that he does." A sudden anger took hold of Marcus. "Under no circumstances is he to discipline the children in any way. Is that understood?"

Seed looked as though he wanted to protest. "If that is what Your Lordships wishes."

"It is."

A sudden weariness settled on Marcus. "The hour grows late, Mr. Seed. Thank you for your time."

He didn't have to state in plainer words that the interview was at an end.

Seed stood, twisting his hat, muttering about what a pleasure it was to have the earl in residence at last. Half hunched in a bowing position, he backed to the door as if he left the royal throne room.

"Mr. Seed," said Marcus, stopping him before he could exit. "The invoices on the fertilizer. Sulphate of ammonia, I believe is what I ordered, to be mixed with basic slag. I'd like to see the paperwork by one o'clock tomorrow."

"But Your Lordship—"

"One o'clock. Also the steam-plow. I know you'll make every effort to see that my requests are met."

In the silence following the land agent's departure, Marcus poured himself a glass of brandy and went to stand by the fire. A long time after the liquor was gone, he continued to stand and to think. Seed and Quirke were a despicable pair, but they knew the land and they knew the ways of farming he was only beginning to understand.

With people they had more trouble. People and orphan lambs.

He would have to keep them in his employ until his education was more nearly complete. And he would have to watch to make sure they didn't—how did Seed phrase it?—to make sure they didn't spit into the stew.

So many things cluttering his thoughts. People, too. As he made his way upstairs to his waiting bed, he narrowed the thoughts to one. A light shone at the base of her door.

He knocked once, twice, listened to the stirring within the room and the whispered, "Who is it?"

"Marcus. I want to ask you something."

"It's late."

"One question. That's all, I promise."

Slowly the door eased open and a pair of black eyes peered suspiciously into the hallway.

"Do members of your class always roam about the night harassing single women?" Raven asked.

Marcus found himself grinning, something he hadn't done in a long while. "Always. It's part of our training."

"As what?"

"Rakes and rascals, what else? Sometimes we get drunk and break down the door."

"Sometimes, I should imagine, you get shot."

"Hazards of the peerage."

He fell silent. Raven was a treat to gaze upon, even with her hair braided and a white gown covering her from foot to throat. Watching her like this was sweet torture. He could stay here all night.

"One question, you said."

"Of course. Do you ride?"

"Why, yes, I do," she said, eyebrows lifted.

He liked the direct answer. Right now, there wasn't much about her he didn't like.

"I'd ask you whether you care to join me for a morning romp except that I promised only one question. Forgive me if I put the request in the form of a command. If your ankle feels strong enough, meet me at the stables as soon as the sun is up tomorrow. Dress warmly. It's sure to be brisk."

He insinuated himself close to the doorframe, his arm propped over his head.

"And another command. No, make that a suggestion. If you don't want a companion for the night, you really should remove yourself from my sight. I am, as you may have noticed, a very weak man."

She closed the door so quickly she almost caught his nose.

"In the morning, Songbird," he whispered. With a lightness in his heart, he turned in time to see a couple of bedroom doors easing shut. The aunts had been listening and watching. As self-appointed chaperons? He could see Aunt Cordelia acting in that capacity, but not Aunt Irene.

Amy didn't bother to hide herself. Instead, she stood boldly in the open doorway to her room, dressed in a pale pink gown and wrapper, her fair hair brushed loose against her slender shoulders.

She looked no more than eighteen.

And she looked angry.

"You can't keep your hands off her, can you?"

"Go to bed, Amy," he said.

"Not just yet. I have one question," she said, mocking his words. "Have you made love to her yet? Or are you saving that little treat for tomorrow?"

"That's two questions," he said tightly.

"I lied. It's a habit I picked up from my brother."

They stared at one another across an ocean of differences. Marcus's weariness returned with a force that staggered him. "It's late. I'm going to bed."

He turned from her.

"Why not take our visitor to Paris? I'm certain she would find things of interest there."

He faced her once again. "I go there for business."

"So you said."

Tears welled in her blue eyes, and in that dampness the distance separating them dissolved. Marcus wanted to hold her and assure her the pains of the past would eventually go away. But she wouldn't believe him. And she would be right.

"Amy," he said, stepping close.

She raised a hand to fend him off. "Treat her gently, Marcus. And most of all, treat her with honesty. I don't know the whole of her story, but something happened to her. Something she can't forget."

A bitter smile erased the youth from her face. "Do you suppose it could be similar to what happened to me?"

Before he could respond, she slipped into her room and closed the door. He heard the key turn in the lock.

He stood for a moment in the darkened hallway, staring at all the closed bedrooms. In each was a woman with secrets and problems. For the time being, they were women dependent upon him.

For just a moment he sympathized with his father. Live life to the fullest had been John Bannerman's credo, and let the world take care of itself.

Marcus should do the same. Graham Seed could continue to run the country estate as he had been doing, stealing no doubt at every chance. There were family attorneys in London who would find a similar manager for Stafford House, if he asked them.

When the money ran out, the valuables of both places could be sold, and then the not-so-valuables, on down until little remained. Then Amy would have to settle on a husband.

The aunts offered a more difficult problem. Cordelia should make a fine nanny; she would have to give up the gin, of course, but everyone would have to sacrifice.

Aunt Irene could find employment as a teacher of geography, a field in which she was surely an expert by now.

And Raven could return home.

As he undressed and fell naked into bed, he found it was the last thought that stayed with him, the thought that unsettled him most.

# *Thirteen*

The morning was indeed brisk, as Marcus had predicted. Raven's Savannah blood would have called it cold.

The Chadwick in her refused to call it impossible, however, and in the thin light of a March dawn she showed up at the stables in a double thickness of undergarments, a blue wool riding habit borrowed from Amy, and her black cloak.

The maid Nancy had helped her into the layers, offering little encouragement for the outing.

"There's things to avoid here," she had said, rather ominously Raven thought, but she attributed the girl's attitude to an unwanted move to the country.

There *were* things to avoid here, like Marcus when no one else was around. But the day was cold and they would be outdoors. All he could do was talk . . . and she could ride away.

As added protection against the elements, Aunt Cordelia had thrown in a pair of earmuffs, an unstylish but very welcome addition to the blue hat under which they were worn, as was Irene's heavy wool scarf wrapped around her neck. With gloves and boots, she was ready for an Arctic trek.

Which was pretty much what Marcus said when he met her at the stable door. The warmth in his eyes robbed the words of offense.

In contrast to her attire, he wore a chocolate-brown riding coat and trousers, his only concession to the weather a cap and heavy gloves and a white wool scarf that made his skin look a disgustingly warm and healthy tan, even in winter.

Didn't the man ever get dirty . . . look rumpled . . . wear ill-fitting clothes?

Wouldn't she ever get used to the long, lean, virile picture he presented and the way he managed to seem both devilishly youthful and worldly wise? Her stomach knotted, and she forgot about the cold.

"I'd like to see you riding through a Georgia swamp in August," she said. "One wonders what you would choose to wear."

He shrugged, all innocence. "Nothing, I should imagine."

Raven got a swift picture of Marcus riding naked through the woods—bronzed arms and legs dusted with golden hair, chest rippled with muscles, his thighs—

Cheeks flushed, she stopped herself.

"When do we leave?" she asked, looking past him to the open stable door while she wondered if she ought to cancel their outing and return to her warm bed. If she had any sense, that's exactly what she would do.

Before she could speak, a red-headed youth emerged from the stable towing a pair of saddled mounts, one a magnificent chestnut, the other an equally beautiful but smaller black. Both bobbed and snorted and stamped at the ground, their breath condensing in the cold.

"Good work, Jason," said Marcus, then turned to Raven. "This is the boy's first day on the job. He's grandson to the man who handled horses for my father when I was a boy. His late father was one of the tenants here."

Raven estimated the boy to be in his mid-teens, freckle-faced and small in stature, yet he held onto the reins of the frisky animals with a command that echoed his heritage.

"Good morning, Jason," she said with a smile.

Shy, the boy kicked a well-worn boot at the ground.

Muscles working beneath sleek coats, the horses looked glorious in the crisp morning light, Raven thought, and it had been so long since her last ride. Her blood stirred, for once because of something other than the earl's proximity.

Marcus stroked the chestnut's strong neck. Two proud creatures, Raven thought, both man and beast, their power primed to be unleashed, although the man's ease of stance left no question he was the one in control. He also looked like a gentleman, she told herself, from cap to calf-high boots. Perhaps today he would actually behave like one.

And they would be outdoors. There could be no harm, she told herself, thrusting aside her doubts.

Marcus gestured to the black. "Miss Chadwick will be riding Héloise."

Raven's brow lifted. "Héloise?"

"Not her original name," said Marcus. "I bought her from the squire when I first arrived, took one look at her ebony mane, and somehow the name came to mind."

"Thinking of a nun's habit, of course. And the chestnut?"

"Abélard."

"A gelding."

"Right."

The black nickered and jerked at the reins.

"Héloise grows restless," said Raven.

"Considering her companion's condition, she should," said Marcus, stepping close. Raven caught her breath as he lifted her onto the sidesaddle. His Lordship smelled of sandalwood, a scent she was learning to like.

"One wonders," he said, smoothing her cloak around her, "what you would wear in a Georgia swamp."

No harm, she reminded herself once again. She could always ride away.

Mounted, Marcus gave the boy instructions to watch out for starving lambs and they started out at a walk down the lane that wound toward the rolling hills behind Beacon Hall. From out of nowhere a figure stepped into their path. Raven felt Marcus's tension even before she looked at the man.

"Quirke," Marcus said, "is something the matter?"

Arthur Quirke, Raven recalled, the bailiff. He'd been present at Aunt Cordelia's rescue from the potting shed. In the midst of the confusion she'd paid him little mind except to note he was big and coarse-featured and kept snarling something about beating the dog.

She gave him a closer perusal. Hatless, coarse brown hair to his shoulders, bristled face, thick lips and a broad, flat nose, beady brown eyes too small for his weathered face. Younger than Marcus by at least five years but equally muscled, he presented a sharp contrast to his employer. Where the earl captured the sleekness of a racing stallion, the bailiff looked more like a bear.

*There's things to avoid here.*

The maid's warning sent a shiver down Raven's spine. Whatever Nancy had meant ought to include Arthur Quirke.

"Yer Lordship oughter be careful on the Downs." The bailiff sniffed, then spat upon the ground. "There's things that'll bring ye harm."

Raven started.

"What things?" Marcus asked sharply.

"Just things," he said, and Raven thought of Amy's talk of witches and their hounds.

"And it don't do to go about hiring the tenants' kin," Quirke continued. "That's a job fer Mr. Seed and meself."

Marcus slapped a riding crop against his thigh. "Are you instructing me as to my responsibilities?"

If Quirke caught the sharpness in the question, he gave no sign. "There's them that knows the country, Yer Lordship, and them that don't."

"Yes," said Marcus. "I'll be speaking to both you and Seed about your job. Very shortly. Now get about your tasks."

Without another word, he brought the crop down sharply on the chestnut's flanks and took off at a gallop. The mare bolted after, throwing Raven backwards in the saddle and forcing Quirke to jump from the path.

They rode in silence, only the horses' hooves against the rutted ground and the creak of leather breaking the early morning stillness. A mist hung low over the Downs, the air damp against Raven's cheeks as she fell into the rhythm of the ride. The bailiff faded from her mind, as did all concerns. She had been too long confined in a city. Her heart pounded in exhilaration at this moment of freedom. She and Marcus existed alone in a world of rolling hills and scattered trees, grasses white with dew in the early light, and a narrow lane that stretched to the end of the world.

From somewhere behind her a dog howled. A witch's hound. She would accept nothing else. Any theater director in the world would have applauded the perfection of the scene.

The howl became a bark, loud over the noise of the horses, and close by. They slowed their pace. She glanced over her shoulder to watch the ghost dog race into view. For an apparition he was decidedly large and brown, his ears floppy, his paws solid as they pounded against the ground.

Albert.

She reined to a halt, Marcus beside her, while the bloodhound pranced excitedly around the stomping horses' hooves.

She cast her companion an innocent smile. "I'm not carrying a flask, I promise."

With a quick grin he lost the tightness around his eyes and mouth. Her heart sank to her boots and rushed to her throat.

"The mutt's envious of us," said Marcus. "He simply wanted to join the party."

Raven held tightly to Héloise's reins. "Party?"

He looked from her to the surrounding hills, the low-hanging sky, the dog, the lane behind them, and the road they had yet to ride, his blue eyes bright with an inner gleam.

"A part of me always feels like celebrating when I

return to my home patch. No matter what brings me here."

Raven forgot the Downs and the dog and the lane. She stared only at him. Strong-featured with unruly wheat-colored hair, scarred chin, and callused hands, he sat astride the gelding with an air of confidence that harkened to ancestors from a distant, noble past.

In that moment she saw him in a new light. A sophisticate, an aristocrat born to London ways, he was likewise a native of the country, equally at home bounding across the hills, a bloodhound racing at his heels.

It was an exciting blend. She admitted to a sense of wonderment and a mix of emotions she couldn't name, emotions so strong her hands trembled as she gripped the reins. All in all, Marcus Bannerman, twelfth Earl of Stafford, was a complicated man, as complicated as her feelings for him . . . for his kisses . . . for his touch.

Ruthlessly she shoved the memories aside. Down such paths of thought awaited danger. If the simple images could stir her to such a degree, what would she do if he actually took her by the hand, clasped her waist, and lifted her from the mare, resting her across his hard thighs, brushing his lips against hers . . .

She stared at the dog. She must be going mad.

The layers of clothes felt heavy against her body, confining, and she removed the bonnet and earmuffs, shook loose her hair, and watched him watching her.

She loosened the scarf at her throat.

"How's the ankle?" he asked.

"As strong as ever," she said truthfully.

"Still, I owe you an apology."

"Whatever for?" she asked, in her confusion forgetting how often she had waited in vain for those words.

"For taking off from Quirke like that. I didn't know you could ride so well."

She secured the bundle of bonnet and muffs to the saddle, pleased despite herself at the compliment. "Papa saw to it that his girls took lessons."

"Your Papa must not be the cad your grandfather thought him."

"He's the dearest man in all the world. Mama was right to fall in love with him."

His eyes traced her face and the flow of her hair against her shoulders. "And her eldest daughter? Has she ever been in love?"

The question took her by surprise. "No," she said, then added, in case he did not understand, "and she never plans to be."

She seemed to be speaking to herself as well.

"Are you sure?" he asked. "Never is a long while."

"I—"

She looked away, her thoughts in a turmoil. For the first time in her life she wanted to say more about a subject she knew to be forbidden, the terrible events of her youth, the reasons she had closed her heart to love.

At least to the kind of love he meant. But her secret could not stand the light of day . . . even a cool, gray morning on a quiet Sussex lane.

Albert barked, the mare started, and Raven welcomed the distraction.

"The animals are growing impatient for activity," she said.

"They're not the only ones."

Her eyes darted to his. There was little chance of mis-interpreting the thoughts behind his heated stare. Beneath her layers of clothes, nerves prickled along the surface of her skin, and she turned coward.

"I ought to go back," she said.

"No." Once again he was the earl. "I want you to see the land."

"Amy can show me later."

"I want to show it to you." He removed his cap and ran a hand through his hair. "I'd like somebody to un-derstand. God knows why, but I believe you will do so more readily than anyone."

She listened for hints of derision in his voice, but she heard only a somber plea. As if drawn by strings of steel, she felt herself pulled toward him, and her heart took another bounce.

"I won't keep you long," he said. "As soon as you're tired, we'll return to the hall."

Raven's chin tilted against the insult. "I'm hardier than I appear. We'll return when *you* are tired."

She dug her heels into Héloise's flanks and set off at a trot down the lane, away from Beacon Hall, an excited bloodhound racing beside her. To the rear she heard the pounding hooves of Abélard.

Marcus soon took the lead to guide her toward a dis-tant grazing field where a herd of fifty sheep munched on the winter grass. He dismounted to talk to the shep-herd boy while Albert and the sheepdog checked each other's private parts.

Pulling himself gracefully once again into the saddle, he urged the gelding on with a click of his tongue and

hey rode cross-country over the Downs. A quarter of a
nile later he reined to a halt and looked over the land.

"The boy's only ten," he said.

Raven glanced in the direction of the grazing field,
now out of sight. "That seems awfully young to be out
here alone."

"It is."

"Isn't there a school nearby?"

"In Ditchling. Not a far walk. But he's needed to work
at home." Tight lines creased the corners of his eyes.
"For me. In the next few weeks his younger brothers
and sisters will labor at bird-scaring and stone-picking."

"How much younger?" asked Raven, dreading the
answer.

"One of the girls is six."

"But that's criminal!"

"You must have known such things occurred." He
looked at her. "What's that old quotation about none so
blind as those who will not see?"

He spoke flatly, but she saw the grip he had on the
riding crop and the helpless fury in his eyes. Here was
another new Marcus, a man moved to wrath because of
children he had never met. She wanted to reach out in
consolation, to at least offer words that showed she
shared his anger.

"Damn my uncle for dying," he said, and the soft
words died in her throat.

Could Marcus be so involved in his land at the same
time he scorned its demands? A complicated man, she
reminded herself, and capable of emotions she couldn't
guess. That had to be why he set up such a tumult inside
her. She hadn't figured him out.

On they rode, stopping only to care for the horses. Sometimes they talked—or rather Marcus talked and Raven simply nodded, listening to his description of the estate, of how iron mines had long ago sustained the Staffords and their people, how the high ground known as Ditchling Beacon had once held fires to warn of the approaching Armada from Spain, how sheep and corn and cattle were the products of the country now.

The anger gone, he spoke with an animation and a knowledge that surprised her, but when she tried to tell him of her reaction, he shrugged it away.

"I was born here," he said, "and rode these hills the first two decades of my life. Without care or supervision. It was a splendid start to life."

Perhaps. An edge to his voice made her question whether he were being completely honest with her—or with himself. Unsupervised meant he had received little attention from his parents. To a woman raised as Raven had been, that translated into little love.

"I didn't realize you grew up at Beacon Hall."

"I didn't. My father's land adjoins Beacon." For a moment a glint of humor returned to his eyes. "Humble Hall, the house is called, for Lucius Humble, a Bannerman ancestor. Father hated the name, but tradition reigned. Humble Hall it has remained."

"And is it humble?"

"Comparatively. Ten bedrooms to Beacon's seventeen, no conservatory, stables half the size. And of course only half the land, five thousand acres in all."

"I grew up in a house behind my parents' store. What you describe sounds quite grand to me."

A shuttered darkness ended the humor in his gaze.

"Grand? I never thought it so, spending as little time as I did indoors."

"Even after you became owner?"

"By then I had grown fond of pursuits in town."

Raven thought of the voluptuous and temperamental Althea Innocent, and a hollowness burrowed inside her.

"You said returning here called for a celebration," she said. "I don't understand."

"Damned if I do either, but that's the way of it. Ever hear of a love/hate relationship? That's the way I feel about Sussex."

Love and hate. Raven wondered if such opposite emotions could truly exist in the same heart. If a man were as enticing and charming as the gods—and if he seduced a woman into acts beyond her nature—she might very well be torn between the two extremes. If she allowed herself to care so very much.

"This past year I've leased Humble Hall to Squire Clifton."

"Margaret's father," Raven said without thinking.

"You've met her already?"

"Amy mentioned her name. I take it they are of an age."

"Margaret's a year or two older than Amy. They never got on. And don't ask me why. I've never understood my sister, and I never will."

Understanding none of the Bannermans, Raven sympathized.

"Amy also wondered if she were still unmarried," she said, speaking casually, wondering why she brought up the subject.

"She's single."

"And wealthy."

"Most definitely."

A perfect candidate for countess, Raven thought, and she took an immediate and totally irrational dislike to the woman.

"And if your next question is whether she's beautiful," Marcus said, "I would have to say she's certainly passable."

"So why is she unwed?"

"I've no idea," he said. "You must ask her when you meet. Perhaps you can tell her why you've also chosen the spinster's life."

Raven had no response. Already she'd said too much.

They rode on in silence, and Albert dropped to the rear, at last turning for a saunter back to the hall. This time Marcus took her down the trails that led to the homes of the tenant farmers.

Shacks, she called them, worse than the slave quarters she remembered from before the war. Cottages whose thatched roofs begged for repair, whose curtainless windows were more often broken than not, whose yards were littered with debris atop the barren dirt.

Occasionally she caught a glimpse of vacant eyes staring from the open windows, shy eyes that hurriedly faded into the dark. Marcus's expression grew grim as he rode past the homes. Once he stopped to talk to one of the farmers, who stood in an empty pen at the side of the lane.

As the farmer looked up at Marcus, his weathered face showed pride and a hint of alarm. His cottage was in better condition than the others, both roof and windows repaired and the surrounding ground free of the litter she'd seen elsewhere.

When Marcus dismounted, Raven started to follow. A glance from him changed her mind.

"Good day to you," he said to the farmer, striding to join him beside the muck-filled pen.

The farmer averted his eyes, mumbling something Raven couldn't understand.

Marcus looked past him to a stretch of thistle-packed ground. "When will the tilling start? Soon, I should expect."

The man rubbed gnarled hands against his stained trousers. "Plow's broke."

"Graham Seed was supposed to provide a steam-plow for the tenants."

The farmer spat into the mud, his rheumy eyes cynical as he looked at Marcus. "Steam-plow, eh? Read about 'em. Ain't seen one, though."

"A literate man," said Marcus with a smile. "Good for you."

"Don't put food on the table. Or keep my boys from the fields."

"What's your name?"

"Joseph Hambridge. Ain't done nothin' wrong."

"I dare say you haven't." He hesitated. "I won't bother you further, Joseph. We've both got work to do."

With a nod, he retreated. When he rejoined her on the trail, he said, "I wanted you to see it all."

Nothing more, and she was left with few clues as to exactly what he meant. She watched him ride beside her, a grim set to his mouth, his blue gaze dark and inward as though he looked upon no more than his private thoughts.

Did demons drive Marcus as they had long driven her? Was he truly disturbed by the plight of those dependent upon him? It was clear his land and his people needed help. It was equally clear he knew it, and her heart warmed ever stronger in sympathy.

Closing her eyes, Raven remembered how the country around Savannah had been after the war. The town itself had been spared, a Christmas gift from General Sherman to his President. Elsewhere, much had been burned and looted, the once fertile land itself laid to waste. She hadn't thought of that devastation in years, but remembering the shepherd and the farmer and watching Marcus's grim expression, she thought about it now.

At last they came to a copse of trees growing close to the banks of a small, fast-moving stream. A dozen yards away sat still another hut, this one looking more forlorn than any they had yet seen, an orphan home abandoned to the woods. It didn't help that here the ground was muddied and the air thick with the scent of rotted leaves and logs.

For all the desolation, winter didn't have its gray grip on the land; here, she caught a scent of early spring.

He dismounted and helped her to the ground. Her legs were shaky from the long ride, and she stumbled. He caught her with hands strong and warm and sure. Laughing, she attempted to make light of her weakness and more, of the heat that rushed through her when she felt his hold on her waist.

She pushed free. "What is this?" she asked, gesturing

toward the hut, hoping he missed the shakiness of her hand.

"The gamekeeper's cottage. Hasn't been used, I don't imagine, since my uncle moved into town and dismissed most of the staff." He shook his head in disgust at the sight of the ramshackle structure. "It's damned certain Graham Seed has not seen to its care."

While he tethered the horses by the stream and a patch of grass, she looked over the hut. The roof appeared to be sound, but the windows were broken, the stone walls blackened, the vines and dead leaves that surrounded it heavy with an air of loneliness and neglect.

Saddlebags in hand, Marcus stepped past her and opened the creaking door.

"Damn," he muttered. "I'd hoped we could take our meal here."

Raven peered around him. Pale light filtering through the windows fell on cobwebs, a chair and broken-legged table, a cold stone fireplace, a carpet of dust and dead leaves.

She also spied a bucket in the corner by the hearth. An idea occurred, brought on, she suspected, by that outdoors hint of spring. She glanced at her companion, a challenge in her eye. So he never got rumpled, did he? Or dirty? She could change all that.

The Bannerman heritage went back two hundred years to noblemen and women he could call by name, to lords and rulers served by vassals to help them survive. Her known family went back one generation, to Thomas and Anne Chadwick, who knew what it was to roll up their sleeves and work. She would put habit against history any day in the week.

And Marcus needed to snap out of the gloom into which he had slipped. He had much to think about, true, and much to do, but not right away. And he didn't look so dangerous. Besides, she was long used to taking care of herself. She could handle him.

An inner voice asked whether she could handle herself, but she refused to listen.

"Can you wait an hour to eat?" she asked.

"Of course. What did you have in mind?"

She stepped close to him, dappled light filtering through the trees onto the path by the hut's front door.

"I'll need your full cooperation," she said, wondering from whence came the urge to tease him when they were so very much alone.

"You have it," he said, bemusement in his eyes.

She removed her cloak and scarf. "Could you find a place for these?"

"Most definitely."

He hung them from a branch of a nearby tree.

"We'll need water," she said, unfastening the top button of her coat.

"An original request," he said, his gaze locked onto the movement of her fingers.

"Not for what I have in mind."

"You intrigue me."

Not for long, she thought.

"The water," she reminded him. He got the bucket, inspected it for leaks, and soon had it filled at the stream.

"You might want to take off your coat," she said. "I promise you won't be cold for long."

Bemusement gave way to a definitely lascivious grin. Raven's heart skipped a beat. It was time to quit teasing.

She spied a fallen branch close to the door.

"Not much of a broom, but it will have to do." She brushed a lock of hair away from her face. "We've got work to do to make this place habitable. That is, if we're going to enjoy our lunch before a healthy fire."

# Fourteen

The cleaning took closer to two hours than to one. Marcus had no complaints. The challenge of following Raven's command was something he would not soon forget. Never having served in the army, he supposed it was how a private felt under the control of a determined sergeant.

He doubted, however, any sergeant had ever looked like his.

Teasing curves and grace of features didn't keep her from thoroughness. Walls and ceilings were freed of cobwebs and dust, the floor swept, the windows washed, the hearth scrubbed.

For battle against the enemy filth, she used a bundle of twigs, the fallen branch, and at last one of her two pairs of underdrawers. He had to leave the hut while she took it off. It took great strength of character not to look through one of the windows, which was just as well. She told him later she had been ready to douse him with water if he took so much as one peek.

The briskness of the day did indeed have little effect on him, just as she had said, but it wasn't because of the hard labor. Watching her work—hair carelessly bound at her nape by her scarf, jacket removed, sleeves of her once-white blouse rolled to her elbows—generated enough heat to melt a glacier.

He especially liked the perspiration that lined her forehead and caused the loose tendrils of hair to cling to her face.

He also liked the dampness that made her clothes cling and the smudge of soot across her cheek. Maybe he ought to clean her the way they had cleaned the room. To do a complete job, he would have to remove her second pair of drawers.

He was still contemplating the particulars of her bath when they sat before the blazing fire, chair and table supplementing logs to provide the fuel, their saddles as back rests, his coat and her cloak cushioning the floor. Meat pasties prepared by the cook and water from the stream made up the feast. He had never tasted anything more delicious.

They ate in silence, each watching the fire. He felt her presence in every nerve of his body, knew without looking how her eyes would reflect the flames. For the first time in a long while he came close to feeling at peace, almost forgetting the scenes of the morning . . . the wrenching poverty . . . the neglect that had laid waste to this once rich land.

He shouldn't have ignored Beacon Hall the first year of his ownership, but more important matters had called—investment worries, a fractious family, and Paris, most definitely Paris—all reasons to keep him away from the scene of his misspent youth.

Not that his life as a man had been spent all that

nobly. It had taken total concentration to change his ways. Surface changes, he knew, as he contemplated the woman beside him. What would she taste like after the hours of labor? To know for sure, he would have to trail his tongue across her satin skin.

"What are you going to do?"

Raven's soft voice startled him from reverie.

*Lick your breasts.* It was an answer more wishful than wise.

"About what?" he asked instead.

"Beacon Hall. The farmers. The children. How do you plan to deal with them?"

The question rankled coming so soon after he'd thrust his worries aside.

"I'll make things right."

"As easy as that?"

"Only the declaration is easy." He looked from the fire to her upturned face. "We both know good intentions don't necessarily bring about change." His sister's image flashed across his mind. "At least the change desired."

"Amy should see what I saw."

How strange, he thought with a start, that their thoughts should run to the same person.

"Why didn't you bring her instead of me?"

"You scoffed at me once for not having a job. Maybe I wanted you to see I have more than a normal earl's share of work to do."

He ran a hand through his hair. "As for Amy, she wouldn't have been interested. You have observed we don't get on."

Raven opened her mouth to speak. He could hear the unasked question: *Why not?*

She had raised the issue weeks ago when he found her breaking into his desk. He hadn't answered her then, and he wouldn't answer her now. Like Amy, she would condemn what he had done, and he wasn't in the mood for censure.

He felt a rise of anger at them both, and then a heat that had little to do with the fire. He was isolated with a beautiful, desirable woman, contemplating pursuits that once had been his way of life. Contemplating, that was the problem. Since when had he stopped with thoughts?

There was damned little he could do at the moment about poverty and child labor and Amy and Paris, but Raven was another matter entirely. She had claimed to want a celibate life, but he had discovered too much passion in her kisses to take her at her word.

He looked at her black eyes, at her black hair, at the smooth, silken line of her neck. Reason had worked him over this afternoon; it was time to let feelings take control. He smiled inwardly. Seduction should be the order of the day. He knew a thousand ways.

The direct approach, he thought. She had been asking most of the questions. He had at least one for her.

"Has there ever been another woman like you, Songbird?"

She swallowed. He watched the muscles in her throat.

"Just because I'm not afraid to dirty my hands—"

"That's not what I meant, and you know it. You weren't afraid to accept my invitation."

Alarm widened her eyes. "Should I have been?"

How innocent she looked, and how totally tempting. She was either the most naive and trusting woman in the world or the most fiendishly clever flirt he'd ever met.

He shifted against the saddle, heard the creak of leather and the pounding of his heart.

"Do you fear me? Even now? Surely you know I have no intention of hurting you."

*Not unless you like it that way.*

The heat within him built. He could see she felt it, could read both worry and wonder in her magnificent eyes. But he did not see rejection, although he did not look too close.

Here was where his conscience should take control, and his recently acquired purity of intent.

What the hell. He'd always been weak.

Besides, there were aspects to her character that he had vowed weeks ago to discover. The time for that discovery had arrived.

Setting his cup aside, he took hers from her hand and did the same. Hands on her shoulders, he turned her to face him.

"I want you, Raven. Won't you show me exactly how much you want me?"

Raven stared in disbelief at Marcus. What a fool she'd been to abandon her well-honed defenses and settle indoors with him. Before a fire, in isolation, so close she could hear his every breath . . . all signs of trouble to come.

She could even count the bristles on his cheeks.

To trust him, to trust herself had been a mistake. But he had behaved for more than half a day—if she didn't count an occasional leer and a comment or two—and she had been hungry and restless, unwilling to return to the house and to the problems facing her there. Most of all, she hadn't wanted to end their outing so soon.

Tingling nerves said it was time to end it now.

But not with missish shock and shy protestations. Such wasn't in her character, and he knew it.

"I don't want you," she said. Quickly, firmly, so he could not misunderstand.

Marcus's blue gaze seemed to look into her soul.

"I don't want you," she repeated, trembling behind the protection of her denial.

"I've evidence to the contrary," he said. Low, deep, insistent. And very sure of himself.

"Can't you for once respect what I say?"

"Oh, I respect you. Especially the lift of your breasts beneath your clothes—"

She gasped at the boldness of his words, but the coaxing rhythm of his words did not miss a beat.

"—the curve of your arms, the way the firelight catches in your hair. That riding skirt has a tendency to shift while you're working, did you know that? It reminded me of just how long your legs really are."

Raven's heart pounded, and shock dissolved into desire that intoxicated her blood. What a worthless wanton she became when Marcus drew near. She would even welcome the night thoughts if they emboldened her to push him away.

"I don't want you," she said for yet a third time, praying the repetition would command belief. He didn't understand her . . . didn't know the terrible things she was capable of doing. She prayed he would never find out.

He shifted closer, until his thigh burned against hers. She shoved against his chest. He did not move, and for her effort she was left with tingles wherever the two of them touched.

"Your body is as hard as a rock, Your Lordship. Is your head the same?"

He grinned. "Strange you should speak of hardness. And very apt."

What would he feel like? Everywhere. She clinched her hands to keep from finding out.

*I don't want him.*

She admitted she lied.

*I can't want him.*

This was closer to the truth.

She tried to rise, but his hands on her shoulders held her against the saddle. Her eyes darted to the confining walls of the gamekeeper's hut, to the wild brush outside the window, the roaring fire in the hearth. And, last, to Marcus with his golden hair and his cerulean gaze and his parted, tempting lips.

Everything she saw was wildly romantic, from the isolated cabin to the small, white scar on his chin. A setting for love. No, for mating, which wasn't at all the same thing.

"I'll not take you by force, Raven."

"Take me?"

"You know what I mean. I'm not a brute."

She wished that he were. Then she could hate him. Then she would have some defense against what he obviously had decided to do.

He kissed the corner of her mouth. "Relax," he whispered, then kissed the other corner.

How could she relax when everything within her threatened to explode?

"You're trembling," he said.

"I'm not."

"Liar." His thumb stroked the pulse point at her throat. "A beautiful, exciting liar."

He pushed her hair back from her face. "Kiss me."

Her skin burned from no more than the way he looked at her. Never had she felt so alive. Never had she felt so in danger . . . except that one time, long, long ago.

From the chasms of her darkest nightmares she saw a young soldier's face emerging from the fog, the alley behind her Papa's store . . . and waves of red that crimsoned the scene like paint flung onto a canvas. Red blanketed her world.

"No," she cried out, denying not Marcus but the old images, the red-streaked blackened mists, the hated remembrances that destroyed a little more of her each time they struck. She had been wrong about the night thoughts. She didn't want them, not ever, ever again. She knew of only one way to keep them distant. One man who might make her forget.

Pressing her body against Marcus's hard chest, she

wrapped her arms around his neck and clung to him with all her strength and will. Senses embroiled, she became the woman whose lustful nature she had so long suppressed.

"You've a strange notion of *no*— " he began.

She covered his lips with hers. The kiss was hard, almost brutal, then softened to something far more desirable. Strong hands gripped her shoulders, easing to stroke her arms, her back, and she gave herself to his strength.

He broke the kiss only for the length of time it took to shift her closer, until she was sharing the saddle he had used as a backrest, his coat and her cloak bundled beneath them both, her legs stretched toward the fire.

Sitting beside her, he gave full attention once again to the kiss. He had given her time to protest, but she couldn't force the words to her lips. Instead, she was inclined only toward frustration at the brief moment they'd been apart. All the years of pretense dissolved into this instant of hunger, of need for a man's touch.

Marcus's touch. She had no wish to harm him or even push him away. He was everything to her, and as his mouth claimed hers, lips parted, he breathed into her mouth the substance of life. She had no guard against his appeal. For so long she had been strong and in the most womanly of ways she had kept herself apart. With Marcus, she wasn't alone.

The kiss deepened, tongues touched, and she ran hungry hands across the front of his shirt, tracing the hard muscles with her palm, her nails scratching against the fabric as though she might tear her way to his skin. She played with danger, but the old reasoning that had for years shielded her from passion shattered under the tender assault of his lips.

He kissed her eyes, her cheeks, her throat, whispering, "You drive me to madness," and doing much the same to her as his lips seared her skin.

Lifting her hair, he kissed the curve of her neck. She turned to liquid, melting against him, desperate to be inside his clothes, inside his skin, no longer a woman separate. Her ignorance allowed no guidance as to how she was supposed to feel. Did women lose themselves in passion so completely? Did they tear at buttons as she was doing, stroke hot skin, rub fingertips against whorls of chest hair and the tight, hard nubs that were a man's nipples?

She didn't care. All of existence distilled into this instant, without mists, or alleys, or red. She thought only of the places he touched her and of the places she touched him. And she shivered with a pleasure so sweet it was almost pain.

His hands were more expert than hers, in swift movements unfastening her blouse and easing it from her shoulders, his gaze burning against the exposed rise of her breasts.

She watched as he looked at her. An eyebrow raised.

"Two chemises?" he asked.

"I was cold," she rasped.

He tugged at the undergarments until they rested just above the distended tips of her breasts and kissed the exposed fullness.

"Are you cold now?"

She answered by lifting herself to him and pulling the garments lower until the dark nipples were exposed.

"Exquisite," he whispered. His eyes found hers, and he repeated, "Exquisite."

The words set off a tumult inside her. When he explored her with his lips and tongue, she hoped that he would never stop.

Rapture possessed her. Instinct drove her hips to press against his, her legs to part. His hand stroked her thigh, her buttocks, pulling her hard against him until her soft body molded to the outline of his solid arousal. Her fingers ached to touch him in the intimate ways he was touching her. A small cry sounded in her throat, a plea of both pleasure and frustration.

He seemed to understand. Working at the fastenings of her skirt and undergarments, he pressed a hot hand against her abdomen. Her muscles tightened, turning somersaults, and she lifted herself toward fingers that fought their way beneath her clothing to the damp heat pulsing between her legs.

He found the throbs, and she slipped into a darkness that had no elements of fear or death, only sweet pleasure and a driving hunger that made the past fade into oblivion. The darkness swirled and stroked and aroused her ever and ever into a formless space both caressing and endless. It all happened so quickly, first a kiss and a touch and, within the space of a blink, this glorious sensation that changed her into a creature she did not know.

She was tight and wild; and when the throbs quickened, she thrust a frantic hand against his to contain the erotic pleasure that drove her out of her mind.

"Raven," he whispered against her ear.

She did not want words. Words were of the earth, and she was hurtling through a dark void toward an unknown place where she had never been.

The explosion shocked her with its all-consuming pleasure and its inevitability. Stunned, she trembled against him, still touching the hand that continued to hold her. The pulses eased, slowly winding out their power, like the fading rolls of thunder after a lightning strike.

She buried her head against his chest, aware of where he held her, of the saddle against which they leaned, of the crushed cloak and coat beneath them, of the fire dying at their feet.

He kissed her forehead and whispered, "Songbird, you sing sweetly today."

Something in his voice made her tighten, made her grow chill.

She forced her eyes to his and saw blue fire. He was not done.

Panic fluttered like a wild dove within her breast, fed by the humiliation of her wantonness and the danger that lay in what he wanted to do.

"Marcus—"

The sound of thrashing horses outside the window stilled her voice.

He bolted upright and muttered an obscenity.

Easing his hand from her, he stood and attempted to shift his erection to a less obvious position.

Stunned, she stared up at him like a child awaiting instructions, little understanding what had just happened between them except that it had been quick and wild and pleasurable beyond all imagining.

Passion had felt too good not to be bad.

He helped her to her feet and smoothed her hair. "Do what you can to look presentable." He shrugged into his wrinkled coat. "I need the cover," he said with a rueful grin. The grin died as he kissed her, hot promise in his eyes.

Raven looked away, listening to the footsteps taking him out the door. Disgust rose like bile in her throat— and scorn directed at them both.

Presentable, he had said. As though she were somehow shameful. All memories of pleasure faded. Shameful described her all too well.

Her eyes darted from corner to corner of the room, searching the shadows for a place to hide, a depression where she could burrow and contemplate her disgrace and the changing nature of her being.

But she had no time for humiliation. He was outside and she heard voices . . . Marcus and another man speaking in deep tones and then a woman's high laugh. Her blood turned to ice. Awkward fingers struggled to tuck her blouse into her skirt, to close the hundred fastenings, to smooth back her hair.

Maybe she could stay inside until everyone rode away. Maybe she could stay inside forever.

"Miss Chadwick," she heard Marcus call, "have you finished with your work?" And then to the newcomers.

"She's a stickler for detail. Wanted to get the last cobwebs before we rode back to the hall."

She forced her legs to take her to the door, lecturing
her knees they must not buckle, telling her heart to settle
properly in her breast. Later she would deal with what
she had done today. Right now she had to put on the
greatest performance of her life.

She walked into an afternoon that had grown misty.
Moisture clung to the leaves and grass, to her riding coat
that hung from a branch by the cottage door, and to the
manes of the matching grays that shifted back and forth
in front of a very placid earl. Marcus smiled at the riders,
playing the part of host as though he were welcoming
the newcomers to Beacon Hall.

"Ah, here she is now. Miss Chadwick, allow me to
introduce my neighbor and good friend Squire Adolfo
Clifton and his daughter, Miss Margaret Clifton."

Raven looked up with every intention of equaling His
Lordship's calm. She made it through a glance at the
squire. A short, broad man of sixty, gray hair and beard
that duplicated the color of his horse, he nodded a
greeting.

Her eyes cut to the daughter and immediately picked
out more details. Diminutive, she noticed, with delicate
features, a turned-up nose, fair skin, brown eyes, brown
hair. Her riding habit was superbly cut to show off her
small frame and disproportionately large breasts.

"Miss Clifton," she said with a determined lift to her
voice.

And then she really looked into the woman's eyes, into
the rage filling their brown depths, a rage so strong it
struck her like a physical blow. Within an instant it sof-

tened to a glow of understanding, along with disdain, and her small tulip lips twitched into something that was not quite a smile.

Raven's heart turned to stone.

*Margaret Clifton knows. She knows what Marcus and I have done.*

# *Fifteen*

During the next two days Raven behaved like a woman possessed. Two women, in truth—the horrified spinster who worked feverishly to stay out of Marcus's path and the wanton who dreamed of sneaking into his room in the dark of night and crawling into his bed.

Neither seemed real to her. She had never harbored fantasies about men or skittered from trouble, not even when she was fourteen. As a child at the edge of womanhood, she had stood tall and determined and fought the most terrible battle of her life.

Afterwards she had retreated to the private world in which she lived her life. Only dreams disturbed her. Never reality.

Not so with Marcus. If she so much as saw his tall, lean shadow in the house or on the grounds, she turned and hurried the other way. If she didn't see him, she thought about him—about the way he held his head as though listening for words no one else could hear, about the thickness of golden hair against his bronzed neck, the way he sat his saddle, thighs gripping the gelding, the curve of mahogany boots along the sweep of his strong calves.

These were the mildest of her memories. When she

thought of the feel of his lips, of the places he had kissed and the intimate places he had touched, stabs of heat penetrated the marrow of her bones.

And she thought about his bed.

Like one of his actress whores, she told herself, but the telling did little good. She must have lost her mind, otherwise she would be thinking of a threatening letter, of hands that shoved her down the stairs. But the fall had done no more than threaten her life; Marcus threatened her soul.

She couldn't avoid him forever. She had pleaded a headache to avoid dinner the evening after their ride, but it was an excuse that once used could not be used again, else she would arouse suspicion among the members of his watchful family. Amy, Cordelia, Irene—she felt their eyes on her every moment she was in their presence. Questioning eyes, especially when Marcus was in the room.

She cursed him as well as herself. In one brief afternoon he had opened something dark inside her, had freed a devil that she had fought to lock away from her proud and private self. He had let loose lust.

Here was the sensation that made the night thoughts so frightening. She had known without admitting it that she had this side to her nature. He forced her to accept the truth.

She wanted him, in ways she had not yet experienced. And she wanted him to enrapture her again and again.

She tried to hate him, but the Earl of Stafford was what he was—a conscienceless rake and a constant temptation—and she had known it full well when she'd sat with him in the gamekeeper's hut. That she would go on wanting him was the most grievous part of the whole situation.

Almost as disturbing was the certainty that their erotic interlude was not a secret.

Miss Margaret Clifton had said not a word to indicate her suspicions, not when she'd sat in judgmental sweetness upon her horse asking Marcus's American visitor about her stage career or on the long ride the four of them had taken back to Beacon Hall.

But she knew. She was far too interested in Marcus to misjudge his secluded afternoon with an actress in the woods. Earlier he had professed ignorance about why his neighbor had not wed. Remembering the woman's momentary rage, Raven understood the reason. She was saving herself to become Countess of Stafford, wife of a handsome earl.

"How long will England be graced with your presence?" the woman had asked as they'd made their way along the narrow, winding trail.

Raven had made her own translation: "How soon will you leave?"

"You Yanks have such a different approach to life, so carefree, unbound by our Victorian precepts," she'd observed, a neatly gloved hand waving prettily in the air.

Thinking of her own chipped nails and fingers stained from hours of work, Raven had gotten her real meaning: "You're all slatterns and sluts."

"We sold the mare to Marcus thinking it was for Amy to ride," said the squire's daughter with a sniff and a wrinkle of her turned-up nose.

Translation: "Get off the horse."

In each instance Raven had responded as politely as

her Mama could have wished, but she hadn't resisted pointing out that her visit was extended at the earl's insistence, as was the ride.

Trailing them, neither Marcus nor the squire had noticed the subtle shots the two women were firing at one another. Just as well. The last thing Raven needed was for him to interject himself into a conversation between the woman who had almost become his whore and the woman who wanted to be his bride.

After two days of avoiding him, she lost the chase one morning while inspecting the conservatory at the back of Beacon Hall's ground floor. She was standing in the middle of the long glass enclosure, looking at the few remaining plants that had not died or gone to seed, thinking that despite the waste, the air still held a damp and fecund scent.

The door creaked open, then closed. She didn't have to turn to know who had entered. She was getting very good at detecting when he was close.

"You can't avoid me forever," a deep voice said. The words caressed her like a draft of warm air, yet she shivered and hugged herself.

She gave a moment's thought to smiling broadly and asking him whatever could he possibly mean. He wouldn't be fooled.

She forced herself to face him. "I can try."

The light was poor; she barely made out his face. But she could see his eyes. They watched her with relentless care.

He moved slowly past the sparse foliage, each step bringing him inexorably closer to her. Stalking her. She felt like his prey.

"Why run?" he asked when he was close.

It was a simple question with an answer so complex he couldn't begin to understand.

She kept her eyes locked with his, although she couldn't keep from noticing he wore a tweed jacket over a pale-blue shirt and dark trousers. Despite the absence of a tie, he showed his usual flair for style.

She ached to touch him, but she kept her hands at her side.

"I ran because I knew if we met in solitude you would not be a gentleman."

"Have I already affronted you?"

"Yes. By seeking me out when you knew I wished otherwise."

He looked her over. She was wearing her emerald-green day dress, a simple design, but its brilliantly colored silk followed the lines of her figure with far too much precision. She suspected he would have looked at her with lascivious intent had she been wearing a sack.

"Tell me what you want, Songbird, and I'll try to comply. An apology? An embrace?"

"Silence would be nice."

He grinned. Her stomach turned somersaults and, worse, she felt the tips of her breasts harden beneath the too-soft layers of silken camisole and dress.

Blue fire flared in his eyes. He'd noticed, too.

"You ask too much," he said.

She turned from him and snapped the dead leaves from what once had been a luxuriant tea rose bush. He stepped closer. With her hair twisted ruthlessly into a bun above her nape, her neck lay bare before him. His breath tickled her ear.

A small cry tore from her throat, as though her hunger for him could no longer be contained. Purposefully she thrust her finger upon a thorn, crying again at the pain.

He took her hand and sucked the blood that welled on her fingertip.

She dragged her hand from his and looked up at him. "You shouldn't do that," she managed, wondering whose thick voice came from her lips.

"I want to kiss more than your hand."

Raven's heart cried for the spinster in her to take control, but it was the wanton whose spirit soared, who swayed toward the devil tempting her beyond endurance.

She whirled from him. "Don't speak of such matters. Please."

"I've told you I'll never force you into anything you don't want. And I haven't."

"You made me want you. You know the ways."

He played with a wisp of hair that curled disobediently against her neck. "And you give me too much credit."

Heat skittered from nerve to nerve as she shook away his touch.

"Your pursuit of me is fruitless, Marcus. You caught me in a moment of weakness."

"You have no weakness."

"Then you don't know me very well."

"Let me know you better. You exploded in my arms. I want to feel that explosion again."

"Then seek out one of your whores."

"No woman, no matter what you label her, has ever made me feel the way you do. When I embraced you, I held the primal forces of the world. You think that happens often? Never to me, and I suspect seldom to any man."

He stroked the whispery silk covering her shoulders. "You invited my kisses, Raven, and my touch. Everywhere. And you held my hand in place. I carried your scent with me for hours. You're in my blood."

She covered her ears, but his words raged in her mind. How could he talk in such a way to her? Didn't he know he had touched her with an intimacy experienced by no other man? And not just her body. He had touched something deep inside her, too. She had given herself to him in more than just brazen passion. She'd given him a part of her soul.

"I wasn't myself."

"You felt like the woman I've held before, and you tasted like the woman I've kissed. What about you was different? Were you more honest? Did you open yourself to what we both wanted to happen?"

"You don't know what I'm capable of." She shuddered. "Terrible things, Marcus, beyond your imagining."

"Then show me. Now. Tonight."

His voice echoed achingly inside her. "You're good at this," she said, wrapping her arms around her middle.

"At what? I don't recall your saying I'm much good at anything."

She separated herself from him and turned to let him read the determination in her gaze. The space between them was too small to keep her from breathing in his scent and catching the twitch of his lips and the tightness around his eyes. But it was space enough to avoid his breath on her cheek.

"You're good at confusing a woman, at making her think she wants what she knows is wrong, at striking sparks within her that should remain dormant."

Her voice grew thin. She took a steadying breath before adding, "You're very good at taking what you want."

His eyes darkened with what she would have taken for despair in another man. With Marcus it had to be disdain.

"You're forgetting the way things went," he said softly. "You put your arms around me, Songbird—"

"Don't call me that."

"—and kissed me as I have never been kissed. I'm an experienced man. I've never felt such a jolt."

"Am I supposed to feel triumphant?"

"I don't know how either of us is supposed to feel . . . except unsatisfied. We haven't joined yet. You know we will."

Joined? Friends joined hands, the betrothed joined in matrimony, and rutting couples joined in carnal embrace. She didn't have to ask which one he meant.

"You've no right to speak to me this way."

"Maybe not, but I've every encouragement."

"Then tell me, Your Lordship, how one discourages you. I'm finding it impossible."

"Convince me you don't burn in the night to be with me."

"That's absurd. People don't burn."

"I burn for you. I wake and look to see if the sheets are seared. They're merely rumpled from a night of tossing about. Can't you see the shadows under my eyes? They're not from the worries that should absorb me. They're caused from hungering for you."

Anguish drove her to a harsh defense. "Oh, I see what bothers you. I'm robbing you of your rest. I'm keeping you from the problems that surround you here. Satisfy your manly urges and then get on with what's important in your life."

"Raven—"

"What happened to Songbird? I never can tell if it's supposed to be sweet talk or a taunt to remind me of Camden Cockloft."

His eyes turned cold, the way she preferred them. "I believe I prefer you trembling under my touch."

"Compliant, you mean. Submissive."

"You weren't in the least submissive the other afternoon. You bared yourself to me, and you were magnificent."

"I was crazed."

"We both were. Can you truthfully swear you don't want to be crazed again?"

"Not like that. I can't be out of control."

"Did it frighten you? Why? What happened that made you afraid?"

"What makes you think I was afraid?" she said, too quickly, but the thought that her secret might become known to him terrified her more than the knowledge of how much she wanted to be in his arms.

"Because I've seen fear in your eyes. Each time we kiss. Except in the gamekeeper's hut. I didn't think you were afraid of anything then. Unless it was being found out."

Raven seized the subject he unwittingly tossed her.

"Margaret Clifton knows."

His brow lifted in surprise. "She told you?"

"She didn't have to. It was in her smirk."

"I'm sorry that you had to endure it. The chances were in our favor we wouldn't be disturbed."

"You planned it?"

"No. Not until after we had eaten. Then it seemed the natural course. I wanted you, Raven; and whether you admit it or not, you wanted me."

How easily he twisted the talk to his own lascivious purpose. But Raven was no fool. And she was fighting for her life.

"Miss Clifton wants to marry you," she said.

"She told you?"

"She didn't have to. It was in the way she looked at you."

"Passionate?" he asked in that self-mocking way that always puzzled her.

"Calculating."

"Ah, of course. I'm not surprised. To an untitled woman of independent means, I'm considered quite the catch."

"She wouldn't be a bad countess. She knows the ways of the country and I doubt she would embarrass you in town."

"Are you championing her cause? Did she offer you a commission if you reeled me in?"

"I'm too inconsequential to be included in her strategy."

"Then she's more of a fool than I took her to be."

"Don't be absurd, Marcus. I don't mean anything—"

The sound of the conservatory door stopped her from continuing. She looked past him to see Amy walking down the narrow path between the rows of dead and dying plants.

"What a dreadful place," the young woman said. "When Elizabeth was alive, the roses in here seemed to me the most glorious sight in all the world."

She looked at her brother with eyes a cold and empty blue. "But all good things have to end, do they not? It's only the bad that lingers on."

"Why not work at reviving them?" he asked. "Make them beautiful again."

"Because I'm no good at bringing what is dead back to life. Surely you know that better than anyone."

She looked at Raven. "Is he trying to put you to work in here? Marcus is expert at getting what he wants out of women."

"Watch yourself, Amy," he said. "You go too far."

Amy gave him not so much as a sideways glance. "Not nearly far enough. If he hasn't already seduced you, Raven, I believe I can dredge up an ancient chastity belt from the small museum in town."

Raven gasped, for a moment losing her composure.

"Goddamn," said Marcus with such disgust that even Amy fell silent. "Apologize," he ordered.

Amy's chin tilted, as though she would defy her brother's command, but when she looked into the anger in his eyes she backed away.

"I'm sorry," she said to Raven. "I grow so used to teasing Marcus that I forget myself. Pay no attention to what I said."

"Of course," said Raven, listening in vain for genuine contrition in Amy's voice, thinking she would remember every syllable the girl had uttered during the darkest hours of night.

"I saw Margaret Clifton in Ditchling," said Amy, sounding no more distressed than if she had just strolled into the room.

"What were you doing in town?" asked Marcus.

"Why, spending money, of course. That's what I always do. Margaret asked us to dine on Saturday. I accepted, for us and the aunts."

An evening alone, thought Raven with a sigh of relief. With Marcus gone from the premises, maybe she could get some rest.

"You are included," said Amy. "Miss Chadwick simply must come," she added, in a fair imitation of Margaret Clifton's chirpy voice.

"I think not."

"Oh, but you must. It's part of the family experience, visiting with the country folk."

"I'm not part of the family."

"Of course you are." She glanced at her brother. "Tell her she is, Marcus. Order her to accompany us."

"If Raven chooses to remain here, that is her decision. I'm sure she has her reasons."

She felt his taunting eyes on her. His words sounded innocent enough, but she heard the challenge in his voice. If she avoided the Cliftons, he would label her a coward. And he would be right.

Besides, she felt an urge to see the house where Marcus had grown to manhood, whether or not he'd spent much time indoors. In her wildest imagination, she would not have guessed he came from a place known as Humble Hall.

* * *

Marcus left the two women to their conversation in the conservatory. Separately, they were difficult to deal with; together, they offered a test even an experienced womanizer wouldn't challenge.

Amy was his constant heartache, a sister long lost to him. Her taunts came as no new pain.

Raven was different. Mostly, he needed to get away from her. He had known her scarcely two months, yet she had become an opiate in his blood. He couldn't get enough of her. What would his dependency be when he actually made love to her? He didn't doubt it would happen. If she would only admit the truth, neither did she.

He threw himself into the waiting paperwork, primarily letters from suppliers he had queried concerning purchases made by Graham Seed balanced against the few actual invoices the land agent had managed to produce.

Except that they didn't balance. The man was a thief. He also knew the land and its needs and he knew the people, things Marcus was belatedly learning about. Now that his employer was on the scene, Seed would be cautious about outright fraud, and Marcus had already warned him against abusing the tenants. But would these be enough?

No child labor, he had decreed in a meeting with Seed the previous day. The agent had howled in protest, claiming without the hundred small hands available, the fields couldn't be cleared. They had compromised on the age of thirteen. Children under that age went to class in Ditchling; their older siblings worked the farmland, but only if they were unwilling to return to school.

"There'll be protests," the agent had warned. "They bring in money, as long as they don't get too tired."

"How much?"

"For a full day? The youngest no more'n four pence, twice't that as they gets older. Have to provide their own food and tools, they do. No sense in mollycoddling 'em."

"How many do you estimate live on Beacon land?"

"Breed like rabbits, they do, Yer Lordship. Must be a hundred or so."

"Get their names and ages."

Seed had not tried to hide his astonishment. "What in hell for? No offense, Your Lordship, but it seems a waste o' me time."

"I want a census taken of the tenants. Hire someone to do it. Someone other than Quirke. The farmer Joseph Hambridge can read and write and cipher. Use him."

"I don't see—"

"You don't have to. Just do as I instruct. Now."

Marcus doubted Seed would enforce the agreement concerning the workers. He would have to be watched.

The conversation with the agent had taken place almost twenty-four hours ago. Impatient for the report, he did some hasty figuring in his head, keeping to the generous side of numbers of offspring and their ages, then multiplied that by the wages Seed had named.

Staring at the final figures, he decided that the impossible idea he had come up with just might be feasible. Unprecedented, most certainly ludicrous to many, but definitely feasible. He sat back in his chair. He had never thought of himself as an innovator, but he rather liked the feeling.

And what would Raven say? Would she discover some way to find fault?

Somehow he doubted it. She didn't disagree with everything he did.

No matter how she protested. God, how he wanted to finish what they had started. And do it again and again and again.

The logistics would be tricky, of course, since she refused to be in a room alone with him. He could imagine what she would say if he offered another opportunity for a ride.

But he remembered the way she had clung to him, her soft, ripe body pressed hungrily to his. There was a wildness in her that matched the wildness in him. And an innocence, too, for which he had no counterpart. He hadn't been innocent since the age of thirteen when the milkmaid had taught him what the private body parts were for.

Was Raven Chadwick, actress and singer, as innocent as she wanted him to believe? If so, she had a damned peculiar way of proving it. Finding the truth ate at him like a cancer. Once he understood her, maybe he would be free of this obsession.

He forced his attention to the papers on his desk, but the work soon grew wearisome. Throwing down his pen, he let himself out through the double doors leading from the library to the once-grand garden behind Beacon Hall.

Everything about the place was once grand. Everything needed work. Strange how the thought didn't tire him as much as it had when he'd first arrived.

He chose a path that took him to the stables. He came upon the boy Jason attempting to load a hunting rifle he recognized as coming from the gun rack in the corner of the library. Not much of a hunter, Marcus hadn't noticed the rack in days.

Slowly he walked toward the boy, whose concentration kept him oblivious to all but the gun.

"What are you doing?" Marcus asked when he came to the door of the stall where the boy labored.

Jason dropped a shell as he jumped to his feet, attempting in vain to thrust the rifle behind him.

Even in the dim light Marcus could make out a fierce determination in the boy's eyes and the fiery flush that darkened his freckled cheeks.

"The gun, Jason. What is it for?"

The boy straightened himself before his master, every inch of him straining to be a man.

"Don't stop me, Yer Lordship. I gots to kill a man."

# Sixteen

Marcus kept his astonishment to himself. Jason looked close to breaking, and the misery on his pale young face was real.

"Whom do you plan to shoot?" he asked matter-of-factly.

"The man what ruined me sister," Jason said, choking on the words.

"I met her the other day, didn't I?" Marcus pictured a red-headed girl a full head shorter than her brother, snub-nosed and freckled, her body still the body of a child. "She's no more than thirteen."

"Jennie's twelve." Jason's voice turned as thin as his spindly arms. "He likes 'em young."

"Who? I need a name."

"Don't matter that you know, Yer Lordship. I'm man o' the house. I'll do what has t' be done."

"By stealing a rifle?"

The boy showed no remorse. "I'll return it when I'm done."

Marcus blocked the door to the stall. The gun barrel lifted in line with his heart.

It would be easy to wrest the weapon from the boy's hands, but Marcus knew he would take the fierce pride with it. He remembered his own fragile boyhood too well for that.

"I'll help you but I need to know whom we're after."

Jason looked at him with defiance, then seemed to crumble inside. Sniffling, he wiped a sleeve against his nose.

"The bastard Arthur Quirke, that's who. He hurt her. She ain't the only one, neither. He's got t' be stopped."

"Is she all right?"

"She's alive."

Marcus didn't ask for details. "You said she's not the only one. He's done this before?"

"Frightened most of 'em is all, or so they said. One family moved on. There's them that blamed the girls, so the talk stopped for a while. Jennie—" His brown eyes locked onto Marcus with something close to desperation. "Jennie's more than just afraid. That's why I got to get him."

"You're a good brother, Jason Murphy. Do you know how to use the gun?"

"I—" Jason began, then snapped his mouth shut.

"You've borrowed it before."

The boy's mouth remained mulishly closed, but Marcus had his answer. Jason had taken the rifle to hunt game. Poaching was a serious offense. But then so was starving.

"If you really want Quirke, you'll give me the gun. We're wasting time."

The boy started to protest.

"Jennie needs us to work together," Marcus said.

Reluctantly, Jason did as he was told.

"When did it happen?" Marcus asked.

"Early this morning. She was outside at the privy. The bastard was quiet about it. She crawled back t' bed without lettin' on. Didn't want to cause no trouble, she said."

"Any idea where Quirke is now?"

Jason shook his head.

"We'll need help. Saddle the horses. I'll look around for Seed."

But the land agent was nowhere to be found. Nor was Quirke. Marcus wasn't surprised.

Within minutes he and the boy were riding Abélard and Héloise across the Downs toward the cottage of the farmer Joseph Hambridge. They found him inside sitting by the light from a window, going over the figures he'd been gathering in his census of the Beacon tenants.

Marcus quickly explained what had happened.

"Do you think you can organize the other farmers into a search?" he asked.

Hambridge shrugged. "They don't take to organizing. I've tried."

Attempting to form a union, Marcus was sure. It was a serious admission to make to the lord of the land.

"Try again," he said. "Most of them have daughters. They'll be protecting them, too."

"Maybe. Maybe not."

"For God's sake, Joseph, convince them. You know these men better than I."

"Aye, that I do," said Hambridge, slowly nodding his agreement, but a hardness in his eyes said the bailiff should never have been hired.

And for that, the absentee lord was ultimately to blame.

As the farmers gathered on the field behind Beacon

Hall, it soon became apparent they felt the same way. They talked among themselves, planned the search, but they held Marcus at bay. In turn, he let them alone.

To his surprise Amy went down to see that Jennie was all right. Raven went with her, bearing a sedative and ointments Aunt Cordelia assured them would ease her pains. They returned to say she was bruised and cut, but most of the injuries were inside.

"She won't leave her bed," said Amy.

"She's so young," said Raven. "Too young to fight back."

It was hard for Marcus to decide which of the women was the more distraught, but when he looked into a pair of stark black eyes, he gave the nod to Raven.

The search turned up only the land agent Graham Seed. He was found in the Bull Hotel in Ditchling, where he claimed to have gone to meet a man about a plow.

After nightfall the men returned to their homes, and Marcus sent word to Seed's cottage on the Downs that he wanted to see him. When the library door opened, he looked up from his desk expecting to see the obsequious agent.

Aunt Irene strode into the room, her black bombazine gown rustling with each long step. She halted as straight as a post before him, gray-streaked hair pulled tight away from her face, her hands with their long fingers and long nails clutched at her side. The zeal of conviction sparked the darkness of her narrow eyes.

"She has to go," she said without prologue.

Marcus was getting good at hiding his surprise. "Miss Chadwick, I suppose."

"Naturally. She's the stranger here."

"She's your cousin."

"Second cousin, daughter to a runaway. And a foreigner. She's trouble, Marcus. She has to go."

Marcus knew the woman better than to ask her to sit and discuss the matter.

"She's also our guest."

"Your guest. Inviting her was a mistake."

Pointing out he could invite anyone he damn well pleased seemed without purpose, as did declaring his life had been disrupted by Raven's presence far more than anyone else's.

"Explain yourself," he said, knowing she would do so regardless.

Her long fingers lifted as, one by one, she counted Raven's sins.

"That dreadful scandal concerning the music hall, the theft of the painting—"

"You knew about that?"

"Everyone did. You've no secrets, you know. She was probably looking for your room when she fell down the stairs."

Marcus came halfway out of his chair. "Aunt Irene—"

But she was not to be stopped. "And now we've this trouble over a bailiff."

He sat back down, fascinated as much as he was repelled by the woman's turn of mind. "You're blaming her for Quirke?"

"I lived in this house when your uncle was earl. Never did we have such a day as today."

He would have asked her how she linked Raven with the attack on Jennie Murphy except that she would have had an answer. Provoked the man, she would have said, and sent him about his mischief.

"I've said what I have to say. She has to go." With the final pronouncement, Irene whirled and exited, leaving the sound of the slammed door echoing in the stillness of the room.

Bloody hell, Marcus thought, then, bone weary, could do no more than think again, bloody hell.

In little more than a minute the door again opened.

Amy? Aunt Cordelia? He wouldn't have been surprised to see Albert padding into the library on a search for gin.

Instead, Frederick announced the arrival of Graham Seed.

The land agent slunk into the room in sharp contrast to Irene with her hearty stride and took his place at the desk.

Seed suffered a major disadvantage. He was a man. Marcus—the one-time champion of London lovers, the scourge of neglectful husbands, the answer to a hundred maidens' prayers—might have lost the upper hand with women, but he knew how to deal with the hapless male before him.

"Did you know anything about Quirke's attacking girls?" he asked.

Seed twisted his bowler hat in his hands.

"There's been talk," the land agent said.

"And you did nothing?"

"Women lie."

"Jennie is a child."

Seed's thin lips twitched into a smirk. "They grow fast in Sussex, Yer Lordship. If you know what I mean."

Fury boiled within Marcus, erasing his exhaustion. He had to clutch the arms of his chair to keep from bounding over the desk and beating the agent to a pulp.

"Get out," he said.

Seed took a backward step. "I'll be seein' about that plow, Yer Lordship."

"Forget the plow. Get off Stafford land. If I see either you or your friend Quirke in this county, I'll have you both arrested for rape and fraud."

Seed's browless eyes widened in protest. "Rape!" he howled. "I didn't touch none of 'em. Don't like women, ask the blacksmith George—"

He stopped himself, realizing his admission.

"You knew what Quirke was doing, and that's as bad. The way he knew you were stealing."

Seed opened his mouth for another protest.

"If you're not out of here by the time I stand—"

He didn't have to finish. Seed was out the door and gone.

Leaving him alone.

He sat back in his chair while his fury settled into a steady throb of frustration and, worse, a sense of futility that ate at his insides like nothing he'd ever felt. What had he accomplished in his week at Beacon Hall? Farmers stirred against him, his primary help dismissed under threat of arrest, Amy at odds with him as much as she had ever been. Even the aunts stayed in their rooms. With the unfortunate exception of Irene's visit tonight.

Raven Chadwick wasn't the problem here; fault for whatever was going wrong lay with the latest earl.

He thought about the dark-eyed beauty, and for a moment the hollowness in his chest disappeared. God, how he would like to have her here to hold in his arms! Not anything more than that, just to hold and talk to. She had understood about the young shepherd and the poverty of the land, just as he had expected. And she would understand how he felt tonight.

If he asked for her presence, she would suspect his purpose. If he tried to embrace her, she would know she was right. He was a victim of his own past sins. But hadn't he always been?

Strangely, he remembered his boyhood, when he had ridden over the Downs undisciplined, unrestrained, as though he were searching for something he never could find.

He had felt alone then, even when Daniel Lindsay had trailed after him. In his wild days in London, there had been friends enough, but with the changes that had taken place in his life, they had dropped off one by one, saying he wasn't *fun* anymore.

Or maybe he had dropped them. He didn't know for sure, but what difference did it make? They were gone.

When the title of earl fell to him, he had hoped to draw his family together, to have something he'd never had. A sense of belonging somewhere, maybe. Of having permanence in his life.

The hope was dying fast.

His thoughts centered on Raven. In ways he didn't understand, it was the image of her that made him feel warmest and at the same time most alone.

Over the next few days Raven threw herself into work on the farm. It wasn't her business to do so. No one suggested she ought. But she felt like a leech taking her bed and board without paying in return. Amy didn't understand; neither did Irene, although Aunt Cordelia smiled encouragement whenever they met.

So she set about gathering up the infant orphan lambs who were wasting away without their mother's milk, organized a half dozen of the farmers' daughters, and set up a program wherein the animals would be fed.

A new pen was needed behind the stables to replace the broken-down enclosure already there. The sons provided the labor, those not already involved in managing the herds of sheep and cattle and in clearing the fields of thistle and stones.

Conspicuous in her gaudy gowns, she asked Nancy about something more practical to wear. The maid discovered a cotton dress left by a former servant and Raven borrowed an apron from the cook. It wasn't the glamorous costume that she had thought about in her dreams of the stage, but it suited the life she led. Sleeves rolled up in the warming day, she supervised the projects, adding her own efforts when she could.

Morning and evening, as he rode to and from the fields, Marcus passed her. Sometimes she dared to look at him sitting high and magnificent on the gelding, his blue gaze directed to her. He was so close, and yet so far away. She knew that since Seed and Quirke had disappeared, he was busy, too.

Two days after the assault, hours away from the scheduled dinner with Squire Clifton and his daughter, she visited the young girl Jennie once again. Her widowed mother, Clara Murphy, met her at the door.

"She'll not see you," the distraught woman said, wringing her wrinkled hands.

"Give us a few minutes alone. If I find I'm upsetting her, I promise to leave."

"Me late husband weren't nothin' more than a poor cottager. You and His Lordship ha' done more'n enough already."

"The girl's heart-sore, isn't she? Maybe I can help."

Raven stayed with the girl a half hour. When she left, Jennie sent word to her mother she would like to bathe and get dressed.

"What did you say to the lass?" Mrs. Murphy asked as Raven prepared to mount Héloïse in the front yard.

"I told her to quit blaming herself for what happened. That the humiliation was the worst part, and the memories. The body would heal and be good as new."

"But that ain't the truth."

"You mean because she's no longer innocent? She's only twelve. Someday there will be someone who won't care about what happened. Someone who will make her forget. In the meantime, the important thing is that she feel good about herself. I'll ask Miss Bannerman about getting her a new dress. And a pair of shoes. Maybe it sounds unimportant, but she needs to feel pretty."

"You're a wise and a good woman, Miss Chadwick. How'd ye know what t' say?"

"I just knew, that's all. Most of all, she needs to feel loved."

"Jason and me'll provide all that, ye can be sure."

Riding back to Beacon Hall, Raven couldn't shake off the mood that had settled on her at the cottage.

*How'd ye know what t' say?*
*I just did.*

It was a simple answer, but the knowledge had come at a terrible cost.

*Someone will make her forget.*

Raven asked herself if she would ever find that someone. *Never* echoed in her mind. He certainly was not Marcus, who reminded her of the past every time they touched. And yet her hunger for him had not gone away. She was beginning to think it never would.

She thought of Papa and Mama and began to make plans for returning home. Once there she would tell Papa he would have to change his plans about bringing Mama to London. If he insisted, she would say he needed to keep her away from Stafford House. "Be tourists, the way you suggested," she would say. "Visit the museums and the theaters. There's no one left that Mama would want to see."

To Mama she would say the letter had been a hoax. It would involve confessing her original duplicity in reading Mama's mail, but she had always planned to do just that.

To the Bannermans and anyone else who would listen she would declare she and all the Chadwicks would keep an ocean between them and England. There was no longer a need for threats or shoves.

But first she had to get through the dinner at Humble Hall.

She returned to Beacon to find Ralph Pickering had arrived from London, along with two distant cousins of the Bannermans, both of them baronets.

Brian Halstead, Baronet of Pettibone, and Douglas

Roe, Baronet of Rathmoore, two full-grown men hovering around thirty, had the light of boys in their eyes.

Informed of the new arrivals, Margaret Clifton sent word they were naturally included in the invitation. It seemed to Raven that three last-minute guests for dinner, all men with hearty appetites, ought to throw any hostess into a tizzy. The mistress of Humble Hall and would-be Lady Stafford was obviously equal to any challenge.

Raven disliked her all the more.

"Good to be back in the country," Ralph said in the drawing room, where they had gathered before the evening ride. "Away from the cursed fog."

Aunt Cordelia and Aunt Irene, dressed in their customary black, sat on the sofa, the latter pinch-faced, Cordelia flushed as though she'd been tippling again. But Raven had walked her into the room without detecting the familiar odor of juniper. Something else had her flustered. Could it be Uncle Ralph?

It was something to consider, but when Marcus strode into the room dressed in formal black, his shirt a blazing white against his skin, she forgot even her name.

"Sorry if I've kept you waiting, but I've only just come in from the fields a half hour ago."

"Really, Marcus," said Amy, who stood by the fire, "if I didn't know you better, I would think you were actually enjoying hard work."

"Impossible," said Marcus with that tone of self-mockery Raven knew so well. "The farmers and I have secretly arranged for orgies in the woods. I'm surprised you haven't heard the women's squeals of delight."

"Count us in," the baronets said in unison.

"For heaven's sake, Marcus," said Aunt Irene with a shake of her head, "watch what you say. There are ladies present."

"How foolish of me to forget." He turned his eyes on Raven, who sat in a chair opposite the aunts. "Miss Chadwick, you're looking particularly fetching tonight."

Raven wasn't sure she agreed. She wore her scarlet gown with the off-the-shoulder neckline and, for jewelry, her mother's teardrop pearl earrings. Compared to the black clothing of the men and the aunts and Amy's off-white *peau de soie,* she felt embarrassingly bright.

The room fell silent as everyone waited for her response. Over the snap of the fire and the hiss of the gas lamps, she could hear the tick of the clock.

"I decided against the cotton gown and apron." Not a clever reply, she thought, but it was all that came to mind.

"It's of little import," said Marcus with more warmth in his voice than the situation warranted. "You look particularly fetching in that, too."

Again silence. Raven tore her eyes away from Marcus. She glanced at Amy, who stared at her brother in bemusement.

Ralph broke the tension. "I don't know about anyone else, but I'm starved. Isn't it time to depart?"

The question set everyone to bustling. Everyone but Marcus, who was somehow beside her when she donned her cloak. Settling the cloak on her shoulders, giving her the slightest squeeze, he turned to help his aunts.

But not before she felt his breath on her neck.

*Raven,* she told herself with a shiver not entirely unwelcome, *go home on the next ship.*

Cousin Brian and Cousin Douglas had brought their phaetons and horses down from London on the train. Together with the Stafford carriage, driven by the footman Roger Hammond, there were ample accommodations for the short journey.

Somehow Raven ended up sitting beside Marcus with Aunt Cordelia and Uncle Ralph on the facing seat. Marcus suggested the older couple might be more comfortable accompanying Cousin Brian, who rode alone. Cordelia gave him one of her rare admonishing looks and settled firmly beside Ralph.

"You visited the Murphy girl," said Marcus when they were under way.

"I did," Raven said, sensing every breath he took and the heat of his body through the layers of her clothing. Or maybe she just imagined that heat, but it seemed very hot and very real.

"That was kind of you."

She looked up at him. The night was bright with moonlight. She saw his face clearly. No sign of mockery. He looked sincere.

She shrugged and looked away, hiding the yearning that surely must be in her eyes.

"I saw Mrs. Murphy," he continued. "She said you and Jennie had a long talk."

"Not so long."

"The girl was better after you left."

"I'm glad, but she would probably have been better anyway."

"Mrs. Murphy didn't think so. She said her daughter actually smiled. What miracle words did you come up with?"

Raven looked at Aunt Cordelia and Uncle Ralph, hoping they would join the conversation, but they seemed lost to their own thoughts. Musing, she suspected, about the afternoon's encounter with Albert in which the newly arrived Ralph had rescued the cornered Cordelia from the potting shed.

Raven sighed. As usual, she would have to handle Marcus on her own.

"I told Mrs. Murphy about Abélard's emasculation," she lied. "I told her that's what sometimes happens to men when they go too far."

Marcus flinched. "I'll have to remember your attitude, Songbird." He found her hand in her lap and held on. "The next time we're alone," he added, so softly she could barely hear over the creak of the carriage, "we'll investigate the boundaries of just where too far is for us."

As he spoke, his eyes drifted across her face, down the slope of her neck and shoulders, to the cloak covering her rounded flesh. Her skin burned beneath the wool, and she wanted his hands to follow the path of his eyes.

She felt a rush of desire that took her breath away.

If they were alone . . . she shuddered to think what she would do.

*The next ship,* she reminded herself as they rocked along through the night. *The very next ship.*

# Seventeen

Wearing a pink, ruffled gown that emphasized her porcelain femininity and her big breasts, Margaret Clifton greeted them at the drawing room door of Humble Hall.

Cousin Brian and Cousin Douglas ogled her openly as they were introduced. Uncle Ralph was more discreet, but he, too, took note of the woman's charms. Raven refused to look away from the three men, but she was certain Marcus, walking in last, followed the example of Ralph.

The room was a clutter of Victoriana: enough upholstered furniture for a plantation, antimacassars on every chair and sofa, darkly floral wallpaper against which hung a hundred prints and paintings, a pair of ornate chests flanking the fireplace, in one far corner an ormolu and gilt-decorated desk, and in another a scarf-covered piano in front of a silk Chinese screen.

Throughout the long, wide room not a table or chair leg went uncarved and no lampshade went unfringed. After the cool simplicity of the outdoors, she had difficulty drawing a breath. She suspected the decor had been like this when Marcus's parents were alive. No wonder he had chosen to ride the Downs.

"We've a surprise for you, Amy," said Margaret. "And

you, too, Marcus," she said, taking his arm, her left breast nestling into the crook of his elbow. She nodded to the far window, where Daniel Lindsay stood, looking as handsome and pleasant as ever in his evening clothes.

"Good God," said Cousin Brian. "Can it be Danny? Haven't seen him since when, '73?"

Cousin Douglas nodded. "It looks as though India did all right by the boy. We'll have to talk."

"Watch them, Daniel," said Marcus with a laugh. "They're touting some investments that'll send you to debtor's prison if you're not careful."

Daniel smiled. "Thanks for the warning." He strode toward the arriving party, a smile on his face.

"Cousin Marcus," said Brian, a hand thrown dramatically against his heart, "you wound me. Diamond mines in Pretoria are no risk a'tall."

"Diamonds, is it?" said Daniel. "Double thanks, old friend." He looked at Raven. "Good evening, Miss Chadwick. You're looking as lovely as ever."

And then he looked at Amy, who stood motionless at her brother's side. Suddenly the air crackled with tension.

"Hello, Amy," said Daniel, the light in his eyes dying.

A lost look flashed across the young woman's face so fleetingly Raven barely caught it. Then it was back to brittle impudence.

Lifting the skirt of her milk-colored gown, she curtsied prettily. "And am I not as lovely as ever?" she asked with a laugh. Bannerman mockery edged her words.

Daniel gazed upon the swirl of golden curls that outlined her features, then locked his eyes with hers. "You know you are."

"By all means you must tell me, sir. We women are fragile creatures and must constantly be reassured."

Like thunder, Squire Clifton's voice boomed into the hard-edged banter. "We're a handsome bunch, no doubt. Let's pop the champagne cork to celebrate."

"Hear, hear," said Uncle Ralph. "Splendid idea."

"What brings you to Sussex, Daniel?" Marcus asked during the pouring of the wine.

"The family land. I sold it, you recall, to pay my way to India. In memory of my parents, I hope to buy it back."

His eyes flitted for a moment to Amy. "And, too, I've always had a fondness for the Downs."

"Some people," she said, "have changeable tastes."

The squire was about to propose a toast when the final guest arrived, a slight man past his youth, plain featured but with a gentle and kindly countenance.

"Ah, vicar, do come in," said the squire. "Marcus, Miss Bannerman, you both know the Reverend Timothy Puddyfat."

"Of course," said Marcus.

The men shook hands, and Margaret introduced the others in the room. She ended with Raven. "Miss Chadwick is most interesting. An actress. She's actually performed on the London stage." Her eyes trailed over Raven's fiery gown. "As a nun, I believe."

"Ah, that is most interesting," the minister said with a noncritical nod.

"She's visiting from the colonies. Her father's in trade." She smiled at Raven. "Runs a draper's shop, is that not so?"

She made it sound as though he fenced stolen goods.

Raven's eyes narrowed and her temper rose. No one made slurring remarks about Thomas Chadwick. No one.

"Papa owns a dry goods store," she said with pride and, with more than a little elaboration, she added, "He's a highly respected member of the community, Reverend Puddyfat. You have to understand in my country we have a different view of making one's own way. We consider it quite honorable."

"As well you should," said the vicar, who went on to apologize for the lateness of his arrival.

"Trouble with one of the parishioners, I'm afraid," he said. "Or rather, with the woman's children."

"Anything we can help with?" asked Marcus.

"Oh, no. She wants to keep her son in school and put the daughter to work. I'm trying to convince her the girl needs to know her letters, too."

He looked around the room as if apologizing for the interjection of a somber subject. His gaze settled on Amy.

"Miss Bannerman—"

A sharp shake of Amy's head cut him off. "Reverend Puddyfat," she said, "I'm sure you can manage the situation with your usual tact and warmth."

The squire toasted the earl's return to Beacon Hall, and Raven found herself beside the baronets.

"About those diamonds," said Brian.

"Don't bother," she said. "I've neither an American dollar nor British pound to invest."

"Don't matter," said Douglas. "We need to practice our touting skills."

Raven nodded as they talked, but she was more clearly aware of the two people who stood by the piano. Marcus and Margaret, both fair-haired and British to their no doubt neatly trimmed toenails. Even their names matched. Perhaps the Reverend Puddyfat should join them to discuss the posting of the banns. Lord and Lady Stafford. The titles fairly rolled off the tongue.

And sickened the stomach, if one thought about them for long. She forced her attention to her companions, who were attempting to entertain her with tales of the Transvaal. She knew little about South Africa, and the baronets could add nothing that was not speculation.

"Marcus says Aunt Irene is splendid with geography," said Douglas. He waved his glass toward where she sat beside Cordelia, finally catching her eye.

"I say, do tell us the capital of South Africa." The baronet's voice carried over all others in the room. "Brian and I have a bet on."

Irene started, visibly unnerved.

"Foolish subject," she snapped. Something in her voice drew the attention of everyone but Margaret.

"Come now, Irene," said Ralph. "Don't be shy."

She feels trapped, thought Raven, remembering a possum Papa had caught in the woods. The same look had been in the animal's eyes.

"Does no one know the answer?" Irene was met with silence. "Well, then, Cairo," she said, then went back to her conversation with Cordelia.

Squire Clifton laughed, but he laughed alone. Clearing his throat, he concentrated on pouring another glass of wine.

"Funny," said Brian, "we rather thought it was Cape Town or Pretoria."

Raven's eyes found Marcus, who looked at her in puzzlement, his thoughts communicated across the room.

Cairo, the capital of South Africa? Irene couldn't have been more wrong if she'd said Liverpool. The mistake was all the more ludicrous given the popularity of Egypt since the completion of the Suez.

What could possibly be in the geography books the woman supposedly read?

At the dinner table, with Raven and Marcus placed at opposite corners, the subject of schooling came up again.

"The economy being what it is," said the vicar with a shake of his head, "there are fewer of our children receiving even the rudiments of an education. Beatrice—"

He looked at Raven. "My sister, who was unable to attend this evening. Beatrice serves as our Ditchling teacher, but she's most disturbed at this recent downward trend."

"It's a trend that can be reversed," said Marcus. He glanced past the candles and the cutlery and the other guests to Raven. She knew he was remembering when they'd stopped by the young shepherd on the day of their eventful ride.

To Raven's regret, Margaret did not miss the sympathetic look. Her stare made up in coolness for all the warmth in Marcus's eyes.

"I don't see how you can get 'em in the classroom," said Clifton. "The vicar's right about the economy. Folk want the pennies their brats bring in."

"They're dependent upon the pennies for food," Marcus said. "Why not pay them to send their children to school?"

Clifton's bushy gray eyebrows lifted to his thin gray hair. "Pay them?"

"I've done some calculating. It would cost little. I

might even give them a raise over what they make pulling weeds and stones, and it's still affordable."

"An interesting idea," the vicar said.

"Revolutionary, that's what it is," the squire growled. "Damned fool idea. You'll be stirring 'em up until they don't know their place."

"Papa," said Margaret in a fluttery voice, "would you like some more wine?"

But Papa wasn't listening to her attempt at peacemaking. "Damned fool idea," he repeated. "Who'll do their work?"

"Youths and men with backs strong enough for it."

"The London fog's pickled your brains."

Marcus ignored the insult. "Education will help them do a better job. They'll learn there's much in the world to experience. And the way to get to it is to find methods for improving their work."

How determined he looks, thought Raven, and how selfless. He made her proud. A fist tightened around her heart. She considered hurrying to his side and rewarding his kindness with a kiss . . . a kiss as generous as he was being. A long, wet kiss with maybe a touching of tongues.

Her cheeks stung, and she stared at her plate of lamb. She must be losing her mind.

Several times during the course of the meal she caught Marcus looking at her. He definitely wasn't thinking about schools. Margaret didn't miss a glance. Once or twice Raven caught a hint of the rage she had seen at the hut. The woman had a temper, she suspected, that was difficult to control.

Without appetite, Raven concentrated on the wine. Her

composure did not improve when they returned to the drawing room for brandy. This time it wasn't Marcus or her shameful musings that disturbed her. It was the anger in her hostess's eye, an anger she alone seemed to detect.

She looked around the garish room . . . at the aunts with Ralph seated awkwardly between them, at Amy and Daniel trying studiously to avoid one another though they chose to stand side by side, at the baronets again ogling Margaret, this time more discreetly, and at the squire and Marcus discussing the various fertilizers for sale.

In contrast to the gaudiness, it was a room of black and white and a touch of pink, and all of it very genteel, the flare-up at dinner evidently forgotten by all but her.

She looked at herself. Crimson-clad and tawny-skinned Raven with her actress ambitions and her tradesman father and her too-passionate heart simply did not belong.

She finished her glass of brandy and accepted another from the squire.

No, she definitely did not belong.

Lightheaded, she sank into a chair with cupids carved into the arms and tried to make herself inconspicuous.

Margaret passed in a blur and whisked the scarf from the piano.

"Miss Chadwick, please entertain us with a song."

Raven blinked in her direction. "I couldn't."

"Nonsense. We'll not have shyness. It doesn't suit you."

"Margaret—" Marcus began.

Margaret smiled across the room at him. "Surely she's not too modest. After all, she's sung upon the stage." Her smile at Raven took on a more ominous cast. "Please. You'll disappoint us if you don't."

Raven looked from face to face. She made out few details, but as best she could tell all were nodding encouragement.

Except Marcus. Seeing past her pretenses the way he so often did, he must have sensed her reluctance. No, her terror. She was close to inebriated and she was certain Margaret was laying a trap.

The object of her suspicions strode over, took her by the arm, and lifted her to her feet. For a diminutive woman, Margaret had the strength of a mule.

"Good show," said the squire. Raven didn't know whether he meant his daughter or her.

Short of wrestling her way to freedom, there was little she could do but let herself be guided to the piano bench. Flexing her fingers, she sat and stared at the keys. Black and white. Like the men in the room. Which should she play?

Marcus.

She almost giggled. That last glass of brandy had been a mistake.

She started with Mozart, but oh, the beast required so many notes. Something simpler seemed in order. A devilish thought occurred. Margaret had openly hinted about her music hall career. Why not demonstrate how it had gone? Without the feathers, of course, and with a decidedly different end.

Her fingers tinkled out the simple melody. She looked up to find herself staring at Marcus, so close she almost gave a yelp. When had the rascal crossed the room?

Never mind. Ignoring the warning light in his eyes, she launched into song:

*He flies through the air with the greatest of ease . . .*

She completed the chorus with a few trills to show she could do it, then, unable to remember the verse, started in again on what she knew. Halfway through, the baronets joined her, and together they gave the song a third go.

She would have gone for a fourth but Marcus closed the piano, almost catching her fingers.

Cousin Brian howled a protest, but one look from Marcus shut him up. The room reeled around Raven. She feared falling off the bench. Strong hands helped her to stand. She focused on a pair of very blue and very solemn eyes.

"Not feeling well, are you?" a deep, sure voice said.

"No," she managed, telling the truth.

She was vaguely aware of his maneuvering her through the drawing room door, into her cloak, and out to one of the phaetons.

The footman Hammond, waiting by the Stafford carriage, cast a leer in her direction that she could neither miss nor misinterpret, even in her discombobulated state. Marcus gave her no time to react.

Sitting beside him in the close quarters, she knew something besides the footman had gone wrong.

"Mama would not be pleased," she said with a hiccough. "I should have said goodbye."

"You did."

"Oh."

With a snap of the reins, Marcus sent the phaeton skimming along the lane. Raven settled back in the plush leather seat and let the movement rock her. The top was up, but there was ample fresh air to whisk away the cobwebs in her brain. Most of them, at least.

The wind whipped at her hair, pulling several tendrils loose from her carefully arranged coiffure. She tried to pin them back.

"Leave it," Marcus said. Then, "Are you going to be sick?"

"No."

They rode in silence, each quarter mile drawing her closer to Beacon Hall, to sobriety, and, inevitably, to regret.

"I'm sorry if I embarrassed you," she said as they neared the lane leading to the house.

She could have sworn he laughed.

Anger replaced humiliation. She made a valiant if awkward attempt to draw away from him in righteous indignation, but the rocking conveyance threw her back against his side.

"Did I appear so foolish? Scandalous, I would have thought."

"Why does that worry you?"

"Because—"

She couldn't come up with an answer that she was willing to tell him. In truth, as she gazed out at the passing landscape bathed in silver light, she couldn't come up with anything that made much sense. She knew only that she wasn't ready to seclude herself in a dark and lonely room.

"The night air feels wonderful. Could we ride for a while longer?" she asked.

"Of course."

He cracked the whip over the horse's flanks, flying past the turn-off, not slowing until they were well down the road.

In the dark, with her head clearing, she felt a need for honesty.

"I didn't belong back there."

"If you didn't, it's understandable. We English are a hypocritical bunch in the country as well as the city. Polite, even as we slice each other with words."

He glanced at her, and she felt a rush of warmth that erased the night chill.

"You're quick to act on how you feel," he said. "There's no disgrace in that. You were forced into singing, so you chose a song that put you back in control."

"Don't make fun of me. I hope never to hear the word *trapeze* again."

He grinned. "A pity. Everyone was enjoying the music. Except for our host and hostess and our curious geographer Aunt Irene. Even Puddyfat was tapping his toes. The only reason I ended the performance was a fear you might be sick."

"You're not making me feel any better."

"Then I need to try harder."

He brought the phaeton to a gradual stop, guiding the horse into a copse of trees off the road. The seclusion wrapped about Raven as warmly as a Marcus embrace.

Drops of moonlight fell on them both through the window. He secured the reins and turned to face her. The lean lines of his face appeared stark in the shadowy light, and his eyes a feral blue. She could not draw a breath.

"Listen to me, Raven. You didn't embarrass me in the least. You were magnificent."

Everything was changing so fast, she thought. From the shame of the parlor to the dizziness of the ride . . . to this, a crystal-speckled night where she and Marcus were alone.

Her fingers tingled to touch his cheeks, his lips. Her heart thundered in her breast.

"Marcus—"

"And if my bratty cousins had got much closer to you, I would have been the one to be disgraced."

"I don't understand."

"Neither do I. But I was ready to punch them out. Jealousy, I believe it's called. I never felt it before."

His voice held a faint teasing quality that both frightened and intrigued.

"Don't lie to me," she said with a tremor. "Not tonight."

"Is there something special about tonight?"

"Maybe," she whispered, afraid to consider the possibilities, yet unable to deny their existence.

He took her hand. "You're not like any woman I've ever met. Surely you know that."

The warmth of his hand sent hot blood coursing through her veins.

"You're not afraid to roll up your sleeves and get to work."

Disappointment stabbed her, and she tried to tug away. "It comes from being a tradesman's daughter."

He held on tight. "It comes from being special. The work you've done with the children, the progress you've helped the estate make in a short while—"

"—could have been started by a decent bailiff." For some reason she felt close to tears.

"Hush." He brought her hand to his lips. "You're different, my lovely Songbird, and that's the truth. Different in all the good ways."

*All the good ways.*

The words applied to him far more than to her. She did what she was raised to do. The Earl of Stafford went against his upbringing, throwing himself into labor, worrying about the people under his care. So many elements went into the character of Marcus, not the least of them the way he made her feel. Whether they were together or apart, he made her heart sing and her spirit soar.

When he looked at her, Raven knew she was in love. Foolishly, hopelessly, completely. She closed her eyes for a moment, lest he read her feelings. But what difference did it make? She loved him, and his scorn or pleasure would do nothing to alter that fact.

The knowledge proved headier than brandy, and far more exhilarating.

She opened her eyes and smiled.

"I'm not different, Marcus. Women want you. I've seen the looks they give you. And it's not just your title, no matter what you think. The talk of schools and children was as wonderful an outpouring of ideas and sympathy as I have ever heard. You were noble. I wanted to jump over the table and show you how it made me feel."

"You're drunk." His voice was husky.

"Not anymore. I remember clearly everything you said tonight. Including how far we would go if we were alone."

He rubbed the tips of her fingers against his lips. She tingled down to her toes.

"Nobility as a technique for seduction," he said with his usual wryness. "I've never used it before."

"Quit denigrating yourself. In case you weren't listening close enough, I just confessed that like every other woman in the world, I want you."

"Raven," he whispered, "do you realize what you've said?"

"I realize—"

He pulled her against him and swallowed her words with a kiss. The heat and the sweetness and the insistence of his lips overwhelmed her and she gave herself to his embrace.

The kiss was long and thorough, eventually involving both their tongues. He thrust his hands into her hair, and the pins fell as easily as her resistance. She was all aches and fire and hunger. He trembled against her. Every part of her body trembled in return.

She was without shame. Marcus and the night consumed her. Marcus, her first and only love. She clutched his sleeves, wanting to be a part of him, needing his lips and his hands to possess her completely.

*Stop,* the Raven of old cried from somewhere inside her, but she ruthlessly stilled the voice. There was no pulling back now. Nothing about Marcus threatened her, except perhaps her sanity. Desire drove her mad.

She loved him. The feeling was too new, too fragile to declare, but she could tell him in other ways.

Images of them locked together seared her mind, vague because there was so much about lovemaking she did not know.

The time for learning was now. The realization was now. The love was now. Her passion had no link with death. No suffocating mist enfolded her. This was life. Glorious, beautiful life, offering itself not in a cloud-soft bed with perfumed sheets, but in a cramped carriage on a tufted leather seat.

But when, she asked herself, had her longings ever been ordinary?

She threw herself into his embrace with the same fierceness of heart that once had driven her to run from love. Afraid to wait, afraid of a thousand circumstances that might drive them apart.

If Marcus truly wanted her, tonight she would be his.

# *Eighteen*

Raven flooded Marcus's senses. In his arms, her breath on his cheek, her words blazing in his mind, she was like a caged bird suddenly set free. He lost his last hold on control. It took the strength of wild winds to pull himself from her embrace and exit the phaeton long enough to secure the horse. Then he was back again, holding her hot fragility against his thundering heart.

Damn him for a rake, but he knew he would have her. Tonight.

He cupped her face and stared into the infinite depths of her eyes, fearful he would see evidence that in the brief seconds of their parting she had changed her mind. He wondered, too, if it would make a difference.

No matter. He saw erotic depths that sucked him like the tide into her passion. He kissed her eyes, sealing her hunger inside her as he opened her cloak and stroked her throat with his thumbs.

He licked her lips. She moaned.

"Raven," he whispered. "A wild, dark creature. Flutter your wings against me. I will possess you as you already possess me."

"Whatever you say. Whatever you want."

The carriage creaked and somewhere in the dark a

night bird sang an earthy song, remindful of where they were and what they were about to do.

"This is madness." He kissed her throat, her neck, her ear. "Sweet, sweet madness."

"I know," she said, tangling her hands in his hair.

He thrust her cloak from her shoulders and rubbed a palm across the swell of her breasts.

She flicked the front fastening of her gown and parted the red silk, offering herself to him.

"Look at me," she whispered, a gentle, fervent order. "Kiss me."

She was a woman he did not know, yet she was the same woman he'd wanted to hold in his arms like this, hold and savor with all the ardor that was his to share. Incredibly, she wanted the same. He would have said the moment belonged to his imaginings, but she felt gloriously real, soft and warm and willing, her urgency firing his.

He freed one breast from its camisole covering and took its crest between his teeth. The tautness was a small, hot counterpart to the engorged shaft he wanted to thrust inside her, again and again until they both were sated.

Impossible, he thought. He could never get enough of her.

"Don't stop," she said, her voice a rasp. "Don't ever, ever stop."

"You like it."

"I like it. You've always known I would." A small cry escaped her throat. "I talk too much."

"No. Nothing you do is wrong."

She bared her other breast. He licked the tip, then drew

it between his lips, embracing her so that he could feel every shift of her body as she writhed against his mouth.

Her hands groped beneath his coat, kneading his shirt, finding with electrifying accuracy his own nipples. He thought he would explode.

He kissed his way to her lips. "This is too fast," he said, torment thick in his voice.

"I want it faster."

"It's awkward. We should be in bed."

"No," she said, the word almost a cry. "You'll know what to do."

He stroked her hair, her throat, the subtle slope of her shoulders. "I want you cushioned beneath me, Raven. Naked, every part of you pressed to every part of me."

"It doesn't matter." She kissed him long and deep, dancing her tongue against his before she eased away. Again the night bird sang. Her eyes blazed with the wildness of her rapture. "I'm not fearful of awkwardness. I trust you'll know what to do."

Marcus gazed in fiery wonder at her, at her swollen, parted lips, at her tangle of hair, at the rise and fall of her breasts as she drew in ragged breaths. She was wanton beyond his wildest dreams, yet she fulfilled all the promise of their earlier kisses and their maddeningly brief moments in the hut.

He had been months without a woman, but it was of little consequence. He had been a lifetime without Raven, and that mattered most of all.

*You'll know what to do.* He did. Oh, God, how he did.

"Open your shirt," she said.

He managed a smile. "I thought I was in control."

"You are. I can't handle the buttons. Help me."

He did as she asked, fumbling like a youth with the milkmaid in the barn, anticipation jumbling his nerves and his mind. She made him feel young and worldly at the same time, but mostly she made him feel hot.

She kissed his chest. "You're hairy," she said. His muscles twitched under the tickle of her breath.

"You don't like it?"

"I like it," she said, kissing him again. "Nothing about you is wrong."

Her hand fell to his thigh. He jerked under the exquisite torture.

"I'll not last much longer," he said huskily.

"Good."

He heard the desperate hunger in the word. He quit worrying about the manner in which they would couple and did what came naturally, kissing her deeply, tasting the dark honey inside her. This was no time for gentleness, for the careful approach. With Raven he could not plan, could not think. He could do no more than rejoice in the spiraling pleasures she brought him and rejoice equally in the pleasures he was bringing her.

The top of her dress was open, but there was no time to undress her more, to touch and kiss all the treasures promised by her dark-tipped breasts. The rustle of silk was music in the night as he eased her skirt to her waist, and then her petticoat. She lifted her body so that he could remove her remaining underclothes. Except for her stockings. He stroked the satin flesh above her garters, his fingers trailing to the inside of her thighs, exploring the textures of her, everything whispery warm and slick.

Her hand tightened against his leg and copied his movements, shifting with taunting slowness toward his throbbing shaft. Exquisite pain shot through him as he fought to hold back the threatened eruptions.

He remembered how she had felt before . . . the thick triangle of hair between her legs, the wet pulsing nub, the flexing motions of her hips and thighs. He wanted all of her pressed against him, enfolding him, sharing the ultimate pleasures that flesh was heir to, at once a weakness and a strength.

He drew back to watch her face in the moonlight as he touched her. Eyes closed, breath ragged between her parted lips, cheeks flushed with the heat of her hunger, she was the most beautiful woman in the world.

And she was his. She pulsed against his palm, at the same time her hand on his leg reached higher. She brushed against the full sacs, and at last she rubbed against his sex. Her fingers trembled, as though in innocence, but she did not stop touching him.

He wanted it harder, rougher. Control was a thin, vibrating wire that could not endure the tension. He had to have her. Now.

He gave her one last thorough massage, then moved his hand from between her legs. He felt her eyes on him in wonder. Unfastening his trousers, he freed himself. He watched her watching him. Her gasp was unmistakable. He hoped he pleased her. She must know how she pleased him.

"Ride me," he whispered.

Her eyes flew to his. "What?"

"Ride me. It's the only way."

"Oh," she said in a small voice. "I hadn't thought—"

She broke off, as though what she wanted to say was

too intimate to share. But they were sharing the ultimate intimacy. They had gone too far to stop.

He helped her to mount him, her thighs pressed provocatively to the sides of his legs, the thickness of his trousers a maddening barrier to the touching of their flesh. Again the silk rustled its own special melody. She held herself above him with tremulous caution, like a maiden, and he wanted her all the more.

He touched her wetness with his shaft, rubbing back and forth while her head fell back in wanton abandon, her hands clutching frantically at his coat. Her thighs, bearing her weight against the leather seat, trembled. She wanted more. He would give her what she craved.

He found the valley he so eagerly sought. He met with resistance, but that made no sense.

He hesitated. She raised her head and looked at him. "Raven—"

He tried again. Still the resistance.

"My God," he said, struck by the impossible truth.

With a small cry she thrust herself upon him, taking the full length of his sex into her tight heat.

His mind reeled with a thousand sensations. He was the first. He couldn't be.

He had hurt her. He couldn't stop.

She wrapped her arms around him and whispered, "It's all right. Make me feel good again, Marcus. Take away the pain."

He struggled for the strength to pull away, but he was too far gone for thought to rule his actions. He tried to keep the drives shallow, tried and failed. He thrust a hand between them, fingers striving to revive her pleasure as she had asked. After a moment of suspended time, the thrust of her hips told him he had not failed.

She shattered against him. Within an instant he soared with her into the sweet savage splendor of completion, pumping himself into her and holding her tight. He wanted to embrace her forever, to hold and protect her, this wild and delicate woman, this innocent, this wanton. This Raven.

Oh, yes, how he wanted to protect her, but that was foolish. She needed protecting from only him.

Neither spoke. In all his experiences with women, Marcus had never been at a loss of words. Not at a time like this.

But there had never been a time like this. His first virgin, and he her first man. Taking her roughly, crudely, assuming that's the way she wanted it, the way she'd had it before.

But she hadn't. Not in any way. Until she had drunk too much wine and considered herself in disgrace.

*Ride me,* he had said, the way he might to a whore. He hadn't meant it that way. She was special and giving, and he had wanted to be inside her. The signs of her innocence were there, but he had thought of nothing beside his wants.

The horse snorted and stamped in the dark, as though he scorned his master the way his master scorned himself.

He was embarrassed. Raven held herself very still. He's too embarrassed to speak. Over her virginity or her eagerness, she didn't know which. Probably both.

She hadn't thought about the afterwards, just the during. So what was she supposed to do now?

She clung to him, wanting to hold on forever, at the same time wishing that in an instant she could be alone in her room.

Marcus stroked her hair from her face, as he might a child's. The gesture seemed ludicrous—her bare breasts were against his rumpled shirt, her legs spread on either side of him, their private parts wetly pressed together. She still loved him but he didn't know it; she was sore as the devil, and the horse had shown poor timing by impatiently jerking at the reins.

Above all else and beyond reason, she felt the afterglow of their lovemaking . . . or their sex or coupling, or whatever it should be called. She didn't know much of anything anymore except that she loved Marcus Bannerman and needed to be alone to consider what next to do about it.

Since the realization had hit her, she had made one dramatic but not necessarily wise decision. She didn't regret it, but the time had come to be smart.

Marcus removed a part of her discomfort by easing her to the seat beside him and smoothing her petticoat and gown over her legs. He discounted the good deed, however, by thrusting a handkerchief into her hand.

"You might want this," he said.

To wipe away the tears that threatened despite her attempts not to cry? She flushed with embarrassment when she realized he meant other places that were damp.

Rumpling the linen between her fingers, trying to ignore the way he was getting his own clothing back in order, she stared at the white underdrawers lying in a heap at her feet. Somehow she had to get them back on.

"Could I have a moment's privacy?"

"Of course." He eased from the carriage and stood with his back to her while he stroked the horse's neck.

Clothes back in place, including the tightly closed cloak, hair pinned without thought to style, she told him she was done.

He stood outside the carriage, arms resting on the window. His hair was mussed, his eyes solemn, his shirt collar a disaster. He looked wonderful.

She stared at the handkerchief.

"Are you all right?" he asked.

Why couldn't he have said she looked beautiful? It wasn't the truth, but he could have said it.

"Nothing's broken, if that's what you mean." Which wasn't, strictly speaking, the truth. He had torn something inside her when she had rashly impaled herself on him.

He choked on an utterance she was glad not to understand. "I didn't know. You should have told me."

Her heart twisted cruelly. She really did feel close to tears.

"I had hoped you would know."

He didn't respond except to stand looking at her as though—if he did so long enough—he would figure her out.

"If I'm not being particularly fair or making this easy for you, forgive me." She concentrated on the horse's rump. "My eagerness"—she had to force the word—"led you to an unfortunate misconception."

"You were wonderful."

Too little, too late. She smiled brightly at him, hoping he would take the glint in her eyes for something other than unshed tears.

"I thought perhaps I was."

He wasn't fooled by her bravado. In a flash he was in the carriage, his hands on her shoulders, his gaze staring through any pretense she might attempt.

"You were wonderful," he repeated. "You *are* wonderful."

"This isn't necessary. I knew what I was doing. And I'd do it again. How about that for being without morals?"

"Amy thought something had happened to you."

Suddenly her blood ran cold. "Happened?"

"Yes. That maybe you'd been hurt at some time, assaulted—"

"Raped?" The word came out a whisper. She wanted to shrink from him, to run and hide.

"Maybe. That could be why you never planned to marry. And then tonight—"

She found the courage to interrupt. "I was making a valiant effort to try it under different circumstances? Therapy, of sorts. If a horse throws you, get back on."

"That's not what I meant."

"Then here's a different scenario, one you've certainly considered. I'm a promiscuous actress, pardon the redundancy. I've pretended to modesty these past weeks. Except when you kissed me and my true nature came forth."

The stricken look on his face told her she'd come upon the truth.

"You were wrong," she said.

"I was wrong," he said, touching her lips.

She sighed, and all her spirit disappeared. There was so much she could tell him, things only Papa knew. And she would have revealed it all to him . . . if she'd thought he loved her in return.

Weariness settled over her. "Enough," she said, pulling away from him. "Take me home."

But home was an ocean away.

"Take me to Beacon Hall."

She saw he wanted to say more, but she stared into the night and at last he got out to free the horse. Clouds blocked the moon, and the stars had faded. She welcomed the darkness. So much to think about. So much.

With the scent of their lovemaking hanging in the air between them and the feel of him still intimately sharp inside her, thinking was very hard to do. Perhaps once she'd discarded her ruined clothes and washed . . .

Perhaps.

They arrived at the stables to find the carriage and second phaeton already unhitched for the night.

"We'll go up the back stairs," he said, helping her alight. Like thieves, she thought, or simply lovers who had something to hide.

She prayed no one would see them, but the disasters of the evening continued even to the early morning hours when they passed Hammond on the stairs. No one spoke, and she wondered who looked guiltier, she or the footman. What had he been doing on the upper floor?

It wasn't her problem. She managed to get into her room without saying another word, past a quick, hard bathing, and through the hours until dawn without a wink of sleep. At the first sign of light, she dressed and hurried down the back stairs to the stable.

Saddling Héloise, she took off on a private ride, desperate to put as much space as she could between herself and the man she loved. Even Albert decided against bounding after her.

The morning was particularly cruel with its cool sunshine. She was more in the mood for storms. Questions besieged her, the main one being how soon could she bring herself to leave.

Without thinking, she guided the mare toward the stream that ran through the Stafford land, toward a particular copse of trees, toward a particular hut. She was already under the shade of early spring leaves when she felt the saddle give way.

She gasped and pulled back on the reins, but there was nothing she could do to keep herself from falling. She struck the ground hard, the saddle landing on top of her, and her last coherent thought was to wonder why she saw stars on such a brilliant day.

# *Nineteen*

Marcus didn't worry when he found the mare gone from the stable. The morning was clear. Raven had taken a ride.

He didn't worry until Héloise came trotting down the lane toward the stable, without saddle or rider, reins trailing uselessly in the dirt.

The sound brought Jason running to the yard. "Where's Miss Chadwick?"

"I don't know." Marcus whistled for Albert. "Did you see her, boy?"

The bloodhound panted expectantly, brown eyes eager for a hunt.

Marcus looked at the sky. The sun rose not far above the horizon. Unless she rode out before dawn, she couldn't have been gone more than an hour.

A great deal could happen in that time.

He made quick work of saddling the gelding, then pulled out a handkerchief thrust into his hands in a darkened hallway only hours ago. He waved it under the bloodhound's quivering nose. "Go find her, boy. Find Raven."

One bark and the hound was loping down the lane, the gelding close behind.

"Should I get help?" Jason yelled, but Marcus waved him away. He and Albert would find Raven. They had no choice.

With few side trips the dog guided him to the copse of trees by the gamekeeper's hut, then ran on ahead into the brush.

Marcus shuddered over what the shadows might reveal. Images of her flashed through his mind, of hair black as storm clouds billowing around her face as she leaned down to kiss him in the carriage, of her lips wet and ripe, of her spirited eyes daring him to denial. And of her slender body lying in the shadows, eyes closed, breath stilled—

He broke off the images and reined the horse through the trees.

"Albert," a woman's voice said loud and clear, "get away."

Marcus sighed in relief. Actually smiled. Then felt the bite of irritation. She had frightened him out of his mind. She had the nerve to be all right.

Dismounting, he tethered Abélard, then walked quietly through the grass. The sidesaddle and blanket lay in a heap under the trees. He bent for an inspection, then stood and looked toward the sound of her voice as she continued to scold the dog.

A cold rage shivered through him. He needed to see her, touch her, know beyond doubt she was well.

He found her kneeling beside the stream, sleeves rolled to her elbows, jacket in the grass at her side. Her hair was half pinned and she was holding a wet cloth to the back of her head. Albert sat close to her water-stained

riding skirt, his tongue lolling as he took her chastise-
ment with regal tolerance.

She, too, had a regal quality about her in the way she
held her head and in the grace of her movements. Regal
and fragile, that was Raven. Marcus looked at her a long
time before he moved to let her know he was there.

She started when she saw him. "You frightened me."

"I didn't mean to. Are you all right?"

She flinched, as though he had said something wrong,
and he remembered he'd asked her the same question a
few hours ago.

"Nothing's broken," she said. He would have smiled
at the same rejoinder, only there was nothing humorous
in what was going on.

He wanted to rush forward and take her in his arms.
A warning in her dark, hollowed eyes held him back.

"I fell off the horse. Didn't pull the cinch tight, I
guess. It's never happened to me before."

She squeezed the cloth into the stream, gave it a shake,
and slowly stood. She swayed once, then found her balance, and Marcus continued to hold back. He hadn't
known he was so strong.

She walked toward him, rolling down her sleeves, fin-
gering a wisp of hair from her eye, stopping more than
an arm's distance away. The sun shone full on her face,
its rays catching in the ebony waves of her hair. Her
cheek was smudged, her clothes wrinkled and wet, but
she showed no sign of injury.

"Really, Marcus, I'm perfectly all right."

She waved a trembling hand. He wasn't fooled by her
bravado. She had taken a bad fall. She was still shaken.

He shared the feeling.

Around them, the forest thrummed with the noises of nature, insects and birds chirping with the insistence of spring, a breeze whispering in the leaves. Something splashed in the water, and Albert's shaggy tail slapped against the grass.

Only the humans were silent.

"I'd like to touch you," he said at last.

She swallowed. "I'm not sure that's wise."

"Still—"

He didn't wait for a stronger denial. When he eased her into a gentle embrace, she did not push him away. For just a moment, she rested her head upon his chest.

"Let's go to the hut."

She stiffened.

"Have you looked inside?" he asked.

"No."

"You'll be surprised."

She slipped from his arms and her eyes met his. "Surprise is the major ingredient of my life lately."

"Mine, too." He stepped close. "Indulge me," he said as he swept her into his arms and marched through the trees and brush toward the hut. She stiffened again, then with a sigh gave up her protest and fell lax against him.

He set her down by the open door. She stared at the clean walls and floor, the new table and chair, the curtain on the window, the quilt-covered bed. A stack of firewood rested beside the clean grate, and there was even a cotton rug on the floor.

Her sideways glance contained the questions he'd expected.

"I've been working on it over the past week. In case it could be used for what it was originally intended. And don't give me that look, Raven. I meant for a game-keeper."

He knelt at the hearth and began stacking wood over the grate. "Besides, it was something I could work on and finish." He looked over his shoulder at her. "Everything else I turn a hand to seems incomplete."

"Everything? Including me?"

Her directness surprised him, although he should have been used to it by now. He didn't answer until after he had started the fire. With the thin flames crackling and struggling for life, he stood to face her.

"Including us."

She looked so pale, so fragile, robbed of her usual vibrancy. He wondered how much was due to him and how much to the fall.

"I might need to sit for a moment," she said.

He caught her before she collapsed. Over her protests, he carried her to the bed, removed her boots, and fluffed the pillow under her head. She stared up at him in silence while he worked over her, black eyes shadowed, searching for something they did not seem to find.

Somehow he disappointed her.

He wished she would tell him what he should do.

He pulled the chair by the fire and stared at the flames. "About last night—"

She groaned.

He started to rise. "Are you sure you're all right?"

"Not if you're going to bring up the carriage ride."

"It's not a subject we can ignore forever."

"Can't we pretend it never happened? Oh, I don't suppose so." She propped herself up and drew her knees under her chin, a girlish sight with her slender figure and her hair giving up the fight for neatness. Girlish until he looked into her eyes, deep as the night, and knew she was deeply disturbed.

"I was like a schoolboy. Fumbling, hurried. It's a wonder I didn't . . ."

"Didn't what?"

"It's a rather personal trait of some men."

"More personal than what you know about me?"

Marcus struggled for the right words. "Sometimes a man's enthusiasm makes him spend himself too soon."

Her brow furrowed.

"I can explain further," he said.

"Oh," she said, lowering thick lashes over pink-stained cheeks. "There's no need."

"In case you didn't realize it, Raven, I was very enthusiastic."

"I realized." She swallowed, and he watched the movement in her slender throat. "So was I."

Their eyes locked. "Yes," he said softly. "And you were magnificent."

Marcus found his enthusiasm once again growing. If she looked in the right direction, she could see visible evidence.

But damn, that wasn't why he had brought her in here. She'd had a bad fall. And worse. His primary concern should be how much to tell her.

"Raven—"

"Please don't say anything more. I've decided to confess something. Something that might curb all that fervor."

"Impossible."

Arms wrapped around her legs, she looked into the

fire, its light reflected in her eyes. "I wish it were so."
A profound sadness thickened her voice, as though she
bore all the tragedies of the world on her shoulders.

"You thought I had been violated," she said. "I almost
was." She shifted her sad, lost gaze to him. "I killed the
man who tried."

How strange the words sounded. Never before had she
said them aloud.

"I killed him," she said, staring right at Marcus, making sure he understood, "and if I could live that afternoon
over, I would do it again."

She almost sighed in relief. *I killed him.* She could
have repeated it again and again. It was at that moment
she realized how close she was to breaking down.

If Marcus so much as blinked, she would take it as
revulsion. And then what would she do?

He smiled. Incredibly, he smiled. "Good for you."

"Papa said the same thing."

"I'd like to meet him and shake his hand."

How would the two get on? Just fine, she decided.
Just fine. She was right to tell him all. Whatever passed
between them, she had fallen in love with the right man.

"I've never told anyone exactly what happened. I'd
like to tell you."

Let him wonder why. Because he was her life and her
love and the reason she felt like a complete person for
the first time in thirteen years hardly seemed a smart
declaration.

"I was fourteen—" she began.

"Goddamn."

"Please don't interrupt. This is difficult enough."

"I don't suppose you'd like to be held—No, sorry I suggested it. Go on."

"It was at Christmas. Sherman's troops occupied Savannah. Papa kept us all in the house. Flame was not quite twelve and Angel seven, and we were as innocent as one of your lambs. But he said things could happen to us, even to Angel, and somehow we understood.

"I was always a dreamy sort, coming up with whole scenes in my head, creating dialogue and acting things out. Flame played a game of trying to catch me whispering to myself. 'Gotcha,' she'd say, the way children do when they play chase." She laughed self-consciously. "You don't want to hear all this."

"I want to hear everything."

She looked past him to the fire, seeing pictures in the flames she had not allowed herself to see in years.

"This particular scene required I go outside. The day was cloudy but not particularly cold, and we'd been cooped up forever. I was going no farther than the alley—"

Her voice broke. A deep breath kept her going.

"He was one of the Yankee soldiers. Probably not many years older than I. Even had freckles on his face." She laughed softly, without humor. "Strange how you remember such details. He appeared out of nowhere, smiling, friendly, you know? He started right out apologizing for the soldiers making life hard for us Rebs and I wasn't to be afraid of them. They'd be leaving soon."

The hard part loomed. She made herself look at Marcus. If she were going to tell this after so many years of secrecy, she would tell it right.

"He made me feel good, Marcus. I didn't know many young men, had hardly spoken to one. And I was fourteen. About to be a woman. He made me feel I already was. Excited, stirred by new feelings. Forbidden fruit, I would call him now, but I couldn't at the time. I imagined we were other people in another place. I returned his smile . . . and suddenly he didn't look so friendly anymore."

"You don't have to do this," Marcus said.

She ignored him. " 'Never had me a Reb,' he said, and he started coming close."

Raven closed her eyes, the images of the past as clear as yesterday, and the pace of her telling quickened.

"He got closer. I grabbed a rock and threw it. Split his cheek and the blood spurted everywhere, all over his freckles, his coat. But he kept on coming. I wanted to run, but I knew he'd catch me. So I ran at him, shoving with all my might, hitting him, getting his blood on my hands."

"My God."

Raven talked faster, wanting to get it said and done. "I took him by surprise. He fell back and hit his head. I remember feeling glad. I don't remember much afterwards except that Papa was there holding me and we were looking at the soldier and he was wide-eyed but he wasn't looking at anything but the sky. The gray sky. Like a Reb's coat. I didn't think about that until later. It must have been the theatrical nature in me that recalled such a detail.

"Papa cut my hand, just a little bit, to explain the blood

on my clothes. He swore me to silence and got me back in the house. Mama thought I'd taken ill. Flame suspected something, and I suppose Mama did, too, but she never asked. Papa took care of things outside. He never said how and, like Mama, I never asked. The Yankees searched for the soldier, but he was never found. I guess they decided he had deserted. There was a great deal of desertion on both sides."

Almost over, she told herself, proud she had not broken down, and she slowed her pace.

"I slipped deeper into my private world, playing out roles in my mind, escaping reality. I became a voracious reader, especially Shakespeare. I wasn't yet twenty when I decided to become an actress. Imaginary settings seemed so much better than the real world. And I was better at playing parts than I was at being me."

She fell silent, empty of spirit, empty of words. Suddenly Marcus was beside her, holding her, brushing at her hair, kissing her temple. Mostly just holding her. She would have thought she would have cried, but she was also empty of tears.

"You've carried this with you a long time," he said.

"I have bad dreams sometimes."

She stroked the lapels of his coat, then clutched them tight, making sure he did not leave.

"I started calling them night thoughts because that's when they came to me. Funny how it was nothing specific, just bad feelings like a mist surrounding me, and red lights. And when I was a little older, I started waking up with a different kind of feeling. I didn't understand it for a long time"—*not until you touched me*—"but I guess it was nature telling me it was time to be a woman."

She sighed. "This is a part Papa doesn't know. That I had these—I guess you'd call them passions—stirring around in me, only I thought they were connected to death."

She pulled away to look into his eyes. "But I was wrong. You're an attractive man, Your Lordship. You've got a way with you. I finally realized that it wasn't death taunting me, but life. Last night you made me feel alive."

He kissed her. Softly, sweetly, but she felt the tensions in him, the holding back of desires to do more.

"Did the night thoughts return after I left you?"

She shrugged. "No. But then, I didn't sleep."

He stroked the purple shadows under her eyes. "Neither did I."

He kissed her again, then eased away. "I'd better stop. You'll think I want to jump you every time we're alone." He grinned, sending Raven's heart into a spin. "I do, but that's a matter for another time."

She almost told him what was in her heart. In a way, she had. A woman didn't reveal such secrets to a man unless for her he was the only man in the world.

"You must think I'm the clumsiest person in the world," she said, proud of her laugh and her casual shrug. "I fall on the stage, I fall downstairs, and now I fall off a horse."

*I even fall in love.* How easy it would be to say it. Before she sailed for home, she would.

Marcus's smile died. "You're not clumsy. And you didn't just fall from the mare."

"Then how did I end up on the ground? A sudden pull of gravity?"

"I didn't know whether to tell you, but you've a right to know. The saddle gave way and took you with it, Raven, because the cinch had been cut."

# *Twenty*

*You will die.*

The words pounded in Raven's head. Mama's threat, and hers.

She snuggled beneath the covers. If only she could get some rest, she might think more clearly. If only she could forget, but that was impossible, given the nature of her troubles. An arranged accident was bad enough. Her need for Marcus threatened her more.

Since her latest fall a week ago, they hadn't been alone even once. She scarcely ate or slept, from shock at first, and worry. And then from wanting.

Looking at him daily, always with witnesses close by, she played the part of stoic. In sleep, she knew no inhibitions; lascivious dreams replaced the night thoughts of old. The dreams varied. Sometimes Marcus approached her from a bank of clouds or out of darkened corridors, sometimes in a field of spring grass. Sometimes even in bed. Always naked, always eager. She would wake up hot, her body bathed in sweat.

And what was His Lordship up to all this time? He was being noble and staying away. She was not impressed.

Right away he had decided Quirke had cut the cinch as revenge for being fired.

"Why get at me?" she had asked. "Surely he knew I'm the only one to ride the mare."

"He could have wanted to do more damage but was interrupted and had to leave the stable before he was through."

Maybe, Raven thought. Maybe not. It could be that the anonymous letter writer had returned to his evil purposes. Or hers. After more than three months in England, she was no closer to identifying so much as the sex of the culprit than she had ever been.

Everyone shared Marcus's assumption and his anger. When news of her fall became known, the farmers banded to search again for the missing bailiff, this time openly and willingly accepting Marcus's guidance. Mrs. Murphy and her daughter Jennie made their first journey ever to Beacon Hall to express their concern.

Amy ceased her daily trips into town to stay by her side, the aunts hovered like shadows in the background, and the Reverend Puddyfat reported he and the Cliftons would do whatever they could to help. Joining in the search, Ralph and the baronets journeyed to the surrounding villages, all the way to Lewes in the east and Brighton in the south, spreading the word that Quirke was to be apprehended on sight.

The household staff let her know how sorry they were.

"Quirke's a bad sort," said the maid Nancy. "Said horrible things t' me, he did, 'til I was scared t' go outdoors."

"Last night the witch hounds howled on the Downs," claimed the housekeeper Mrs. Reardon when she caught Raven lingering over breakfast. "Now, I don't hold with all the stories about witches turning to hares, you understand. But I heard what I heard. The hounds are searching for him, too, I'll be bound. He's a man what's doomed."

Overhearing, Frederick ordered the woman to cease her nonsense. "I heard no such baying. Wind, that's what it was. Anything else is superstitious nonsense."

The footman Hammond kept his feelings to himself, about both the witch hounds and the accident, but at least he ceased casting sideways glances that made Raven's skin crawl.

Everyone was so certain of the bailiff's guilt.

But they hadn't read Mama's letter. And they didn't know the intended victim had been pushed down the Stafford House stairs.

Dwelling on the incident led only to worry. Dwelling on Marcus brought a more tantalizing concern. Shifting restlessly in bed, she thought about what she would do to him if she got the chance. To begin, she would shake those broad shoulders of his. She couldn't remain in England much longer, that much was certain. He ought to know they were wasting time.

Raven sighed. What a lonely place a bed could be when a woman was in love. As oppressive as reality. That's why she had always sought solace in make believe. If only she could do so now.

A thought occurred. It was ridiculous, but it would not go away and she let it grow, working on the beginnings of a plan. Given the restrictions that Marcus had placed upon her, did she dare carry it through?

Of course she did. He would be furious. But not for long, not if she set up the scene right. Not if he were the man she knew him to be. And if he weren't, best to find out now. The only things lacking were a few items to set the proper scene—and all the backbone she could muster.

She elaborated on the idea, adding touches of dialogue and costume, crawling from bed to assemble her supplies. All those years of dreamy solitude, of studying Shakespeare, of acting out scenes in her mind would be put to good use, she thought as she settled back in bed. For the first time in more than a week, she enjoyed a good night's sleep.

She arose early, forced down a light breakfast—if things went as she hoped, she would need her strength—and strode determinedly to the stable.

Reluctantly Jason helped her saddle the mare.

"His Lordship's already gone out to look at some new fencing," the boy said. "He said he'd be back soon. He won't like it that you're gone."

*Not at first,* she thought, then with a moment's faint heart thought *maybe not at all.*

It was too late for cowardice. She handed Jason a note for Marcus and, with the day still soft-edged by the lingering remains of night, set out at a brisk pace, a small bundle strapped behind her and Albert running by the horse's hooves. The ride to the hut took a half hour. Ordering the dog to serve as outside sentry, she lit the fire and set the scene.

Her own appearance took the most time. When she heard noises signaling Marcus's arrival, she draped herself across the bed, satisfied she had done her best. Satisfied and terrified, both at once. She must be insane.

She thought of Marcus, riding tall in the saddle through the shadowed grove.

*O happy horse, to bear the weight of Antony!* It was a quote from her favorite Shakespearean play. She hoped it suited the occasion.

The door slammed opened and Marcus strode inside. Whining, the bloodhound chose not to follow.

"Damnation, woman, what do you mean disobeying—"

He stopped short and rocked back on the heels of his boots. For the first time since they had met, he was speechless.

She smiled tentatively, swallowing her heart, wondering what had happened to her backbone. It probably lay somewhere in the corner with her discarded clothes.

Too late for retreat. She looked up at him with heavily kohled eyes, fingered the hair she'd brushed mercilessly into straight strands beside her face, arranged the toga—actually a sheet from her bed—so that one shoulder and one leg were clearly bared, and she waited. Waited and trembled and went through a thousand deaths.

His eyes burned a blue trail from her smoothed-down hair to her bared toes, then slowly back again. His lips twitched. Such a little sign made her spirit soar.

"Cleopatra," he said.

She sighed. He understood.

"I'll be damned," he added.

Understood, she thought, but perhaps did not approve.

"I tried to roll myself in the rug, the way she did for Caesar, but it's harder than I thought. Besides, you're Antony."

"I am, eh?" He looked at his riding trousers, waistcoat, and jacket. "I don't look the part."

"I can correct that."

She rose from the bed, kicking aside with more efficiency than grace the long train of the sheet, adjusted the gold cord she'd borrowed from her bedroom draperies to use as a belt, and stood before him. She didn't think he realized the weak condition of her knees.

"I know a toga's not Egyptian, but it was the best I could do."

"Have you heard me complain?"

Her eyes met his, and it was her turn to be rocked back on her heels. Goodness, he had a look about him that curled a woman's toes.

"The day is young," she said softly. "I promise to give you little opportunity."

Bold words said with a buzzing in her ears. She was two people, a weakling and a wanton. Yearning drove her on.

He allowed her to strip him to the waist. She didn't move very fast, taken as she was with observing the contours of his body. She had never seen anything like him. Wide shoulders, smooth golden skin pulled tight over sculpted muscles, a dusting of pale chest hairs that thickened close to the band of his trousers.

Every inch a soldier, a leader of men and of one very aroused woman. She felt an almost uncontrollable urge to lick his nipples. Would he like it? In the ways of lovemaking, she had much to find out.

Reluctantly—unwilling to cover anything—she helped him don the jacquard waistcoat. Oh well, he wouldn't have it on very long.

She went for his trousers. He stopped her hands. "A man can take only so much," he growled, working at the buckle himself.

She handed him a towel.

"What's this for?"

"It's the best I could do. Strip and put it around your waist."

"Listen, Cleo," he began.

"Not romantic, my Antony. He called her Egypt in the play."

She tiptoed to the fire, stoked the embers, stirred a bowl of rosewater on the hearth. Sweet fragrance filled the room, blending with the acrid scent of burning wood.

"I'm not sure about this," he said.

She turned to face him. He stood before her in the waistcoat and towel, boots tight against his calves. He had great thighs. No other way to put it. And the rest of him looked even better from the tips of his leather boots to the furrows of uncertainty on his boyishly handsome face.

"I'm sure about it, Roman," she said, heat and firelight licking at her skin. Was that movement she saw beneath the towel? She rather thought so.

"You look like a conqueror," she added, taking a step toward him. "I do believe you can conquer me."

He shrugged. She liked the subtle play of muscle in his upper arms.

"I don't know any dialogue from the play."

Her heart caught in her throat. He was going along. She loved him all the more. The world and all its problems ceased to be.

"That's all right, Roman. We'll improvise." She stepped closer. "I'd like to feed you grapes, one by one, but they're out of season and it seemed too early in the day for wine."

"You'll satisfy my appetite."

She was in his arms so quickly she didn't know quite how it happened. His mouth claimed hers as her eager fingers stroked the outline of his arms. His skin was smooth and hard. He ran his hands over her shoulders and down her back, moaning when he realized she had nothing on beneath the sheet.

His sex pressed against her stomach. He cupped her buttocks and held her tight. She shook, fighting herself. She must not make a fool of herself by going too fast, by making demands that might prove impossible. But oh, she remembered how he had wanted them both naked and her lying beneath him on a bed. She wanted it, too.

And she had already danced dangerously close to the edge of absurdity . . . of rejection . . . with her charade.

Her breasts swelled for his touch and his kiss, and she felt a dampness between her legs . . . all natural, she supposed, when a woman was ready for love. Her first time had passed so quickly she could hardly remember the preparations. Only the shattering explosion and the awkward aftermath.

She would not feel awkward this morning. Queens never felt awkward, and today she was a queen.

"Let me go," she said in her best monarch's voice, and he obeyed.

She pulled the cord from her waist and tossed aside the brooch pinned at her shoulder. Quiet as mist, the white linen slipped to the rug, and she stood before him naked.

His sharp intake of breath fell like poetry on her ears. Her Roman didn't need to know Shakespeare; he spoke a language all his own.

He stroked her breast, then took the dark, hard tip

between his thumb and forefinger. She swayed, clutching his arm for support. Somewhere between the undressing and the touching, she forgot about being queen. Her lover took control.

His costume quickly discarded, he led her to the bed, lay beside her, and touched and stroked the places he had not been able to reach in the carriage, reacquainting himself with the places he already knew.

She tried for compliance, but eagerness got the better of her and she returned the favors, touching and stroking and kissing. He was perfect, hard-muscled where she was soft and knowledgeable in ways that sent her blood coursing hotly through her veins.

She touched her tongue to his, tasting the coffee he'd had for breakfast and the flavor that was uniquely his, then kissed his throat, his chest, her hands working at his body all the while. Sweet agony drove her on.

Marcus was not idle. He seemed to touch her everywhere at once, her breasts and buttocks, her belly, the private triangle of pubic hair, the backs of her knees, her thighs, and at last the pulsing nub between her legs. Her body wept intimate tears, begging for their joining.

His fingers found the dampness. "If you are Egypt, I've found your valley of the Nile."

She smiled and trembled and writhed beneath him all at once.

"Explore me," she whispered. "Now." She thought to make it a monarch's command, but it came out a plea.

Brave soldier that he was, he eased his fingers inside her, stroked in and out, moistening her pulses, exciting her to madness. She found his sex, but her touch was tentative, unsure.

"Explore me," he said. She did, stroking, caressing, increasing the fervor of her motions as his tense, low cry drove her on.

"A sword for a conqueror," she said, staring up at him, falling into the endless blue of his eyes.

He grinned, raggedly, and kissed her for what seemed forever, tasting her, sucking out her breath, her sighs, her life.

He settled between her thighs, skin hot and slick against her. Instinct drove her to wrap her legs around him as he answered her body's silent pleas, burying himself inside her. He was big and strong and powerful, yet he slipped into the hot, wet corridor with ease, resting against her with a weightlessness she would not have believed possible for such a muscled man.

He knew just where to touch and how to stroke her to the edge of velvet madness. Pleasure exploded around her, inside her, in her heart and soul. She felt a mighty tremor shudder through him, and his soft cry was a symphony.

They held tightly to one another until the poundings ceased, every nerve in Raven tingling with the echoes of slowly fading rapture. She felt his seed on her legs, knew the danger it presented, but she also knew there could be no other course for her but submission to her one true love, her only love.

She smiled against his neck. Submission? She felt rather like the conqueror, with Marcus the vanquished.

She kissed his neck. Muscles twitched beneath her lips. Strong hands moved with surprising delicacy against her hair, her shoulders, her arms. He didn't seem too

vanquished; he probably believed that somewhere, sometime he had taken control.

Let him believe it. She knew the truth.

Slowly they parted, but she stayed nestled in his arms.

He stroked the damp hair from her face. *"Other
women cloy the appetites they feed, but she makes hungry
where most she satisfies."*

She looked up at him in surprise. "You do know the
play."

"I was inspired to remember."

She hugged him hard, and in her heart she hugged the
memory of the moment.

"I don't suppose now's the time to chastise you," he
said.

"No." Then with a sigh she said, "Get it over with.
You'll choke if you don't get it out."

"You show your Antony little respect."

"Respect was not what Antony seemed to want."

He chuckled. "Damn it, Raven, I'm trying to be serious."

Worry fluttered like a caged bird in her chest. She was
not ready for seriousness. Not ready to vacate their private world.

"The mighty soldier can be as serious as he chooses,"
she said, trying to still the flutters.

"I'm not so certain the mighty soldier is in command.
I asked you to stay close to the house."

"Asked?"

"Don't quibble. We're all being careful until Quirke
is caught."

"I don't see how he could be within a hundred miles
of here."

"There are rumors he's been spotted."

"I can well imagine. With most of the countryside watching for him, there are bound to be supposed sightings. Mrs. Reardon swears the witch hounds are after him."

"I hope."

Raven grew weary of arguing. They would return to reality soon enough . . . but not just yet. She traced the skin around his nipples. "So I should have given up my plan for the morning."

The taut skin twitched. "You can't always retreat from the problems of the world," he said, but she thought he put little effort into what he said.

"Why not? It worked during the bad times. Why not the good?"

"You make arguing difficult. Whatever made you pick *Antony and Cleopatra?*"

"It's my favorite. Besides, the costumes were easy."

"Easily discarded, you mean."

They looked at one another and grinned.

"That, too," she said.

"What's next on your playbill? The saga of Héloise and Abélard?"

"Considering the man's condition, what would be the point?"

"I definitely agree, Songbird. I'll shed a towel for you, but that's as far as I will go."

Raven's heart turned chill, and she looked away before he could read distress in her eyes. *Songbird.* There was much in the name that reminded her of how things stood between them. She was an actress, a singer, a foreigner who intrigued and entertained.

She was not his one true love.

A momentary panic seized her. She couldn't go on like this forever. The best thing was to make a clean break and leave.

Eventually. As the Bard had put it, *Tomorrow and tomorrow and tomorrow.* One of those tomorrows would be soon enough.

She kissed him. If he caught the urgency in the act, he gave no sign.

"The quote you remembered. It's about still being hungry, isn't that right?"

Understanding glinted in his eyes. "Right."

"Then I suggest we return to the cloying of appetites. We both need to be sated if we are to accomplish any work today."

# *Twenty-one*

Raven's awakened passion became Marcus's as well. He couldn't get enough of her.

The days turned sunless, rainy, compounding his problems with the land, yet for all the work into which he threw himself, it was thoughts of Raven that quickened his pulse and heated his blood.

The steam-plow arrived, but it proved of limited benefit. A new land agent, both knowledgeable and honest, worked side by side with him to teach the tenant farmers the plow's use. With capricious nature turning even the highest ground to mud, the plowing went slowly.

Planting delayed, he should have been close to panic. The month was quickly moving on. Instead, his thoughts turned to Raven's legs wrapped around him, to her thighs holding tight. He thought, too, of her quick smile, a sight rare in the early days of her visit, and he thought of her inventive mind.

Never had he known a woman with such imagination. He had never considered the trait of much import; because of Raven, he did so now.

He worked hard, beginning at dawn; and in the evening, he pored over paperwork, paying bills, ordering supplies, pondering how to finance the expansions he wanted in livestock and seed.

On misty afternoons he made love to Raven in the hut. She came to him in many guises, always characters from her world of make believe. After that first time of *Antony and Cleopatra,* she never asked for his participation except as lovemaker. For him she played a range of parts— a young and eager Juliet, tremulous beneath him, offering her treasures with a cool innocence that soon burned hot with knowledge; an all-wise Portia who begged for mercy when he made her await his kiss; the shrewish Kate who let him tame her in a dozen different ways.

He learned a thousand things about her—the shape of her breasts and the sweep of her hips, her satin texture, the small dark patch of skin at the base of her spine, the way she liked him to kiss the backs of her knees.

Too, she liked his occasional attempts at humor. At least she laughed, which he took as approval. She also willingly shared the brief moments they gave to the land and its problems. Almost always she agreed with his assessments, and he decided she was a genius.

She was like wine, dulling the pains of the world; and she was the promise of spring, convincing him that nothing was so wrong that it couldn't be made right.

He wasn't so mesmerized that he couldn't see the purpose of her pretense. Assuming roles, she held back her own true self. Playing a part, she hid secrets whose nature he could not perceive.

This was the ultimate irony of his obsessive need for her. He knew her and he didn't know her at all.

A stormy morning in late March he sat at his desk in the library, trying to concentrate not on her but on the clutter of bills that lay before him. He met with little success.

Thunder rattled the windows, almost covering the knock at the door.

The cousins entered.

"Marcus," said Brian with his usual jovial smile, "thought we'd find you here."

"There's something we want to discuss," Douglas said, his expression not so serious it obscured the glint in his eyes.

"I hope it's not diamonds." Marcus lifted a dozen invoices, then let them fall like snow. "I haven't a tuppence to invest."

Douglas shook his head in mock disgust. "Nay, cousin, we're not daft enough for that."

"We are daft enough, however," said Brian, "to have an alternate proposal for your problems."

"Speaking of proposals," said Douglas, "whatever happened to your plan to take a wealthy wife?"

Marcus looked from one baronet to the other. "Does everyone know my business?"

They shrugged silently.

"The plan has been postponed," Marcus said curtly, not wanting to discuss the issue. He hadn't removed it from his options, not totally; but as the days passed, he found it less and less desirable.

He didn't miss the look that passed between the cousins. Did they know about his afternoons with Raven? The assignations were supposed to be secret; but when they were together in the hut, discretion ranked far below their top priorities.

For her sake, he ought to leave her alone.

He'd sooner walk into fire.

If he had any decency, he would make an honest woman of her. The idea came to him in full flower, and he realized it had long been germinating at the back of his mind. Marrying her seemed the most natural thing in the world. He certainly couldn't imagine marrying anyone else.

Lady Stafford . . . He pictured her in flowing white.

Lady Songbird . . . He pictured her in nothing at all.

The names enticed, as did the images; but bloody hell, there was so much working against them.

And yet . . .

He smiled to himself. No wonder he'd postponed choosing a bride. He already had one in mind.

"We've lost him," said one of the cousins, and the other echoed the sentiment. With a start, Marcus realized they were speaking of him. He pulled himself to the present.

"What did you want to talk about?"

"Your problems and how to solve them. At least how to make a start," said Brian.

"Unless one of you has inherited the crown jewels, there's little to suggest. My problems center around money. Or lack of it."

"We know," said Brian. "As we told you, that's why we're here."

The two looked so hopefully determined that Marcus could only grin. "No diamonds, you say?"

"No diamonds," said Douglas.

"The Ditchling Gooseberry and Copper Kettle Fair," said Brian.

"I see," said Marcus, not seeing at all. "We're to move about the crowd and pick pockets."

Brian sat forward in his chair. "In a way."

"Before you became a noble lord," said his companion, "how did you pay for your wayward pastimes?"

"Ah, lads, that seems a lifetime ago. Gambling. Cards, mainly, and an occasional boxing match. And of course, there were the races."

The baronets nodded.

"I assume you're not thinking of whist or fists. Which leaves a race."

"There's also a prize for the heaviest pint of gooseberries," said Brian, "but we doubt there's much money in it."

"I can come up with berries more easily than a horse. Abélard's no racer."

"What about Lightning?"

Marcus sighed, thinking of the sleek, black stallion as quick as his name. "I sold him ten months ago."

"He's available. Squire Clifton was telling us he's on the market. The owner's fallen into bad times, but he wants to see the animal gets a good home."

Marcus allowed himself only a moment's excitement. "Giving him away, is he? That's the only way I'll put Lightning into Beacon stables."

The cousins glanced at one another.

"The squire's willing to loan the money," said Brian. "Out of gratitude for leasing Humble Hall."

"Generous of him."

Douglas shrugged. "Not exactly. Instead of interest, he'd like the option of buying the hall and its grounds. He's taken a fancy to it—"

"No," said Marcus.

Both men looked surprised at his ready response. "Were you so happy there?" asked Brian.

"Happiness has nothing to do with it. My father lived in Humble Hall, and before him a half-dozen other Bannermans. Amy and I were raised there, and it was Cordelia's home for years."

"Ah, tradition. I see. You've become quite the family man."

"Don't tell the family that. They might laugh."

The baronets made a few more pitches in favor of the race, but Marcus declined to agree with much they said. Selling his ancestral land was more than he was willing to do.

He couldn't say why, other than what he had already told them. He had been so determined to hold his family together, and that meant holding onto their land.

An inner voice asked the difference between selling and leasing the property into perpetuity, as his financial condition indicated he must do. He couldn't come up with an answer.

"We're off to Brighton for a while," said Brian, standing. "Soon as the weather let's up. Think it over. That's all we suggest."

"You'll find, cousin," said Douglas, "it's the only way."

When the two were gone, Marcus stared out the window at the rain. He thought of Amy and Cordelia, of his parents who had never been close by when he wanted them to be. People made families, not dirt and rocks and trees. People like sisters, aunts, and even almost-relatives like Ralph and Irene. And wives. Selling Humble Hall would provide the money for a swift wedding.

Maybe he could do it. The thought of riding Lightning stirred his blood. Racing was a young man's game, and at thirty-five he wasn't young anymore. But he had been good at it. He and the stallion had been a fine match.

For a long period in his life, racing had brought easy money. Could it do so again?

A bolt of lightning rent the air, its jagged white light blindingly close to the window, and thunder crashed loud enough to crack the brick walls of the house.

He took it as a sign.

"Raven," he whispered to himself, "wilt thou be mine?"

He grinned at his foolishness, but the question remained. Would she have him? He remembered the eager innocence with which she threw herself into their lovemaking, as though each coupling were the very first time. Despite her willingness to meet with him, she wasn't like the other women he had known, women who expected his gifts. Raven seemed to want only him. She had probably been waiting weeks for him to ask the important question. Her wait was about to end.

Marcus felt younger than he had in years, and better for having chosen the right path.

Did he love her? He had no knowledge of love between a man and woman, had never seen it in his years of growing up, never felt the love of parent for child. He knew only that Raven obsessed him. He wanted to live his life with her in his bed.

The rain continued throughout most of the day, precluding a ride to the hut. In late afternoon he took the carriage to Humble Hall and arranged for the squire to purchase Lightning.

"I'll take care of the details, if you don't mind," Clifton said, and Marcus was forced to agree.

During dinner he couldn't keep his eyes off Raven. She looked radiant, her gown an emerald green that brought a dark glow to her skin. He imagined his mother's locket resting at her throat. Lovely, he thought, although its burnished gold held no more beauty than her high, smooth cheeks, and rubies no more lustre than her lips.

Her eyes were like the blackest ink still wet from the pen, and her hair as dark as the bird for which she was named. Damn, he was turning into a poet. It must be those plays in the afternoon.

He kept his musings on only those parts above the slender slope of her neck. Shoulders and below would have him vaulting down the table toward her, something earls simply did not do.

Countess of Stafford. If she were, he could take her to his room.

She avoided his frequent stare, but he knew she was aware of him. He knew it from the slight shake of her hand holding her fork and the way she sometimes held her breath, as though, thinking of other matters, she had forgotten her need for air.

He felt other eyes on him. Aunt Irene took special note of his attention to their guest. He smiled at Irene once, but the frost in her returning stare sent a chill across the table as potent as a fist.

The temptation to ask about Egypt's capital played at the edges of his mind, but that would be beneath the lofty goals he'd set for himself. Still, the temptation did not quite go away.

Amy watched him, too, speculation darkening her blue eyes. He avoided looking at her, for to do so reminded him of Paris. He needed to go abroad; he *wanted* to go abroad, but there had been much to do at Beacon. And there was Raven.

What would she think of Paris? She would have to know.

Neither Ralph nor Cordelia had much to say, and the table conversation lagged. After dinner he secluded himself in the library for a glass of brandy and a few quiet minutes to consider the timing of his proposal.

"Mind if I join you?" asked Ralph, who strode in without waiting for an answer.

Over the brandy, fondling the locket he'd brought with him to dinner, Marcus found himself wanting to share his news.

"I've decided to marry."

Ralph's Dundreary whiskers twitched. "It was only a matter of time. Margaret Clifton will make a fine countess. Small, but not so much in the hips. She should bear you a number of strapping sons."

"Not Margaret. Raven."

Ralph's eyebrows shot to his hairline. "Good God, have you lost your mind?"

Marcus's stare turned as frosty as Irene's. "You find something wrong with the idea?"

"In many ways she's a wonderful woman. Charming, lovely, considerate, and no one can fault her for laziness. She makes me tired just observing her with the children and the lambs."

"So why the disapproval?"

"She's an American, half-Irish on top of that. An actress. And more than likely, she's a thief."

"The painting, you mean."

"The painting. Surely you've not forgot."

"Of course not. But there's nothing to link her to the theft," he said, refusing to consider how he had caught her breaking into his desk. She had said she wanted to learn the mysteries of the Bannermans. He had long ago decided to believe her.

"She's an exciting woman, I'll give you that," said Ralph. "Don't deny you've noticed, or that you've wanted to sample her offerings. And we all know such ungratified feelings can lead to a softening of the brain. Driveling idiocy, too. I've not seen you driveling, m'boy, but there's evidence of a definite softening. Marriage. Bah."

Marcus regretted selecting Ralph as a confidant. He should have remembered the man's proclivity for lecturing. He should have kept his mouth shut.

"I'm not changing my mind," he said.

Ralph sipped at his brandy, for a moment lost in thought. "Then take her as your mistress for as long as she is here. Might do you both good. Few women are bothered by sexual feeling of any kind, I can attest to that. If she's the exception—and I suspect she well might be—then satisfy her nature. And yours. But take Miss Clifton as your bride."

Marcus knew Ralph spoke of common beliefs, but that didn't keep him from growing angry.

"I'll marry Raven. If she'll have me. I have no idea whether she'll accept."

A gasp, a cry—both very feminine sounds—told him someone was listening outside the library door. When he investigated, the hallway was empty, but he heard footsteps scurrying up the stairs. Refilling the snifters, he joined Ralph by the fire.

"Who do you suppose that might have been?" Ralph asked.

"I haven't the vaguest idea," he said, uneasy over the possibility it might have been Raven. He wanted to approach her in a special way.

He shook his head. "The women in this family remain a mystery to me."

Unwilling to listen further to arguments against Raven, he turned to the topic of the race. For this, Ralph showed much enthusiasm. "I'll wager a pound or two myself. Didn't know you helped me get by, did you?"

"You bet on me?"

"Whenever I heard you were racing. I've missed your old ways."

"And I thought everyone wanted me to be upstanding."

"Not everyone," said Ralph, brushing at his whiskers. "Not in every way."

Except where women were concerned. In matters of sex, Ralph Pickering was a typical Victorian gentleman.

The door crashed open, and Amy strode into the room.

"What's all this talk about your marrying Raven?"

"Do come in, Amy," said Marcus without a blink. "I should have known you would find out long before the prospective bride."

"You haven't asked her?"

"No. And I do not know that she will accept."

A dark figure loomed beside his sister.

"He wants his own actress," said Irene, her voice hard and ugly. She clutched a small carved box close to her bosom. "I've tried to warn him against her but he paid no mind."

"You're the one who eavesdropped, Aunt Irene. Haven't you heard you never hear good news that way?"

"Humph!" Irene rejoined. "I certainly didn't this time."

"I haven't said it's bad news," Amy said. "Not for you. I like the woman. I'm not sure it's a wise move for her."

"Thank you for the vote of confidence."

"Did you expect anything else?"

Aunt Cordelia stepped inside the library. "Goodness," she said in a flutter, "so much commotion."

"Ah," said Ralph, "please join us, Cordelia."

"By all means," Marcus said. "You'll want to cast your vote."

Everyone talked at once. The Pickering siblings, Ralph and Irene, lined up against the betrothal; Cordelia thought it a wonderful idea, and Amy withheld her opinion, not of Raven but of him.

"Enough," said Marcus over the babble. "This is absurd. I'll do what is best for Raven and me, and that's the end of it."

Everyone fell silent. Everyone but Irene. Knuckles white against the box, eyes wide and feverishly bright, she spoke at a piercing pitch. "The painting, Marcus. Don't forget she's a thief."

"What did you say?" Amy asked.

"The Landseer painting," said Irene. "The one that was stolen from Stafford House. Surely you knew."

"But Raven Chadwick the thief?" Amy said. "That I hadn't heard."

"Only because Marcus is so taken with the woman he refuses to admit the truth."

Amy turned to her brother. "Is that so? Are you in love with her?"

"My feelings, little sister, are as private as yours." He looked around the room. "It would seem my choice is not popular."

"She didn't take the painting."

Marcus stared in surprise at Amy. "You seem quite sure."

"I am." Her voice dropped even as her chin tilted defiantly against him. "I was the thief."

"Good God," said Ralph.

"Oh, dear," whispered Cordelia.

For a change, Irene was the silent one.

Marcus saw in his sister's eyes that she spoke the truth. "Why?" he asked. "Did you think I was partial to it?"

"I'm not going to tell you. I sold it. The money has long been spent."

Brother and sister stared at one another. No one spoke. Only the clock dared to intrude its measurement of seconds into the stillness of the room.

"Marry Raven or not," Amy said at last. "But don't ever accuse her of things she did not do."

Something made him look toward the open door, to the figure standing silently in the shadows outside the library.

"Raven—" he began.

"Get away," hissed Irene, waving catlike at her. "This is family business. You don't belong."

Raven stepped inside just far enough to reach the door-knob.

"Of course I don't belong," she said, her eyes never leaving Marcus. "I never did."

Backing away, she closed the door, leaving them to themselves, to their looks of guilt, to the high-pitched laughter of Aunt Irene.

# Twenty-two

Raven stared for a moment at the closed door. Everything within her collapsed—composure, pride, will—all destroyed along with happiness. The noble family of the house discussed her suitability as a bride as though she had been waiting around for a proposal. As though she thought Marcus cared.

The worst part of the moment was the realization they were right.

Whirling from the library, rushing past the butler, who suddenly emerged from the dark behind her, she ran from Beacon Hall as though a thousand hounds snapped at her heels.

The cold night air, empty of rain, fluttered the chilled silk gown against her skin, and her cheeks burned from the briskness, but she felt no discomfort save a tortured mind and the twisting of a broken heart.

The world seemed an alien place, as it used to be when she was young, full of shadows and clouds and winds that moaned through the trees, everything threatening harm. She flew down the steps and rushed toward the stable, her skirt trailing in the puddles from the day's storm. Her only desire was for solitude, her only prayer a sanctuary far away from Marcus and his kin.

Inside the stable, she leaned against the door to catch her breath, glad of the warmth that the well-built walls provided. The horses nickered in their stalls. She felt her way past them in the dark, stopping at the last small empty stall where she had once seen Marcus feeding a baby lamb.

The stable door creaked open. Holding her breath, she fell to her knees on a carpet of dry straw.

"Raven."

Marcus's voice struck terror in her heart. She didn't want to face him, didn't want to hear his apology, his explanation of what she had overheard. She needed no explanation. Already she understood too much.

A match snapped; in the dark it sounded like a shot. Light flickered and grew brighter as his footsteps approached her hiding place. The horses stirred restlessly as he passed, but Raven could not draw a breath. He halted at the entrance to the stall, a lantern held high in his hand. Her eyes trailed from his mud-spattered shoes up the straight line of his trousers, the impeccable jacket, to the shock of golden hair across his forehead.

He looked so damnably aristocratic in his evening clothes, his shirt and tie as white as ice against the ebony coat. Aristocratic and concerned, and more than a little embarrassed. If she weren't so crushed by the sudden turn of events, she would be embarrassed, too.

She stood to face him, wishing she had brushed the tears from her cheeks. She must not cower before him. No matter what he threatened, no matter what he said.

"That was unforgivable of us," he said.

"Not at all," she managed. "I intruded where I was not asked."

"It was not a family conference, no matter how it appeared. Ralph joined me, and then Amy, and the next thing I knew everyone was there." He ran a hand through his hair. "Hell, I don't know how it happened, but I'm sorry."

He looked so sincere, so worried, she almost reached out to comfort him. What a fool she was.

She took a steadying breath. "I accept your apology," she said, formality her only shield. "Now please leave. I don't want to talk about it right now."

He hung the lantern on a nail at the entrance to the stall. "No." He stepped deeper into the stall, the straw crunching under his shoes. "I want to explain."

Her heart quickened. She couldn't let him get closer or she might—

There was no telling what she might do. She dug her nails into her palms. "Get away from me."

"You're crying."

"Not anymore. And if I am, it's because I'm angry."

"I've seen your anger often enough, Raven. I don't see it now." He touched her arm. She pulled away. "Let's have no pretenses tonight," he said.

The words stung. "You didn't like my roles? You certainly seemed entertained."

"That hardly describes how you made me feel. But you never presented yourself in any part that had a happy ending. That's what I wanted to offer you."

The overheard discussion in the library seared into her mind; and the hurt, the humiliation, swept over her once again.

"Marriage, you mean."

"You've got something against the institution?"

"I told you once it was not for me."

"But that was before we made love."

Raven closed her eyes, but only for an instant, lest she break down completely. *Love,* he'd said, the one word she yearned to hear; but he used it to mean the sex they shared. He offered nothing to mend her broken heart.

"What happened between us has not changed my mind," she said, the strong words issued in a far-too-timid voice.

He stood so close she had only to sway and she would lean against him. Her pride cried for him to go away, but all the sensations within her begged otherwise.

"Are you saying you didn't like what we did?" he asked.

She stiffened herself against his power, against all the hungers and the hurts he so easily aroused. "Of course not. The assignations in the hut were my idea."

"Yes," he said. "And this one's mine."

He brushed his lips against hers, with no more pressure than the flicker of a flame, but with all the heat.

"Tell me you don't want this," he whispered.

"I don't—" She could not say more. When she raised her eyes to his, she saw blue fire. He took her by the shoulders, not letting her pull away.

Somehow she found a spark of resistance, a sense of the madness of the moment. "It's over between us, Marcus. Let me go."

"I can't," he said, crushing her against his chest. His passion wrapped around her, as real as his arms; his lips covered hers, and he swallowed her angry response. Her fists pounded against his chest. He embraced her tighter, his tongue plundering her mouth. This couldn't be happening, her mind screamed, not his unyielding hands holding her, his iron body refusing to leave a quarter inch between them, his tongue insistent as i danced against hers . . . and the worst part of all, the realization that she didn't want to fight him at all.

She struggled to find her sense of self, her pride, but even her anger was fast dissolving, leaving her with nothing but the hurt.

And desire.

What a pathetic creature she was. She had run from the house, run from Marcus, but she couldn't run from herself. Suddenly she saw the way things would be. He didn't want pretenses. He wouldn't get them. She would love him one last time, not as Cleopatra or Juliet or Kate, but as herself.

Raven Chadwick, an Irish storekeeper's daughter and would-be actress, giving herself to an earl in a straw-strewn barn.

Giving herself and her heart.

With a low cry, she returned the kiss, thrusting her tongue inside the sweet darkness of his mouth, holding him tight, rubbing her full, taut-tipped breasts against his chest, thrusting her hips against him until she felt his arousal against her belly.

A long, ragged breath shuddered through him as he pulled her to the straw, hungry hands running over the silk that covered her breasts, down her side, her thighs, between her legs, pulling up her gown and petticoat, massaging between her legs until the wetness came through the last thin garment that separated his fingers from her heat.

"Raven," he whispered hoarsely against her tumbling hair.

"That's right," she whispered back. "Raven. No one else."

Her fingers flew to the front buttons of her gown. She exposed herself to him. He licked her nipples. She trembled under his tongue.

He left her long enough to toss his coat and tie aside and unfasten his shirt. She licked his nipples. He trembled under her tongue.

They both went wild. Her undergarments joined his coat and tie and his hands roamed at will, stroking, rubbing, arousing. With head thrown back, she gave herself to his explorations, her silk gown crackling against the dry straw until she wondered why a fire was not struck. But the only fire burned between her legs.

When his mouth pressed urgent kisses against her inner thigh, she stiffened. He'd never done this to her before. Her body throbbed painfully for release. He gave it to her with his tongue, kissing her so intimately she couldn't breathe.

Rapture became the color red behind her closed eyes; ecstasy lay in his lips and tongue. He stopped before she slipped into madness. Easing himself under her, his trousers lowered to his knees, he lifted her on top of him. Through the haze of passion she realized he was protecting her from the roughness of the straw.

She slowly lowered herself, kissing him as she took him inside her, tasting herself on his tongue. It was a strange sensation, but everything about her love for

Marcus was strange because it was so completely impossible.

He thrust deep, again and again, and they shattered against one another, their climax coming at the same time. She felt his seed flow into her, warm and natural. She gripped her thighs against him, her hands stroking his face, her head buried in the curve of his neck. As the tentacles of completion slowly relaxed their hold on her, she kissed the damp hairs that swirled across the contours of his chest.

He held her tight, whispering her name, blowing at the wisps of hair at her temple, gradually relaxing his embrace. He stayed inside her and she listened to the pounding of his heart.

Forcing her breath to steadiness, she eased from his arms, not wishing to let him be the first to push away. She knelt beside him in the straw, smoothing her gown over her thighs, feeling the wet fabric, beyond caring about such inconsequential matters as clothes.

Her eyes fell to his lax manhood. Even in repose he was beautiful. She looked at the dark pubic hairs, the hard, flat belly, the muscled chest. She lingered at his corded neck, the pale scar on his chin, the strong nose and bristled cheeks, and at last his eyes, no longer as blue as a morning sky but as dark as dusk.

How like the first time this was, her gown at her waist as she impaled herself on his erection.

*Ride me,* he had said. She had done it then. And she had done it now.

The first time, so like the last. She looked away before he could see the tears in her eyes. She wanted to stand, to walk, to run as far away as her strength could

ake her, but she doubted she could get to her feet.
With shaking hands, she eased into her undergarment,
listening to the sounds of his breathing, the crackle of
straw, the hammering of her heart as he straightened
his own clothes.

They sat in silence for a moment. Something glinted
in the straw. He scooped it up and held out his hand.
"Marry me."

She stared at the small gold locket resting against his
callused palm. "I've given you my answer." The words
came hard.

"Marry me," he said again.

"You can't keep asking me."

"Of course I can. Until I get the answer I want."

*Why?* That's what she wanted to say.

*Because I love you beyond heaven and earth and I
want you at my side forever.* That's what she wanted to
hear.

*Because it's the right thing to do, no matter what
anyone else believes.* That's what he would say if he
did not lie.

"I want you for my wife, Raven."

"Don't be so honorable. I wasn't forced into anything."

He slipped the golden jewelry into his pocket, his anger and frustration so strong they frightened her, but she
could not relent and tell him so.

"I said I want you for my wife, and I meant it. I
can't imagine sharing my bed with anyone else. Not
ever. I'll do everything in my power to make you
happy."

He stroked her hair, half-pinned, a mass of tangled

ebony curls. She shifted away. Anguish struck, a horrid hollow pain within her, worse than the terror in a Savannah alley, worse than anything she had ever known.

"I can't marry you, Marcus. We come from two different worlds. They were right in the library. Irene was right. I don't belong here. I know it, even if you don't."

"That's insane."

She looked at the rough-hewn walls enclosing them, at the rafters, at their bed of straw.

"I can read the scandal sheets now. 'His Lordship made love to a would-be countess in the stable of Beacon Hall.' It would be worse than the music hall story."

"I imagine it's been done before."

"You would know more about that than I. Most women would say I am indeed insane to feel as I do, but I can't help it. Countess is not a role I can play. For a long while I've been telling myself it was time to leave. I should have listened to that inner voice."

She found the strength to stand, awkward, stumbling. He stood beside her in an instant, his steadying hand on her arm.

"It doesn't matter what anyone else wants or believes," he said. "We're all that matters."

He sounded so sure.

She turned to leave, but hard images stopped her. Of Marcus approaching her the day she first visited the Lyceum, of Marcus kissing her in the library at Stafford House, Marcus always insistent, always doubting, taking whatever she had to give. Eventually she'd given him everything.

"Don't touch me."

"Raven—"

His voice was dark and deep and insistent. She couldn't hold the anguish inside her anymore. She couldn't hold back the tears.

She whirled to face him, arms at her sides, cheeks damp, her head held high.

"Damn you, Marcus Bannerman, for making me feel things I never wanted to feel. I reached the age of twenty-seven handling things all right. Alone. Until you."

"Maybe not so all right. You kept things to yourself you should have talked about."

"The talking came at a very high price.

"Goddamn it, Raven, I don't understand."

"I hardly do myself. Except that I've always known what we've been sharing was for a little while. Tonight I realize the time is done."

"I asked you to become my wife. Is that such an insult?"

If he had told her he loved her, she almost said, she would have lived with him as a peasant in a gamekeeper's hut.

"Not an insult. Just not enough."

She didn't wait for his response. He might tell her things he did not feel. Out of honor. She could read the need to do so in his eyes.

She turned her back to him and stepped from the stall.

"What if you're carrying our baby?" he asked.

She caught her breath, unable to take another step. He knew how to fight for what he wanted. She hugged herself, struggling for a way to fight back. She couldn't look at him, otherwise he would know she yearned to bear his child.

And she could not bring a bastard into the world.

*If I'm increasing, I'll marry you and when you get used to sex with me, I'll look the other way while you visit your actresses. But I'll love our children none the less, and I'll love you all the more.*

The declaration remained in her heart.

"It's possible," she said, being as honest as she could manage. "I won't leave England until I know for sure." She glanced over her shoulder. He stood so close, and yet a world away. Not a world, she amended, just an ocean. But it was enough.

"I'm through with pretenses, Marcus. I'll let you know."

She started toward the stable door.

"Let me straighten your hair," he said.

"I said I'm through with pretenses. If your family sees me, they'll know for sure what they've already guessed."

He didn't stop her from leaving. When she walked through the front door of Beacon Hall, gaslight fell on her tangled hair, her swollen lips, her stained and wrinkled gown. It fell, too, on a piece of straw clinging to her dampened skirt.

Frederick closed the door behind her. "Miss Chadwick, are you all right?"

"Jim-dandy," she said, knowing others watched and listened. "That's an American expression meaning I'm just fine."

Head high, she walked up the stairs to pack.


Raven left early the next day, leaving each member of the family and several members of the staff formal notes of gratitude for their hospitality. To the family she also apologized for causing them inconvenience or distress.

The rains lifted, and Marcus threw himself into work, but a cloud hung low over Beacon Hall, blocking out the sun. Amy and Cordelia divided their days between reviving the roses in the conservatory and journeying to town. What they did in Ditchling, he could not imagine. Irene went around the house clutching the wooden box to her bosom and talking to herself. Each time he saw her, he felt a chill down his spine. The woman was not well.

Ralph and the baronets contented themselves with planning for the fair, arranging the bets, gathering what funds they could to lay on Marcus and Lightning to win.

Marcus worked, throwing himself into every task with an abandon that had even Amy asking him to slow down. And he drank. What he tried not to do was think about Raven. She had made her choice. She was gone.

Squire Clifton, as jovial as ever, visited often to talk about the race and, more importantly to him, his eventual ownership of Humble Hall. On several occasions Margaret joined him.

"Has the actress gone?" she asked on the first visit.

Marcus looked at her without answering. She did not mention Raven again.

Two weeks after Raven's departure, he received a letter saying she did not carry his child. Throwing the paper into the fire, he packed away the locket that she'd declined.

The day before the fair several of his former gaming

companions journeyed down from London; he joined them in drinking through the night.

As the time for the race neared, Marcus admitted to two mistakes. He hadn't worked with Lightning as much as he should have to get their rhythms right, to pace the layout of the race. And he had not totally reached sobriety.

As a consequence, he lost.

"A close second," Ralph said, trying to put the best face on it.

But his friends and family had gambled he would win. He owed them for the loss. As soon as he received payment for his ancestral property, he would see they were reimbursed. The rest of the money would go to pay his bills and to relieve the hardships of the families dependent upon him.

When Margaret came over to commiserate, somehow the talk of marriage came up. Close to the precipice of betrothal, he narrowly escaped by pretending to be drunker than he was.

He should have proposed. Her wealth would go far in helping the people of his estate. And, as Ralph pointed out, she would bear him healthy sons. Since the idea of fathering a child with Raven had first occurred to him, he had often thought of how pleasing it would be. But he had always pictured black-haired little girls, dark eyes flashing as they crawled upon his knee.

Marriage to Margaret? Maybe, but not just yet.

With the new land agent taking over as supervisor and the tenants working in the field, he saw no need to remain in the country. He did what he should have done weeks ago, during the time he was under a song-bird's spell.

After a cool goodbye to his sister and aunts, he went to Paris.

# Twenty-three

Raven spent most of her days and all her nights in the Soho boardinghouse where she had stayed the first few weeks in London, waiting until she could leave for Portsmouth and for home.

When her monthly flow began, she had told herself it was best she was not carrying Marcus's child; his proposal had been from his conscience, not his heart.

She had sent him a letter to relieve his worry, then booked passage for Savannah. She was scheduled to sail in two weeks. It seemed a lifetime away, yet it was little time to decide how she would tell Mama and Papa all that she had done in England. And why. They had to know before they journeyed to London in the upcoming summer and knocked at 22 Bolton Row.

How much to tell? Everything. No, almost everything. There were some details she would keep to herself, most of them involving the gamekeeper's hut. She would say she had made poor decisions, emotional choices that proved her undoing. She would blame no one except herself.

She ought to laugh at the situation. Reserved, self-assured Raven, the practical daughter who didn't allow herself to feel, was returning to her beloved family hollow-eyed and subdued, a world of hurt in her heart and a sense of loss in her soul. At least she wouldn't cry in front of them. Her tears were shed.

In organizing her belongings for the sailing, she had come upon the raven's feather Amy had given her at the Tower of London long ago, claiming that if the birds flew away, the Tower and the kingdom would fall. As she stroked the long black plume, the legend and her disastrous music hall costume mixed in her mind.

"This Raven is leaving," she whispered, flushed with a lingering shame. "The kingdom must fend for itself."

She tried not to be embittered. Her wounds were self-inflicted. Willingly she had thrust her hand into the fire of passion; somewhere deep inside herself she must have known she would get burned. The worst part was, feeling as she did about Marcus, she would probably do it again.

It was a shameless, selfish realization.

No matter how long or hard she pondered, she came up with no way to keep from passing her hurt on to her parents. And their welfare was the reason she was here. The irony did not escape her. She would make up her failures to them if it required the rest of her life.

She rose from her chair by the window, ready to take her daily afternoon walk, when a knock sounded at the door.

"You've a visitor, lass," said the landlady Mrs. Goodbody.

Raven's heart stopped. "I don't want to see anyone."

"Miss 'alstead looks 'armless enough, she does. I put her in the parlor."

It took Raven a moment to realize whom the landlady

meant. Aunt Cordelia! Why was she here? Was Marcus all right?

She flew past Mrs. Goodbody and down the stairs, skidding to a halt at the parlor door. Cordelia sat on the sofa, her hands folded over the reticule in her lap, a kindly smile wrinkling her face.

"Is anything wrong?" Raven gasped.

Cordelia's smile creased into a frown. "I didn't mean to frighten you, dear. There's always something wrong with the Bannermans. Nothing of an emergency nature, you understand. Not like an accident or anything. I thought we should talk."

Raven sank onto the sofa beside her, a hand pressed to her heart. "Let me catch my breath."

"I'll get some tea," said Mrs. Goodbody from the doorway, not bothering to hide her curiosity.

"That will be nice," said Cordelia, setting her bonnet and purse on the table beside her.

"How did you know where to find me?" asked Raven.

"You wrote Marcus at Beacon Hall. I saw the envelope. The letter had him quite upset. For days not even Irene would dare cross him."

"Oh," said Raven, puzzled. The only time she'd written Marcus was to inform him she wasn't *enceinte*.

"They found the body of that dreadful bailiff," Cordelia said, as calmly as though she were discussing the weather, startling Raven from her thoughts. "In a lonely part of the Downs, a few miles from Beacon, where the grass grows tallest. One had to pass right by to see him."

Before Raven could come up with a response, she continued in the same sweet voice. "Carrion mostly, from what I've been able to learn. He had been in the rain for days. They don't like to tell ladies about such matters. Ralph let me know."

She smiled conspiratorially. "He didn't want to. He's dreadfully old-fashioned."

Raven had never heard Aunt Cordelia ramble on in such a manner, and imparting such gruesome details. She had changed since they had last seen each other, and not just in her speech. Something—

The full impact of Cordelia's news hit her. Arthur Quirke was dead.

"I hadn't heard. Did they know how long he'd been out there?"

"The doctor said no more than a few weeks."

"After my fall from the horse."

"Oh, he was certain it was days after. Apparently the man broke his neck in an accident not unlike yours. His manner of death seems quite appropriate, don't you agree? The housekeeper swore it was the witches' hounds that got him, but I'm convinced it was meanness."

"I don't think that's possible."

"You're much too innocent, my child. Mr. Quirke was not a very nice man. He liked to beat his horse. The animal must have thrown him and run away. Marcus said it proved he was the culprit who tried to harm you. Apparently he was lurking about at the time and was clever enough to avoid apprehension." She sighed. "I suppose everyone is good at something."

Mrs. Goodbody returned to serve the tea. Studying the two women, apparently satisfied no emergency troubled her boarder, she quietly left, closing the parlor door behind her.

Raven absentmindedly reached for the sugar bowl.

Had a vengeful Arthur Quirke really **sought** redress by hurting her? Had he crept into the stable and cut the cinch, as Marcus had always believed? She had been **quick to** doubt it, but Marcus had a maddening way of being right about things. He was probably right about Quirke.

And she had probably imagined that someone shoved her down the stairs. All the creaks in the hall must have stimulated her imagination. She had expected trouble. People, she knew too well, often got what they were looking for.

She settled back on the sofa and lifted her cup to her lips, grateful she wouldn't have to tell Mama to fear for her life. For that, she owed Cordelia thanks.

"Marcus was a lonely little boy," said Cordelia.

Raven choked on her tea. Cordelia pulled a handkerchief out of nowhere and passed it to her.

"What makes you say that?" Raven asked, wishing she had said she didn't care about His Lordship's youth, that Cordelia had passed on the news she'd come to deliver and shouldn't be detained any further.

But the woman had an air about her that said she was just now getting to the reason for her call.

"I was there to care for him." Cordelia sighed. "Poor tyke. Someone had to, and my sister wasn't inclined. Neither was my brother-in-law. It's not polite to speak ill of the dead, but they were far too selfish to succeed as parents. They were rarely kind, even to each other. Amy got what love they had to give."

Raven pictured a fair-haired boy roaming around the countryside alone. "I guessed as much," she said, her heart twisting. "From things he's said."

She got hold of herself. "That was all a long time ago," she said as though the topic was covered and they should go on to something else.

Settled comfortably on the sofa, Cordelia gave no sign she was done with Marcus's past.

Suddenly the difference in the woman hit her. No excessive color stained her cheeks, and she smelled of lavender water, without a hint of gin. She was sober. Raven thought back over the weeks in the country. With Marcus absorbing her every waking moment, she had given little thought to Cordelia. Only now did she realize that in the final days before her departure Albert had ceased cornering the poor woman in the potting shed.

Cordelia had a faraway look in her eye, oblivious to Raven's musings.

"He was a wild thing, a fair young god riding across the Downs on horses much too big and strong for him. But there was no one to tell him he shouldn't engage in such a dangerous sport, nobody but a dithering maiden aunt, and nobody listens to such creatures."

"I can tell you right now, my sisters and I would have."

Cordelia patted her hand. "I know, dear. That's why I'm here."

She took a deep breath before continuing her narrative. "Daniel Lindsay was younger, but like most of the boys in East Sussex, he worshipped Marcus. Amy tried to keep up with the two of them, but she was a girl and was not tolerated." She shook her head. "Poor Amy. But that's a story for another day. Marcus cares for her, more than most of us realize. She finds it difficult to return the affection."

Her gray eyes warmed as she looked at Raven. "The

boy needs someone to care for him. Someone to teach him how to love. He doesn't know the way of it, you understand. I've decided you're the one."

Raven shook her head. "I can't believe I'm hearing this."

"I would give you awhile to think the matter over, but we haven't the time. Before my nephew does something foolish, he needs you to teach him how to feel."

Raven looked away, struck by the absurdity of the suggestion. *I tried,* she thought, blinking away tears she didn't know were still inside her. *I tried with all my heart.*

Sipping her cold tea, Cordelia pulled a face. "Margaret Clifton is all wrong for him," she said, half to herself. "If something doesn't happen soon, they'll be betrothed."

Raven looked away to hide her pain. "Surely that's for the best," she managed.

"Not at all. It almost happened right after the race, with Marcus needing the money after he lost."

"Marcus raced and lost?"

"By a nose, Ralph said. Everyone thought the engagement was inevitable. Certainly Margaret did." Cordelia sighed. "She's a determined woman. She'll catch him yet."

Raven's head reeled. She felt like a kite on a string, jerked from one topic to another, with nothing solid beneath her to steady her feet. She needed to write everything down in some kind of order, asking Cordelia to fill in the empty spaces.

"That's why I decided you must go to Paris. I'll give you the address to look for, and I'll help you make the arrangements. Marcus will be gone by the time you arrive, but that's all right. He's not the one I want you to meet."

"I can't go to Paris," said Raven, feeling a strong jerk on the kite string, wondering if perhaps someone hadn't sneaked some gin into her own cup of tea. "I'm sailing for home in two weeks."

"Perfect. If you leave tomorrow, you can get there and back with time to spare."

"I can't go to Paris," she repeated, emphasizing each word.

"Oh, but you must. It's imperative."

"Why?"

Cordelia shook her head. "I'm sorry, dear, but that's the one thing I won't tell you. There are some things best learned for oneself."

"No," said Raven. "Absolutely not. This is insane. Whatever concerns Marcus in Paris is his business. If he needs someone to teach him about love, he'll have to find her on his own, someone who comes from his own world. That someone is certainly not a shopkeeper's daughter from Georgia who tried to pursue an acting career. I don't belong here. I'm surprised you don't realize it. It's certain Marcus does by now."

Throughout her monologue, Cordelia had sat quietly, hands folded in her lap.

"Is that your final decision?"

"Yes. The next country I plan to see is the United States of America. It most certainly is not France."


Early the next morning Raven left on the boat train for Paris. She wasn't quite sure how she got there, except that Cordelia had proven a formidable force to reckon with. How Marcus ever managed to ride the wild horses of his youth over her objection she couldn't imagine.

Except that he possessed a stronger sense of will than the woman who had fallen in love with him.

In her heart she suspected why she had agreed to the journey, even though she would have paraded on a thousand music hall stages before admitting it to Cordelia.

She wanted to learn all she could about the man she loved. It wasn't to harm him in any way or embarrass him with her knowledge, but to understand him, to know why he behaved the way he did in his dealings with everyone—the Beacon tenants, Cordelia, Irene and Ralph, Amy, and an unexpected distant cousin by marriage who showed up at his door.

Raven had long thought she knew little about anyone connected to him. In the short time she and Cordelia had spent together arranging the journey, she learned about the woman herself.

"I've decided not to accept Ralph's proposal," Cordelia had announced when she accompanied Raven to Victoria Station. Like most of her pronouncements, this one came without warning.

"I didn't know—"

Raven had been unable to continue. There was so much she didn't know. Where should she begin?

"He asked me quite awhile ago, the first time, I mean, when we were young. But Marcus needed me, and neither of us had the resources to have a family. I realize now I didn't love him, otherwise nothing would have mattered except saying yes. We could have managed our problems well enough."

"It takes two people to be in love."

"It most certainly does. During the years I lived in town, he supplied me with gin. I shouldn't have accepted it, I know, but it seemed harmless. And then, when we returned to the country, which I really do prefer, and that horrid monster attacked me, I knew what I had to do. It wasn't easy, but Amy helped. She really is a dear girl, even though she doesn't want people to realize it. She was teaching the children of Ditchling to paint, did you know? I thought not. Marcus was sure she was looking for ways to spend money. He really ought to trust the girl more."

Every syllable of the woman's discourse came back to Raven as she rocked along toward the English coast in the first-class compartment of the London, Chatham and Dover Railway. Especially her final words.

"A man has to be trusted if he is ever to learn how to do the same with others. Remember that, Raven, when you're in Paris. Trust Marcus. No matter what you find."

*Trust Marcus, trust Marcus, trust Marcus.*

The words echoed in the chug of the train. They lingered with her throughout the channel crossing, on the final train ride into Paris, and in the carriage as she made her way through the crowded streets, across the River Seine, past Notre Dame Cathedral, to a hotel Cordelia had recommended for her stay. The next day the English-speaking *concierge* summoned a carriage to take her to a small house tucked beside a narrow lane near the Sorbonne.

She arrived at her destination in the middle of a sunny April morning. Nothing about the dwelling gave the least hint of what she might expect inside, and she wondered if she might not add this journey to the list of mistakes she had made since leaving Georgia.

With the sound of the departing carriage ringing in her ears, reminding her of the day she had first approached Stafford House, she knocked at the door. At least there was no brass lions-head knocker to intimidate her. If only she knew what to expect. If only she knew what to say. All her cogitating since London had left her with only the sinking feeling that, despite Cordelia's avowals, she was doing something wrong.

A young woman answered the door. A very pretty young woman with sparkling brown eyes and a slender figure beneath her simple dress.

She wasn't the voluptuous and fashionable mistress Raven had sometimes imagined Marcus kept in France. She was worse. Though the spate of French she threw at Raven precluded any real communication, she seemed very nice.

*"Parlez-vous anglais?"* Raven asked when she got a chance.

*"Pardon, non,"* the girl said, looking as though she would rather eat dirt than disappoint her visitor.

Raven pondered what to say next. She spoke little French and understood even less. Cordelia's written instructions and scribbled phrases had gotten her this far, but she had refused to provide Raven with further guidance.

*"Père,"* the girl called over her shoulder. She said more, but to Raven it all sounded like one long word.

A thin, graying man in loose-fitting coat and trousers appeared behind her. He smiled at Raven. *"Bonjour, mademoiselle,"* he said. "How may I help you?"

Raven sighed in relief. "You speak English."

"Not so good, but we will try, how you say, to converse."

"You sound wonderful."

He looked expectantly at her, waiting for her to go on. "I'm a friend of Miss Cordelia Halstead."

His Gallic shrug gave proof he did not know the name. Raven's heart sank. "And Marcus Bannerman."

"M'sieur Bannerman," said the girl with a wide smile.

*"Mon dieu,* I would not have thought you could arrive so soon."

"You were expecting me?"

"But of course. We knew M'sieur Bannerman would not ignore the letter. But I sent it only a week ago. This is a puzzle."

He caught his daughter's frown. "She says I have the manners of a goat. You did not hear her? My daughter speaks with her eyes." He stepped aside. *"Entrez, s'il vous plaît."*

The door opened into a parlor, charmingly decorated in upholstered furniture, a round braided rug in the center of the wooden floor, ruffled print curtains at the window.

"Allow me to introduce myself," he said, guiding Raven to a chintz-covered chair. "I am Claude Jenet. *Je vous présente ma fille* Arianne."

*"Enchantée,"* said Raven. *"Je m'appelle* Raven Chadwick."

He spoke rapidly to his daughter, who promptly left the room. "Arianne prepares a small repast. *Vin,* with a little cheese and bread, nothing more, but my wife baked the bread only this morning and Arianne brought the cheese from the country. It is never too early in the day for wine, *n'est pas?"*

"*Merci,* M'sieur Jenet, but I'm truly not hungry."

In truth, she doubted she could swallow a bite. What to say next? She faced a courteous gentleman who expected to hear from Marcus about an obviously important matter, but she had no earthly idea what it was. She started to present him with her problem when Monsieur Jenet slapped his forehead.

"*Pardon,* Mademoiselle Chadwick. I keep you here when you wish to see the others. On such a fine day as this they have removed themselves to the park. *Le Jardin du Luxembourg* is a short distance away. Allow me to walk with you. Later we will have the wine."

He left long enough to speak to his daughter, then guided his visitor through the busy streets to a tree-lined park that covered several city blocks. At one end rose a magnificent structure, three floors of buff brick, its many wings and turrets built in the grandest style Raven had ever seen.

The Luxembourg Palace, Jenet explained, once the private home of Marie de Medici. "During the Terror it was a prison. Now"—he shrugged dramatically—"government offices. We treat our Parisian officials very well, *n'est pas?"*

He paused to look around the stretch of grass and trees and early-spring flowers. Raven would have been charmed by the vista were she not occupied with calming her rising anxiety.

"Ah," he said with a broad smile. *"A droite."*

Raven followed his gesture to the right. Dozens of Parisians, children and adults, strolled along the paths in front of her. "My wife, do you not see her near the pond? She sits beside the boy. She has seen us. She waves."

Raven found them, a gray-haired matron and a fair-haired tot sitting in the grass, a toy sailboat between them. Anxiety turned to dread as she walked beside Jenet, and a cold fist clutched her heart. Whatever she was about to learn, she knew she wouldn't like it.

"Odile will be pleased to see you have arrived," said Jenet. "We have much on our minds, with the birth of the triplets, but we also love the boy. We have, you know, cared for him since his birth. It will be difficult for us both when he leaves."

Raven could not take her eyes from the child. Four, perhaps close to five, he waved excitedly to Jenet. The distance closed slowly, too slowly, between them. They drew within twenty yards, close enough for Raven to make out the wheat-colored hair, the blue eyes, the still-developing features that promised to grow strong as he became older.

Had she borne a child for Marcus and had he taken after his father, he might very well have looked like this.

She was scarcely aware of putting one foot in front of the other. The boy struggled to stand.

*"Faites attention!"* Madame Jenet warned him.

"You coddle him too much," her husband said. He glanced at Raven. "It is perhaps natural, but still, the boy must learn to be strong. We speak English before him, as M'sieur Bannerman has instructed. John calls him *Oncle* Marcus," he added with a shrug. "It is best, *n'est pas?"*

The boy took an uneven step toward them, and then another, his left leg stiffer than his right.

Raven fell to her knees, putting her on his level, as Jenet introduced his wife. She scarcely heard him. What came through was the name of the boy, John Bannerman, the same as Marcus's father.

"Hello," said the boy with an awkward bow, "and *bonjour.*"

He was beautiful, with his golden hair, sky-blue eyes, and already a strong chin she easily recognized. He was also lame, but that mattered not at all. With a shaking hand, Raven reached out to Marcus's son.

# Twenty-four

*Trust Marcus.*

To do what? To have done what?

Raven brushed the hair from the eyes of the boy beside her, then settled back on the uncomfortably stiff train seat. They were on their last portion of the journey from Paris to London. The English coast was behind them. Ahead lay Victoria Station. What else awaited, Raven had no idea.

"Will *Oncle* Marcus meet us when we get there?"

Raven hesitated, unwilling to tell him Marcus had no idea they were in the country.

"Would you like that?" she asked.

John's face brightened, as if a light had been turned on inside him. *"Oui.* Very much."

He yawned widely.

"Put your head in my lap and try to sleep. The time will go by faster."

John wrinkled his nose in disbelief, but, polite child that he was, he held his tongue as he stretched out on the bench. Raven rested her arm across his slender young body, feeling his warmth against her. Was this what it felt like to be a parent, to pillow a young head, to assure a worried mind, to protect an innocent child from harm?

Was that what she was doing? Since leaving Paris, she had seen to his needs for warmth and food and shelter, but there were other matters equally important. Family matters that would affect him the rest of his life.

Maybe she should take him aboard a southbound train straight to Portsmouth, smuggle him onto the ship that would shortly be awaiting her, and sail all the way to Savannah. That way she wouldn't have to explain to Marcus how all of this had come about.

Too, she would be taking a part of her one and only love back with her. John Bannerman was clearly his son. The name, the features, the coloring were all signs, and Claude Jenet had practically told her so.

Raven stared out the window at the rolling landscape. Keeping the boy must join the list of her never-to-be-realized dreams. She would have to face Marcus. She could hear herself explaining the situation, speaking fast so that he could not interrupt.

"Cordelia asked me to go to Paris, and when I arrived, the Jenets were preparing to leave for Provence to help their oldest daughter who'd just given birth to triplets. They had written to tell you they couldn't take John with them, but would return within a few months to resume their caretaking. Assuming I was there to escort their charge to his uncle, they wouldn't accept any of my half-hearted excuses.

"In truth, I fell in love with the boy. I couldn't leave him to whomever you might send, not when he was so certain he was returning with me."

The words were true. They also showed exactly what

she was, an interfering woman who brought trouble wherever she went.

She had other words seething within her, comments about his inquiries into her being *enceinte*. She had assumed that if she were with child, their marriage would be a natural consequence, but such was not necessarily true. Perhaps he had wondered whether to make room for another offspring in France.

Cordelia said the letter she had sent him at Beacon Hall absolving him of worry had upset him so much everyone had decided it contained bad news. Cordelia and the others must have been wrong. He could have been concerned about a hundred other matters—the price of fertilizer, the weather, the dwindling market for beef.

Not the Songbird. She had already flown from his life.

Raven caressed the sleeping child tightly for a moment, then eased her hold when he stirred restlessly. His lashes were dark against his pale round cheeks, his lips parted as he drew in even breaths. She smoothed away a small bubble at the corner of his mouth. She'd been with him for only two days, but she didn't know how she could let him go.

What a mad thing it had been to bring him with her, mad and impetuous, something Flame might have done. But she had felt such a tenderness for the boy, something Angel might have felt. It was possible, Raven thought with a warm glow in her heart, that the three Chadwick daughters were more alike than anyone had believed.

The boy slept most of the way to London, awakening to a drowsy excitement. From Victoria Station they took a hansom cab to the boardinghouse, where Mrs. Goodbody cooed over him as she might have a grandchild.

Raven gave her no explanation for his presence, nor his identity, save to report she was helping out a friend.

The first order of business was to dispatch a letter to Cordelia at Stafford House, notifying her of their arrival. Sweet, kindly Cordelia had proven to be a troublemaker of the grandest proportions. And a schemer, too. She must have opened Claude Jenet's letter to Marcus and decided, without consultation with anyone, to send Raven to Paris, knowing she would either fetch John home or remain with him while the Jenets were gone. In either case Marcus would involve himself.

Was Marcus supposed to look at Raven and his son together and decide they were all he wanted in life? Cordelia should know by now that His Lordship could not be maneuvered into anything, most of all love.

The woman's action had brought Raven one last devastating blow. Gazing upon the child, so like his father, feeling more than ever like an outsider, knowing she would be leaving them both, she felt the shattering of her already broken heart.

Cordelia's answer to her letter came immediately. The following afternoon she would be alone at Stafford House.

"Bring the boy," she wrote, "and I promise that together we shall decide what to do next."

Raven's frustrations mounted. She didn't like the woman's suggestion, nor did she trust her, but with the sailing date a week away, she could not waste time in quarrelsome correspondence. In her sobriety, Cordelia was proving a formidable manipulator.

She took the boy's belongings with her. In the carriage, he bombarded her with questions.

"Will *Oncle* Marcus be waiting?"

"Will he be pleased to see me?"

"Will he help me play with my boat?"

Raven tried to explain they were visiting his uncle's house and would meet a member of his family, but the boy only half listened, deciding for himself that Marcus would be there.

To her surprise, Cordelia answered her knock. "You must have been watching for us," Raven said.

"Oh, I was," answered Cordelia breathlessly. She smiled down at the boy, who was peering around her to the front hallway. "What a handsome lad."

She bustled them inside. Frederick appeared, staring at the boy, muttering something that sounded most unbutlerlike.

He glanced toward the winding stairway behind him. "Does—"

"Now, now," said Cordelia hurriedly, "just go about your business, Frederick. Don't be concerned."

He shook his head. "Things weren't like this under the old earl," he said, walking away.

"Let's go up to the drawing room, shall we?" Cordelia said, starting for the stairs, Raven and John beside her. The sound of men's voices from the upstairs hallway stopped them.

"I thought you were alone."

Cordelia did not meet her eye.

A woman's high giggle made Raven's blood run cold.

"Margaret Clifton," she said, willing her feet to turn and run, but they refused to obey.

Cordelia had the grace to smile sheepishly. "Accompanied by her father. My nephew has invited a few acquaintances over to meet the Cliftons. I fear she's in London to purchase her trousseau. And, of course, to make the betrothal a fact."

"You planned this."

"Not exactly. But it is working out rather nicely."

Cordelia the schemer. Was there no end to her duplicity?

Raven was too torn to plot revenge. Her gaze trailed up the staircase, pulled there by a force beyond her control. She took a step forward and then another, until she could see the shoes and trousers of the man standing on the landing where the stairway curved. She knew already who it was. It didn't take a child's laugh to tell her.

Setting the boy's valise on the marble floor, she looked up to meet Marcus's cold stare of disbelief and shock.


Marcus's heart missed a beat, then began hammering in his chest. He had thought never to see her again. Yet here she was, the boy and Cordelia by her side, all of them looking up from the base of the stairs.

It took a moment for the significance of the boy's presence to register. John, so long hidden away, stood in the middle of Stafford House, looking lost in the vastness of the entryway.

My God, Marcus thought. He had never imagined things would happen this way. All the years of secrecy . . . gone in an instant.

John looked up at him shyly, expectantly. He could do nothing but smile encouragement. The boy's stiff leg made climbing the stairs awkward, but his excitement sped him on. Marcus went halfway down to meet him, to sweep him into his arms.

"You're a long way from home, rascal," he said, giving him an affectionate shake, ruffling his hair.

John rested an arm around Marcus's neck. "It was the three babies, you see," he said, then added all in a breath, "Papa Jenet said it would be difficult and then Miss Chadwick arrived, and here I am."

Marcus did not try to make sense of the boy's outburst.

"Darling," said Margaret from the top of the stairs, "who is the child?" She took a step lower, and another, stopping when she saw Raven. "What is that woman doing here?"

Bloody hell. He'd been on the brink of proposing to Margaret, before company lest he lost his nerve, and now . . .

Cordelia hurried up the stairs and took the boy. "Let's go to my room, shall we? I'll get us some biscuits and we can get to know one another." The boy started to protest. "We'll see Marcus soon, I promise. The adults have matters to discuss, and he won't be able to join you in play for a while."

By the time she had finished speaking she was beginning the second flight of stairs that led to the bedrooms, climbing hand in hand with John. He moved slowly but surely, his uneven gate hampering him not in the least.

"Biscuits?" he asked, gazing up at her.

"Wonderful English biscuits. Better by far than the rich French pastries you're used to, I'll be bound."

The boy's response was lost as they reached the upper level, leaving Marcus in the middle of the stairway, his almost-fiancée behind him and the only woman he had asked to marry him standing in front.

"Margaret, return to the drawing room. I'll be there in a moment."

"But—"

"In a moment." Her features screwed into a pout. It was a look he had long grown tired of.

"Well, all right. But don't be long. We have guests."

*We,* he thought, as though she were already hostess of Stafford House instead of an afternoon visitor. Conscience forced him to admit she wasn't entirely wrong.

He turned back to Raven, and he forgot all else. She looked pale, he thought, in her black bonnet and cloak, and there was a lost, questioning look in her eyes. Sensations he'd never felt swelled in him, twisting his heart, robbing him of breath. The boy's presence shocked him, inexplicable as it was, but Raven's dear face looking up at him stunned him all the more.

He wanted to run down the stairs and take her in his arms, then tell her how much he had missed her. It had been a long while since he had done what he wanted. The last time had been in a stable. So much had gone right with that last precious hour he'd spent with her, but in the end he had handled things wrong.

He must go slowly here. His life depended upon this moment.

"It's good to see you."

"It can't be. I brought bad news."

"Bad news?"

"Your son." Her voice caught on the words.

He hesitated, considering how to go on. "John is not bad news."

"Then why—"

"Why keep him in France? Not because I wanted him there. It seemed simpler."

He saw puzzlement in her eyes, then anger. How quick she was to take offense when she detected injustice or injury or any kind of wrong, which she had to assume was the situation here.

"I'm sure you're wondering why he's here with me," she said. "It's a complicated story."

But Marcus didn't care about the *why*. For now he felt only relief and a sense that, against all odds, things might turn out right after all.

"Do you like him?" He could see the question took her by surprise.

"Like him? He's—" Tears dampened her eyes, but she tilted her chin against him, the way she had done a hundred times. "He's wonderful and brave and beautiful. He's perfect."

"It wasn't his lameness that made me keep him in Paris, Raven."

She started. He had struck at what was bothering her. She was as she had described the boy—wonderful and brave and beautiful. And perfect. He loved her with all his heart.

He smiled to himself. Oh yes, he loved her, and he would do so the rest of his life. The admission, the realization, freed his heart, his spirit, his soul. He could have whooped for joy. He wanted to leap down the remaining stairs, to take her in his arms, to whirl her around and around until she grew too dizzy to reason away his love or his presence in her life.

He was a civilized man with responsibilities, but he

was a savage, too, where Raven was concerned. There were no rules that would keep her from his side.

For now, the civilized man must be in control. When they were alone, all his savage instincts would dominate.

They looked at each other in silence. She turned, as if she would leave.

"No," he said. "Please don't go. After the others have gone, we have to talk."

"But I—"

"If you say you don't belong here, I'll throw you over my shoulder and carry you into the drawing room."

"You'd do it, too, wouldn't you?"

"At last you understand me."

"I've always known you wanted your way." She said it with no sign of rancor. He wanted to believe she smiled.

As if summoned, Frederick appeared to take her cloak and bonnet. Lavender silk shimmered against her slender body. She held her head high as she walked up the stairs to him, passing by so close he caught her natural sweet scent. It filled his nostrils, quickened his blood. How easily she aroused him. He clutched his fists at his side to keep from touching her, making silent promises to touch her later. Whenever, wherever, and for as long as she wished.

How close he had come to proposing to the wrong woman, to doing what was expected of him, to denying his heart. He felt like a condemned man who'd received a gallows reprieve.

He guided Raven to the drawing room, where a small gathering awaited, both men and women, acquaintances of Marcus, as well as Ralph, Daniel Lindsay, the squire, and Margaret.

"I believe most of you know Miss Chadwick," he said. Daniel nodded a greeting to Raven, but no one spoke.

Margaret sat stiffly on the sofa, hands together in her lap, her eyes narrowed as she stared into space. One of the men said something about leaving, but no one moved. An inquisitive group, thought Marcus, but it was time they were gone. He felt guilty about having led Margaret on. Later he would apologize to her. Much later, after he and Raven had talked.

"Thank you for coming today," he said, his eyes sweeping across the room, "but something has arisen that needs my attention."

They all nodded, but still no one moved.

"What's going on?" asked Ralph, who stood with Daniel by the piano.

"A private matter," Marcus said. Then to the room, "Perhaps we can visit longer some other time. I'm certain Amy will be arranging another gathering. She regretted not being here today."

It was a lie. Fearing a betrothal announcement, she had refused to stay in the house.

He glanced at Margaret. She stared back with startling fury. He hardly recognized the genteel woman who had assumed she would be his bride. She was seething over his dismissal . . . over the unexpected child who looked so much like him . . . over the woman she had thought long gone. From the feral look of her right now, the hard eyes, the tight, open mouth, the small white teeth, he saw that he wasn't the only savage in the room.

"Who is he?" she hissed, an angry cat prepared for assault.

"Margaret—" the squire began. His daughter waved him to silence.

"You're concerned about the boy?" asked Marcus.

"Who is he?"

"Not here, Margaret."

But she was beyond reason. "Who is he?"

Marcus had never seen her like this. He hoped he never would again. She gave him no choice but to go on. Rumors would fly anyway; he might as well tell the story he wanted everyone to hear. It would be the truth, as far as he could go.

"A boy from Paris, a boy named John. I plan to adopt him."

"And have him live with us? You want me to accept your bastard son?"

Several women in the room gasped, including Raven, who stood behind him.

"See here," said Ralph.

Marcus thought of nothing but Margaret's harsh indictment. "Be careful what you say. We are not betrothed." He bit out the words, cold and sharp, but she seemed beyond all warning.

"Now, Margaret," said the squire.

"And the mother?" Margaret asked.

"None of your business."

"You plan to parade him around our friends?"

"What friends I have will accept him as they accept me." He glanced at one or two of the men. "In every way John will be my son."

Margaret cast a sideways glance at Raven. "I should

have known if there were scandal to be unearthed, she would be a part."

Never in his life had Marcus struck a woman, but he had difficulty restraining himself now.

Margaret was not done. "The child is crippled."

"Oh!" Raven's cry echoed across the room. "What a cruel heart you have."

"My God, yes," said Daniel. "You speak the truth, Miss Chadwick."

Squire Clifton looked at his daughter as though seeing her for the first time.

"You don't have to do this," Marcus said to Raven, but she kept her dark and angry eyes on Margaret. She looked magnificent, glorious in her righteous fury.

Suddenly his anger eased. Let Raven with her quick temper and her sharp wit fight this battle for him. Margaret ought to know it was an uneven match.

Unwisely she blundered on. "Are you his mother?"

Raven's response shot back as true as an arrow. "Any woman who wouldn't claim him is a fool."

"Marcus," said Margaret, her thin voice squeaking with fury, "aren't you going to defend me?"

He shrugged. She looked at him, at Raven, and back at him. A trapped look, a sense of loss, darkened her eyes. Clearly, she saw where her mad rage had led. She looked around the room, as if seeking support; but no one, not even her father, offered help, and she returned to her almost-fiancé.

"It's obvious my presence is no longer wanted here."

She stared at him as though waiting for his protest. It took all of Marcus's control not to sigh with relief.

"Leave if you must, Margaret. You must follow your conscience."

"Well!" Margaret glanced over her shoulder at the squire. "Come, Papa, take me home. To Sussex. I'm glad I made the journey to the city and learned the kind of man Lord Stafford truly is. No title is worth such abuse."

She strode from the room. The squire took a moment to mumble his regrets, then hurried after. A buzz of whispers broke the momentary silence.

"Good riddance," said Ralph. "I never cared for the woman anyway."

"I don't know about you, Marcus," Daniel said, "but I'd like something stronger than tea."

"Good idea," said Marcus. He looked at Raven. Her cheeks were flushed with anger, and she looked at him as though she had never seen him before.

"You goaded her on purpose," she said.

"Little was required to raise her wrath."

"You're glad she's gone."

"I'm glad—"

He stopped. Now was not the time to tell her all, but he could contain himself no longer. He started to take her hand when he saw Amy standing in the doorway, the child in her arms. Her face was white, her eyes wild with an emotion he could only imagine.

All joy in the moment fled. "Amy."

"I knew I'd hold him some day," she said, her words catching on a sob. "I knew it." Tears dampened her cheeks. "So many lies. Let them all be done."

"You don't have to do this," he said as she walked into the room.

She stroked the boy's face. John stared back at her, wonder in his bright blue eyes.

"Marcus said you were with another family," she said to the boy. "That he went to Paris only for business, but I knew better." And to her brother, "Forgive me for hating you. You've done a wonderful job. He's perfect."

She looked around the room until she saw Daniel by the piano. "There's someone I want you to meet," she said, walking toward him.

Daniel paled as he watched her approach.

She stood before him, blinking away the tears. "Marcus is probably claiming the boy as his own, but as usual, he lies. Allow me to present to you our son."

# Twenty-five

So much happened in the next hour that Raven had no chance to be alone with Marcus, to apologize for thinking rotten things about him, to tell him that one day he would find the right woman, to bid him a final farewell.

The guests departed immediately, practically shoved out the door by their host. Cordelia returned to add her support in clearing the room.

Raven wanted to leave, too. Somehow she ended up close to Cordelia as the bittersweet story unfolded, everything coming out in a rush, Daniel and Amy standing face to face, embracing the boy between them.

Marcus stood quietly close by. Sometimes she felt his eyes on her, but she couldn't look at him.

"I left for India because I thought you didn't love me," Daniel declared, not caring who was in the room.

"I showed you how I felt," said Amy. "I gave myself to you."

"I needed to hear the words."

"And so did I."

"I had no money."

"You were a fool."

"You should have told me you carried our child."

"You were already gone when I knew for sure."

"You should have written."

"Why? To force you back to England to do the honorable thing?"

"I would have been here on the fastest clipper, the happiest man in the world."

"But I didn't know that. I couldn't write. Marcus took me away from London to protect me. I refused to name the father. He had no idea it was you. We were good at keeping our secret."

Tears streamed down her cheeks as she looked at John. "I gave him up. I didn't want to, but Marcus said for the boy's sake I must. It was the worst mistake of my life."

"Mine was worse. I never should have gone."

The boy squirmed, his dangling legs twisting between them. His parents laughed, but they did not put him down. Raven wondered if it were wise for the tot to learn of his parentage in such a way, but other than a restlessness at being confined, the only emotion he showed was fascination with his mother and father.

Raven could stand the intrusion no longer. This was a private moment. Perhaps Cordelia should hear, and Marcus. They were family. Ralph had the good sense to stand aside and be quiet. Irene had the best sense of all. She didn't appear.

With attention focused on Daniel and Amy, and on the wide-eyed child between them, Raven slipped from the room. So many things were clear now—Amy's harsh feelings toward her brother, Marcus's frustrations, the frequent trips to Paris, his need to establish his family and his estate so that everyone in both countries could be cared for.

She would try to be happy for them all. It might take awhile, selfish creature that she was, but eventually she would see that everything had truly worked out for the best.

Behind her she could hear Daniel asking Marcus for his sister's hand in marriage.

"How wonderful," she whispered. She meant it. Why did she feel so empty inside?

She stood in the hallway, willing her feet to get to work, but she could not move.

"Miss Chadwick."

She looked toward the stairs leading to the bedrooms. Irene beckoned from halfway up. There was something compelling in the woman's gesture. Raven walked toward her, planning a quick goodbye.

Irene clutched a small wooden box to her breast. "Come with me," she said. "I want to show you something."

"No, I have to—" But the woman had already reached the top of the stairs.

Reluctantly, Raven did as she was asked. Irene took her to her bedroom, which was plainly furnished, all the essentials without frills, like the manner in which Irene clothed herself. There was nothing to see that Raven would not have expected, except for the array of books on the bed.

"My treasures," said Irene. A lilt in the woman's voice made Raven glance at her. She had a dreamy look in her eyes, as though she saw things no one else could see.

A chill ran down Raven's spine. She backed toward the door, but Irene skirted around her, closing it, turning the key and slipping it into her pocket.

"Don't you want to see my treasures?" she asked.

"Later," Raven said. "I really must leave."

"Now."

Thinking to humor her, Raven walked closer to look at the books, expecting geography tomes, but the titles were all wrong: *The Lustful Turk; The Romance of Lust; The Convent School, or Early Experiences of A Young Flagellant.* The thickest of all was a scholarly looking work called *My Secret Life.*

She had heard mention of such publications. Mrs. Goodbody had said they were for sale in Soho.

"If the Queen only knew about 'em," the woman had said, "she'd join Prince Albert in 'is grave."

Surely the contents couldn't be as erotic as the landlady had hinted. Surely Irene wouldn't possess them if they did. Shocked and fascinated at the same time, Raven reached for *The Lustful Turk.*

"No," said Irene sharply. "They are mine." She stepped beside Raven and set the box onto the bed. "Here," she said, lifting the lid, "is the greatest treasure of all."

Inside the box, on a bed of crushed black velvet, lay a brooch beyond all imagining, a diamond the size of an acorn set into a network of gold filigree, smaller diamonds and rubies wreathed around it. Exquisite and garish at the same time, it had to be worth a king's ransom.

"No one knows about it," Irene said in a hoarse whisper. "Not even Roger."

Raven barely heard her, all her attention devoted to the jewel. It sparkled back at her, at once beautiful and somehow evil. She felt no urge to touch the stone. All she could do was stare and wonder at its presence in this room in the possession of a woman supposedly impoverished, dependent upon a family that was not really hers.

"You shan't have it."

Irene's voice exploded behind her. She whirled to see the woman standing an arm's length away, the poker from the hearth gripped in her hand, a wild and determined look in her eye.

"It was to be your mother's heritage and, in accordance with her father's will, the property of her first-born child. But I took possession of it. No one knew, not even my stupid brother. After your mother left, your grandfather squandered most of his money. The brooch was his secret treasure, but I stole it from him. Now it is mine."

"You were the one who wrote Mama."

"She was coming for the diamond, but it was all I had, all that kept me from poverty. They thought I was a poor relation, living on charity. The fools. Then you arrived."

"I wasn't after the brooch."

"You would have found it. Marcus would have let you take it. I had to stop you."

The unreality of the moment turned to horror as Raven saw the truth. "You pushed me down the stairs."

"You should have died."

"And the cinch? Surely you didn't—"

Irene laughed. "Roger did it for me."

"Roger," Raven said, puzzled. Of course, she thought, the footman. Roger Hammond, the hawk-eyed footman who liked to leer.

"He delivered the letter to the music hall, too. Had you followed, he did, at my request. He does everything for me. Everything."

Irene waved the poker. Raven backed against the bed. A familiar fear gripped her. She thought of the alley behind her Savannah home, of a mean-eyed Yankee soldier rushing at her, of a dark hallway and hands shoving her down the stairs.

She thought, too, of the terrifying moment the saddle had given way beneath her. So much . . . too much . . . and in an instant her fear was gone.

She stared at her assailant, at her lined face and graying hair, at the weapon in her hand. Could she fight a woman more than twice her age? Of course she could, if she were given little choice.

Irene lifted the poker high, and Raven went on the attack, her fist catching Irene on the chin. The woman's eyes rolled back in her head, and with a small grunt, she fell to the floor.

Raven sank back on the bed, sitting on *The Lustful Turk,* barely aware of the discomfort as she stared down at the unconscious woman. Old images whirled in her mind, red-streaked mists, oppressive as they were vague.

**Someone** pounded on the door. "Irene! Raven, are you in there?"

It was Marcus. He sounded furious. Marcus. Thinking of him, she forgot the images, forgot all threats of harm. How she wanted the comfort of his embrace. Without a qualm, she felt through Irene's pockets for the key, then ran toward the door to let him in.

They stared at one another for a moment, neither moving.

"I thought you'd gotten away again," he said.

How dear he looked, boyish and manly as always.

"No," she said, "and I'm not likely to, either. If you want to get rid of me, Your Lordship, you'll have to throw me out."

Without giving him a chance to respond, she threw herself into his arms and held on tight, as though her life depended upon him.

Which it did.


"I love you," Marcus whispered into her ear.

The hour was late. They were alone in the library, on the sofa, before a crackling fire. Raven, wearing a golden locket at her throat, rested in his arms. He did not intend to let her go.

"You've told me," she said. "But don't stop."

"Stop what? Telling or loving?"

"Neither." She stroked his cheek. "I love you."

She had said it a dozen times, but not often enough. "You should have mentioned your feelings for me in the stable," he said.

"It didn't seem like the right time."

"I'd asked you to marry me."

"And I told you it wasn't enough."

Marcus grinned. "Stupid man that I am, I didn't understand what you meant. I also hadn't figured out yet why I couldn't let you go. I know now I've loved you for a very long time." He thought a minute. "Probably since you so courageously showed up here to apologize about the music hall."

She shuddered. "Do you have to mention that?"

His grin broadened. "Not if you don't want. But I can't promise not to think of you staring at me from the stage. I wanted to bound over the footlights and carry you off into the night. Of course, I told myself it was righteous rage, but I was behaving a bit pompously at the time."

"Do you know what your smile does to me?" she asked, stroking the corners of his lips.

He answered her with a kiss. "I'm not letting you go until I've made a lady out of you."

"Fat chance of that."

"Lady Stafford."

"Of course, m'lord."

"You say that very well. It sounds almost dutiful."

"Don't get your hopes up."

"My darling, darling Songbird, everything about me is up right now."

"You're incorrigible."

"Among other things." He grew solemn for a moment. "Do you mind if I call you Songbird?"

"Not anymore. Not when you say it that way. It might be best, however, if you save it for special occasions."

"Like now."

She nodded.

"And bed. And stables, too, don't forget. I have particularly fond memories of one in particular."

"But no carriages," she said. "Ladies can go only so far."

"We'll see," was all he said.

She snuggled against him, her head close to his chin. He kissed the top of her head.

"So much has happened," she said.

Marcus stared into the fire. "Did I tell you that as soon as they're married, Amy and Daniel are going to India? I hate like the devil to see John leave, but they don't seem inclined to leave him behind."

He thought of his sister and their young days in Sussex. "I never realized they took a serious look at each other. Cordelia knew, of course, but Amy swore her to secrecy. She stood by all these years, watching her niece and nephew grow further apart. I imagine it's why she drank."

"When she sobered up, she became a formidable force. Like all the Bannermans. Of course she's only a Bannerman by marriage, but it's close enough."

"Formidable. Right," Marcus said. "And don't you forget it."

He sensed a change in her mood.

"Roger Hammond is safely locked away, Raven. He can't harm you anymore. I hope they toss him in the deepest hole at Tyburn and throw away the key."

She sighed.

"Irene's troubling you, right? She threatened Amy, you know, claiming that if she didn't receive adequate payment she would tell the scandal reporters about John.

She wrote anonymous letters, the same as your mother's, instructing where the money was to be placed in Green Park."

"How did she know about John?"

"Probably overheard Cordelia and Amy. It was Hammond's idea to write Amy for money. She had no funds of her own, so she pawned the Landseer. It's another mark against the footman. We found the envelope of bills in his room."

"Surely Irene's not responsible for what she does. She was out of her mind when she tried to hit me."

Marcus held her tight. "She's sick. I don't know if we'll be able to help her. The doctor has her sedated. There's a special home he's recommending, a place where she'll be cared for. Ralph has sworn to stand by her. He's being far stronger about this than I would have expected."

"Pickerings can be a force to reckon with," said Raven. "And don't you forget it."

"Pickerings and Chadwicks," Marcus pointed out. "I'm a defeated man."

"A lucky one, you mean. I'm also wealthy, you know. Ralph said the brooch, which he had thought long ago stolen or lost, was supposed to go to the first grandchild in the family. So you're getting a rich wife after all."

She sat up, eyes wide as she looked at him. "Here I am rattling on about myself, as though I'm the only person to consider. I'm a selfish brat. I haven't thought once of Mama or Papa, not since I told you about the letter that brought me here."

"So what are you thinking?"

"That when they look at me, all giddy and laughing and silly in love, they'll not recognize their solemn-eyed eldest daughter. The minute they meet you, my darling, they'll understand exactly why I changed."

# Epilogue

In April of the second year of her marriage, Raven Chadwick Bannerman, Lady Stafford, appeared in the Irish play *The School for Scandal* at the Lyceum Theater. It was a limited run, but that was all right with Raven. She had other things on her mind.

In the Bannerman box were her parents, who were making their second trip to London, Amy and Daniel on a visit from India, and her sister Angel.

And, of course, Marcus.

The family was almost complete. Cordelia was caring for the Lindsays' two boys at Stafford House. Ralph stayed to help her, although Raven thought the woman would rather be alone.

In celebration of their successful South African diamond mine, the two baronets had sailed for a holiday in New York.

The only sad note was the death of Irene, who had succumbed to pneumonia the previous winter, never having completely regained her senses.

At the conclusion of the play, Raven stood on the stage to take her bow. She could hear her husband's applause above all others. She wasn't the star. That honor went to the Lyceum's wonderful Ellen Terry. But she knew that for an upstart American—which the stage manager Simon Normandy regularly called her—she had acquitted herself respectably.

So much had happened since that night two years ago when Marcus proposed, yet some things remained the same. Roger Hammond was in a cell at Tyburn Prison, much to everyone's relief. Margaret Clifton had married the owner of a northern mill and moved to Liverpool, and the squire had given up his hold on Humble Hall, returning it to the Bannerman family where it belonged.

And she had married her one true love, the man who had taught her to feel. It was no small satisfaction to know she had done the same for him.

Backstage the family gathered around her. Marcus presented her with a dozen roses and a kiss. Everyone congratulated her, but Papa beamed the proudest of all.

"You've a lot of Irish in you, lass. You make me proud."

Raven hugged him. "I've more to thank you for than words can say," she whispered in his ear.

Thomas Chadwick backed away to brush a tear from his eye. "I'll be breaking down in front of your fine husband if ye don't stop with the kind words."

"You know how I am," she said, winking at him. "Wildly demonstrative, openly affectionate, extravagantly emotional."

Angel laughed. "You're more like Flame than any of us ever knew." The laughter died, and her gentle face grew solemn. "I wish she and Matt were here. With their son and daughter."

Anne Chadwick shook her head. "One child in Texas,

another in England. Angel, I'm going to lock you in your room to make sure I keep one of you at home."

"It's natural," said Amy, "for the women of the family to follow their men. Look at me, in India of all places, and with two children."

"The two boys like it, do they?" asked Thomas.

"The baby's too young to see beyond his cradle," said Daniel. "But John, now there's a happy child." He looked at his wife. "We'd best be getting back to them. Cordelia is a wonderful caretaker, but we don't want to overtax her."

Amy took his arm. "What you mean is you've been away from them as long as you can stand."

The two excused themselves and left for Stafford House.

Thomas stared with unusual gravity at his eldest child. "Do ye plan to make a career of the stage?"

Raven glanced at Marcus. She hadn't meant for the news to come out this way, but on this wonderful night it seemed an appropriate time to speak.

"I've already told Mr. Normandy that after the play closes, I won't be trying out for another."

"She swears she prefers the country to the city," said Marcus. "We're going to live at Beacon Hall most of the year."

"I might work with the children and the adults who show an interest, perhaps start a local theater. It will be a challenge." She looked at her husband. "But not the greatest one I'll be facing."

"And what's that, my love? Marriage to me?"

"That's easy. I was thinking more of motherhood."

"Don't worry, love," Marcus said, stroking her hair. "We'll start our family soon."

"Sooner than you think. It's April now. How would you like a son or daughter born in October?"

She didn't have to explain to him exactly what she meant. Thrusting her roses into Angel's hands, he took her in his arms.

"You're sure?"

Raven nodded. "Are you pleased?"

"I'm pleased." The warmth of his kiss showed her just how much.

Angel sighed. "My sisters have found perfect mates, have they not, Mama? I'll settle for nothing less. Someone honest and strong and true. I don't care what he looks like or how much money he has, as long as he honors me above all else."

Anne patted her youngest daughter's hand. "I'm sure you'll find him, dear." She winked at her husband of thirty-two years. "After all, it's a family trait that Chadwick women only settle for the best."

# AUTHOR'S NOTE

*Raven* is the second book in a trilogy about the Chadwick sisters of nineteenth-century Savannah, Georgia. Book One, *Flame* (a March 1994 release), tells the story of the impetuous middle sister who discovers happiness with a Texas rancher. In the third and final tale, the youngest daughter Angel finds her good and gentle nature tested by a vengeful rake from her beloved Papa's native Ireland. Book Three will be published in the fall, 1995.

Evelyn Rogers
8039 Callaghan, #102
San Antonio, Texas
March, 1994

## SURRENDER TO THE SPLENDOR OF THE ROMANCES OF F. ROSANNE BITTNER!

CARESS                          (3791, $5.99/$6.99)

COMANCHE SUNSET                 (3568, $4.99/$5.99)

HEARTS SURRENDER                (2945, $4.50/$5.50)

LAWLESS LOVE                    (3877, $4.50/$5.50)

PRAIRIE EMBRACE                 (3160, $4.50/$5.50)

RAPTURE'S GOLD                  (3879, $4.50/$5.50)

SHAMELESS                       (4056, $5.99/$6.99)

# STALEMATE

"It's Paris, isn't it?" she said with sudden insight. "Something about Paris. Amy cried when she told me that's where you'd gone."

A shuttered look darkened his eyes. "A coincidence. She grows emotional at times."

"She's rarely emotional, not below the surface where emotions count. That is what has me worried about her. She's brittle. And things that are brittle tend to break."

"Ah, all is clear. You broke into my desk to learn more about my sister."

"I wanted to know more about you." Surely he could sense the truth in what she said.

"I fascinate you, do I?" The self-mockery was back in his voice. *More than you know.*

"You're a hard man."

"I tend to be that way around you."

He stood a whisper away. She caught the scent of sandalwood, of soot from the train, of the outdoors, of Marcus himself.

"Is there no gentleness in your soul?" she asked.

"None. I do not possess a soul."

He took her in his embrace; she could not pull away, even had she tried.

She looked at his lips, still slightly swollen where she'd struck him, and his strong, scarred chin. Another woman's mark? Perhaps. She could not look into his eyes.

"It always ends like this between us," she said.

His lips twitched into a partial smile. "It's the only way I can stop your accusations."

At last her eyes met his. "And what about the things you say to me? Do you think I want them to continue?"

"I don't know what you want." He slanted his lips across hers. "This?" Again, more firmly. "Or this?"

He tightened his embrace. "Or maybe this . . ."

# TODAY'S HOTTEST READS
# ARE TOMORROW'S SUPERSTARS